ARIADNE
unraveled

A MYTHIC RETELLING

ZENOBIA NEIL

ALSO BY ZENOBIA NEIL

Psyche Unbound

The Jinni's Last Wish

The Queen of Warriors: Alexandra of Sparta Book One

In loving memory of John Leopold

In Crete

Royal family:
Queen Pasiphae and King Minos
Their named children: Androgeus, Ariadne, and Phaedra
Pasiphae and Poseidon: Asterion/ The Minotaur
Ariadne's Handmaidens: Thalia, Zoe, Melia, and Alexa
Ariadne's bodyguards: Manko, Talos
Phaedra's bodyguard: Tios
Others:
Zakros: Ariadne's previous husband
Cilix: Thalia's stepfather
Kaira: Pasiphae's Oceanid handmaiden
Melas: innkeeper
Seer: high priestess
White Foot: the bull
Bull leapers: Tanziz, Agri
Tamar: lyre player
Daedalus: Royal Architect

Named Athenians:
Aegeus: King of Athens
Athenian Tributes: Theseus, Chrysippos, Iris, and Echo

On the Seas:
Ahumm: Phoenician sailor
Seadog: Phoenician navigator
Medon, Dictys: Tyrrhenian sailors
Acoetes: Tyrrhenian navigator

On Naxos:
Chalkio: high priest
Palitia: older woman

On Lemnos:
  Hephaestus: god of the forge
  Milos: guide
  Polydorus: blacksmith of Hephaestus

Waves crashing on the shore awakened her. She opened her eyes to a night sky speckled with stars. Sand scratched her naked limbs as she reached out an arm for her lover. Nothing. Only the cold blanket they had lain on. Panicked, she sat up, calling his name.

The full moon rode low on the horizon, close to dawn. The sea foam flashed for a moment, reflecting the moonlight of the goddess she had forsaken. The emptiness of the beach set her heart pounding.

"Theseus!" she screamed in fury, already up and running, scanning the vast expanse of the black, empty sea. The boat that had brought her was gone. Rage burned her every breath, tingling in her hands.

"Theseus!" she screamed again, anger ripping through her vocal cords. If only she could summon a wave to crash down on his ship, destroying him and all aboard. But she was not a powerful sorceress like her Aunt Circe or her cousin Medea. To survive this, she would need her strength for herself and the child growing in her belly.

She pulled down the shawl he had insisted she wear to hide her breasts from his men and knelt. She licked her forefinger and dug it into the sand to draw a curse, her tears falling onto the lines.

"Shame unto you, Theseus, son of Aegeus. No matter how great your deeds, let it never be forgotten that you abandoned me here." Her voice wavered, tears falling harder. She had given up everything only to be cast aside. Her fingers trembled with anger and with magic. "I will live to hear of your shame, Theseus. May you be the death of your father. May you be remembered for your treachery." She spit into the sand, sealing the curse.

The moon stared down at her with cold vengeance. This was what she deserved. Her betrayal had been unforgivable, and now she had been betrayed unforgivably. *The gods are just*, she thought. Abandonment and slow death. After all she had given him: a sword, a way out of the labyrinth, a boat to escape with and, above all, her own body. And in exchange, he had taken everything from her: her home, her priestesshood, even her sister. Little vixen. Phaedra would surely warm his bed now. She would make a perfect Athenian bride, ready to hide her breasts and bow her head to her husband. Ariadne was too strong. She understood now.

"I curse you, too, sister. May the gods give you what you deserve!" She whispered this, cupping her hand to her mouth, so her prayer would travel on the wind.

He had left her with nothing more than the blanket and what she wore. No food, no water. He had promised to make her his queen in Athens, to never forget how she had saved him. The promise of a man was worthless.

She glanced at her hands, which had cast magic and spilled blood. She wore two rings: one a snake biting its own tail, and the other an odd hair ring made from a coil of black hair. She had taken a liking to it and never removed it. Clearly it was of no worth—just like her. Giving in to hopelessness, she lay down on the beach and let the tears come.

PART ONE
WHAT SHE DOES NOT REMEMBER

ARIADNE, HIGH PRIESTESS OF CRETE

THREE YEARS EARLIER

CRETE

"Priestess, I cannot find the honey," Melia said after setting out the olives, grilled fish, and flat bread on the blue wool blanket.

All around them, red poppies and purple and yellow irises bloomed, their fragrances mingled with wild mint and sage. A perfect day for making an offering to the goddess. After they dined, they would weave crowns from the wildflowers in honor of the goddess and leave them, along with the honey, in the sacred cave.

"Manko," Ariadne called out to one of her bodyguards.

Like all palace guards, he wore little more than a white kilt, which shone brightly against his dark skin. The border of his kilt was red, marking him as one of Ariadne's guards. Despite his muscular build, he bowed gracefully.

"Yes, High Priestess."

"Go back to Knossos to fetch the honey."

He bowed again and sprinted to her other bodyguard, Talos, who stood in the distance to allow privacy. After exchanging a few words, Manko ran toward the palace.

"He'll be back soon. Pour the mead," Ariadne said. Perhaps all was not lost. The bull's-horn mark on her thigh still tingled as it did when the goddess summoned her. Though it had been a long while since Ariadne had felt anything from the mark, surely the goddess had called her to the meadow.

Since this was not a formal occasion, Ariadne wore her daily clothes: a light crimson shawl over the small vest that left her breasts exposed, a leather corselet, and turquoise, saffron, and burgundy flounced skirts that fell to her ankles. She hoped the goddess did not mind her lack of headdress.

Her handmaiden Zoe poured five cups and passed the first to Ariadne. She took the golden cup ceremonially and held it high.

"Great Goddess, we honor you as you honor us. Our Lady, we are here to serve." She poured the mead into the earth, thinking of all the libations and blood she had given to the goddess this way. Zoe and Melia repeated her words.

Ariadne settled back onto the blanket, listening to the rushing river and the soft buzzing of bees in the wildflowers. Thalia passed around the bread, cheese, and olives as a butterfly fluttered in the breeze.

"I hear another girl was badly beaten by Cilix," Melia said after finishing her first cup of mead. Her words were aimed at Thalia. On an island where almost everyone had dark, almond-shaped eyes and pure black hair, Thalia's blonde hair and green eyes marked her as an outsider. No matter how Ariadne loved Thalia, Melia and Zoe found ways to taunt her. Bringing up Cilix, Thalia's stepfather, was an easy way to upset her.

Thalia twined a strand of golden hair around her finger.

"Did he kill another one?" Zoe asked.

"Not this time. Good thing, since he can't afford to buy any more slaves," Melia said.

The tip of Thalia's finger reddened as she pulled at her hair and glanced toward the copse of plane trees.

"I'll talk to my father again," Ariadne said. King Minos

considered himself a just man, but since no one had brought a formal complaint against Cilix, he continued beating women. Perhaps she should send Manko and Talos to visit Cilix in the night.

"What news have you heard from abroad, Melia?" Ariadne asked.

"There is talk of a new god traveling about, causing all kinds of trouble."

"A new god? How can we know who is a god and who is not? Every bastard can claim Zeus as his father," Thalia said, her green eyes flashing with daring. "Perhaps I, too, am a demigoddess."

Zoe laughed more loudly than she did in Knossos. There was a bite to the sound like the edge of a knife. The idea of Thalia as a demigoddess offended Zoe greatly.

Yet for Ariadne, Thalia's golden, wool-like hair made her a perfect possible bastard child of Ariadne's grandfather Helios, the sun.

"Demigoddess, pour me more mead," Ariadne said.

Thalia crawled over to the amphora. Her small, pert breasts hung down as she reached for the jug. On her knees, she moved to where Ariadne lay on the blanket and tipped the small amphora to the cup. Nothing came out.

"How strange, Priestess, I could have sworn there were two more cups' worth in here," Thalia said.

"You must have drunk it all, Thalia," Zoe said. She offered Ariadne her cup. "Have mine, Priestess."

Ariadne took it and sipped, but the mead tasted bitter.

"Perhaps you should not have mocked the new god," Melia said.

"I meant no disrespect." Thalia paled. "Priestess, do you think I offended the new god?"

"No." Ariadne finished the cup. "We who follow the goddess need not fear a foreign god. She will protect the devout."

"Goddess protect us," Melia whispered.

Thalia gasped as she glanced down at the amphora. "Priestess, it is full." She lifted it to her nose. "But it is not mead. It is dark red and smells unlike anything I know."

Too stunned to respond, no one said anything. Melia gazed at Thalia, still on her hands and knees, and said softly, "You should drink it."

A cloud drifted over the sun. Frozen in place, Thalia stared at the amphora. The mark on Ariadne's thigh buzzed. Compared to when the goddess summoned her, this sensation was lighter, like a small breeze, barely enough to raise the hair on her arms.

"Where is Talos? Manko should have returned by now," Zoe said.

Across the meadow, a young man strode toward them, his form tall and regal. The wind shifted, and the skies cleared, revealing a blinding burst of sunlight. Ariadne shaded her eyes, and then the stranger was standing before her. The pale quality of his skin reminded her of stars. Beardless, he appeared to be a youth at first glance, but carried himself like a man of quiet power.

His long, curly hair, darker than a starless night, could brand him as a fellow Minoan. But none of her countrymen would wear such outlandish garb. His purple chiton was clasped over one shoulder with a golden pin in the shape of a grape leaf. He wore a crown of myrtle as if he were a victor. Yet there were no contests taking place today. In his right hand he clutched a thyrsus, a wand of giant fennel entwined with ivy and capped with a pinecone. His purple-stained fingers suggested he was a laborer—perhaps a mad laborer who styled himself a king.

He was pretty, not handsome as a man was supposed to be. Though she wanted to stare at his strange beauty, she tore her gaze away and pulled the picnic basket closer, aware that Thalia had settled next to her, clutching the amphora to her chest.

The stranger did not bow but spoke plainly as if he had every right to approach her.

"I'm sure many tell you you're beautiful, Priestess, but what draws me to you is your power. I felt it from across the sea."

Though his words shocked her, she was not offended. Unlike her parents, she did not need commoners to speak to her with fancy words, their tongues dripping with flattering falsehoods.

The power that emanated from him made her aware of the blood pumping through her veins, of her heart beating in her breast. He had strong, muscular calves, and his taut thighs made her imagine lifting his chiton to see what was underneath.

"Please forgive me for interrupting your time together. This was simply my best chance to speak to you." He tipped his thyrsus in their direction. Zoe and Melia stood, not to protect their mistress, but as if awaiting his command.

Zoe unbound her long, black hair so it flowed freely to her waist, and Melia ripped off her vest, as if she couldn't bear to have fabric near her breasts.

Thalia gazed at the stranger with a wild hunger. "Forgive me, Mistress," she whispered, setting the amphora down and standing.

Appearing not the least bit surprised by this, the stranger glanced at Ariadne, who remained seated on the blanket. Her handmaidens, usually so demure, suddenly reminded her of dogs straining on the leash to go after a deer.

Before she could formulate a response, the stranger spoke to her women.

"Go," he said. "Find one deserving of my punishment."

And Melia, Zoe, and Thalia ran, faster than Ariadne thought possible. She opened her mouth to call them back, but was so shocked, she could not utter a word.

"I am here to serve you, Priestess. Whatever you desire from me, I would be glad to give." When he returned his attention to her, she questioned her own strength.

"I..." she began. He took three steps closer and stared at her as if she were his prey. His power was almost too much to bear. The desire to rip off her own clothes and lie naked with him under the blue sky overtook her. "I..." she said again, fighting the urge as he drew closer.

Where had he come from? Why was she so drawn to him? Her hand rose to her belt, and it took all her willpower to place it back in her lap. Without permission, the stranger sat on her blanket. He smelled of grapes and earth. His presence was more intoxicating than the mead she had drunk.

"How can I serve you?" he asked, his voice like a caress.

She yearned to stroke his thighs, to run her hands underneath his purple chiton. She was certain he would give her pleasure unlike any she had ever known.

No. She could not. Should not. "I am a priestess of the Great Goddess. No man can serve me."

"But don't men serve the goddess?"

"Not men who are long for this world, stranger." She hoped this would frighten him, but instead he grinned.

"I do not worry about dying, Priestess. I would very much like to serve you. Simply tell me what you would like."

His large, strong, purple-stained hands seemed to have seen work, though the rest of his body was like that of royalty. He touched her wrist gently. Heat shot up her arm.

"I need not take your maidenhead to give you pleasure. Do you think the maidens of Artemis deny themselves desire?" he asked lightly. "All those girls and women together. Even the Great Huntress herself. Do you not think she has a favorite maiden she takes to her bed? In fact, she has several." Visions filled Ariadne's mind as the stranger continued. "They remain virgins and are faithful to her still."

"But you are not the goddess." Could he be? He was effeminate and had an air of the divine. Desire surged within. If the goddess came to her as this pretty boy, she could take her pleasure as she wished. Or, if he were the goddess, was this a trick? A test of her loyalty?

No. The way the mark on her thigh tingled was different than when the goddess summoned her. This being before her was not the goddess. Despite his thin build, his high cheekbones, there was something deeply masculine about him. Something divine that sent her into a frenzy of desire. She wanted those purple-tipped fingers on her skin.

"Does your goddess forbid you from lying with a man?" he asked. He was obviously a foreigner. None of her people would dare be so forward, so unaware.

"That is between the goddess and me. It is none of your concern."

"Forgive me, Priestess. I am only trying to understand, so I can give you what you want."

There was no need to tell him she was not a sworn virgin. That foolishness was all the rage on the mainland. The rules on Crete were different. When the goddess or the king decreed it, the high priestess took a husband for one to three years, depending on his status. She wed him, bedded him, and sacrificed him to the goddess. Her mother Pasiphae had done the same, but she had angered the goddess by keeping her husband Minos. Ariadne had been allowed to continue the line, and the goddess had permitted her parents to live and prosper.

When the goddess demanded Ariadne take a king for a year, Ariadne had allowed Zakros to become her husband. She had lain with him in the fields and allowed him into her bed, but he had not given her a child. And at the end of the year, she gave the goddess his blood, slitting his throat herself. It had been his honor to die for her, for the goddess, for Crete—that is what he had sworn, and what she had repeated to herself. Zakros had shown her deference, desire, and fear. This stranger who longed to please her was unafraid of the goddess and of death.

"Are you a god?" she asked. *The new god we were just talking about?* Had Thalia somehow summoned him?

The stranger surprised her by laughing, a deep sound full of mirth.

"A good question to which there is no answer. My nursemaid told me my father is Zeus, but are not all bastards told the same thing?"

"No." Thalia's mother had been raped by a Spartan, and everyone knew her origin. "Some bastards are told the truth."

"I spent my childhood hidden in a cave made of amethyst. My bed and curtains were moss. Satyrs raised me; my nursemaids were rain nymphs. A satyr named Silenus acted as my father, and a shepherd named Hermes visited often."

She could not tell whether he was joking or serious. His fine black tresses distracted her. Though she sensed danger, she only wanted to stare at his perfect ringlets falling over his rounded shoulders.

"My nursemaids made me dress as a girl when we left the cave. They warned me that if my father's wife found me, she would try to kill me again."

"Again?" she asked.

"Yes, so perhaps I am indeed the son of the Lightning-Striker. I have many gifts as well as an inexplicable power over women. Though not, it seems, over you."

"You do." If he would be truthful, she would be as well. "I feel your power. I want to raise my skirts and feel you deep inside me, but the goddess I vowed myself to is not one to be trifled with."

"No gods are." A fire lit in his eyes.

She pulled away, but that only intensified the yearning.

"Perhaps just one kiss, Priestess?"

"No." She knew how this usually went. A woman unguarded. A stranger. If the seduction did not work, he would try to rape her. That's what men, what gods did. Which is why she had slid the dagger from the picnic basket beneath her skirt. If need be, she would cut him and see whether blood or ichor flowed beneath his skin. "I will not kiss you."

"I will not force you, Priestess. There is no need for the knife." He glanced at her hand under her skirt. "I am sure you are quite skilled at cutting the throats of beasts and men, but I am no sacrifice. At least, not today." He stared into her eyes, and she understood that the stranger's charms were irresistible.

"Swear not to take my maidenhead." It did not matter that she was no maiden.

"Priestess, I swear on the name of Zeus the Father. May he strike me with his bolt if I take your maidenhead against your will."

An odd oath. Zeus the Father would likely applaud any man who took a woman by force, and he had twisted his oath to properly bed her if she wished it.

The stranger smelled of grass, grapes, and earth. Gazing at him made her feel drunk. His full lips beckoned, and she could not wait much longer. Though she wanted to kiss him, instinct told her that if she allowed his lips on her own, she would give herself to him completely and never recover.

"I will not kiss you, stranger. But I will permit you to show me the pleasure you spoke of." She untied the shawl which had kept her breasts hidden. The stranger grinned.

"With your permission." He lowered his head to her breast. Divine pleasure consumed her. The sweet, earthy scent of his hair made her want to drink him in. She hesitated only a moment before plunging her hand into his black tresses and drawing him harder against her.

"Yes, Priestess," he whispered against her skin. "I am here to serve."

He tried to unknot the belt at her waist, but she would not let him. Instead, she lifted her multicolored skirts up over her ankles, then her knees, and finally her hips. She wore no undergarment. The stranger stared at her mound, the hair there dark against her thighs.

"Lovely," he said, stroking her hip.

Of course, Ariadne played with her handmaidens. Thalia was her favorite bedmate. Yet it had been a long time since she had desired a man.

She allowed him to gaze at her, his face hovering closer than any man's had in years. The desire to kiss him pulled at her. The need to satisfy him, to satiate her own yearning, so intense, so immediate.

She fought it. Although she wanted to allow him to take her completely, she would permit him only to serve her. Be he a god or be he a mortal. What she would not do was yield to him completely. She would take what she needed from him. His sole pleasure would be in serving her.

He caressed her, beckoning desire she could barely contain. She gasped, pushing herself to him until she exploded in ecstasy: sudden, urgent, hotter than blood. She gripped his forearm, her nails sinking into his skin, her need for him so complete, but still, still she held back. Instead of putting her mouth on his, she kissed his neck. As pleasure overcame her, she bit him hard, harder than she meant. Liquid warmed her tongue, sweet and salty, a hint of nectar. His blood. She wanted more. He pulled away.

"Did I hurt you?" she asked, shocked to have drawn blood.

He touched his neck, fingering the wound, and appeared even more intrigued by her. "No. It was only unexpected."

"Go on then. Serve me as you promised."

They had come to an understanding. He looked into her eyes as he lowered his head to her waist. He kissed her belly through the multicolored fabric of her gown and then moved between her thighs. She stared up at the blue sky, glad the moon did not witness her betrayal.

"If you are a god, show me the power you have to possess the High Priestess of Crete."

The stranger moaned, husky and low. He pulled back and nipped her inner thigh. She yelped but pushed his head back to her center. She would give him all but her kiss.

His purple-stained fingers worked their magic until she moaned and finally let out a roar of pleasure, the kind of which would have shamed her had she cared for such things anymore.

The sensation seemed to last an eternity. A wave she rode and rode and rode, expecting it to crash, and yet it continued. Nothing else existed in the world but her essence and this stranger who had offered to please her and had been true to his word.

Finally, the wave came to a crescendo, and she released his hair, relaxed her back, and let her legs fall to the blanket. Tears leaked from her eyes, and she stared up at the bright blue sky.

There was no sound but her jagged breaths, the rushing river, and the buzzing bees. She closed her eyes. She felt around in her mind for shame or regret. She found none.

"Did I please you well, Priestess?" he asked.

"Yes." She wanted to permit him to take her into his arms, to nestle her head into the hollow of his shoulder. But she had already let herself go too far. The goddess would not approve of this unsanctioned dalliance.

She pulled down her skirt and sat up. "What do you want in exchange, stranger?"

"Only the chance to do that again, Priestess. And perhaps to call you by your name."

She laughed then, like bells on a spring morning. His words surprised her, but she had never lost track of the hidden dagger.

"What did you do with my bodyguards?" she asked. Manko and Talos would not easily abandon her.

"They distinctly heard you calling them and telling them to return to Knossos."

"How?"

"They heard your voice in their heads. I did not think it proper to have them watch."

She straightened her skirt and adjusted her corselet. "And my ladies?"

For a moment he appeared to not know what she was talking about. "Ah, yes. Your women have gone on a hunt for me. But do not worry, they will not hurt anyone who does not deserve it."

"What do you mean?"

He placed his hand on hers, and an image of her handmaidens filled her mind. Thalia's eyes were wild, her teeth set in a snarl. Blood splattered her chest, her hands stained red to the wrist. Zoe appeared drunk, delirious with the joy of murder. And Melia's smile was wider than Ariadne had ever seen. Her dark hair fell loose and free, so unlike the proper lady Ariadne knew.

Ariadne pulled away from the stranger. "What have you done?"

"Priestess, you asked whether I was a god, and I told you I do not know. But if I am, I am not like Zeus-Lightning-Striker or Poseidon-Earth-Shaker. I am more like Aphrodite or Ares. I do not create the feeling in mortals; I only allow the feeling to come to the surface. Every woman is a leopard or wolf. By day subservient, obedient, full of mother-love, but there is a wild creature hidden beneath. I simply bring it forth."

Nausea pitted her stomach. She had given in to the stranger's sway, had nearly allowed the lust he inspired to consume her, but he had sent her handmaidens on a hunt for blood. What would become of them now?

Dressed, with the dagger in hand, Ariadne rose on unsteady feet. Even overcome by disgust, she was drawn to him still. As she struggled to take a step away from him, she imagined kissing and biting his neck. No. If she gave in to these desires, she would lose herself. She owed it to her family, to all of Crete, not to stray from her duty and incur the wrath of the goddess.

She turned away before he could entice her back to the blanket. Leaving the picnic baskets, she ran like she had never run before. For the first time in her life, she ran from something—not to something.

He could have stopped her. Not only with speed, but with his will. She sensed he could easily draw her back. He could have seduced her easily, convinced her to finish what he had begun, and a part of her longed for it. But he said nothing more. He let her go.

And she went, running all the way back to Knossos, shaking and exuberant, fearful but still full of desire, feeling the thrum between her legs. Yearning to see him again, terrified of what would happen if she did.

DIONYSUS THE YOUNG GOD

Dionysus waited on the dock for a boat to come in. Phoenician traders chatted with Tyrrhenian merchants while a crew of Spartans loaded their new purchases onto their ship. A delegation of Nubians had come to discuss a trade deal, and the Minoans around him speculated what this could mean for the future.

How Ariadne, High Priestess of Crete, captivated him! When she ran away, he was delighted. He had never met a woman who could resist him. Her power inspired him to stay on to pursue her and his craft. The very soil of Crete seemed to call to him, begging him to plant seeds and instruct the people in the ways of the vine.

After Ariadne ran away, he had walked along the meadow. Following the river, he went to the fields, knelt, and plunged his hands into the earth. How rich the soil was, how ready to take the grape and help transform it into wine. Soon he would introduce Crete to the new art of tending the vine, and everything would change. That was not the initial reason he had come here, but thinking of the vintages that were to be born and grow on this island thrilled him.

A heavily laden ship from Attica pulled into port. The sailors were yelling fiercely, trying to untangle the gray sail, dirty and worn from travel, as rowers worked to come in at the right angle. Some of the Phoenicians on the dock watched, amused.

"Go back to your farms. You're no sailors," one of them yelled, bellowing with laughter. The men on the incoming boat could not hear or understand, but Dionysus let out a laugh. This was the boat he was waiting for.

The boat from Attica pulled into the dock with its sail still in a tangle. The red-faced captain yelled at the men who had dropped the sail and tangled the lines. The Phoenicians laughed loudly when they saw that the deck was full of sheep.

"They brought the farm with them," the Phoenician captain called, making everyone who heard hoot.

After docking badly, the crowd was rewarded with the fun of watching the chaos of sailors herding the sheep off the boat and onto the quay.

After the sheep disembarked, the man Dionysus had been waiting for staggered off the ship. Time had not been kind to him, but Dionysus would recognize the uneven gait of his foster father Silenus anywhere. His curly black hair had receded, showing his high forehead, now creased with lines. He had the same upturned nose and scraggly beard as always, and his large ears appeared ready to transform into ass's ears. To blend in, he had transformed his goat legs into those of a mortal man, though his new legs still appeared bowed.

"Little Liber," Silenus said, embracing him. The old satyr smelled of sheep and weak beer.

"It has been too long, Silenus. Come, let's go to the market. I'll buy you a cup of beer and a skewer of octopus fresh from the sea. Everything I've eaten here is delicious. Can you feel the magic of this place?"

Silenus cupped Dionysus's cheek. "It is so good to see you, Little Liber. I meant to come back to you on Nysa. When I returned, you were gone, and every place I went, I heard tales of your deeds—and misdeeds. How you have grown." He took in

Dionysus's purple robe, the thyrsus clutched in his hand, the small wineskin on his belt, and the crown of myrtle in his hair. "You no longer doubt your divinity, do you?"

"Not the way I did before." He led Silenus out of the port town. They followed the road next to the river full of smaller boats laden with cargo. "This is how they transport the oil and grain to the storehouse under the great palace-temple of Knossos. One day, they will export wine."

"Of course, Little Liber, of course." Silenus noticed his first woman then and became transfixed, watching her walk toward them and then past them.

"It is not considered polite to stare. You are in their land now," Dionysus said.

"The women here do not cover their breasts."

"No. They reveal them proudly, for they are part of their power."

Silenus glanced about, taking in the Minoans around them. "The men don't wear much either. What fine forms they have."

"They are a skillful, artistic people. This place is full of acrobats, dancers, divers, and bull leapers. I'm glad you got my message to meet here."

"Oh, yes." Silenus started to stare at an older woman walking toward them. He caught himself and turned his attention back to Dionysus. "I looked for you in Brauron. I heard nothing of you when I asked. What occurred there?"

It was hard for Dionysus not to be truthful, but he was not ready to tell his foster father the whole story yet. "Let's get something to eat first."

"And drink," Silenus added.

Having been in Crete a few days, Dionysus had sampled several of the food stalls and found a favorite. He ordered skewered octopus, which was deliciously salted and paired perfectly with a cup of beer. They took the stools the place offered for an extra price and sat in the half shade.

"What an amazing city," Silenus said, taking in the grand

buildings and squinting up at Knossos. "What is that on top of the building?"

"The horns of consecration. They're both crescent moons and bull horns. Both are sacred here."

"Ah, this is delicious." Silenus sucked the octopus from his skewer. "Tell me all, Little Liber. What adventures have you had?"

"After you left Nysa, I waited for you or Hermes to return. The nymphs said I should stay, that they had been instructed to hide me from Hera. You know I never really believed them, and I grew tired of being in the same place for so long.

"I went to Thebes, to meet my mother's sister. She didn't believe I was her nephew at first, but she saw a resemblance in my eyes, so she offered to take me in. It was intriguing to live with them, and all was well until her husband went mad and began to whip us all. We had done nothing to rouse his anger. He had been god-struck. In a panic, we ran toward the sea." He didn't tell Silenus how terrified he had been, how he regretted not listening to the nymphs, how he wished he had worn girls' clothes and never left Mount Nysa. He didn't ask Silenus where he had been.

"I jumped off a cliff, wondering whether I was going to die."

"But I've always said you are the son of Zeus and immortal."

"Isn't every bastard told the same?" Dionysus had finished the beer and needed a better drink for this discussion. He pulled out the small wineskin on his waist and poured some wine into his empty cup, doing the same for Silenus.

"Ah, yes. How I've missed this divine brew. Little Liber, how can you doubt your divinity after a single sip of this?"

"The moment I truly believed that Zeus was my father was the moment I didn't die in the depths of the Ionian Sea. The nereid Thetis rescued me. She hid me in her grotto where she shared many secrets. In her depths, with her blue-black hair swirling around us, she told me about the other gods and suggested I meet Hephaestus. She had rescued the Smith God when Hera threw him down from Olympus. The God of the Forge was not at first friendly, but after I gave him some wine, he became vivacious and jolly. He said if I ever needed to seek him on Lemnos, I would always be welcomed there."

Silenus's attention was drawn away from Dionysus by the farmers who had come from the villages to inspect the livestock from Attica. "I spent all my time on the boat with those sheep. I do hope they go to good homes."

"I'm sure they will. Where have you been all this time, Silenus?"

"Ah." Silenus glanced down into his empty clay cup. "I've had women and raised families. How long has it been, Little Liber?"

"I don't know, generations, centuries? Who's to say?"

"Yes, I buried three wives and outlived all my children. After that, I just traveled. Sometimes it's easier to live with the animals."

Grief washed over Silenus's face. Dionysus had forgotten this sorrow that overcame his foster father after drinking.

"Little Liber, I was not a good father to you. I never meant to leave Mount Nysa. You know how easily I lose my way. I never forgot you, and I kept trying to return, but there was always a beautiful woman in the way and then children." He passed his hand over his face, wiping away tears.

"You were a better father to me than my own," Dionysus said, trying to keep the bitterness from his voice. Two women sitting nearby were staring at Silenus, and Dionysus did not want to draw attention.

"Come," Dionysus said.

"I'm sorry." Silenus stood up, upending his stool.

Dionysus wrapped his arm around Silenus's shoulder and led him away from the marketplace, away from the city. The old satyr needed to be in nature. Once among the trees, he would recover his spirits.

Without thinking, Dionysus returned to the meadow where he had encountered Ariadne. He smiled at the memory of her pleasure and how her strength had surprised him. He had not expected to be so drawn to a high priestess. Never had he met one so powerful.

"Ah, this place smells lovely," Silenus sniffed, inhaling the scent of wild rosemary, sage, and thyme.

On the edge of the meadow, a grove of trees beckoned. While on Crete, Dionysus had spied finely tended olive groves and vast fields of organized farmland, but here, the trees grew as they wished. Once beneath the shade of the branches, Silenus sighed, as if the large oak leaves would take all his cares away. The wind blew gently through the branches.

"I did not mean to leave you, Little Liber, and am so glad to see you again."

"You as well, Silenus. I need your help here teaching the people how to make wine and..."

"I am weary from my journey. A nap is what I need, and there is the perfect spot." He staggered to the shade of a plane tree, made his cloak into a pillow, and lay down.

Dionysus stared at his already sleeping foster father.

He wanted to tell Silenus what had happened in Brauron and the real reason he had initially come to Crete. Perhaps he should keep the shame to himself.

In truth, he had sought Ariadne to take revenge on his half-sister Artemis. He had only met the Maiden of the Hunt once, but her words and her arrows had stung.

He had traveled to Delphi to find Apollo, but the far-shooting god was not there. The oracle told him to go to Brauron, for his fate lay there. He went happily, eager to meet Artemis, the Mistress of Wild Things. He sent his satyrs and maenads away. They made such a racket, it would be impossible to find the Maidens of Artemis, and that was exactly who he was hoping to come upon. He did not mind the days of solitude. Being alone among the trees under the clear sky was a gift enough. If he wanted to make plants grow, all he need do was ask.

He did not know how long he wandered in those sacred woods. Left to himself, he could spend months, years, decades away and feel as if it were only days. He had no need to pay attention to time, for there were no mortals who mattered to him.

Solitude created its own magic as he enjoyed the wind singing through the trees and silently observed roe deer nibble grass and hares dart from their hiding places. This place was enchanted. The Mistress of Wild Things and her troop of maidens were near. He could sense it with a new awareness. One of his father's children was not far away.

The next day, he heard the shouts and cheers of women through the trees. Their voices drew him, the way his own maenads compelled mortals to come dance. He crept to the edge of the tree line and peered out. About fifty young women in various stages of dress stood in a circle intently watching a match. He had never seen such athletic women—their naked limbs exposed to the sun, strong arms and muscular thighs shining with oil.

They stood riveted, shouting, "You can do it, Lippodie!" and "Don't let her pin you, Little Hound!"

He guessed they were watching a wrestling match. Unable to resist, he crept closer. He had often been told he looked like a girl. Perhaps they wouldn't notice him. Pressing into the crowd, he stared over the heads of the onlookers. In the center, two maidens wrestled, naked and oiled.

Admiring their gleaming bodies and caught up in the sport, he stared in awe at their glistening forearms; slick thighs, grasping to pin the other around the waist; their mounds, coated in oil and sweat, so close to touching. Lippodie was closing in. Little Hound was almost completely pinned, Lippodie's breasts so close to Little Hound's mouth.

The crowd surged closer against him. A pair of breasts pushed up against his back, a firm calf brushed his own. He stood transfixed among the swell of female bodies, wanting nothing more than to stand unseen and watch.

But the girl in front of him took a step back and brushed against his manhood. Turning, she glared at him in shock.

"Who are you?" she asked, pushing her hand against his chest. She clutched at his breast, squeezing. "You are no maiden," she yelled over the noise of the others. "You dare to trespass against the goddess?"

Raising her arms, she began to shout. "There is a man here. A man has dared to come to the camp!"

The Maidens of Artemis all turned their attention toward him. The wrestlers stopped. Disentangling themselves from one another, they stood, naked, coated in oil and dust, fists clenched, cords on their forearms standing out.

The beauties who just a moment before had been so alluring now snarled, yelling in startled fury. He wondered whether he should use his power on them. What maenads this mob would make! Well-muscled and much stronger than the average woman. He was considering his choices when a brown-haired girl stepped to the forefront. She wore a saffron colored tunic and carried a bow, which she quickly raised and aimed at him. The maidens around him scattered, giving their mistress a clearer target.

Realizing she was about to draw, he put out his hand, and a vine sprung from the earth, tripping her. Her arrow faltered and grazed his arm instead of hitting his heart.

Seeing their mistress distressed, the Maidens of Artemis swarmed to attack, but Dionysus raised his hand again, summoning his own power. Drumbeats sounded from the forest, and the women turned, unable to resist the pull. They held still for a moment, fighting him; some turned their eyes to their goddess as if to beg forgiveness. His sway overtook them, and one, then two, then five, then all raced away from their mistress and into the woods, leaving the two gods alone.

"Who are you that you dare to trespass and disperse my women?" Artemis spat. Her young face radiated fury as she again raised her bow, nocked an arrow, and drew back.

Dionysus lifted his hand. A vine sprang from the earth and pulled her bow from her hands.

"I am your brother."

"Brother?" She said the word with disgust. "Phoebus Apollo is my brother. You are just another bastard my father got on a mortal." She narrowed her eyes, which shone with golden fury. "The new god, is it? From what I hear, he did not care enough for your mother to let her birth you."

Her words were like a punch to the gut. Overcome with anger, he growled. Vines sprouted from the earth, snaking up the goddess's calves, tightening and rendering her immobile.

"Stop that!" she said and threw an arrow at him.

The point penetrated his shoulder, hurting far more than he had expected. The vines went slack, and the drums stopped beating in the forest.

"I'm not impressed with your tricks, bastard!" the Goddess of the Hunt said. "I've heard about you—your wild women and your new drink. They mean nothing to me. You mean nothing to me. My maidens are skilled archers. When they return, they will arm themselves and hunt you like the wild beast you are. My father has sired countless bastards—most mortal, few divine. I don't know whether you're immortal, but I would be happy to find out. If you value your life, you should run."

He probed his wound with trembling fingers. Blood seeped from his shoulder. He did as the Huntress advised and ran.

He had escaped with his life. His wound healed, but his desire for vengeance remained. He made it his mission to find the priestesses of Artemis and seduce them. It had not been difficult. He had gone all the way back to Thebes, where he seduced a priestess of Artemis and fought with his cousin Pentheus. In Athens, he had converted a doe-eyed beauty to his new religion, and in Sparta, he had taught the cultivation of wine while bedding the high priestess of the upstanding Artemis temple.

He travelled around the isles, sharing his gift of wine and enraging women if their kings did not honor him. Mortals came to him easily, drawn by his gifts. Boys and women eagerly joined his retinue, spreading the word of his wonder, honoring him with sacrifices and songs. Every priestess of Artemis he encountered easily fell under his spell.

Buoyed by his success, he had left his entourage behind and set sail for Crete, bringing amphorae of wine and a desire for his next conquest. The famed island nation rivaled Egypt in her astounding architecture and art. A feat befitting the gods, the palaces stood four stories tall, and Dionysus had heard they were equipped with running water.

The people were strikingly beautiful: dark-skinned, almond-eyed, with hair black as night. He would have come here just to meet rich King Minos and give him the gift of wine. The fertile Cretan soil would be perfect for harvesting grapes, but more than that, he longed to see the High Priestess Ariadne. He had come hoping for a challenge. But he had never suspected she would be able to resist him—to deny him, even. She was the granddaughter of the sun, but he did not think that was why she was able to withstand his power. That strength seemed to come from her alone.

He had at last found someone worthy of the chase. Now that Silenus was here to help him, he had a new idea, one that would have shocked him only a few days before.

✵ 3 ✵

ARIADNE AT KNOSSOS

As she neared the bull gates, Ariadne regained her composure. She pushed away her fears that she had angered the goddess, that something terrible had happened to her handmaidens and guards. She must always appear calm in public. Hopefully, no one had raised the alarm that she returned alone.

A small boat was docked in the river that ran by the palace. The shouts of sailors unloading amphorae of oil and grain floated on the wind. Hearing their voices calmed her. Knossos continued to prosper. Everything was still in its place. Her people needed her to appear at ease and in control.

Her father's guards bowed as she passed the bright red columns. None of them dared address her, but she could tell they all noted she entered alone. Talos and Manko could lose their lives for abandoning her. If questioned, she would claim to have ordered them to another task. Clearly the stranger had a power they could not resist. She would not let them be executed.

Once inside the inner courtyard, she wiped the sweat from her brow and readjusted her garments. *You are the embodiment of the goddess,* her mother had told her. If she showed distress, the whole city could erupt in terror. *Even if the omens are bad, even if they spell out disaster, never let your expression betray your fear.*

Ariadne entered the main building through one of the many side doors. Visitors said the palace was a labyrinth, but Ariadne had spent her childhood navigating the twisting corridors, running up and down the stairs, and playing hide and seek with her sister Phaedra and her many brothers.

She wended her way past the hall of shields, up the grand staircase, and to the second floor to her mother's rooms.

Though Pasiphae was no longer the high priestess, her status of witch-queen remained. Nowhere in Knossos did Ariadne feel magic as she did in her mother's rooms. Festooned with fresh flowers in exquisite vases, her mother's outer chamber was abuzz with women sorting wool and herbs. As always, women came from all over the island bringing gifts of honey, flowers, and herbs in exchange for spells and curses. The scent of chamomile and lavender hung heavy in the air. A common sleep aid for children and demanding husbands, this was what most women needed.

"Greetings, High Priestess," Kaira, Pasiphae's Oceanid handmaid, said. Her long blue hair glittered with gray.

"Kaira." Ariadne clasped her worn hands.

"It is good to see you, child." She laughed, and though it had been years since she left the sea, Ariadne could still hear the surf in her voice. "Though you are a child no longer. Did you come to help sort the wool as you used to?"

Warmth flooded Ariadne. How many days had she spent here with her mother, Kaira, and her sister Phaedra sorting and spinning wool for her mother's visions? Those days of her childhood seemed so long ago. Everything had changed after her brother Androgeus was murdered in Athens.

"No, Kaira, I came to see my mother, but perhaps now is not the best time."

Pasiphae sat on her throne of cedarwood painted with gold, her hand on a woman's belly. Some of the women and girls in her audience hall sat on the gypsum bench that surrounded three of the walls. One of the walls was painted with images of girls gathering saffron, an aid for menstrual cramps and headaches. Other flowered frescoes held secrets as well. While women waited, they could learn which flowers would aid different ailments.

Tapestries on the wall glittered, woven with gold or silver thread. There were many of great, glistening bulls' horns or a majestic white bull swimming in the sea—a sea that seemed to foam and move as if animated.

Nursing women and naked children sat on the saffron-colored carpet and waited their turn for an audience with Pasiphae. Ariadne inhaled scents of chamomile, lavender, rosemary, and sage, willing herself to calm. She wanted to speak to her mother about what had occurred, but she had not thought of what she would be interrupting.

"You are always welcome here, child," Kaira said.

Pasiphae noticed her. Her eyes flashed pure gold for a moment. *The sun saw what I did.* Ariadne tried not to panic. No. Her grandfather did not speak to her mother, and Ariadne had broken no laws. She could bed who she wanted. But how could her handmaidens leave her like that? Where were Talos and Manko?

"High Priestess," several women murmured and held their arms up in an honorary salute. A heavily pregnant woman waddled toward her, and Ariadne touched her belly.

"May the Great Goddess bless you with an easy labor and a healthy babe."

"Thank you, High Priestess." The woman moved away slowly.

Ariadne blessed a woman with a sallow baby, a woman hoping to conceive, and a girl who suffered debilitating cramps.

One of Pasiphae's handmaidens offered Ariadne basil tea flavored with honey. She took a long sip to quench her thirst and focused on not betraying her worries.

Tamar, the most skilled lyre player in Knossos, began a song everyone knew.

"Great Goddess, my goddess, shine through us."

The chorus buoyed Ariadne's spirits. She was here now, in her mother's chambers among the women she lived to protect. She took another sip of tea and went to her mother.

As always, Pasiphae was beautiful beyond measure, golden eyes glittering, her skin and demeanor cool as marble—a divine being.

"Daughter, I see a great change for you on this day."

Ariadne's cheeks warmed as she pictured the stranger between her thighs.

"The gods shine a light through you. Your destiny has shifted." She smoothed Ariadne's hair. "You are bound for greatness, but the path is crooked. Your journey is to walk the labyrinth. A change comes for us today, and the gods themselves do not know the outcome. As far as Athens and all the way to India, the winds shift. We are destined to a new age, but we will not be forgotten."

"Mother," she wanted to cry like a child. Instead, she lifted the necklace she always wore—polished bull's horn shaped into the form of bull's horns and the crescent moon—and dug one of the points into her breastbone.

"Your destiny will not be easy, child, but there is little point in fighting it." Pasiphae laughed lightly, the sound like rock crystal shattering on marble. "I fought my own destiny once when I first came here. I did not want to marry a mortal, but the gods had plans for me—as they do for you. Love comes for you, daughter." She spoke these last words lightly, yet Ariadne could not help feeling she was being cursed.

Zoe, Melia, and Thalia crept back into the palace before the guards closed the gates for the night. They came to their mistress wild-eyed, with their hair loose. Ariadne did not ask where they had been. The vision she had seen was too terrible. Thalia knelt before her; leaves and dirt crowned her head where she had once worn flowers.

"Mistress, I do not know how it came to pass, but we ran and ran and fell upon a deer. It was..." Her lips parted in an unbidden smile. Scratches and flecks of blood marred her arms; her nails were coated with blood. She glanced up into Ariadne's eyes, and her pale face transformed to one of grief. "It was unforgivable that we left you. We await your punishment." Thalia bowed her head, her curly blonde hair cascading over her face. Zoe stood and handed Ariadne the whip as Melia got down on her knees. They helped each other remove their vests and bared their backs.

Ariadne lifted the whip in her hand. For merely displeasing her, she could send them to work in the laundry or the kitchen instead of having the honor of serving her. For abandoning her, her handmaidens could be sent away. If King Minos discovered their true crime, he would sentence them to die.

"Zoe, Thalia, and Melia, I value the service you have rendered me. Yet your crime is unforgivable. You must be punished, but I will not have you lose your lives for this. This will remain a secret among us."

Did they even know what they had done? No. Their downcast eyes and tears were for abandoning her.

It would be better for her handmaidens to stay out of public view. Suddenly inspiration struck.

"I will not beat you." She put the whip down. "Your punishment will not be that easy. Instead I will send you to the cave shrines with an offering. Your journey will appease the goddess since we forgot to leave her honey yesterday. Sleep in the temple tonight. Tell Priestess Seer what I've commanded. In the morning, she will give you all you need to take."

Melia and Zoe stood and dressed, but Thalia knelt. "Don't make me leave you, Mistress. Whip me instead. Please."

Ariadne caressed Thalia's face. She wished Thalia could stay with her. Ariadne would suffer without Thalia—and that was another reason her plan was perfect.

"You will redeem us by going to the cave shrine. When you return, all will be as it was." Ariadne hoped this was true.

Thalia glanced at the bed they had slept in together for the last eleven years. "Should I return to help you ready for sleep?"

"No. I will attend to myself," Ariadne said.

Zoe gasped aloud, and Melia said, "But..." before remembering herself. Thalia gazed at her, lowering her head, and began to follow the others out the door. Then, as if attached by an invisible string, she ran back and knelt before Ariadne, placing her face on her mistress's left foot. Thalia's tears fell hot against her skin.

"Please, punish me however you like, Mistress, but do not let me go. Please, you are my..."

"Thalia, enough." She sank her fingers into Thalia's hair, wishing she could pull her to standing, forgive her, and invite her to return to their bed. But she could not. She stroked Thalia's cheek, wiping away her tears. "I do this so you can return to me." If anyone accused Thalia, if anyone had seen, Ariadne would not let her die. She would go against her father if she had to. She would exile Thalia, Zoe, and Melia from Crete rather than allow them to be executed.

Loneliness descended once they were gone. She washed her face but ignored her hair. Thalia would have unraveled the complicated strand of gold entwined in her many braids, would have brushed it out gently and rubbed her arms, legs, and breasts with lavender oil. She did not deserve such luxuries. Though her stomach growled, she did not eat. This and sleeping without Thalia was part of her punishment.

She had been eleven when she first saw Thalia in King Minos's audience hall. As part of her training, Ariadne observed her father as he sat as judge over his subjects. The cases usually bored her—farmers arguing over cows or land, an occasional military issue. Children and foreigners were seldom brought to court. Ariadne spied the blonde girl the moment she entered, eyes downcast, tangled hair hiding her face.

"Great Minos," the bailiff announced. "Melas the innkeeper begs your wise judgment against the swineherd Cilix. They each claim to own this girl." This brought whispering among the audience chamber.

Cilix's greasy black hair fell unevenly over his bare shoulders. Though she suspected he had donned his finest clothing to go to court, his white kilt was stained with mud, and he stank of swine.

He pulled the girl toward King Minos, clutching her wrist. Bruises like bracelets snaked their way around her forearm. Pity for the girl and fury at the man overwhelmed her. *Kill him, Father*, she thought. King Minos often said that justice could not be decided without evidence. But one look at Thalia's stepfather, and she knew he was guilty, the way a girl can know the crimes of men.

As Cilix raised his eyes to the royal dais, he noticed her. His gaze made her shudder. She was safe in her status as the daughter of the queen and king, but one glance from the swineherd, and she knew that if she met this man alone in some deserted place, he could overpower her and do what men often did to helpless girls. Do to her what he had likely done to the bruised blonde girl. But Ariadne was not afraid. She was not helpless.

Melas, a muscular man with broad shoulders, bowed and stepped forward. "Great Minos, I bought this girl, Thalia, from Cilix two days ago in exchange for coin and a jar of mead. He drank the mead and spent the coin, but when I went to collect the girl, he denied selling her to me."

Thalia glanced up at Melas, as if wondering whether he could offer a better future than Cilix. Blondes were rare in Crete. But it was not only the uniqueness of her hair color. The girl was strikingly beautiful. Even bruised, her tanned skin was exquisite when juxtaposed with her golden hair.

Ariadne saw the girl's future in an instant. Serving one horrid man or another—that was a common woman's lot, but this girl with her strange beauty would attract a monster, one who would rent her out or beat her just for being so stunning. Such a creature would not live long on Crete as a peasant.

"I never sold my stepdaughter to this man, Great Minos,"

Cilix said. "Everyone knows he whores out girls to sailors. I would never allow the girl to be defiled."

"With respect, Great Minos," Melas interrupted. "Cilix does not remember his agreement to me because he was drunk. He was all too happy to sell the girl to me for mead. I paid a good amount for her. It was only when he realized he could get more by keeping her that he reneged. I've lost money on the deal. If he won't give me the girl, I at least want my money back."

Ariadne's father stroked his black beard, a crinkle of pity in his eye and a hint of lust. If Minos took Thalia for himself, the girl would have jewels and fine gowns, but she would still belong to a man.

Ariadne pictured a different fate for Thalia. Without thinking, she stood. All her father's subjects turned their attention to her.

"How much did you pay?" she asked Melas.

"Two coins of silver."

"I will pay you for the money lost. I want the girl for myself."

It seemed the court had never been so silent. Had anyone else spoken without permission, the bailiff would have been upon them in an instant. Ariadne turned toward her father. "With your permission, Great Minos."

Beneath her father's beard, she spied a hint of a smile. He motioned for her to continue.

"Cilix." Even speaking his name left a bitter impression on her lips. "You will give her to me in the name of the goddess." Ariadne was not sure whether the goddess was speaking through her, but she did know that her destiny was intertwined with this girl.

"My daughter speaks. The future High Priestess of Crete makes demands. Her will and the will of the goddess are just."

Cilix had begrudgingly surrendered Thalia to Ariadne. Thalia had stared at her, stunned, tears of gratitude streaked her dirty cheeks. She had been the most obedient servant from that day since. And now she was a murderer. What had the stranger taken from her?

The next morning Ariadne dressed herself and attempted to

fix her hair. The golden strands of jewels had become badly tangled, but the braids still held. Her hair would do for the day. She would decipher how to fix it later. She slipped her golden earrings in and applied a little makeup. There was no need for ceremony on this day.

When she was dressed and ready, she strode from her bedroom, past the empty side rooms where Zoe and Melia usually slept, to the outer chamber.

"Talos," she called. He and Manko had been waiting outside her door when she returned from her mother's rooms. They had appeared dazed, and she had said nothing about their disappearance.

Talos opened the door to her outer chamber. "Good morning, High Priestess." He appeared to have returned to himself. He scanned her rooms, frowning to find them empty.

"My handmaidens are taking an offering to the goddess in a cave shrine. No need to tell anyone but Manko."

"Yes, High Priestess."

"Tell me the news."

Talos's handsome face changed. Excitement lit his black eyes.

"A trade deal with Nubia has been reached, and a contingent will stay to train with King Minos's soldiers. Among our own, everyone is talking of how Cilix the swineherd is dead, torn apart near his home. It seems to be the work of wild creatures, though no one can figure out what might have killed him in such a grizzly manner. No one weeps for his death. I'm glad for Thalia. I know his crimes haunt her still."

Ariadne grasped his forearm. The strong, corded muscles and his warmth gave her comfort. "She will be glad to learn of it, I'm sure. Is there a hunt for the wild creatures?"

Talos shrugged his broad shoulders. "I have heard of no search. His neighbors do not mourn and have already divided his lands among themselves. Many have wanted him gone. Perhaps the prayers for his death have finally been heard."

"The gods are mysterious," she said, hoping she sounded convincing.

Talos and Manko accompanied her to the temple where she checked with the priestesses, listened to complaints, and gave counsel to supplicants. Then she walked the sacred path in privacy, listening for the goddess. But the goddess did not speak to her, and the crescent mark on her thigh did not tingle as it had before the stranger came.

Ariadne returned to the east wing eager to take a bath, drink some mead, and fall into a dreamless sleep. She had no plans to dine in the small dining hall. She could not stomach watching nobles, sailors, and statesmen discuss business with her father over coriander cuttlefish and beer. King Minos would forgive her, and Pasiphae wouldn't notice.

She walked by the hall of shields, passing the great gallery that split off in the direction of her rooms. Phaedra sat playing with a monkey.

"Sister, come see Zek," Phaedra said.

Zek was her sister's favorite new plaything. The little gray vervet monkey screeched and climbed up to Phaedra's shoulder.

"How old is she now?" Ariadne asked.

"Six months." Phaedra stroked Zek's fuzzy back, and the little monkey played with Phaedra's braids. "I can't wait to see what animals arrive next. Maybe someone will bring a griffin."

"Perhaps, or a dragon or a golden sheep. She is very cute."

Phaedra fed Zek a piece of fruit. "I hear Father has a suitor for you."

Ariadne laughed lightly. "I'm not interested."

"That doesn't matter. Isn't a part of your job as high priestess to marry and kill?"

"Phaedra, now is not the time."

"Father says now is exactly the time. All of Crete would breathe a sigh of relief if you were with child. This might be the perfect match. Besides, you'll have to sacrifice him anyway, so perhaps it's best if you don't like him." Phaedra laughed, and the monkey let out a little bark.

Ariadne turned to go, but Phaedra, with Zek on her shoulder, followed. "I think this suitor would suit you." She giggled at her joke. "Father has taken a liking to him. He comes bearing all kinds of gifts from across the sea."

"A foreigner?" King Minos must be serious then. Ariadne sighed. She would have to don her ceremonial gown and go to dinner. She shouldn't have dismissed Thalia. She could do her own makeup, but the golden strands were tangled in her hair, and she couldn't remove them on her own. She wasn't even sure she could lace her corselet by herself.

Talos opened the chamber doors for her. Phaedra strode right in, taking in the emptiness.

"Where are your ladies, sister? I'm sure Zoe is off flirting with Daedalus, and perhaps Melia is getting you mead, but I expected your little Spartan slut to be here, eager to undress you."

"Phaedra, stop that," Ariadne snapped.

"Really though, where is Thalia? I heard about Cilix. She must be overjoyed."

The hair on Ariadne's neck stood up. "I sent them to purify themselves for touching a possession of the goddess."

"Is that so? I don't recall mother teaching us about that."

"Well, you were never the most observant during our lessons."

Phaedra glared at her and then smiled, sharp as a knife. She put Zek down, and the monkey ran to the fruit bowl on a low table.

"Well, since your ladies aren't here, let me help you."

"That is kind, sister." She went to her cedar chest and pulled out her ceremonial corselet and a turquoise, amber, and blood red flounced skirt.

"I always forget how grand your rooms are," Phaedra said, walking through the bedroom and out to the balcony. The monkey followed, leaving a smear of apricots in her wake.

Ariadne's head ached from not eating. She wished Thalia were there to rub her temples and help her dress. Sending her ladies away had seemed the right thing to do last night, but now, with the sun in the sky, it was clearly a mistake.

Ariadne picked up her mirror and examined her hair. To the untrained eye, the gold glittering in her black tresses would still be impressive. She just needed to re-oil some of the coils on the sides.

"Not too bad," Phaedra said, coming back from the balcony. She hovered behind the mirror and pulled one of the golden strands entwined in Ariadne's hair. "You're like a true goddess, with gold coming out of your head."

Ariadne didn't reply or let on how much the tug hurt. She slid off her short-sleeved vest and slipped the corselet over her head until it was around her waist.

"Let me help you," Phaedra said, pulling the cords tight. "You have the smallest waist. Hopefully this new husband will plant a child in there, and then we can all watch it swell and rejoice."

"Phaedra, I'm in no mood for this."

"But that doesn't matter, High Priestess. This is part of your duty. You are the chosen one." Phaedra spoke lightly, but her words did their damage. "Just look at your breasts, so full of power. Do you want me to paint your nipples gold?"

"No. Another suitor is of no concern. I'm sure he's not a worthy sacrifice for the goddess—few are."

"If he is not worthy of you or the goddess, I'll take him—either to my bed for the night or as a husband. I saw him going in to meet Father. Just from his profile, my nipples got hard, and I was wet between the thighs. He's not the same kind of boring local king father usually has you parade your tits out for."

Ariadne clenched her fist, wishing she had a snake wrapped around her wrist to fling at Phaedra. Though even if she had, her sister would not be worth potentially damaging a sacred snake.

"And how do they look?" Ariadne asked, standing up straight. Women, men, and eunuchs had complimented her breasts. They were full but somehow light, as if they were meant to be displayed to the populace. Her breasts were not a private thing to be fondled by one man in the dark. Her breasts were meant to be shown to the people to give them confidence. These were the strong breasts of the High Priestess of the Goddess, full of promise for her people.

"The left one is hanging a little low," Phaedra said.

Resisting the urge to slap her, Ariadne adjusted herself. "Don't forget your monkey, sister." She turned and walked down the stairs.

The delicious scent of roasted meat filled the small dining hall. Ariadne expected a large gathering, but King Minos was not there. She did not see any men except the guards who stood by the doors.

Queen Pasiphae sat on a grand chair surrounded by her ladies.

"Daughter, glad you are here. Try some of this." She passed Ariadne her golden cup, engraved with a scene of the goddess descending and dancing among swaying palms.

"It's very good," Kaira said. Her old eyes appeared bluer than usual.

"It's like mead, but instead of honey, it's made of grapes. It's called grape-wine, a gift from the gods. Go on, try," Pasiphae said.

Ariadne could not describe the flavor, but she wanted more. Taking a second sip, the liquid flowed over her tongue—plum, flower—she could almost taste the earth and the sun, imagine the vines crawling up from the earth.

"Your father is sorting out the details of your new marriage. For once, he might have found the right husband for you. Eat and then go to him," Pasiphae said, taking back her cup.

Phaedra followed Ariadne as she took her customary seat on the gypsum bench.

"High Priestess." A servant offered her a skewer of roasted lamb, which she took gratefully. Seasoned with honey and lavender, the lamb melted in her mouth.

"Princess." The servant offered a platter full of delicacies to Phaedra.

Phaedra scooped up some sea snails with rosemary in flatbread. Zek leapt off her shoulder and ran across the room to the doorway where the new dishes were being brought out.

"Mother will be furious if that monkey makes a mess in here," Ariadne said, taking a bowl of seafood stew in both hands and bringing it to her lips. The stew was delicious and just what she needed to strengthen her.

"Someone will put Zek back in the menagerie. I want to try the new drink."

"High Priestess, Princess." Another servant brought them cups full of dark red liquid. The scent of the wine and the feeling of intoxication it gave made her think of the stranger.

She must forget about him and all that had passed between them. She would wed this new suitor, probably an Egyptian or Phoenician, a minor prince perhaps who came to offer his hand and later his head.

Yet with the next sip, she imagined the stranger's tongue in her mouth, as smooth as the wine she swallowed, his hands stroking her neck, his purple-stained fingers trailing slowly down to her clavicle. Her nipples hardened at the memory. Phaedra noticed.

"Looks like you're ready to meet your new husband. Do let me know if you don't care for him."

Ariadne ignored her sister and stood. She maintained her regal air and strode to the room next door.

"Daughter!" Minos exclaimed, rising from his couch. His cheeks glowed like hot coals, his smile too large and carefree. His purple teeth gave his secret away. Clearly he had drunk too much —what was it called? wine—grape-wine, the new invention of the gods. She hardly noticed the frescoes of the sacred bull that foreigners always commented on, the cedarwood tables and luxurious couches covered with Egyptian linen. Two men attended her father, though in the flickering light of the brazier she could see neither clearly.

"Ariadne," King Minos said, swaying on his feet, "at long last, I have found the perfect husband for you! He is god-touched. Worthy of your blade—and he has agreed to be your husband for a great year of three years' time."

She could not make out the man's face at first, only the perfectly coiled tresses of his hair and his purple robe embroidered with gold. She gasped upon seeing his high cheekbones, his eyes dancing in amusement.

"Princess," he said, bowing to her, "Priestess, I am honored."

"Daughter, this is Dionysus, a prince from across the sea, and his foster father Silenus."

Dionysus's companion rose from the couch—or attempted to rise. His short, curly black hair peppered with gray gave the impression of hiding horns or ass's ears.

"An honor, Lady," Silenus slurred, adjusting his chiton which puffed awkwardly in the back, giving her the distinct impression that he failed to hide a tail. Looking at Silenus made her feel drunk, and the proximity of Dionysus roused her far more than she'd ever admit.

Resist. But she could barely restrain herself from grinning like a fool at the sight of the stranger she had lain with.

"Dionysus has come bearing gifts of this magical elixir he calls wine. He and Silenus have agreed to teach us how to cultivate it. In exchange, Dionysus asks only for the chance to be your husband."

Delightful. She wanted to slap herself for how excited she was to see the stranger. She could not allow herself to be enchanted by Dionysus as her father was.

"He will be a good match for you, daughter. Of that I am sure."

Dionysus awaited her reaction. She refused to give him one.

"Would the priestess like to try the wine that is my wedding gift?" he asked.

"Yes!" King Minos's eyes lit up at the idea. Her father had never been one to share.

"Not tonight. Thank you. I must retire to bed," she said.

Perhaps this folly would be forgotten in the morning. How long could the enchantment last?

"Go then," her father said. "But do not go alone, daughter. Take your new husband with you."

Dionysus grinned, his teeth white in the light, his eyes clear. He took two steps and was suddenly holding her hand.

"Please, Priestess, show me the way."

4

DIONYSUS LEARNS TO SERVE

The high priestess dropped his hand as soon as they were out of sight of her father. She neither glanced at him nor spoke as he followed her through the pathways of Knossos. Some of the corridors were lit with torches; others only had light from wide windows and light shafts. Guards with daggers at their waists stood throughout.

They passed a great corridor painted with huge cow-hide shields. He remembered this from his entrance. Though the Minoans had no high walls or apparent defenses, this very palace was the defense. In the many places he had traveled, Dionysus had seen men armed for combat with shields and breastplates, yet these nearly naked, wasp-waisted men of Knossos appeared more fearless and certain than an army of Thebans.

Ariadne did not glance back as she ascended the grand staircase. The steps were more evenly spaced than any others he had climbed. The ox-blood colonnades on the sides of the stairs caught his eye but were not as intriguing as the woman he followed. She moved like a snake. The way she walked was its own dance.

In his youth, Dionysus had a young satyr friend named Ampelus. He was the best athlete of all the satyrs and nymphs.

Yet when Ampelus wanted to race Dionysus, the young god easily outpaced him. When Ampelus wanted to throw the discus, Dionysus simply flicked his wrist and hit the target. Always he would see his friend exhausted, having given his utmost while Dionysus had barely even tried.

This is how it had been for Dionysus with lovers as well. All he needed do was appear, and women, boys, men all eagerly offered themselves to him. It was not simply that they wanted him and he obliged. No. His joy was in their desire for him. Their delight in him fueled his passion.

Ariadne stirred a feeling he could not name. He desired her as a lover, of course, but he wanted to know her. He wanted her to know him. Strange. He had never cared what mortals thought before—not like this. Or rather, they had all felt basically the same about him—attracted, curious, intoxicated, satiated.

He had expected Ariadne to be delighted to discover what he had arranged with her father. Instead, he sensed fury and a distinct hope to lose him somewhere within the palace.

Her rooms could not possibly be this far from the dining hall. She must be taking the longest route possible. The torch light flickered off the oiled muscles of a bare-chested guard, and Dionysus imagined pulling out the small amphora of wine he always carried and stopping to have a drink with one of the guards. Despite their training, he could easily coax them into having a drink and then a quick tryst. That's what he would do if he were not so intent on following this woman. No, that was what he would have done before meeting Ariadne. He had no desire for anyone else now.

They passed an open terrace with a view of the land below. Dusk had come, pinkening the clouds in the azure sky. How pleasant it would be to pause and gaze out at the fields, to see whether he could spy the river that flowed to the sea, but if he stopped, she would disappear, leaving him lost all night. He grinned with the certainty of deciphering her plan and strode after her.

At last he recognized her two personal guards outside a grand ox-blood door. Dionysus had observed their muscular ochre skin and black coiled hair before. Now he noted their beautiful faces. One had a stronger, firmer jaw. They were both lovely.

They bowed to Ariadne and stared vacantly over him. All that mattered was their priestess. He had worried she would lose him in the labyrinth of Knossos, but she could simply have her guards throw him out.

Sudden gratitude surged as she permitted him to enter. Manko, the one with the firm jaw, sized him up. How often did Ariadne bring men to her chamber? He had thought her a virgin, but after talking to her father, he realized he knew nothing about her people and their ways. He could not wait to discover more.

He expected her handmaidens to help him out of his sandals and cloak, perhaps wash his feet with scented water, but no one greeted them. Unattended, the brazier burned low. Ariadne added some wood. As the flames rose, he took in her chambers: a cedar couch with red pillows, two small tables, a large Egyptian cedar chest painted gold. This main chamber was one of at least three interconnected rooms.

The frescoes rivaled those he had seen below. In one panel, blue monkeys on a red background gathered flowers to offer the goddess while birds sang in others. In another, a dolphin leapt in the water. In a third, three women were shown in profile.

"Such artistry," he said of the frescoes. "Such beauty," he added, staring at Ariadne.

She glared at him. "What have you done to my father? What lies did you tell to even get an audience with him?"

Did she not like him? All mortal women liked him; only goddesses hated him—Hera and Artemis, anyway. Some said Ariadne of Crete was a goddess. Perhaps that was why.

"I've angered you. Did you not enjoy lying with me? Did we not have a connection?" He licked his bottom lip, remembering her taste and how he had made her moan. She shuddered as if remembering, too.

"That was outside the palace. You wended your way in, enchanting my father. Do you think you can trick me into marrying you?"

He stroked her hand gently and stared into her almond-shaped eyes. He could not recall ever seeing a more beautiful woman, and he certainly hadn't met any who captivated him half as much. She did not gaze back longingly. But something in her eyes flickered behind her anger. Was it concern?

"Do you even understand what you've promised, stranger?"

"The price to be your husband? Oh, your father made it quite clear. I am willing to give my blood, my life in exchange for being yours for three years. Three years only. Right now I would settle for three days, or months." He smiled. "Or three hundred or three thousand years."

"What?" Her confusion and the slightest hint of understanding delighted him even more. There was a secret he wanted to tease out of her, like a forgotten dream. A connection between them, beyond them, as if they had always been lovers.

"Why do you promise to lay down your life for me? If you agree to be my husband, at the end of three years, I will slit your throat as if you were an animal sacrifice instead of a man. This is the price for marrying the priestess of the goddess."

"You do not like doing this? You do not like to kill men?"

"I do what I must for the goddess."

The old gods and their old ways. Surely a time would come when they would no longer demand the blood of mortals. He took her hand again. "I have many worries, Priestess, but death is not one of them. If in three years, you still desire to kill me, I will yield to your knife." He tilted his head back, exposing his throat. The weight of his hair slid down his back, and when he lowered his gaze, he saw the gesture had worked.

Curiosity lit her eyes as it had the day before when he had sworn not to take her maidenhead unless she desired it. By the end of three years, she might be ready to throw off her goddess and worship at his altar instead.

"Would you like some wine?" he asked, lifting the amphora. He expected her to call for her serving women, but she inclined her head toward a low table carved with lions' paws near the veranda that held cups and a carafe of water. He poured the wine.

"I will be honest," he said, offering her a cup, "as I always strive to be. My desire to marry you is rooted in my own past. Do you know the story of my mother?"

Ariadne accepted the cup in two hands. "I've heard the gossip." She sat on her red pillowed couch. Though she did not offer him a seat, he sat next to her.

"Will you tell me what you know, Priestess?"

"My nurse, Karia, used to tell me a bedtime story from Hellas about a son of Zeus who just couldn't seem to die." She scrutinized his face as if trying to decide whether he was the god of legend. "Semele, daughter of Cadmus and Harmonia, was a strikingly beautiful priestess in Thebes. When Zeus spied her bathing, he was overcome with lust as he normally is, but this time Eros struck him hard. He loved her above others and offered her Hera's place. Hera came to her in the form of her nurse and tricked Semele into making Zeus promise to give her anything to prove his love.

"When Zeus next visited, he promised once again to elevate her to the heavens so she could be with him always. She asked for a promise. He said he would do anything and swore upon the River Styx. She demanded proof of his divinity and to see his true form. He begged her to reconsider. He would give her anything else. But she refused. Zeus summoned clouds in vain hope of protecting her. Then he showed his beloved just a small flash of his power, but even that was too much for her. As she turned to ashes, he grasped the baby from her belly, tore open his own thigh, and put the child inside. The pain, they said, was nothing compared to what the loss did to his heart. Back home, on Mount Olympus, he threw lightning bolts at his wife. But she, being a goddess, only stepped aside, smiling at his rage."

Ariadne took a sip of wine as if that were the end of the story, but for Dionysus it was beginning and end both.

"Go on," he whispered.

"Seven months later, Dionysus was born from his father's thigh. Zeus took the baby to Mount Nysa, hiding him there with the nymphs. They dressed him as a girl, so Hera would not see him, for she hated him still."

Dionysus wiped his eyes. He had not expected tears, but they had come unbidden. Hera still hated him. Every goddess he had met wanted him dead. He would not dwell on that now. "There is another tale about my mother. One that paints her rather badly. I suspect you've heard the other version."

Ariadne took a sip of wine and looked into his face as if really seeing him for the first time. "It is also said that when Semele claimed Zeus had impregnated her, no one believed her. She swore on Zeus's name that everyone would soon witness the truth. When her bedroom was struck by lightning, her family and all of Thebes saw it as divine retribution for her lies. No one mourned for her. The child died when she did."

"Yes. That is the story most people believe. Do you understand why I'm here, Priestess?"

She glanced up at him, her almond eyes flashing with a hint of desire and a bit of mischief. "I hope you don't plan to murder me."

"No, quite the opposite. I want to lie with you and not dishonor you in doing it."

She laughed at this, her voice like bells. "You could not dishonor me. I am a priestess of the goddess. You can only dishonor yourself by not respecting me by keeping your vow. And you have already dishonored yourself by making my handmaidens killers."

He put his cup down on the side table and clasped her hand in both of his.

"Forgive me for that. I did not mean to possess your ladies. I have not yet learned to control my power. Priestess, I have come to Crete for you. Will you have me?"

Her face softened, but she pulled her hand away.

"I have sent my handmaidens away because of you."

"Oh, I hope..."

"What do you hope? What you did—what you brought out in them." She lowered her voice. "What they did for you, they could be executed. My father does not allow unsanctioned murder—even if the man who was killed deserved it."

He brought his hand to his head and stroked the myrtle in his diadem. Fool. He shouldn't have let her ladies go so far. He hadn't even used much of his power; just being there with them had been enough. He had rarely worried about the effect his actions could have on mortals. But now that had changed.

"I am a young god—if I am a god at all. There are times I do not understand my power. I encountered your ladies for only a few moments, but during that time, I observed they are dear to you—especially the golden-haired one. I do not want any harm to come to them because of me. How can I make it right?"

She considered him and glanced toward the other small chamber. "For a start, you can do their work. Draw me a bath. You claim you came to serve. Come, young god, and be my servant."

This made him happier than he would have guessed. He stifled a laugh, imagining how any of his half-brothers or sisters would react to such an idea. *Be her servant.* Oh, he loved it.

The bath chamber stunned him as much as the rooms below. A small room, separated from the rest by a single wall, that smelled of lavender and mint. A red and white design of lotus blossoms swirled along the top, and a fresco of colorful fish and octopus filled the wall. A high-backed tub sat in the center, made of polished stone with paintings of fish and dolphins on the inside. A terracotta pipe protruded from the wall toward the tub —an odd decoration.

He had watched mortals bathe in lakes, in ponds, in large buckets, and occasionally in hot springs. More often, he had seen mortals wipe themselves with a small cloth or use oil to get clean.

But this, to easily bathe in the comfort of one's own room. A clean floor and towels at the ready. Delightful.

"Where do I get the water, Priestess?" They had climbed up three flights of stairs, and there was a lower level as well. Was he to bring buckets from the kitchens? What a laborious job for her handmaidens. Perhaps there were other slaves who carried the hot water all that way. He would carry the water easily and very quickly if it meant she would disrobe when he was done.

"Turn the tap. One is hot; one is cold."

He turned the handle, staring at the magic of water flowing out of the faucet. He had never heard of such a thing. Even the stories of Mount Olympus did not include hot and cold running water.

"What magic is this?" he asked. He had underestimated the power of these people. Once again he was out of his element, but he did not mind.

Ariadne smiled at his amazement. "We have the most renowned craftsmen. Daedalus is the main architect now. In my youth, he built the pipes as well as the labyrinth. It is said there is nothing he can't create. He is one of my father's favorite possessions. Now, make sure the temperature is right and then come help me undress."

He turned the other tap, marveling as hot water poured out. He would have to meet this Daedalus. After making the water warm, he stood up to attend to her. She held up her slender arms, and he helped remove her short vest. He forced himself not to stare at her breasts as he helped loosen the leather corselet she wore around her tiny waist. She pulled off her multi-colored skirt and handed him her clothing, standing naked before him. Beautiful and fierce.

He would happily stand there forever just to behold a woman who displayed herself so proudly. He thought of the Maidens of Artemis and how they had no need for modesty, but in Athens, in Thebes, in Delphi he had never encountered a woman who did not feel the need to cover herself.

"Put my clothing in the other room, on the cedar chest," Ariadne said, turning to step into the bath.

He surveyed the finely crafted furnishings of her room. The brilliantly painted Egyptian wooden box must be her cedar chest. He traced his finger over the gold paint portraying symbols he could not read as he laid her clothing upon it.

When he returned to the bathing chamber, she had settled into the tub, her back to him. He had not properly appreciated her onyx-black hair. Swept up in several parts in complicated knots, it was adorned with a long strand of gold with star-shaped bangles. He had been so taken with her face and body, he had missed this great joy.

"Did you come to ogle at the architecture? Or to be my hand-maiden?" she asked, not turning her head.

He laughed, surprised by the mirth she stirred in him. "Neither. I came to seduce you, but instead you have seduced me. Now I stand at your service. What would your handmaiden do next?"

"Probably wash my hair. But that is far too complicated for a man." She turned her head slightly, her gaze challenging him.

"Oh, no, I would be glad to assist."

"Really? I suppose you have the patience of a god then."

"Of course. Do you want me to remove your jewels?"

"If you think you can."

He liked the challenge in her voice. He began to unravel her braids, releasing the scent of iris oil. Her hair was mostly unbound, but how could he possibly untangle the golden jewels entwined in her dark tresses? He slid a finger under the chain of star-shaped designs. Tangled. Tangled and complicated. Impossible. How did her handmaidens manage?

Impossible for a mortal man, but he was a god. With her back to him, she would not see how he got the jewels out. Vine tendrils slid from his fingertips, ever so gently disentangling the golden chains from her hair. Even with the finest vines, he could not help pulling her hair a little.

"Am I hurting you, Priestess?"

"It does not bother me. I do not think you will be able to get it out." She sighed with the resignation of one expecting disappointment.

He worked slowly, carefully pulling at the golden strands. Untangling the gold from her hair was surprisingly satisfying. When he finished, he came around and presented the golden chain to her.

"How did you do that? And so quickly?"

"I have many talents, Priestess. I am especially skilled with my hands."

She laughed, her note of surprise ringing in the small bath chamber. "Go set it on the table and then see that ewer? There, fill it with water and wash my hair. That container, the one with the dolphin painted on it, has the soap."

He lifted it, enjoying the scent of rosemary and verbena, and gently spilled the water over her hair. He could spend the whole night enjoying how her silken tresses loosened. Unbound, her hair cascaded down her brown shoulders, losing its curl as he covered her with water. Then he plunged his hand, slick with oil, rosemary, and verbena, into her hair, rubbing her scalp and lifting the heavy locks off her back. She sighed and allowed the weight of her head to fall into his hands. He continued to massage her, moving his hands down to her neck and shoulders.

"You are a much better handmaiden than I imagined, stranger."

"Please, call me Dionysus."

"I will consider your request."

He rinsed her hair with fresh water and passed her an Egyptian linen towel. She stood to take it, her body glistening as the water slid down. He held the towel open. She grasped his wrist as she stepped over the lip of the tub. He could not recall desiring a woman this desperately, yet he was completely willing to wait.

She took the towel and began to dry her arms, breasts, belly, and mound.

"See that jar with the lady painted on it? I use it after the bath."

He reached for the jar, breathing in the scent of iris oil.

"Would you like me to apply it?"

She wrapped her hair in the towel and assessed him. "You're not a bad handmaiden after all, Dionysus. Bring the oil to the bedroom. I have other duties for you to attend to."

He followed gladly.

TRULY ARIADNE OF CRETE WAS A GODDESS IN HER OWN RIGHT. He would happily worship at her altar again and again. After he pleasured her the first time, she agreed to drink another cup of wine.

"I am not sure whether this is the right thing to do, but I believe our destinies are linked," she said after the second time. She caressed his throat; her fingers slowly trailed down his shoulder and traced the place she had bitten him the day before.

He always reveled in the joy of pleasuring his lovers multiple times, but this connection was more than physical. In the dim light of her room, he whispered secrets he had told no one, not even himself. They emptied the amphora, and he refilled it several times, but the desire for her far exceeded his desire for drink.

"If in three years you wish to kill me, I will bare my throat to you," he said before dawn.

Her lips parted, but no word came. He grasped her hand. "I do not fear death, only failing to become who I should be... and I believe that if you kill me, I will come back to you. Do you not feel, Ariadne, as if we've been together before?"

Her arms broke into goose flesh, and her nipples hardened. "Perhaps," she whispered, caressing his thigh.

He smiled slightly and let go of her hand. "Tell me about your mother. There is much said of her abroad."

Ariadne twisted her crescent moon-bull's horn necklace, partially digging the point into her chest.

"None good, I'm sure."

"I heard she bore a bull-headed god."

Ariadne clenched her fist. "There are malicious lies about my mother spread by the Athenians. They do not understand our people or our ways."

"Tell me." He cupped her fist and stroked her wrist until she relaxed. "I will understand."

Ariadne sighed and rose from her bed. Her long black hair hung loose and wild. He savored this sight of a powerful woman naked and willing to tell him a tale.

"There is a tradition of women and gods and bulls. It began long ago with Io, a semi-divine priestess. The Father of the Gods lusted after her and turned her into a cow. She traveled the world in disguise. Her daughter, Memphis, founded a city, and her granddaughter, Libya, a nation."

"Priestess, I wish to journey the world. Perhaps one day we can visit these cities together."

She laughed and strode to the balcony. He could imagine the cool night air surrounding her skin and rose, taking a blanket to warm her.

"I have no plans to leave Crete, Dionysus. And you should have no plans to live beyond the next three years."

"True," he said, placing the blanket over her shoulders. "Please, go on with your story."

The night air hung heavy with the scent of jasmine. She scanned the sky and stared up at the crescent moon.

"Generations later, Europa, a Phoenician princess, was gathering flowers when a beautiful white bull appeared holding the sacred crocus flower in his mouth."

Dionysus had not yet seen the beautiful purple flowers other than in the frescoes he observed earlier. He had long heard of this magic flower that shot out threads of red and kept the secrets of saffron.

"Europa went to the bull and put a wreath of flowers around his neck. The bull radiated magic; she knew he was her destiny. When he lowered himself for her, she climbed astride his broad back but was unprepared when he charged into the sea. She held fast to his neck, whispering into his ears, prayers not to die, but also prayers for her future.

"'Give me a land of my own,' she said. 'Do not let me ever be forgotten. Give me powerful sons and brilliant granddaughters. Let my name be ever remembered.' The white bull, who was Zeus in disguise, listened. He swam across the sea until they came here, to Crete. The Great God gave her three sons: my father Minos and his brothers Rhadamanthys and Sarpedon.

"She was not the first priestess here, but the others gladly followed her, and the bull became even more sacred. The priestess-queen and the priest-king kept a balance between the Great Goddess and the bull—both worshipped equally, and both giving bounty to Crete." Ariadne stared out at the dark land, small lights from the houses, the fields dark.

Dionysus felt the magic of this island. The fertile soil called to him, but there was more to it than that.

"My mother was drawn to Crete and welcomed as a new priestess of the sun. She took husbands when the goddess commanded it, made them king for a year or a great year—and then sacrificed them to the goddess. But then the goddess marked Minos, son of Zeus, to be her husband, and the balance between the gods and the Great Goddess was in harmony, until it came time for the sacrifice." She stopped and looked into Dionysus's face.

The golden flecks in her eyes glowed, and though he wanted to hear the rest of the story, he also wanted to kiss her.

"My mother refused to sacrifice my father. Zeus not only intervened but gave the kingship of Crete to him. In celebration, Poseidon sent a bull for Minos to sacrifice. The bull was so beautiful that Minos decided to keep it, sacrificing another in its place. When Poseidon learned what Minos had done, he was furious. To save Minos's life, my mother went to the seashore with a garland of flowers and stood naked, waiting.

"Poseidon transformed himself into a bull. White as milk, glittering like seafoam, his horns shining like stars. The bull-god lowered his head, and my mother placed the garland around his neck. Then, following the tradition of Zeus and Europa, my mother climbed on his back and allowed him to carry her away.

"They say that months later, when Pasiphae walked out of the sea, the sentries who had waited for her every day since she left raised a cry of joy. A crowd formed, chanting praise as they escorted her back to Knossos. Naked except for a crown of seaweed and a necklace of pearls, her belly swollen with a demigod, her people bowed to her as a double queen, worthy of wielding the ceremonial double axe.

"They say my mother gave birth to a bull-headed child. He would be the one to receive the sacrifices that had been denied Poseidon. My mother made a choice and a sacrifice. She bore a monster to pay for my father's crimes, but she bore him with a god, not a bull, like some say.

"My brother Asterion has always had the gift of prophecy and a blood-lust to match my father's, but Asterion keeps the balance below for the bull, and I keep the balance above for the goddess."

"I would like to meet this brother. I've never met one with a birth story as complicated and contradictory as my own."

"He doesn't like strangers," Ariadne said. "Or rather, he likes them too much, but they do not enjoy meeting him. I haven't seen him since my brother Androgeus died in Athens." She sighed and pulled the blanket tighter around her shoulders. He had let her get too cold.

"There are malicious lies about my mother, too, priestess. It is said I was born with horns, that I was a bull-headed god. Perhaps that is why being here with you feels like I am home."

5

ARIADNE SWINGS

truck by Eros, that was what foreigners called it. And it had happened to her. She had tried to resist, to focus on her devotion to the goddess, on the path set by the stars. As High Priestess of Crete, she would sacrifice all the goddess demanded. But perhaps this was the path set by the stars. This stranger, this god had come for her. Had they been lovers before? His scent and the comfort of his touch was so familiar.

The sacred olive grove, which usually gave Ariadne such peace, was dry and brittle with the heat of the long summer. Leaves and a few neglected olives crunched under her feet as she walked with Thalia. Manko and Talos followed behind at a distance.

"I brought honey and oil if you desire it," Thalia said.

"Thank you, Little Leopard." Years ago when Zoe had teased Thalia for her freckles, Ariadne had given Thalia the name to show how much she liked the spots.

Ariadne had told no one that the goddess had ceased speaking to her long before Dionysus had come. The goddess did not always speak to her high priestesses, but this felt different. Sometimes a high priestess could reach the goddess by swinging to epiphany.

They stopped before the sacred swing that Daedalus had built for Pasiphae. In early spring, novice priestesses wove flower braids around the two cedar posts. Musicians would play, and priestesses and novices would sing while Ariadne swung.

But now, at the height of summer, the swing appeared dried out, as if the sacred doorway would yield nothing. Still, Ariadne would try. She smoothed her skirt down and sat on the swing.

This is as close as you will come to flying, her mother had said when she and Phaedra first learned how to pump their legs on the swings designed for children. This one was different. The pillars were wider at the top, so the ropes hung at an angle. She had to work much harder, but that often led to epiphany.

She gripped the hot ropes and kicked off. As a child, she had thought Phaedra would travel this path with her, believing the two daughters of Pasiphae would both become priestesses. Ariadne's crescent-shaped mark had begun to tingle at her first blood, but the goddess had never spoken to Phaedra.

Ariadne pulled back and pushed. The wind rushed through her hair, whooshing in her ears. She let the rhythm carry her to and fro. Sweat beaded her brow. The sun beat down. *Let this be another show of my devotion, Goddess. Please tell me what to do.* She pumped her legs, leaned back on the ropes. Had she angered the goddess by marrying Dionysus? Had the offerings Thalia, Melia, and Zoe left not appeased her? Or did the goddess no longer care?

She swung higher, pumped, and extended her legs over and over again, until her mind cleared. Now the goddess could enter and convey what she wanted Ariadne to do.

Fully entranced, Ariadne let her mind search for the goddess as her body continued to swing. She traveled to the cave sanctuaries. First, the one in the hills above Knossos, but the darkened cavern where women left offerings and came to give birth was empty. Her mind's eye flew high, leaping from one peak to another. An old priestess alone in a cavern, staring out from the rocky crag to the sea below. Two girls who had just started their moon blood climbed up to another, eager to be able to enter the sacred space for the first time.

But the goddess was not there.

Ariadne swung, searching in her mind, calling the goddess by her names.

Mistress of Wild Things, Great Goddess, Our Lady, Artemis.

She searched across the island, from temple to temple to the uninhabited wild lands. She spied mountain goats asleep in the shade, and a griffin vulture circled above a canyon. Ariadne felt herself soar with the bird, the wind on her wings, her vision keen.

Great Goddess, where are you?

This sensation of flying with the bird, of going from cave to cave was a new one. Her power had never been this strong before.

She swung higher and higher, ignoring the pain in her hands and legs. Intense heat enveloped her, and she imagined jumping straight up into the sky, directly into the sun. Bright light and searing heat surrounded her.

Granddaughter.

The Titan Helios stood before her, his bronze skin giving off its own light. His eyes glowed with the sun itself; a crown of flames danced on his pure gold hair.

I have had a vision of you, child. Your fame will be great, but you will be abandoned and remembered as a girl left behind, though you will be far more than that. Your service to Crete is near its end.

Ariadne gasped. What did he mean? She could not speak. The fire of the sun consumed her, blinding her so she lost her connection to her strength. She put her hands up to feel where she was and began to fall, out of the sky, plummeting to the earth below.

She imagined falling into the sea, being extinguished by the water, but no, she fell toward Crete, past the griffin vulture, gliding on the wind, past the sleeping mountain goats and back toward her vacant body in the dried-out grove.

Thalia screamed as Ariadne's body pitched backwards off the swing. Ariadne opened her eyes to see a flash of blue sky, the crooked olive branches. She had flown, and now she fell. She had reached an epiphany only to be thrown back to earth. Was she to die? Was that the goddess's message to her?

A whoosh from behind her. Thalia's muffled scream. A terrible ripping of skin upon the hard packed earth and a sharp impact as her buttocks hit the ground. Her back and head followed, but the hard crash she feared was softened by strong arms cradling her.

Talos. She gazed up at his noble jaw line, grateful for his protection. She tried to cry out a warning of her own as the hard wooden swing bench came back and hit him hard in the brow. His eyes rolled back as he lost consciousness and ever so gracefully fell back, still gently holding her as his head hit the ground.

Thalia stepped forward and caught one of the ropes. The swing bench jerked as if objecting to being handled in such a way. Manko grabbed the other rope, stilling the swing completely as he knelt next to Ariadne.

"High Priestess, forgive us." He helped her sit up. Ariadne's head felt heavy as it did when she drank too much mead. Thalia squatted down, slipped her arm around Ariadne, and helped her stand.

"Talos?" Her voice sounded strange in her ears. She glanced up at the blinding sun and at the prone body in the dirt. She had flown too high, and now her bodyguard suffered the consequence.

"Is he...?"

"He lives, my priestess," Manko said, feeling his friend's wrist.

Thalia guided Ariadne to a nearby olive tree with a thick base and leaned her against the rough bark. She stroked Ariadne's brow and examined her rope-burned hands, kissing each palm.

"You are here, Mistress. Back at home. All is well. Talos will be fine."

They watched Manko lift Talos's torso off the ground and straighten his bloodied knees.

"He bore worse in training, and he has always been thick-headed." Manko took a flask from his waist and wetted Talos's lips. Talos did not at first respond, but then his tongue darted out, and Manko smiled.

"You saved our priestess, Talos. The Great Goddess blesses you."

His words chilled her. Did the Great Goddess bless her still? She could not say.

"Mistress." Thalia offered water, which she took with a shaking hand.

"Have some honey." Thalia dipped her finger in the pot and offered it to Ariadne.

"That is for the goddess," Ariadne said.

"You are my goddess." Thalia had been whispering such things in her ear for years in the seclusion of their bed, but here in the grove, her words added new strength. Had the goddess left Crete? Did she journey to another island, accept the worship of another people?

Sucking on Thalia's finger, sweetened with honey, brought Ariadne back from the liminal world. She had journeyed to the peak sanctuaries in her mind before, but she had never flown with a bird or soared all the way to the sun. *I have had a vision of you, child...* She couldn't think of her grandfather's words now.

"What did the Great Goddess say?" Thalia was her friend, her lover, her handmaiden, but she was not a citizen of Crete, not a devotee of the goddess. She sacrificed and honored the goddess, gave a tithe to King Minos, but in her heart Ariadne suspected Thalia was a non-believer.

Ariadne stared at the swelling forming on Talos's forehead, at the blood running down his calves, and told Thalia what she had told no one.

"I have felt nothing from the mark since the day we went on our picnic. I thought it was the goddess calling to me, but now I suspect it was Dionysus. When I go to the temple, she does not respond."

Thalia rubbed her thumb against Ariadne's skirt over the mark, as if her touch could invoke the goddess.

"You've grown more powerful since Dionysus came. When

you were swinging, a golden light shone over you. Perhaps you are becoming the Great Goddess of Crete."

"Hush, Thalia. I am only a mortal."

"You are half divine on both sides. The wife and sister to demi-gods."

"Don't speak like this."

Manko helped Talos to stand. Talos wobbled unsteadily, his eyes unfocused. His soldier's training served him well; even injured, he stood erect, though she feared if Manko let him go, he would fall forward.

"Mistress, it is his honor to save you from harm," Thalia said, switching to a more formal tone. "As for the Great Goddess, there have been times before when she has not spoken to you for months. You've said she likes to travel. Perhaps she has gone to her worshippers across the sea? She'll return. She always does."

Ariadne clasped Thalia's thumb under her hand, pushing it against the mark, wishing to feel a return of sensation to the sensitive spot. "Thank you, Little Leopard—that is what I will say if anyone begins to worry. If pressed, I'll tell them a leopard told me in a dream." She attempted to laugh, but it came out brittle.

"Should we return to Knossos?" Thalia asked, offering Ariadne her arm.

Ariadne pushed away from the tree. Talos needed to see the healer. She could sense his pain and his determination not to show it.

She let Thalia guide her through the dappled sunlight. Confessing the goddess's silence to Thalia had lifted a weight she hadn't realized she was carrying. While they were still in the sacred grove, she wanted to tell her everything.

"I do worry," Ariadne said, her voice little more than a whisper. "I've asked the goddess for advice, for permission, for guidance, and she says nothing. Yet it is done. I've married the new god. He agreed to be the goddess's sacrifice. My father is happy. The people have faith the crops will do well. Silenus is teaching the farmers how to cultivate the vine, and everyone is delighted that we will be able to make wine. Yet, I don't know what will happen in three years' time."

"I don't know either, Ariadne, but I will be here by your side."

Thalia's words brought tears, sudden and strong. To have a friend like this! She glanced back at Manko and Talos limping behind them. To have these devout followers. She rarely thought of her station in this way, but the Great Goddess had blessed her.

"Perhaps Lord Dionysus will give you a child," Thalia said.

The image of their baby came quickly. She could almost feel the babe in her arms, almost smell its little head. And Dionysus's child would be a fighter—fierce, ever shining. Raven black hair, an irresistible power. The image of her daughter rose over her, so clear she could almost see her in the flesh. Yearning overcame her, a desire for a child so desperate, she could almost taste it.

The image disappeared, but the warmth remained.

"I would like one with him. If the goddess gives me a child to continue the line, perhaps it will mean forgiveness." Crete would rejoice when she had a daughter—the line ensured. "You know I tried with Zakros."

"Zakros was too weak for you. He was a perfect sacrifice for the goddess though—a good first husband. You don't have the nightmares anymore, do you?"

"No." Ariadne hadn't thought of her first husband in some time. A deep-sea diver from the east of the island, he had come to her in the late fall. A light emanated from him, and she knew before he spoke why he had come. Her father and mother had agreed to the marriage, and the goddess had sanctioned it, telling her to sacrifice him after one year. He had not been clever, but he had been devout. Giving his life for the goddess was his greatest joy.

Pasiphae had instructed her how to slit his throat, how to give him opium-infused pomegranate juice first. The night before the sacrifice, he had confessed all his fears. She in turn could not confess hers. She pretended to be strong and unwavering in her devotion. In the end, he had offered her his throat, and having drunk some opium-laced pomegranate juice herself, she had done her duty. The nightmares had haunted her for two years.

"Do you think you've angered the goddess by taking Lord Dionysus as your husband?" Thalia asked softly.

"There is no reason for me not to take him as a lover. Though he is a stranger, there is nothing in the law that says I can't. It's just that the goddess..." She glanced up at the moon in the bright blue sky. Could her goddess see her? "Perhaps she would not like me to associate with another god—even one who is so deferential to her. But it is done. My father ordered it, Dionysus agreed to it and, goddess forgive me, I like the new god."

She paused. The wind blew. The hoopoe birds hooted. Bees buzzed. She stared up, wondering whether the goddess watched. Did she listen to Ariadne's words? Did she care? Perhaps the goddess only cared for blood sacrifice and adoration. The desires of the goddess had changed since Ariadne's brother Androgeus was killed in Athens. She was less interested in Ariadne and Crete. Pasiphae said that was the way of the gods.

"The goddess has not made it clear to me what she would like. My father has. I've always been obedient to the goddess, and I will always adhere to her laws." Ariadne adjusted her bull's horn-crescent moon necklace. She had given one to Dionysus as a wedding present, and touching it now made her think of him.

She glanced up at the moon in the sky one last time. Soon she would have to prepare for the ceremony of womanhood for the girls who had gotten their first moonblood in the spring and summer.

"The moon is always changing, Little Leopard. Together we have grown from girls to women, and if the goddess grants it, we may be mothers. Do you feel as if something is changing?"

"Yes," Thalia said more quickly that Ariadne expected. "There is much talk of it down at the docks and among the slaves. New peoples are gaining strength. They say that Athens grows strong. The Spartans are developing strong weapons of bronze. And strange new gods of Hellas and Egypt are gaining followers—

especially among men who are losing their devotion to the goddess." Thalia whispered the last part, just as she whispered the word Sparta; both had potential ill-fortune.

"And Dionysus?" Ariadne asked, fascinated to realize how much Thalia knew of life outside the palace.

"There is much excitement when people speak of his new drink. The farmers and tavern keepers are especially eager. Though I think people are worried you might not sacrifice him as your mother did not sacrifice your father."

Ariadne stopped walking and plucked a low-hanging fig, holding it in the palm of her hand. Late summer, the seasons about to change. Yet it also felt as if the whole world were about to change.

"I will always honor the goddess and ensure that she is worshipped properly in Crete. But I do not believe that means I can't be wed to the new god. I will fulfill my obligations. I will keep her worship and my vows as her priestess." She would do all that she had done before, but she would also allow this new feeling she had never permitted herself to have for a man. Love.

❦ *6* ❦

DIONYSUS LOST

He should have taken Ariadne's offer for Thalia to escort him to find Silenus in the west fields. Fearing he made the golden-haired girl uncomfortable, he had declined. Now lost somewhere beneath Knossos, he regretted it.

Only in Knossos did he experience this complete loss of direction. Even deep in the sea with Thetis, in the heart of the woods, in Sparta or Thebes, he always knew which way was west, but here his sense of direction abandoned him. Something in this dark, mazelike place bedeviled his mind so he could not think clearly. It was as if flies buzzed, keeping his thoughts from forming clearly.

Ariadne had told him to turn left to find his way out of the west gate, which would lead to the west garden. But he had made a wrong turn. He had not seen anyone since the hall of shields. The Minoan guards were like fleeting shadows, lurking when he did not want them nearby and vanishing when he needed aid. He no longer cared whether he came out near the west garden. He only wanted to be out of this monstrous palace.

He took another set of stairs leading down. Knossos was terraced, so eventually he would find his way out. He had seen the lowest floor—the one near the river where the storehouses could receive goods from the boats that brought them from the sea. If he couldn't find a guard, some miller or storehouse worker would give him directions.

Though this part of the palace seemed deserted, occasional torches marked the way. The white and red of a fresco flickered in the dim light. This painting was in a different style than the ones above. Instead of nature or a ceremony, the face of a beautiful royal Minoan youth gazed at him from the wall. Though most Minoans shared common features, Dionysus immediately recognized Ariadne's smile on the painted lips. It must be one of her brothers.

In all the frescoes, males were painted red and females white, but this face, seeming to float in the empty corridor, had much darker reddish-brown skin, as if it had been painted in blood.

Even as he turned away, the beauty and tragedy in the image haunted him. He glanced back down the corridor. The last flickering torch was just around the corner. He been following the torches without realizing it.

He walked back to the previous torch, making out another image, which he hadn't noticed in the darkness—the same Minoan youth. Serene eyes stared out at Dionysus as if he wanted to share a secret. In this fresco, he wore a bull's horn necklace painted bone white, so bright it shone in the darkness. Dionysus stroked the necklace hanging over his own breastbone. The boy in the frieze wore the same one he did. Ariadne had given him this after their marriage—the crescent-shaped necklace that could be either the moon or the bull's horns. King Minos had one in silver; Queen Pasiphae's was gold. Ariadne's was on a strand of beaded amethyst and quartz, and Phaedra's— he hadn't paid attention, but he thought hers was on a strand of carnelian.

Footsteps echoed down the corridor. A guard! At last, he would find his way out of this maze. But the approaching footsteps did not sound like a man's—the uneven gait of a hoofed creature clomped closer. He closed his eyes to sense what was coming—power, like Pasiphae's, and divinity, like his own, but also torment and madness.

Dionysus had a sudden urge to run. His spine tingled, and the hair on the nape of his neck stood up. Having been both the hunter and the hunted, he knew that those who run are chased, those who are chased are hunted, and those who are hunted die.

He stroked the wineskin on his belt. He was a god. The only Minoan who could kill him was Ariadne. He would not run.

The hoofbeats paused and turned the corner. The creature came into view—a bull-headed, bare-chested man wearing the same necklace as Dionysus. A red linen kilt adorned his narrow waist along with a short dagger.

The Minotaur. Ariadne's eldest brother Asterion, son of Poseidon and Pasiphae.

"Please forgive my intrusion. I am Dionysus, your sister Ariadne's husband."

The Minotaur stopped. Dionysus wondered how long it had been since someone had spoken to him instead of fleeing. The creature's great brown eyes swiveled, peering at him as if from a distance. Stepping closer, the Minotaur sniffed. Dionysus observed that the nostrils did not flare. The Minotaur walked around him slowly—this move was designed to create fear, but once the shock of the creature's appearance had worn off, he did not fear for himself. Instead, the deep sorrow and rage emanating from the creature lashed at him, creating an emotion he could not name.

"I got lost on my way to the west garden." He noticed the blood encrusted in Asterion's fingernails, the sandals with hoofed heels strapped to his feet, and the lack of a tail. "My apologies for disturbing you, though I am glad to make your acquaintance."

"You are not afraid of me?" the Minotaur growled, his voice like gravel.

"I am. You have a heavy aura that creates fear." He watched the Minotaur's unmoving face. "Yet I am pleased to meet you. They say I, too, was born with horns. Perhaps I, too, could have dwelled here below, eaten by fury and bloodlust, but instead I was destroyed and born again. I have wandered far. Perhaps part of the reason I landed on Crete was to meet you."

The Minotaur stared at him. The golden flecks in his eyes appeared almost red. The prickle of fear came again. He forced himself to remain calm.

A low rumble began in the creature's belly and unfurled, becoming a laugh in his throat. He let out a bellow of mirth, the shout of surprise echoing in the emptiness of the labyrinth.

"Dionysus, the God Who Comes," Asterion said, as if recognizing an old acquaintance. "At last. I have expected you since my brother died. Even before I knew what I was to become." He held his arms out, elbows bent so his fingers pointed back at himself. His golden seal ring glinted in the light. Dionysus noticed the bracelets of a priest-king. "I received a prophecy in my youth that your arrival would signal the beginning of my end." He sighed and stroked the fur on his forehead, then reached to grasp the tip of his right horn, pushing his first finger on the sharp point.

"I mean you no harm," Dionysus said.

"No. Of course not—and as you are my sister's husband, my sister's sacrifice, I could never harm you. Not only that—" He thrust his hand onto Dionysus's chest and clasped his breast, as if they were comrades. "—even if I wanted to kill you, I could not. Yet it is not you I want to kill. I hunger only for the blood of Athenians."

"I saw your paintings, Asterion." Dionysus cupped the hand on his breast. They stood in silence, until Dionysus feared the sorrow of the Minotaur would drive him to madness.

"Come, Asterion, have a drink with me."

Asterion let go of Dionysus and bellowed out a laugh, as if he were easily remembering how laughing was done. "You invite me to drink in my own lair? What manners are these? And yet, I see no mead in your hands, no servant carrying a krater."

"Forgive me if my request appears rude. I have something better than mead, here in my wineskin."

"I don't have many visitors these days and welcome a chance to talk to another..." Dionysus waited eagerly to hear what Asterion would call him—another horned one, another man, another forgotten son of a god? But the Minotaur did not call him anything more.

"Come with me."

Dionysus followed. Was this the same way he had come? Had he passed this place several times, or was it new?

The sound of the hoofs attached to the Minotaur's sandals clopped in front of him, echoing off the walls. This was the sound the Athenian youths heard before they died. This was the sound that tormented them as they ran down these halls, desperately trying to find a way out or a place to hide.

Their fear emanated from the walls as if their terror had burrowed there. This was a place of no return—a maze where the only way out was death. At intermittent lamps, the baleful eyes of the youth painted in blood stared out.

He followed the Minotaur into a darkened corner. No lamps were lit here; not even a glimmer of light penetrated now. Dionysus reached out a hand to brush the wall and met only air. The sensation of bees buzzing filled his mind, and he lost all sense of direction. Terror overwhelmed him. Was this the last place Athenian youths had begged in vain for their lives? If he were a mortal, if he were not Ariadne's husband, he would never return from this place.

"Come, Dionysus." Asterion's voice, like gravel in the dark. "Come to me, God Who Comes. You have found the Minotaur in his labyrinth. It is time to have a drink." Asterion's rough hand grabbed his and pulled him into the darkness. Dionysus closed his eyes and thought of the fermented grapes in his wineskin. They were more than the power to transform—they were transformation itself. They had changed from grape to wine, and now, they could change anyone who drank into something else. Dionysus would help Asterion transform from a Minotaur into a man, even if for only a moment.

He let Asterion pull him. Amid the darkness, he spied a lamp. It had only been a few moments in the dark, but it had only felt much longer. As he stepped toward the glimmering light, he gasped.

He had believed the stories of the mad Minotaur, a wild creature penned below, content in his maze. But this was simply another floor of the palace-temple that was Knossos. This grand chamber eerily mirrored Ariadne's throne room two floors above. The red walls had been painted by an expert craftsman. White rivers made clean lines leading the gaze to the gypsum throne. The only difference between Ariadne's chamber and this was that instead of griffins framing the throne, white bulls faced each other, their horns tipped with gold.

A brazier warmed the room, and the sky-blue ceiling had an air shaft which carried the smoke away. Couches lined one wall, their arms and feet painted gold. The rug was designed to mimic a maze; meander patterns in dark blue created a labyrinth over undyed wool. The rug covered the whole floor and kept the room warm.

"My king." A beautiful girl appeared. Black tresses fell over her bare chest. "I did not know you were expecting a visitor."

"I was not, Alexa. He surprised me."

Dionysus had grown used to Minoan women not covering their breasts, but he had not expected to find a woman here.

"Should I bring your dagger my King?"

"No. He is my sister's sacrifice, and my guest. Bring mead and cheese and bread."

"Yes, my King." She bowed her head slightly while glaring at Dionysus.

Asterion chuckled. "She hates it when she doesn't know something is going to happen. I enjoy her company, but she wants to dip her fingers in every pot. Still, I will miss her."

Dionysus let the silence engulf them. So quiet. For a moment upon entering the room, he had forgotten he was underground, but the stillness here was the stillness of the crypt.

"So, you have married my sister. Will she keep you alive for one year or three?"

"I made a vow to her for three years."

"And then you will flee?"

"No, I will be with her forever. I have never loved a woman like Ariadne."

Asterion stared at Dionysus, his deep eyes distant.

"Come, sit." Asterion sat on one of the pillowed benches, gesturing for Dionysus to take a camp stool opposite him. It was not the most comfortable seat, but resting brought its own pleasure after being lost for so long.

Alexa returned with cups full of mead and came to stand by Asterion's side.

"Dear one." He cupped her hip. Dionysus could not help but marvel at the incredibly narrow waist of this girl. He could not tell whether she was the Minotaur's wife, concubine, or slave. "I need to speak to my guest alone. Tell the others not to disturb me. We will commence our activity after he leaves."

Dionysus felt her surge of anger, though her face remained calm. "Yes, my King."

Asterion took a sip of the mead and passed Dionysus the cup. Dionysus had seen this ritual before. He took the cup with both hands, drank, then passed it back.

"You are the first stranger to come visit me by choice," Asterion said.

"I am glad to meet you. Your fame is known far and wide."

"As the Minotaur." He stroked his right horn. "As a killer of Athenians—a monster to be feared by men."

"But I see you as a priest-king who loved his brother and has taken revenge on the kin of those who slew him."

"Androgeus was the best of men, the best of brothers. He would have ruled after our father while I kept the will of the gods." Asterion's voice cracked. "I should have gone to Athens with him. Two days before we were to leave, we climbed up to a sanctuary in the mountains. I slipped and broke my leg. In all the confusion of getting me back home, no one left a dedication to the goddess. I blame myself for her curse. My clumsiness caused it all… If I had been with him, the Athenians wouldn't have killed him." He turned back to Dionysus, all trace of grief in his voice erased by vengeance. "But I've made them pay. I've bled them dry. And they will never again forget who their masters are."

Dionysus wanted to tell him how foolish this was. The Athenian tributes Asterion killed were not the same people who had slain his brother. The Athenian youths he slaughtered in his guise as Minotaur were innocent, but none of these words would matter.

Asterion drained the cup, poured more mead, and passed it to Dionysus. Dionysus rarely felt drunk, but this mead was stronger than his wine. The thick, sweet honey taste lingered on his tongue and befuddled his brain as Asterion refilled and handed him the cup again and again.

"You see through me in a way other foreigners do not. Is that why Ariadne chose you?"

"To be honest, I chose her—at first. Then I fell into her thrall."

"Yes, the women of my country are powerful. More beautiful than any other. I used to travel with my father, and plenty of outsiders have come here. Minoan women are the strongest. But the Athenians can't handle their power—they cannot see breasts and control their lust. So they degrade our women." The edge of anger that had been in Asterion's voice all along grew sharper.

"Is that why you kill them?"

"I kill them because my father asked me to. The Athenians grow strong. He wants them to remember their place. It is also payment for what they did to my brother. They invited him to their country and killed him in the streets. And I do it for my mother. Do you know what they say about her?" He was slurring now, and Dionysus almost believed he saw the bull lips moving. "They call her a bull-fucker!" Asterion bellowed. "Pasiphae, daughter of the Sun, former High Priestess of Crete. A bull-fucker. Do you know how weak those Athenians are to make up that lie? They cannot even see the god. They do not understand our ways, so they make up lies, and the lies become myths, and people believe them."

"People believe many such things, especially if it is about a foreigner." Dionysus passed the cup back. "I understand your anger. People have called my own mother a slut, saying my father was not Zeus but a palace slave. I, too, have killed those who wronged me."

Asterion's gaze changed from one of anger to sudden attraction. Dionysus was familiar with this look of lust, especially coupled with drink. Asterion moved back on the bench, spread his knees, and showed himself to Dionysus. For a moment the young god believed Asterion could be the son of a bull.

"Take off your mask, Asterion," Dionysus said softly.

"When did you know this was a mask?"

"A moment after I met you. The light was dim, but there is not enough of the bull about you. Let me see your face."

With both hands, Asterion lifted the bull's head off and placed it on the couch next to him. Long black hair fell over his shoulders. He wiped his sweaty face with his palms.

His eyes were like Ariadne's, black with hints of gold. His nose was squat and his eyes too close together, so he did partially resemble a bull. Without the mask, his shoulders seemed broader.

"It is not easy to wear, but I grew used to it."

"Pain can be like that," Dionysus said. "I can feel your heartache from here." He touched Asterion's large hand, then clasped it. "Let me see how I can help."

❧ 7 ❧

ARIADNE RECEIVES A MESSAGE

What a fool she had been! Why in the name of the great goddess had she trusted him—worse, let herself fall in love? Where was he? Probably off fucking a slave girl or romping with a guard. She had seen the way he ogled her people. Their taut, naked flesh was too much for him. For a demi-god like Dionysus, one woman would never be enough.

You will be abandoned and remembered as a girl left behind. The memory of her grandfather's words came to her. She had pushed the vision away, but now with her husband missing, they made her fear turn to rage.

Had Dionysus already left Crete? Would he stay until she was meant to sacrifice him? Had he already lost interest? He had her heart, and she had nothing.

She got out of bed again. What was the point in trying to sleep? Even after all the wine, sleep would not come. When she closed her eyes, all she could see was him, mounting a nubile girl, a muscular boy, walking the hills alone—his presence making peasant women rush from their houses, throwing off their clothes to beg for an orgy.

"Mistress," Thalia whispered. She had fallen asleep on Ariadne's couch after trying to console her.

"Where could he be?" Ariadne asked.

"I should have gone with him."

Ariadne pictured Thalia leading him toward the west fields, Dionysus stopping her in a darkened corridor, getting her to raise her skirts. She remembered how Thalia had stared at her helplessly before she ran off to kill Cilix. *Forgive me, Mistress.*

"Ariadne." Thalia was next to her now, her hair shining in the darkness. "Punish me for your anger with your hands or belt. It will make us both feel better."

Ariadne cupped Thalia's cheek and plunged her hand into Thalia's golden hair, gripping it at the roots. Thalia moaned from the base of her throat and bent her head back, offering herself up.

"Your pleasure is mine," Thalia whispered, the very words visibly arousing her further.

Ariadne pulled her close, kissing her savagely.

"Little Leopard, I wish the games of our youth would satisfy me now, but I am too distracted." She let go of Thalia's hair. Thalia said nothing as she silently poured Ariadne a cup of water.

"Did Manko come back?" Ariadne asked.

"No. He sent men in every direction. No one saw Dionysus leave the palace, Mistress."

"He could still be gone. What makes him honor his vow to me? If a mortal man married me, he would keep his word. He would be bound by duty and by fear, but Dionysus fears nothing, not even death—why stay with me?"

"Ariadne, how can you even ask that?" Thalia's voice broke as tears trailed her cheeks. "You are the most beautiful, most powerful woman in the world. The people of Crete obey your every order. You are the vessel of the goddess. The very snakes and bulls obey you. Men offer their lives for the chance to lie with you. You alone do not see your power."

Ariadne wiped Thalia's tears with her fingers and rubbed the wetness on her lips. "Little Leopard, I am honored to have such a friend. You are as good as you are kind, and if I weren't so drunk and angry, I'd make you beg for me the way I know you like."

Thalia brought Ariadne's hand to her lips and kissed the palm. "It is a shame you are so drunk and angry. Enough stewing, Ariadne. Lie down then. I will massage you, and you will sleep. He will return. I believe in him. I believe in you." Thalia let out a bitter laugh. "Imagine, I, the one non-believer in Crete, have more faith in you and Lord Dionysus than you have in yourselves. Now, take off your gown and get in bed."

Thalia's hands cast their magic, rubbing her mistress's shoulders and head. Ariadne fell into a deep sleep, but even from the depths of slumber, a burning pain from the mark on her thigh made her moan.

"Ariadne, daughter of Pasiphae." The voice was rough. She wanted to ask the Great Goddess where she had been, why had it been so long, but she did not. They were in the temple now. Snakes slithered on the ground, and the braziers sent off smoke. Normally, dreaming of this space with the goddess speaking to her would comfort her, but fear pitted Ariadne's stomach.

"Whose priestess are you, Ariadne?"

"Yours of course, Great Goddess."

"But you serve the bull as well."

"Yes, as you have commanded."

"And what if I command it no longer?"

Ariadne could not comprehend this question. The bull was the symbol of Crete. Seeing her father wear the bull mask was one of her first memories. The way the bull's horns and the crescent moon aligned—the way one thing could be two was one of first lessons every Minoan learned.

"No longer serve the bull?" Ariadne asked. "Why?"

"There has been a dispute."

Ariadne had not been able to see the goddess this whole time, but now she made out an outline of white smoke, as flittering and luminous as moth wings. The image began to harden, and the vision grew stronger. An essence sparkled beneath the outline of the goddess's form—a cosmic mixture of divinity and starlight. Ariadne saw her then, the Great Goddess she had always known, Protectress of Crete.

Ariadne's only goal in this world was to be a vessel for this deity. This was the goddess she had seen when her moonblood first came. This was the goddess who had summoned her and made the crescent-shaped mark on her thigh buzz. In the forest, on the sacred swing, this goddess had come to her. This goddess stared at her with sorrow; her bare breasts did not emulate power as they once had, and tears glittered in her eyes.

And then, the goddess began to morph. Her skirt and vest were replaced by a long, draped robe. Her face, her body, and her whole countenance shifted into a deity hard as steel. A war helmet covered her head, and her eyes, once as black as Ariadne's own, became gray.

"You've changed," Ariadne whispered. Tears filled her eyes, and sorrow burrowed deep in her soul.

"Time changes all. Crete may continue as it has before, but across the sea, mortals change as well. Backwater towns become cities and will make their own navies and nations. I will not be forgotten, and so I, too, will change."

Ariadne pictured a faraway place, a dispute between the gods for who would be patron of a city. She saw the Bull from the Sea, the Great Earthshaker hit the ground with his trident and bring up a spring. The people of the faraway place ran toward it in joy, then dismay when they realized it was saltwater. The helmeted goddess struck the ground with her spear, and an olive tree began to grow. The people ran forth and danced around the still-growing tree. It provided shade, food, and oil. The small town began to grow; a single marble structure shone bright as the moon among the rocks and dirt. The olive tree continued to grow, and the small city-state grew with it.

"Who are you?" Ariadne asked.

"I am the Great Goddess still." She grew like the tree, larger and larger. The fabric of her gown floated on the wind of her power. Ariadne saw now that snakes rose from her back.

"When the world was new, I was the Great Mother Earth. When mortals came, I was the Great Mother. Then I became the daughter, the sister, the wife, the goddess of motherhood, of women, of childbirth. I am in everything: the moon, the sky, the sea, the world below, but then the new gods came. New male gods. One claimed the sea and another the sky, and another the world below, but he needed a consort. So my essence split, and I became one face of many. My strength comes from worship. You and your mother did much to strengthen me here in Crete, but there are others—new people who see me differently." She gestured to her helmet. "What I need from you is changing. So I ask you now, whose priestess are you? Mine or his?" The question struck like a slap.

"Yours, of course." Even as she spoke, she doubted her words.

"Are you?" the goddess asked. "We will see."

She awoke shuddering, her face sticky with tears, her hands cold and the crescent mark on her thigh stinging as if she had been branded.

"Mistress," Thalia whispered.

Ariadne could not speak, nor could she stop trembling. Thalia wrapped her in an embrace, slowly warming her with her body. "You had a nightmare. Too much wine."

She inhaled Thalia's familiar scent of verbena and rosemary. A nightmare.

Was it? The goddess did not speak to her in dreams. The goddess spoke to her in the temple, or the sacred grove, or on the swing, but never had she come in a dream. And that had not been her goddess. She had drunk a lot of wine because, because...

"Dionysus..."

"He is in the antechamber. He lost his way and spent this whole night below with your brother."

Do you serve the bull or me? The memory of the words sent her heart racing again.

Lost. He had been lost this whole time.

What had she lost?

"I told him not to wake you, and I did not allow him in your bed since you were so furious."

"My brother... Did he..." She pictured Asterion, wearing that damned bull head.

"He did not harm him, Mistress. Lord Dionysus said he's never been so lost, or so grateful to return to your rooms. Shall I admit him?"

"Bring me some water and a cloth for my face first."

When Thalia called him in, he came to her immediately. She had never seen him so serious. Even when he had sworn to let her sacrifice him, a hint of mirth danced around the corners of his lips. Now all hints of mischief had disappeared. He did not speak; instead he strode straight to her bed and knelt before it. Staring into her eyes, he cupped her cheek. She saw stars in his eyes, sparks of divinity. "Ariadne, I feared I'd never see you again. While I was lost, I thought I'd spend eternity below, forgotten."

She had not known whether rage or love would erupt upon seeing him, but instead of either, she only felt compassion.

"My brother can be fearsome. He was not always so." Gold glittered on his chest. "You are wearing his necklace."

"Yes." He stroked one of the gold-tipped bull's horns. "I promised to take a part of him with me to the world above, while something I valued stayed below."

"You gave him my wedding present to you." Anger blazed up, but only for a moment. Her brother was persuasive.

"They say I was born with horns," Dionysus began. "Asterion and I came to an understanding. I do not know how to explain. He wanted an exchange, something I valued. I understand if you're angry."

She burst into laughter, surprising herself. Of all the reasons. Dionysus stood up, a hint of mischief returning to his eyes.

"What's he like, my brother. Is he mad? Does he think he's a bull now?"

"No. But he has become the monster others say he is." Dionysus sat on her bed. "But are we not all monsters sometimes? This is something he and I have in common. I was glad to meet him and gladder still to return to you. If you will have me."

Ariadne did not speak. Instead, she dug her hand into the base of his long hair and pulled him toward her, kissing him mercilessly.

8

DIONYSUS: BASTARD SON OF ZEUS

The last three months with Ariadne had passed like one long, delightful day. The cool mornings and evenings made Dionysus realize the summer was ending. Time had never mattered to him as it did now. Three years would come soon. Existence had been an easy thing before. He had always done what he liked, gone where he wanted, never paying time any mind. He had never truly known the terrible pressure of his grandfather Chronos until he lay awake in Ariadne's bed, inhaling her scent of iris oil and listening to her breathe.

He had come to Crete in search of vengeance and had instead found love. The seasons would fly by. Three years would pass, and soon he and Ariadne would have to make grave decisions. Would he bare his throat for her? Would she sacrifice him to her goddess? Much could change between now and then.

Permanently dying did not worry him. He believed himself to be one of his father's kind—an undying god—or rather, a god who died but did not stay that way. He could not be certain, but he thought he had died before, been resurrected, been torn apart, and then been made whole again. Even if he yielded to her sacrificial blade, he would return. But what would his sacrifice do to her?

He suppressed a laugh at this concern. He did not want to wake her. How she had changed him! He had lain with many mortals and rarely wondered about them after. But this woman, this priestess of the Moon Goddess had truly shown him love. His desire to be honest with her surprised him. More than once, he had almost told her about his feud with Artemis. He wanted her to understand that though he had come with dishonest intentions, his love for her was real—so real he wanted to confess. But his understanding of women kept him from revealing his original intent.

He stared at Ariadne's face, beautiful in the darkness as it was in the sunlight. What was she dreaming about? Him, the goddess, or a future he could not foresee?

Suddenly, like a magnetized stone to a meteor, something tugged on him—a divine calling from one god to another. Wrapping a kilt around his waist, he rose from bed and strode to the balcony.

The crescent moon hung in a clear black sky. The stars twinkled. He made out the constellation of the sky serpent, the hydra, and recognized the triangle of the eagle, swan, and lyre. Ariadne had told him these three stars were the Three Mothers to the Minoans and they watched down on Crete. The stars were eternal. Their stories had already passed. His was just beginning.

The gentle Cretan breeze had shifted with the coming of fall. The night air prickled his naked torso and bare legs. Deciding to get a cloak, he turned to go back inside when a voice in his mind stopped him.

Bastard son of Zeus, I know how you've bedded my priestesses, trying to break their ties to me. Is this your idea of revenge, little godling?

He froze. The goddess, She of the Silver Bow, the Mistress of Wild Things—Artemis. She did not show herself but continued speaking in his mind.

You want to trifle with me, little godling? You want to play? You've picked the wrong enemy, for I am much older and far more powerful.

I am not afraid of you, sister. He sent his thoughts toward her.

Even as he simmered in fury, he delighted that he could communicate with another this way. Despite her animosity, this was the kind of connection he had longed for with the other gods.

You are truly a fool. Your control over humans is to cause madness through wine. My power is far greater. Every woman's health is in my hands. You seduced my priestesses and then abandoned them. Yet you tarry in Crete for more than three months. Pasiphae's daughter has made you her husband. Why do you not leave her with a broken heart as you did the others? Do you wish to take the crown of Minos—try to be a son Zeus is actually proud of?

Her words flew forth swiftly, piercing him like arrows. He gritted his teeth to keep from responding like a jealous child. Was Zeus ashamed of him? Did the Father of the Gods complain about Dionysus to his acknowledged children, the Olympians? Emotions he had never recognized threatened to overtake him. Dionysus pushed them away. The goddess was still speaking.

Find another land for people to worship you. There are plenty for the choosing, but this one belongs to me.

We started wrong, goddess. I did not mean to offend you by coming upon your maidens. I only wanted to meet you. Please, have a drink with me, and we can talk, as one god to another.

Her bitter laughter filled his mind, all the worse for sounding like the barbed giggles of a young girl. *You want to be friends? You really have no idea what it is to be a god. So incredibly naive. How unfortunate for you that you chose one of the only gods who has neither the desire to fuck you nor to drink with you.*

Red, the color of newly spilled blood, flashed before his eyes. *Then come down and fight me.*

I will fight you, little godling, the way a true goddess does. You have taken one of my priestesses and made her your wife. If you get her with child, it is for me to decide whether she lives or dies.

He stared up at the moon as if pinned in place. He had not lived very long compared to Artemis. With her words alone, she revealed that he was nothing more than a child playing at being a warrior. He was still formulating a response when Artemis spoke again. *This is how I fight, bastard son of Zeus. This is how gods fight. Your weakness is the woman, the one you had betray me. Leave her, and I will spare her life.*

Dionysus clenched his fists. Without his consciously bidding it, vines erupted from the earth and began climbing to the sky.

Artemis's laughter filled his mind, merry with surprise.

Will you build a tower of vines to the moon? You are impotent in this, little godling. Yet there is something about you I rather enjoy. Perhaps it is how feminine you appear, and I appreciate that you do not foolishly attempt to threaten me when you know you are beaten. Keeping quiet is a skill many need to learn.

Please, he thought before he could stop himself.

Ah. He could hear the smile in her voice. *Yes, I do like how humble you are.*

His cheeks burned with shame. How easily he could grovel. How badly he wanted to beg the goddess for mercy, not only for Ariadne, but for his own heart. He bowed his head, letting his long hair fall around his shoulders. Now was a good time to listen.

I will make a deal with you, son of Zeus. If you leave this woman for three years, I will let you have her after that time, if she will have you. If you get her with child, I will allow her to live. In fact, I will give her twins.

"Why do you really want me to leave, sister?" he said aloud, quietly enough not to wake anyone in the palace, but loud enough for his voice to be carried on the wind to Artemis.

Ah, pretty and clever. I have seen her future. Ariadne, daughter of Minos, has a destiny to fulfill with another. When she is done with him, you may have her back.

"Him?" He was willing to share her with the goddess, but with a mortal man? His pulse raced at the thought. He could not give his wife to another.

Do you prefer her dead? Would you rather watch her die trying to birth your child? How many women have you lain with? Do you think she belongs only to you now?

Her questions struck him hard. He wanted to be different

from his father, but never had it occurred to him that his wife would sleep with another man. He stared up at the moon, his mouth slightly agape.

Artemis let out a small, soft laugh. *Why is it that men can bed as many women and boys as they like, but women are meant to only belong to one man? That is part of why I chose to remain a virgin.*

You are wise, sister. I wish we were not enemies.

Well, little godling, you should have thought of that before you spied on my camp and fucked my priestesses.

Dionysus cast his head down in shame. She was right. He had behaved terribly. But it had led him here to his destiny. He could not let Artemis take Ariadne away from him. Though if she decided to, he would be helpless to stop her.

Little godling, do you want this woman again in three years, or will you let her die in childbirth?

"Is she pregnant?" he whispered, glancing back into the room at her sleeping form, her dark tresses spread over her pillow.

Not at the moment, the goddess replied. *If you bed her after the sun rises or any of the days after, your seed will take root, and a child will grow, a boy to make you proud. He will be too big for her to birth, and she will die. Eileithyia, the goddess of childbirth, owes me. She will do as I bid.*

Dionysus gulped the night air and tried to fight off the sorrow creeping up from his belly as Artemis began to slip away.

"Wait," he said to the moon. "You must make a vow, on the River Styx, and I will do as you say."

While the Goddess of the Hunt made her promise, sticky tears flowed down his cheek. He wiped them away, noticing the purple streaks on his finger—wine, weakened by saltwater.

He was not strong enough for a wife. If he were truly a god, he could match one of the Olympians. He would take the next three years to build his godhead, to gather a following, and learn more about his powers. It would break his heart to leave Ariadne, but at least she would be safe. And he would have her again.

He watched her sleep as the moon rose high into the sky. After slipping back into bed, he took her in his arms, kissing her cool skin. When at first she did not rouse, he imagined her dead. He put his ear to her heart and not only heard her blood pumping but also felt the divine energy emanating from her. He kissed her breasts, and she moaned softly.

He nestled his face against her, searching for the source of her energy. He trailed his tongue down from her breast, tracing the outline of her waist. He put his ear to her navel; perhaps that was the root of her power, for he knew it came from her matrilineal line, but her navel served only as an enticing distraction, and he continued his search. He stroked her mound, still sticky from earlier in the evening. The smell he had left on her mixed with her own aroused him further, and he slipped his tongue inside her.

She spread her thighs and gripped his hair. He teased her gently, knowing she wanted him to stroke her harder. Then he moved his head away to kiss her inner thigh. She moaned and arched her back, trying to entice him back to her center. He licked her inner thigh on one side then the other.

"Dionysus," she whispered, tilting her pelvis. But he continued to run his mouth along her inner thighs, feeling the pinpoint of her power. When his tongue connected with it, a bolt of electricity shot through him.

"What is this spot?" He probed it with his tongue, and sparks bit against his mouth. Ariadne gasped.

"Am I hurting you?" he asked.

"No. It is a strange sensation. That mark has always overwhelmed me with a feeling I cannot name. It is both arousal and fear. A call to the goddess—a pull from my normal life and away from all I know but also toward the divine."

He licked the spot again. She offered her inner thigh to him, her fingers fully entwined in his hair. He opened his mouth wide and sucked on the flesh surrounding the mark.

She moaned from deep in her throat, a low, begging sound. He thrust a finger into her womanhood, and she immediately climaxed, spasming hard against him.

He kept his lips fastened against her thigh, sucking on the mark harder and harder until she climaxed again and again.

"Yes," she whispered, "though I fear I will die of pleasure."

For all the nights I will not be with you, he thought, continuing to make her orgasm.

"Please," she gasped. "Come inside me."

The sky was still dark. He mounted her and thrust into her hard. She wrapped her legs against him and held on tight, taking him deep. He wanted to stay with this woman, to give himself to her nightly, but he could not cause her death.

"Please," she breathed, gripping him tightly.

He had already pushed her beyond the mortal limit of pleasure. He lowered his head to her breast and licked her nipple once before resuming his thrusts in earnest and finally coming into his pleasure.

She fell back asleep quickly after, and he wondered whether she would be sore in the morning. He had not meant to hurt her; he did not want to break either of their hearts. He cursed Artemis. He cursed his father Zeus, and he cursed himself for falling in love with a mortal, though even with his heart on the point of breaking, he would do it all again.

IN THE MORNING, SHE GAZED AT HIM WITH LOVE. "THAT WAS A nice surprise, husband. A fine way to start the day."

Should he tell her the truth? No. If he told her why he had sought her out, about his rivalry with Artemis, she would hate him. If he told her he had to leave, she would curse him as a coward. He had sworn to give her his life at the end of three years. When she found him gone, what would she think of him?

She would despise him no matter what. Perhaps she would not take him back after all. Perhaps she would fall in love with the other man the goddess planned for her to lie with.

In this same situation, Zeus would impregnate her and leave

her to die alone. If Dionysus was indeed a god, he was a new god. He truly loved her and wanted her to live more than anything. To live and fulfill her own destiny. He had thought they were meant to be together—she seemed the perfect consort. Ariadne was enough of a goddess for him, but he was not enough of a god. Not yet.

"Mistress." Thalia had entered the room, carrying a tray of fruit. "Lord Dionysus." The golden-haired girl liked him better than Ariadne's other two handmaids, who narrowly hid their disdain that their mistress had married a foreigner. At least Thalia would be here to console Ariadne after he left.

"Little Leopard, is my bath ready?" Ariadne asked, taking a plum and rising naked from the bed. He watched her walk away, loving the way her hips swayed. He hated leaving her for the day. How would he last three years?

In all his travels, he had never been so sad about leaving a place. He would miss these cultivated people, but he would leave Silenus here. Silenus could fulfill Dionysus's promise to King Minos. When he returned, the vines would be growing. He enjoyed giving his gift to the Cretans, if nothing else.

"Master, what ails you?" Thalia asked when she returned to gather Ariadne's brush and hair pins.

Without meaning to, he had let his face morph into an expression of pure grief. Soft as a feather, Thalia brushed his cheek with her finger.

"Forgive me," she whispered for trespassing against her station. Her fingertip came away purple red. He was crying and hadn't realized.

"It's nothing. Perhaps I drank too much last night." He hoped to jest, but Thalia's brow furrowed with concern as she returned to Ariadne in the bath.

After slipping on a kilt, Dionysus stood in the entrance of the bathing chamber. The damp air smelled of iris oil, verbena, and rosemary. He savored the scent and the sight as Ariadne rose from her bath. He envied the droplets of water sliding from her hair to her breast and dripping down her waist until Thalia dried her with an Egyptian linen towel.

He watched Thalia anoint her with honeysuckle oil. Her nipples were slightly bruised to a beautiful shade of purple, and the memory of pleasure shot through him. She caught his gaze and smiled as Thalia brushed her hair, oiling every sleek tress so it shone. She put on her golden hooped earrings that resembled blossoms and a red beaded necklace in addition to the bull's horn-crescent moon pendant she always wore. Thalia tied the sacred knot around her waist and helped her into her vest and long skirt.

"I'm to oversee the rites for the girls who got their first moon-blood in the last three months. I'll be back late."

"Do not worry, Ariadne. I will find my own entertainment. I always do."

"That is what concerns me." She came to him, twisting his hair in her finger. "Look, what a perfect ring this would make. She twined a dark strand of his hair around her finger.

"It does not match your fancy gold or jewels."

"I grew up wearing these golden bracelets, gems of amethyst, and rubies. But the hair of a god, that is a new thing." She kissed him, and his eyes prickled. He could not let her see him cry.

"Go," he said. "Your temple and your people await you."

She kissed him again on his neck and turned, walking out escorted by Thalia.

He gazed around the chamber where he had known such happiness. There was nothing much he needed to take with him, only his traveling cloak, his thyrsus, a small amphora, and a wine flask. He wanted something of Ariadne's. She was wearing all her finest jewels, but he knew which ones were important to her. He opened her cedar jewelry box inlaid with mother of pearl. None of her rings would fit him, so he took a golden armlet and a silver bracelet. Feeling a bit like a thief, he pulled out her dagger and decided to leave her something of himself to help ease her pain.

Talos and Manko had accompanied Ariadne to the temple. The guard who stood outside her door glared at him. Dionysus could occasionally hear mortals' thoughts. This time they were as loud in his mind as Artemis's words had been.

You're not worthy of our priestess. No one approves of this marriage. He had not realized how much the guards detested him. *You don't belong in the priestess's bed. One of us should be there. We are all worthier sacrifices.*

Dionysus pulled his purple cloak closer, his skin prickling. He walked down the corridor, turned to the right, and promptly got lost. This place was a labyrinth. He had been married to the Mistress of the Labyrinth, and now instead of leaving her, perhaps he would wander lost here forever. He tugged on one of his ringlets to bring himself back. He could not give in to self-pity—not yet. Once he took a ship, he could let the sorrow come. Out on the sea, with the wind in his face, he could cry, howl even. But now he had to get out of the palace. He had to find Silenus and leave a message with one of Ariadne's handmaidens.

Finally, after turning left and right countless times and realizing he was going back where he had come from, he somehow found himself in the hall of shields and knew where he was. He did not see any guards but suspected they watched from the shadows.

In the courtyard he asked for Thalia, Zoe, or Melia. None of the guards responded. They treated him with respect when he walked next to Ariadne, but without her, he was nothing but a foreign sacrifice.

Proceeding down the hall, he continued to what he hoped was the west gate. A flutter of motion caught his eye, a pretty girl dressed in saffron, a veil over her head, her breasts bare. Phaedra.

"Brother," she said, addressing him. This struck him as odd since they had hardly spoken.

"Little sister," he said, using what he hoped was their form of address. "I have a message for my wife. I have sudden business and must take a ship today. Please, tell her I will come back for her. Even if I am gone long, I have not forgotten her."

Phaedra's face twitched. "Oh, you think you might be gone for some time. That is a shame." She laughed suddenly, almost like a hiccup.

"I wanted to tell Thalia, to leave my message with her, but I could not find her."

Phaedra gained control of her face and now appeared grave, her seriousness reflecting his own.

"You can't find Thalia," she repeated.

Was she stupid? Women often reacted to him like this. Ariadne had never acted foolish or easily swayed. Perhaps Phaedra was dumb or stunned, but at least she did not take down her hair or shuck off her clothing.

"Will you tell Ariadne? Will you ask her to forgive my absence and tell her I will return?"

"Oh yes!" Phaedra brightened, her eyes clear with understanding. "So sad, you must go... I wonder where Thalia is... You!" she called to a passing guard. "Go find the blonde girl who serves the high priestess. Bring her to me." She turned back to Dionysus. "Go ahead, brother. I will give my sister your message when she leaves the temple tonight. Go and get yourself a ship. Any of my father's fleet will be happy to take you wherever you want to go. Where exactly are you sailing to?"

"Ah, well, my business is... to the east."

"Oh, brother, allow me to help you. Tios," she called to her personal guard. "Take Lord Dionysus to the harbor. Find a boat for him."

"I must find my friend Silenus before I go," Dionysus said. Having a guard to guide him would make negotiating Knossos much easier.

"Very good. I believe he is in the east vineyard." Phaedra seemed to know more than he realized.

"Thank you, little sister." He took her hand in thanks.

"I will be sure to tell my sister you have left."

"And that I will return."

"Of course, that, too." Her lips twitched. "Tios, be sure to follow Lord Dionysus's every desire."

He did not understand mortals. Already his heart hurt to leave Ariadne behind. Even when he was full of power, she remained calm. He did his best to keep his essence contained, but Phaedra acted as if he was pouring out cups of wine.

"Thank you," he said, following Tios to what he guessed was the east vineyard. He did not understand why she thanked him in return.

9

ARIADNE AND THE RITE OF FIRST BLOOD

Overseeing the celebration of the girls' first crossover into womanhood was one of Ariadne's greatest joys as high priestess. Though it left her exhausted, passing on secrets of womanhood to the next generation was one of her favorite ceremonies.

Nervous excitement mixed in the air along with the scent of mountain mint, lavender, and dittany. The girls and their mothers, aunts, and grandmothers formed a circle while Ariadne and her priestesses stood in the center of the temple.

One by one, she called each girl up to receive her cycle counting necklace of red beads. This bond between the women of Crete strengthened them all. Their dark eyes shining with pride, their hands nervously twisting their gowns or fidgeting with their hair, these girls on the brink of becoming women now entered the sacred sisterhood.

"You now have magic men cannot fathom. Your strength comes from the goddess, from your foremothers, and the moon. This necklace is more than a symbol that you are women now. It is a counting tool. With it you can learn about yourself and decide when you are ready to have a child."

Some of the girls smiled knowingly, having learned from their mothers or sisters. Others held the agate stones delicately—at odds with their necklaces and with themselves. There was no going back. The unknown pleasures and pain of fertility awaited them now.

Ariadne let one of her priestesses lead the first part of explaining the cycle. The girls listened, following along on their own necklaces. These daughters of Crete were so beautiful even in their awkwardness.

Ariadne thought back to her own first-blood. Thalia's had come first, but she had not wanted to go to the ceremony without Ariadne. They had sat where these girls sat now, rapt with attention, shy and excited at their possible futures.

Pasiphae had led the ceremony with Seer at her side, and Ariadne imagined herself and Phaedra taking their places.

Ariadne stepped up to continue explaining the cycle counting. She spoke more slowly than usual as the girls followed along on their own necklaces. A few stared at her as if unable to comprehend what she said. Girls and women could come as many times as they liked to hear her talk about their cycles. It was too much to take in the first time. The mystery of a woman's body was not easy to comprehend.

"Eat honey on this day." Ariadne held up a bead close to the end and moved on to the next. "Be kind to yourself on this day, for dark thoughts may come. On this day, you may discover a blemish on your skin, and you may desire sex suddenly."

The older women laughed at this as they always did. The other priestesses had already explained how to encourage or discourage pregnancy.

"Just because you can bleed, doesn't mean it is time to have a baby. You have magic now," Ariadne added. "You can bleed without sickness or dying. You are a part of the goddess, and she is a part of you. Let yourself feel your new body. Use the necklace to help you understand where you are in your cycle and what that means to you. It is not the same for every woman." She paused. The mothers and aunts always appreciated this part.

"When you come to the fourteenth bead, you will be at your most fertile." She was on her thirteenth bead today. Would the goddess bless her with a daughter this month? It finally seemed like the right time. For the first time, she wanted to have a baby with a specific man. She caressed her thirteenth bead. She and Dionysus would have to try hard tonight and tomorrow. She could clearly see the babe they would have together. Their daughter, beautiful and intelligent, would be the perfect heir to carry on the divine line of priestesses.

Ariadne would not think of what would happen in two years and nine months. Perhaps she could find a way out of sacrificing her husband. Perhaps he would not die even if she slit his throat. He claimed to be an undying god. She did not doubt him.

"When you are ready to get pregnant, have intercourse on these days." She held up the beads, separating them from the others and giving the girls time to check their own necklaces.

"For most of you, that will not be for a while now, but you must know and understand your cycle so you can better understand yourselves. Sometimes on these days," she indicated the beads toward the end, "you will find yourself feeling angry or worried about small things. Remember you can always come to the temple. You can help the priestesses sweep or weave or go to the caves with an offering or just sit in silence. The more you understand your moods, the better you can help yourself."

She continued explaining the beads. Not bleeding did not always mean pregnancy. There were other ways to tell. She had given this talk so many times that she let her mind wander while she spoke. As soon as she returned to the palace, she would sup with her husband. She had grown quite fond of his new drink. She had always liked mead, but wine was transformative in a completely different way. After they talked about the day, he would entertain her in bed. He pleasured her in ways she had never experienced before his arrival. Each night was a revelation. Even if she could only have him for three years, she would enjoy every moment.

The ceremony ended when the sun set. Ariadne stayed long after, speaking to girls, chatting with their mothers. On such a special day, no one wanted to return home just yet.

Finally, Ariadne said goodbye to the last girl, leaving the novices to see to the cleanup. She allowed herself a moment of anticipation. She could almost taste the wine on her tongue, taste Dionysus's skin in her mouth.

Manko and Talos followed her back to the east wing. All the guards she passed along the way bowed even lower than they normally did. Filled with divine power and blood magic, she was even more revered on this special day.

Tomorrow she had little to do. Perhaps she and Dionysus could picnic in the late afternoon. There were still many parts of Knossos he hadn't seen. He wanted to meet Daedalus. The engineer's workshop would astound her husband. She pictured how big his eyes would grow upon seeing the life-like statues Daedalus had built. She also wanted to take him to other parts of the island. He had not seen the sacred caves. She especially wanted to show him where some believed baby Zeus had been hidden, the cave that bled honey.

She did not notice Phaedra waiting for her in the courtyard until she spoke.

"Priestess." Her voice was solemn, falling like a stone. "Sister."

Ariadne's heart began to race. Their parents, something must have happened. An argument? An accident? Had her father finally pushed her mother too far?

"I have sad news, Ariadne. Your husband..."

Dear gods, no! How could anything have befallen him? He would not succumb to fever or a fall down the stairs like a mortal, drown in the ocean or get gored by a bull.

"... Dionysus has abandoned you. He was seen taking a ship east."

A blazing light flashed behind Ariadne's eyes—bright as the sun. Searing as seeing her grandfather Helios while her body swung in the sacred grove.

Abandoned. Images flashed through her mind—depictions of her alone, unwanted, forgotten.

All her rage from the night he had been with her brother flooded forth. *Never trust the word of a god.* She had given him her heart, but gods were nothing more than liars, and she a fool to have fallen for him. She would never give her heart so easily again. She would never love a man again. She stood up straight, wishing for a sacred dagger to grip, for a victim's throat to cut—for Dionysus's throat to cut.

She laughed bitterly. And if he had offered her his throat, it would have broken her heart to cut it.

Phaedra clasped Ariadne's hand. "And, dearest, we cannot be certain, but he had a blonde girl with him. His arm wrapped around her waist in public is what the people say they saw. I am afraid that Thalia ran off with him."

"No." The word came out like a shard of broken glass, and she bit her lip so as not to say more.

"I am so sorry, sister. I don't understand it myself. I only know what I was told by those who saw."

This could not be true. She had believed in Dionysus, not just as a god, but as a man. And Thalia—to betray her in such a way after all they had been through. No. She would return to her chambers and find them both there. They would laugh over this... A cruel joke that Phaedra had made up to hurt her.

No, people did not joke about these things. Phaedra, no matter how mean-spirited, could not make this up.

"Sister," Phaedra asked softly, "did you fight with your husband? Perhaps do something to displease him?"

Ariadne slapped her before even realizing it. Phaedra cradled her cheek in her hand, tears of shock streaming down her face, smudging her kohl.

"I'm sorry," Ariadne said. It wasn't Phaedra's fault if she was only repeating what had been reported.

"Why did you do that?" Phaedra asked. Fury lit behind her

eyes along with a flash of a malicious smile. Then it was gone, and Phaedra once again became a wounded, innocent girl.

"I'm sorry," Ariadne repeated. "I cannot believe he would leave me."

"Why? What do you know of him truly? He was a stranger. A stranger who convinced Father to make you marry him. Did you really think he would stay and give his life for the goddess?"

Ariadne wanted to drop to her knees in pain and sob on the cold floor of the courtyard. But with her little sister and the guards watching, she stood up straight. She was the high priestess, the keeper of the future of Crete. She could not crumble over a man. She could not fall to pieces over the betrayal of her hand-maiden. *Thalia*. No, she would not think of the little blonde whore.

"I must return to my rooms, Phaedra. We will not speak of Dionysus again. We will forget that I was ever married to him, that he ever came here. We will drink wine, and we will forget." She laughed suddenly, a broken sound she had wanted to keep in until she was alone.

She did not hear Phaedra's response as she turned and walked away, barely seeing the corridors or the brightly colored columns as she made her way back to her rooms.

Her chambers were so empty without him. Without Thalia.

"Wine!" she growled at Melia. Zoe came timidly, not commenting on her tears or her rage. With shaking hands, Zoe helped remove her vest and loosened her colored skirt.

"I'm sorry, Mistress. I do not know where Thalia is."

Not knowing what she was doing, Ariadne's hand fastened around Zoe's slender throat.

"Never speak her name again!" she yelled. Zoe dropped the ceremonial gown on her feet, gasping for air. Zoe's nails dug into her wrists, but Ariadne hardly saw anything through her tears.

"Mistress!" Melia shrieked, opening the door. The small amphora of wine fell. It shattered, making a dull sound. As wine, dark as blood, oozed across the floor, Ariadne released Zoe, who dropped to her knees before her mistress.

Coming back to herself, Ariadne observed her naked body from a distance—her servant at her feet, the broken amphora, the wine puddled on the floor. Outside, Manko called out, asking whether they should enter. Melia told them to wait, then quickly picked up a blanket and wrapped her mistress in it as the door burst open. Ariadne barely saw their faces filled with fear and fury as they assessed that their priestess was not in danger.

"You are not needed," Melia said. "It was my fault. I dropped the wine and screamed. It was foolishness. Manko, send a boy for more wine. And some bread and cheese. My mistress is hungry."

Manko glared about the room, waiting for Ariadne to speak.

"Go." The word came out broken, as if *Go* were a terrible thing she could hardly utter.

Melia said nothing as she helped Zoe up. She said nothing as Ariadne wept. She cleaned up the broken amphora and mopped up the wine, then cleaned up the second and third amphora Ariadne threw across the room after emptying their contents.

Shame, Ariadne thought. *I have been shamed. Everyone will know of the husband who left me. They will wonder what I did to deserve being abandoned.* The urge to cry returned, but she had no more tears.

"Mistress," Melia said softly. "You must sleep now."

Ariadne let her handmaiden lead her to the water closet and then to her bed. The sheets smelled like him. She wanted to jump up and demand the bedding be burned. But she also wanted to lie there one last time, savoring the memories she would have to forget on the morrow.

She had never thought she could have love. Yet it had been hers briefly. Now it was gone. She had been betrayed. He had used her after all. All his words, lies. She laughed to herself because now the only solace she could find was in wine. She would drink and drink and drink until she died, and then the shame would be no more.

"Daughter! Open this door!" Ariadne had not heard her mother sound this angry for a long time. She did not know how many days had passed or how many amphorae she had drunk. Zoe and Melia attended her, meek and quiet, yet brave just being there.

Pasiphae strode into the room, the glow of her rage surrounding her. Ariadne never forgot her mother was the daughter of the sun.

"Have you lost your head, child? What is all this?" A hint of concern lingered behind her mother's smooth skin and painted lips.

"Do you not know, mother? My husband has left me."

"Husband? You have no husband."

"Indeed, I do not."

Pasiphae glanced at Zoe as if to assess whether her daughter had gone mad.

"Do you mean you foresaw that your husband would leave you? These prophecies are never clear until they occur. There is little point in fretting about the future."

Ariadne stood up to protest or shout, but once she did, her crumpled robes and knotted hair shamed her. Pasiphae's gaze reminded her of her station. The high priestess of Crete had no right to self-pity. Her face sticky with tears, she suddenly smelled her unbathed body, the room stuffy with the scent of old wine.

"I did not misunderstand. My husband left me, and he took..." *My friend, my slave, that whore.* "...Thalia."

"I heard that Thalia is missing. Odd. She was always so faithful to you. Your father sent guards to look for her." Pasiphae placed a cool hand on Ariadne's forehead. "Are you sick, daughter?"

It was then Ariadne noticed the ring around her mother's finger. Black and slick, a perfect curl, so odd next to Pasiphae's jeweled gold rings.

"What is this?" she asked, grabbing her mother's hand.

Pasiphae laughed. "Oh this? Your father's new horticulturalist, Silenus, gave us these rings. He swore it would help the new vines grow and bring great prosperity to our kingdom if we wore them for seven days. It is quite foolish, but he was so charming and persuasive. He gave one to me and your father, and to many of the servants. He said after seven days we should give them to others in the kingdom. He promised if everyone on Crete wore them, we would be remembered for all eternity. Foolishness, I know, but they are rather fun. I feel good when I wear it. As soon as I put the ring on, it was almost as if I was floating. Your father hasn't been this pleasant since before that whole business with the bull. Daughter, what are you doing?"

Ariadne had gripped her mother's hand and tried to pull the ring off her finger. Once her finger touched the silken hair, she, too, felt her sorrow lift slightly. *Bastard.*

She strode to her desk and opened her jewelry box. Of course, he had left her one, too. She lifted out the ring of Dionysus's hair. A perfect, magical curl. It did not shed or become unwound. *Bastard*, she thought again, then slid it over her finger and thought, *Who?*

10

DIONYSUS LEAVES CRETE

Once Dionysus caught the last glimpse of Crete, he strode to the prow and let the wind come at him. He had experienced loss and grief at the death of a friend, neglect and abandonment by his father, but never had his heart broken to leave a mortal woman. Even as anguish overcame him, he delighted in the newness of this sensation. Any pain, no matter how small, was a comfort.

It had been kind of Phaedra to have her personal guard Tios find him this Phoenician merchant ship. When the grizzled captain had offered him passage to Cyprus and then on to Tyre, he had hiked up his traveling cloak and clambered onboard. As the ship sailed over the calm sea, he marveled at the carefully carved horse head adorning the prow. Sailors had strapped a large amphora of grain to the foremast. Was it an offering to the god or just a safe place to harness such a large container?

Small clay amphorae filled with olive oil and covered bales of goods lined the sides of the boat. Dionysus followed the lines from the handles of the amphorae tied with rope to the bundles to the covered chests, all strapped down. Skilled as spiders, the sailors had intertwined all their cargo. Their talent to secure their goods was as impressive as their ability to maneuver on the water.

At least he was among such worldly men. The Phoenicians made it possible for Egypt to have cedar and Crete to have Egyptian luxuries. They brought spices from Arabia and gold and jewels from Nubia. Now they carried olive oil east. One day those amphorae would contain wine. One day thousands of ships would cross the seas with wine as part of their cargo.

Above, the elegant saffron-and-purple-striped sail billowed on the breeze. He closed his eyes as the fresh ocean air caressed his face. Perhaps in time Ariadne would forgive him. Perhaps the magic hair rings would work, and she would forget him. He would not forget her, but a few distractions would ease his pain.

Travel was always a balm for sorrow. The future and other intriguing mortals lay ahead. The captain had said they would sail to Rhodes, then Cyprus, stopping at Ugarit, Byblos, Sidon, and finally arriving at Tyre—the land of the purple. In Tyre, he would watch as they extracted the dye from the sea snail. He would garb himself in the most expensive purple cloak.

A Phoenician youth strode toward him. Nothing but a dark blue kilt covered his lithe, muscular body. A white cap barely contained his curly black hair. The sailor's dark brown eyes drank Dionysus in. He held a cup of water in his hands like an offering. "My Lord, I am called Ahumm." He licked his bottom lip. "Are you thirsty?"

Dionysus could not help but grin at the very clear suggestion. He took the cup from Ahumm and drank.

"It is an honor to have you on board, Lord Dionysus. We understand you were an esteemed guest of King Minos. I would be happy to assist you. There are spaces below deck if you desire anything."

Dionysus glanced at the opening in the deck—a gaping black mouth on the otherwise clean, bright cedarwood. When he focused his mind on the area below, fear shot through him. He could picture the darkness, the cramped quarters, but more than that, he sensed a great terror down below. It was not the rowers, free men who chose this life of adventure. No, there was...

Ahumm adjusted the knife on his belt, sliding down his kilt ever so slightly and exposing the light brown skin undarkened by the sun. Dionysus glanced at his taut belly, the fine line of his hip bone. Taking Ahumm below decks would be satisfying and a good way to forget his troubled heart, at least momentarily.

The young man's lips turned up in a smile. *I give myself to you, Lord.*

Dionysus had caught this thought many times. Mortals had made this gesture to him throughout the years; as his power had grown, so had their need of him.

Ahumm allowed himself a full smile. Dionysus easily read his mind as the Phoenician's dark eyes shone at the very thought of being taken by Dionysus.

Many mortals had been overcome by his power, but not Ariadne; that was one reason he loved her.

"I am content for now, Ahumm, but I will not forget your generous offer." He patted Ahumm's hand in acknowledgement.

Once they had anchored and eaten, the Phoenicians gave him a pallet to recline on. The sailors spread out on the deck, and two remained awake to keep watch. Ahumm had laid his pallet near Dionysus. Soon the sound of the sailors' snores mixed with the sea lapping against the boat.

Dionysus enjoyed sleep, though he did not require it. Tonight that ease of mind would not come. He stared up at the stars, the memories of so many myths.

Was he truly a god? If his father was indeed Zeus, that simply made Dionysus another semi-divine bastard. The Great Thunderer had never come down from on high to talk to him. When Dionysus was a youth, Zeus had allowed him to be whipped by his uncle and chased into the forest, into the very sea. The God of the Sky had offered no help. Thetis the Titan had saved him. Among the gods, only she, Hermes, Hephaestus, and Pan had been his friends. The others hated him or worse, were completely indifferent.

He dreamed of being a new kind of god, yet he could not even compete with the old ones. He had tried to befriend Artemis and instead had made her his enemy. He had hoped for kinship among the gods, acknowledgment that he was indeed one of them. But he was not. He had held the truth at bay long enough—he was a failure.

He possessed nothing more than a few tricks of transformation. His powers were far from impressive and completely unpredictable. When Zeus sent a lightning bolt, it struck. When Zeus decided to bed a maiden, he did. No matter the cost. When Poseidon sent a wave or an earthquake, it did as he bid. When the Earth Shaker wanted something, he took it, caring not at all who suffered. And Artemis's twin, Apollo—giver of prophecy, keeper of medicine, unleasher of plagues—his will, too, became action, smiting his intended victim. Just like his sister.

Dionysus could not save the woman he loved. He could not change the way gods or mortals behaved—at least not for the better.

He let the tears come. It did not matter whether the stars saw. They, like the gods themselves, did not care. He was little more than a man with a bit of magic, not a god at all. Other sons of gods were heroes—not gods. Why would he fancy himself any different?

He allowed himself this shameful pity. He uncorked his small wineskin and took a sip. He rarely allowed himself to wash away his sorrow with the tonic of his gift, but out on the dark sea, forced from the mortal he loved, unsure of his future—this was the perfect time to indulge.

He pictured Ariadne in her rooms, entrenched in fury, throwing anything he had left behind against the wall, calling for a fire to burn his possessions. He did not blame her. She would assume he had left for fear of being killed, or worse, out of boredom. For her right now, all his words had been lies. She hated herself for trusting him. She should have been more wary of a stranger claiming to be a new god. Perhaps there had been something between them—something true. But he was gone now.

Her rage would frighten Zoe and Melia, but Thalia would stay by her side through the storm of fury, through screams and tears. The girl would find a way to keep Ariadne from the worst of it. He loved the High Priestess of Crete, but Thalia loved her more.

And for that he was grateful. He was not his father, or Poseidon, or Hades. He didn't want to be anything like the generation before who demanded women be faithful while the men were not. Thalia loved Ariadne, and of course Ariadne delighted in Thalia. Dionysus didn't have perky breasts with pink nipples, lighter than any other flesh tone in Crete. He had not transitioned through girlhood to womanhood with Ariadne as Thalia had. He was not jealous.

Perhaps the magic rings would work. He had never attempted anything like that before. He tugged on his hair, some of the tresses partially shorn, others growing long and curling like vines. Sacrificing some of his hair meant nothing if it would ease his wife's heart. And she was his wife still. She would always be his wife.

The dark of the night, the quiet sounds of the sea, and the cool breeze gave him peace. Perhaps after he drank with Ahumm, after their bodies entwined under the night sky, after the boy showed his devotion, perhaps then, rocked by the waves, he could sleep. Perhaps he could have a moment without feeling this terrible ache of loss. Perhaps...

A woman's scream rent the silence. Immediately recognizing this kind of shriek—a last attempt at stopping a violation—he jumped up and grasped his thyrsus. A few sailors sat up in surprise, cocking their heads to listen, and then lay back down. Men were not meant to intervene when a woman cried out. Dionysus was halfway across the deck. He would follow no mortal's rules—only his own instinct.

He descended the stairs. Bitterness rose in his throat. He had sensed this woman's fear all along. Yet he had not allowed himself to realize it. The gaping mouth on the deck had led to this place of torment. He could not call himself a god if he ignored her pain any longer.

The darkness below engulfed him. A faint flicker of light and a moan gave him direction. Scents of cedar, clay, and olive oil lingered in the air. A small lantern glowed behind a curtain. Dionysus parted the ox hide. In the dim light of a lantern surrounded by sand, the captain stood with his fists clenched in the golden hair of the weeping, naked woman crumpled on the ground.

"Stop," Dionysus commanded.

The stout captain turned away from the girl, not letting go of her hair.

"What? You want some? Maybe tomorrow night after I train her better. She's still fighting too much. A few more lessons with my fists, and she'll be docile enough to share." He pulled her hair, making her moan and growl as he forced her to rise to her knees.

"Stop," the girl cried, digging her nails into the captain's wrist. Her pale forearms and chest bore bruises and freckles. Dionysus glanced at her face.

"Thalia?"

"Lord Dionysus!"

He did not touch the captain, but vines sprang from his hand, wrapping around the Phoenician's wrist.

"The woman's mine, stranger," the captain snarled, "given to me by the Princess of Crete as a gift."

Ariadne? She was willing to slit men's throats for her goddess, but would she discard her favorite like this? Could her heart be this cruel? Had he misunderstood everything?

"My Lord, I prayed you would come. This is all a terrible dream. Please, help me," Thalia said.

It did not matter whether Ariadne had given her to the captain. It did not matter whether or not he was a real god. He had a few tricks, and he would use one now.

"Thalia, I free you. Not just from servitude to this man, but from your mortal form. Go and be who you will!"

He tilted his thyrsus, and she began to transform. Her long, golden hair flowed over her shoulders and back until it covered her arms and legs. The markings from the man's fists darkened and shrank into a majestic pattern of spots. Her hands, which had been clenched, transformed into paws, her ears sharpened into tips, and a long, balancing tail grew from her rump.

Where a frightened girl had begged for mercy, a giant leopard crouched, ready to strike. She growled, low and deep, and pounced on the captain. He let out a shriek as he fell, weakly trying to fend her off. She slashed at him with her claws. Streaks of blood gushed from his forearms and palms as he screamed in terror and pain.

From all around the ship, sailors came running. Those who had ignored Thalia's screams responded immediately when their captain cried out. There was only enough space for a few men below; once they glimpsed the leopard, they froze.

"Help me!" the captain cried.

Not one man moved.

"What's happening?" those above called down.

The men below did not respond. How could they admit to what they saw? The captain screamed as Thalia stepped closer.

"By the Great Goddess, what is happening down there?"

"Leopard!" a sailor cried, slowly moving back to escape above deck.

Thalia swiped at the captain's chest with her claw; red gashes ran like rivers.

"Please," the captain pleaded, "spare my life. I will give you anything you desire."

Thalia turned to Dionysus, her eyes still the same shade of brilliant green.

"Your choice, Little Leopard. You are the one who has suffered."

She lowered her head as if in thanks, then returned her attention to the man who had planned to rape her. She growled and sank her teeth into the captain's throat. Dionysus tried not to smile too broadly, though pride was one of many emotions that played through him as he watched Thalia demolish the man who had planned to rape her.

Above deck, men shouted in panic.

"Leopard on board!"

"We have angered the gods! Forgive us, great gods of the sea. Forgive us, great gods of the sky!"

"The captain is dead! The monster eats him even now! Will she eat us next?"

"Prepare to jump! A sailor dies in the sea rather than as prey!"

"Enough!" Dionysus bellowed, coming above deck and raising his thyrsus. Two sailors appeared ready to hurl themselves overboard, several had their knives unsheathed, and one waved a torch dangerously close to the olive oil while Ahumm tried to calm him.

"I am the god the captain has angered! Calm yourselves, or you will continue to feel my wrath. If you want to live, quiet your terror."

A gentle breeze blew. The sailors sheathed their knives. One of the sailors jumped into the sea. The soft splash of his death seemed to break the trance of the other, who stepped away from the side.

Ahumm took the torch and strode toward Dionysus. "Tell us how to please you, Lord Dionysus."

Dionysus allowed the men to stare at him as the firelight danced over his features. He did not appear too different than they were, but every one of them was aware of his divinity.

"I do not abide rape. Not of girls, women, boys, or men. Some of you have had this done to you as boys and think that it is the way of the world. But it is not. Not on this ship, and not in the new world to come. Your captain tried to rape a woman—a woman he thought was his slave. But she was not his slave, and she was not a woman. A leopard eats him now, gnawing on the hands that held her down."

The men stared, slack-jawed with horror. One or two had their hands back on their knives, as if doing anything other than obeying could save them now.

"I yield to your command, Lord Dionysus," Ahumm said. Several others repeated his words.

"Your old captain is dead for violating the will of a god. Who is captain now?" Dionysus asked.

Silence followed. The moment stretched until an older man stepped forward. Gray hair sprouted from his chest. He removed his pointed white cap to smooth down his short, grizzled locks. "I suppose I am, my Lord."

"Seadog is our navigator, Lord, and a good man," Ahumm said. "We are honored to witness the justice of the new god! Blessed be Dionysus!" He bowed deeply, and Dionysus placed his hand on the cap covering the boy's silken black hair.

"I am a new god—a god for new men and women. The woman who is now a leopard was my wife's friend. I found her at the mercy of the captain and gave her the freedom to transform." He eyed the crew, suddenly able to see what shape each man would take if he gave them the same gift. Seadog, not surprisingly, would become a dolphin. Ahumm, an otter; a thick-throated man, a turtle; another, an octopus. "I am a just god. You need not follow me, but I will reach my destination, and I will not have the woman who is a leopard misused. You decide what course you wish to follow."

Leaving the crew to discuss matters, Dionysus brought Thalia above deck. With the cool, fresh air surrounding them, Thalia calmed. The sailors backed away, warily eying her rust-colored muzzle as she licked her forepaws clean.

"You're enjoying that tongue of yours, aren't you?"

She glanced up, a hint of mirth in her green eyes.

"I can transform you back." He placed his hand near her head. She surprised him by growling, *No*. It was clear in her voice, clear in his mind.

He withdrew his hand. "I understand. You are welcome to keep this form as long as you wish." She rose and nuzzled his leg.

Her soft, thick fur rubbed against his calf, and he stroked her head. When she responded, he dug his fingers into the space behind her ears.

"Thalia, you shouldn't be here."

She lifted her head, eyes flashing. Streaks of dark fur trailed from her eyes as if she had been crying.

He could not understand her message. Anger? Fate. Calm, acceptance... gratitude.

"I am glad to be here with you as well, Little Leopard." His wife had called her that. "I would rather you be with your mistress, but if we were abandoned, it comforts me to take you with me. Though I do not understand why your mistress would sell you to that captain. If you displeased Ariadne, I can think of many ways she might punish you—many which you would both enjoy. There is much I do not understand about mortals, but your desires with Ariadne were very clear, and I faulted neither of you for it. But giving you away. It makes no sense. She cared for you deeply, Thalia." He scratched behind her ears, and she began to purr.

He had never transformed a woman like this. When he was younger, he had reveled in shedding his own mortal form and taking on the body of another. As thrilling as it was to be women, boys, or men, there was a different kind of pleasure to be obtained by inhabiting the body of an animal. The shift of perspective was astounding—relaxing and basic and infinitely wiser.

He had been a bull, a ram, and many horned creatures. He had also spent time in the guise of a dog, a cat, a mouse and, most exhilarating, a hawk. Each body he experienced had offered its own gift.

Some mortals did not see it that way. They feared being transformed into animals. A great insult. A divine punishment. As if they believed it was so far beneath them to be other than human. But Thalia, ah, Thalia appeared completely comfortable in her new form. Beautiful and deadly—that's how she should have been all along. He only wished Ariadne were there to appreciate her splendor and to explain why she had given her away.

The air on the deck had cooled. Dionysus did not mind the cold, and Thalia was well cloaked in fur. The first rays of sun began to peek out beyond the sea.

"Lord Dionysus," Ahumm said, bowing before him. "We offer you our service gladly."

The Phoenician sailors stood behind Ahumm. They feared Dionysus and did not doubt his godhead. They did not question his power.

"I want to travel east. As far east as we can."

Seadog did not flinch, though some of the other men paled. The new captain stepped forward.

"I will take you where you wish to go, Lord. After Rhodes, after Cyprus, after Tyre."

The sky began to change from deep blue-gray to a weak shade of early light.

"A new day," Dionysus said.

Some of the sailors stared at him; others glanced out at the sea, as if comprehending how far they would have to journey.

"None of you need accompany me any further than you wish. If you want to disembark at Cyprus, I will not punish you for it. I only ask that you spread the word of the new god, the Twice Born, the one who comes bringing the gift of wine."

Some of the men raised their arms in thanks.

"I will accompany you, my Lord," Ahumm said. "As far as you wish me to go. Once I saw you, I felt your power. I will follow you on your journey."

"I as well!" the man who would be an octopus cried out.

Others also pledged themselves. As the sun crested the horizon, Dionysus smiled. He would gather followers on his way. Soon all would know of the new god of wine. And those who did not show proper respect would know his vengeance.

PART TWO
ARIADNE'S SACRIFICE

11

ARIADNE'S SACRIFICE

TWO YEARS LATER

"What are the Athenians like, Priestess?" Ariadne's newest handmaiden Alexa asked. They sat with Phaedra, Melia, and Zoe in the common room, weaving together.

"Odd," Ariadne replied. "Different. The Phoenicians, the Egyptians, Etruscans, Ethiopians, Nubians, even the Trojans are all foreign, but the Athenians are stranger still."

"They're paler than we are, and some of them have very light hair," Phaedra said.

"They cover their bodies and keep their eyes to the ground. When curiosity overcomes them, they slowly peek at our breasts, as if they have no breasts in Athens," Melia said, making them all giggle.

"Is it true that the Athenians have new names for old gods and want everyone to worship them as their own?" Alexa asked.

"Yes. They worship a goddess who wears a helmet and fights like a man. They say she is wise because she will take no husband. The old goddesses do not like her, but the Athenians say she was born from Zeus's head."

Zoe and Melia chuckled, though Alexa stared in shock and bit her lip. Ariadne had a vague memory of having a dream once of such a goddess, but she could not remember the details. If she had ever had such a dream, surely it was from the rumors she had heard instead of an actual visitation.

"They are very strange indeed, but the tributes are attractive enough," Phaedra said. "They are not acrobatic like we are. They sing and dance gracefully—not like foreign sailors. The tributes are all high-born and well-mannered. The best of their people."

"And they come here to die?" Alexa asked, a hint of excitement in her voice. Phaedra had told Ariadne that Alexa had been an apprentice in a distant temple the last time the tributes came.

"To be sacrificed," Ariadne said. "To appease the gods." *And my father's bloodlust.*

"They come as punishment for killing our brother, Androgeus," Phaedra said. "And making our brother Asterion go mad."

Ariadne had heard whispers that Phaedra visited Asterion in his maze, that she brought him honey and girls to keep him company. Ariadne had visited him when she was a newly ordained high priestess. But the brother she had known was gone. She had found instead a mad priest-king in an underground maze of sorrow. He had refused to remove his bull's-head mask, saying he would become the rumors that people believed, just as she would become a goddess.

Asterion had always possessed the magic of prophecy—like all dark gifts, it came without warning. She feared what he might say if she visited again, both of himself and of her. Now she wondered whether she should have gone to see him again. All these years... had she forgotten the brother she once loved? Had fear gotten in the way? Or had she, too, begun to believe the stories that her brother was in fact a monster? Some nights when the moon was new and the night completely dark, she heard screams from below. She never knew whether they belonged to her brother or his victims.

"It is good the Athenians know their place. Everyone knows the power of Minos and the power of Asterion," Alexa said.

Ariadne sensed suddenly that her new handmaiden knew Asterion. She hadn't wanted to replace Thalia, but Phaedra had convinced her that Alexa would be perfect. Ariadne still could not believe Thalia had run off, but Phaedra had brought several men from the docks who had seen her get on a Phoenician ship.

The crescent mark on Ariadne's thigh tingled, and she had a vision of Alexa holding the sacred dagger. Was Alexa marked to serve the goddess? She had an air of quiet power. She appeared the very model of a Minoan noble: a beautifully angled face, wide almond eyes, and a fine, perfectly shaped nose. Her wavy black hair fell to her waist, her fingers were quick and nimble, and her figure was made to be replicated in statuary.

"I am grateful to be here to see the Athenian tributes this year," Alexa said.

"It is always fun," Phaedra said. "Days of feasting, entertainment, bull dancing, and then," she giggled, "to the labyrinth, from which there is no return."

Zoe's mouth had become a thin line of disapproval. One year she had fallen in love with an Athenian youth. After drinking too much mead, she had confessed to Ariadne how much she detested the slaughter of the high-born Athenian tributes every three years. "Are we not better than this, Mistress?" Even though that had been years before, Ariadne had heard this plea in her mind each time the Athenians went into the labyrinth. Was this tribute what the goddess wanted or simply what her father and brother desired? No amount of bloodshed would bring Androgeus back.

THE NIGHT BEFORE THE ATHENIANS WERE TO ARRIVE, ARIADNE and Alexa went to the temple as it grew dark. She had come the last time the moon was new and the time before that, but the goddess had remained silent. Still, Alexa had dressed her in ceremonial garb, a turquoise and saffron flounced skirt, her bodice extra tight, the sacrificial blade on a belt around her waist.

"So many beautiful new frescoes," Alexa said as they passed new designs of blue monkeys, griffins, and lilies in the inner corridors. "I was using some of the old images to find my way, and now I am lost again." She laughed and glanced at Talos and Manko. "Fortunately, I have a guide—unlike the Athenians."

Alexa was trying to make her smile, but Ariadne could not. Why had the goddess not spoken to her?

The temple was only across the courtyard, but it was still a long walk. Guards lit the braziers; the freshly painted frescoes danced in the light of the flames.

"This will impress the foreigners," Alexa said.

"Yes." Ariadne had accepted Alexa as a novice priestess but had not yet grown used to being accompanied to the temple.

"Have you ever gone abroad, Priestess?"

"No. The world comes here to us."

"Indeed. I've heard that only the great halls of Egypt and Troy compare to Knossos. It is an honor for the Athenians to spill their blood for the Minotaur. They will make a worthy sacrifice."

Had Ariadne ever been so devout? She had until... until what? Was it Thalia's disappearance? No. Something happened before. The goddess had grown more and more distant. Once she had been the chosen one. The sacred birthmark on her thigh had designated her to continue her mother's legacy, but something had changed. Every time she tried to recall exactly what had occurred, no memories came.

The guards bowed as they approached the temple. Talos and Manko stayed outside. Alexa followed her in.

A worthy sacrifice, Ariadne thought as the priestesses of the temple saluted her with open arms. Ariadne and Alexa removed their shoes and entered. Ariadne saluted the statue of the goddess in the center of the room. The goddess stood with her arms raised, her breasts full of sacred power, her face impassive. Ariadne mirrored her stance and whispered a prayer.

Despite all the painting outside, the temple had not changed. The old frescoes, even the ones that needed to be touched up, brought comfort. Images of the goddess descending, of worshippers dancing among the trees. If only the goddess would come to her now. Every thought she had seemed only half-formed, as if her mind were full of the buzzing of bees.

"Always an honor, High Priestess," Seer, the priestess of the temple, said, clasping her hand. The warmth in the older woman's smile made Ariadne want to go into the smallest chamber and confess all her worries. Perhaps Seer could help her. But Ariadne was the high priestess now. Her time for confiding and weeping was done.

"Seeing you is a gift, as always. Is all well?" Ariadne asked, letting go of Seer's hands.

"Yes. We had a complicated birth here on the night of the half moon, but the goddess granted the mother and babe life."

"A blessing."

"Yes, but you have come to speak to the goddess, not chatter with me. Come." She grasped Ariadne's hand to lead her deeper into the temple.

In the smallest room, the braziers burned bright, filling the chamber with smoke. The snakes slithered out of their holes, as if to greet her.

"The Athenians will be here soon," Seer said, handing her a sacred pitcher in the form of the goddess filled with a concoction of hawthorn and poppy milk. "May the goddess bless us."

"May the goddess bless us," Ariadne replied as Seer left.

She swallowed the sacred drink, bitter at first with a lingering sweetness, and inhaled deeply. The scented smoke made her stomach contract, and she forced herself to relax. *A worthy sacrifice,* she thought again, taking the next swallow. The little pitcher shaped like the goddess had been made for this. How many priestesses had drunk from it and divined the future? Did any struggle as she did? When Pasiphae was high priestess, she only needed to enter the sacred space before the goddess spoke to her. Even now, she could communicate with the gods.

Ariadne drank more, shuddering as she emptied the pitcher. Asterion's prophecies came to him without even trying. She used to think he would be such a perfect priest-king before their brother went to Athens. She should go see Asterion. They had been close once. She should try. She should... focus.

She let the snakes come to her, picking up two gently.

"Great Goddess, what will come of this year's sacrifice? How can I help my people?" She began to hum softly, to sway with the snakes in her hands. One snake coiled around her wrist. Ariadne raised her arms in the position of adoration. Like the poppy-milk pitcher, she was just a vessel.

Her sway turned into a slow dance. Her body began the steps even before her mind knew what she was doing. She had learned this dance as a child, following her mother. She did not know how long she followed the steps, humming and dancing, the room growing thick with smoke.

Ariadne, daughter of Pasiphae. The goddess spoke in her mind, her voice clear and strong. *I have a special task for you.* Warmth filled her. Finally, the goddess saw her, needed her. She would not disappoint.

A little king comes for you, and you will go with him. Help the little king at your own peril. But help the little king you must.

"Goddess, I do not understand." Ariadne opened her eyes. In the dark temple, the flames danced, throwing shadows on the wall: a man's form, strong shoulders, a short skirt. A black-sailed boat leaving Crete.

Will you be true to me? Will you fulfill your oaths to me?

"Yes, Goddess. Your will is mine."

The goddess laughed, like stones crumbling. Cold shot up Ariadne's spine. She wanted to drop to her knees, kiss the goddess's thigh, and beg for mercy.

Your destiny is with the Athenian. The words were as sharp as a sword severing a head for sacrifice. One solid chop, and it was done.

"I thought my destiny was here in Crete, like my mother before me."

You are too much like your mother. Perhaps the offspring of Titans are not who I need as my high priestesses. I think a simple mortal will be good enough. You belong here no longer.

Ariadne choked on the goddess's words. Hot tears filled her eyes and rolled down her cheeks before she could even comprehend what she had been told. This could not be. She was a chosen priestess of the moon goddess. She had the mark, the power of vision. She could not leave this place, her people, her family.

"What have I done to displease you?" Her voice came out broken, cracked, inadequate.

The goddess did not respond. Ariadne swam in the darkness of the cavern, the smoke threatening to swallow her.

You don't know? Never had the goddess's voice sounded colder. The smoke formed into the shape of the goddess, and an icy hand struck Ariadne's breast.

Images of a dalliance in the grass danced before her. A man, glittering like lightning, his black hair sparkling with stars, lay with her on a blanket. Warmth from love she had forgotten overwhelmed her. The sparkling man kissed her reverently. A phantom of a taste she could not recall flooded her. Knowledge and yearning on the tip of her tongue—on the edge of her memory.

Do you deny it? The images were replaced with others: Ariadne and the sparkling man in her bathing chamber, in her bedroom, walking by the river, through the palace.

He left you, as he leaves every priestess. He left you disgraced, a traitor.

Who? She adjusted the odd hair ring she wore on her second finger. She almost remembered. The emptiness left her bereft. This had something to do with Thalia's disappearance—and everything to do with the goddess punishing her.

Daughter of Pasiphae, I gave you the gift any woman would envy—I permitted you to kill men—and in return you chose a foreigner, a male god, over me.

"No, Goddess."

Had she? Even amidst her confusion, the idea of loving a foreign god warmed her.

No. Her only goal was to serve the goddess. She must repair this misunderstanding. Any mistrust lost would be mended, or she would die trying.

Ariadne released the snakes and slid the sacred knife from its sheath. "If I do not belong to you, Goddess, I do not belong in this life. I will give you my blood. If that will not appease you, I will give you all." She slashed at her inner arm. At first she did not feel the bite of the blade, but then it stung, sharp and bright. Her blood, dark as the columns of Knossos, dripped from the gash. She sliced another part of her arm, tears blurring the snakes on the floor and the flickering lamps.

The pain of her arm matched the pain of her heart. This was more shameful than being born without a mark like Phaedra. She had been given a chance and had ruined it. The goddess no longer wanted her. She would bleed to death in the temple rather than betray her people.

She lifted the dagger to cut again.

Enough. I do not want you to die.

Relief washed over her. Did the blood dripping down the knife show her loyalty? Perhaps they could be reconciled; her crimes—whatever they might be—could be forgiven.

Your punishment will not be so swift. Your traitorous ways have taught me to look beyond Crete, to the new people whose star is on the rise. They will not forget me, and they will not be forgotten. Your destiny is with the foreign king. He is the future. Let him and his people escape the Minotaur. To hide your shame, when he leaves this place, go with him.

Ariadne fell to her knees. Her blood dripped from her arm, like the blood of any other sacrifice. The goddess paid her no mind.

She could not betray her people, her parents, her followers this way. Yet she had sworn to do what the goddess demanded.

She did not know how much time passed until she came out of the room. Seer was not there. Only Alexa waited for her. Her dark eyes widened. Alexa reached for Ariadne to offer assistance, but she pushed the girl away.

Her guards were used to seeing her disoriented, but tonight Talos's brow furrowed in concern, though he said nothing. Once they left public view, he slid his arm around her waist, his forearm warm against her cold skin.

"Priestess," he whispered. *I am here for you. I will give my last breath to fight for you.* His unspoken words strengthened her. He and Manko were by her side, always ready to hold her up. She must stand tall for Crete.

Once Talos opened the door and Manko delivered her to Zoe, she gave in to exhaustion. She barely stayed awake long enough for Melia to undress her. The girl fussed over the wounds to her arm, cleaning and wrapping them, but not daring to utter a word of complaint.

12

WITH THE ATHENIAN TRIBUTES

"Daughter, get dressed. You must be there to greet the Athenians." Her mother's words ripped her from slumber.

Opening her eyes to the late morning brightness brought pain. Pasiphae frowned down at her. Ariadne's eyes hurt from crying, and the wounds on her bandaged arm throbbed.

"Have you displeased the goddess, daughter?" Her voice fell like a stone.

Ariadne had longed for her mother's comfort, but the Pasiphae who stood above her was not the mother she wanted. This Pasiphae was the witch-queen of Crete, still worshiped on far-off isles. Her beauty shone sharp as obsidian; the flecks of gold in her eyes flashed with disappointment.

Ariadne pulled the blanket up to her neck, covering her arm. It burned her heart to remember what the goddess had commanded.

"She favors me no longer, Mother."

Pasiphae stood still as a statue, regal in a ruby red vest and stunning saffron and turquoise skirt. Gold and amethyst necklaces adorned her chest, her breasts still filled with power, a sacral knot tied at the base of her throat.

"Wash your face, daughter." Pasiphae motioned for Alexa to hand her a wet cloth. "The ways of the gods are strange. We are not mortals, and we are not gods; we are women, somewhere in between. All you can do is adhere to the will of the goddess."

"But you..." Ariadne paused. What she wanted to say was disrespectful. She should not speak so to her mother.

"But I slept with the god?" Pasiphae asked, raising one perfect eyebrow. "I did. I vexed the goddess. She never forgave me, though she let me live, and she let you keep our family's seat as high priestess. That is another reason why you must obey where I did not."

A knot formed in Ariadne's throat. *But she wants me to betray you and Crete and run off with some foreign prince. I would rather sleep with a god and remain here, even if shamed.*

"Melia, prepare my daughter's bath. Alexa, go to my rooms and ask Kaira for an ointment to calm the skin around her eyes. When Ariadne's ready, cover her sorrow with makeup. She will appear lovely to all who see her. Zoe, choose her best garments and jewels." Ariadne's handmaidens hastened to obey.

"Now," Pasiphae said when they left, "the sentries in the mountains say a boat bearing black sails will dock today. Everyone is curious. We've heard the king was sending his own son as a tribute. The rumor is it's the work of my niece Medea." Pasiphae had lost much, but the women in her family still had strength.

Your destiny is with the foreign king. Ariadne could not make the first move toward this unwanted fate. "I am not curious, Mother. The Athenians can come to shore without me."

"Ariadne." Her mother said her name tightly with a perfect mixture of disappointment and contempt. "Do not make me remind you that it is your duty as high priestess to welcome this ship, as it is your duty to prepare for the sacrifice."

Ariadne shuddered. She did not want to greet the Athenian youths: beautiful boys, nubile girls who would be sacrificed to her father's vengeance.

"No excuses, now. Bathe quickly and dress in your ceremonial attire to welcome them. If you do not, the citizens of Crete will worry that something is amiss. Make the goddess proud, and perhaps she will forgive you."

ARIADNE STOOD UNDER A BRIGHT RED CANOPY WITH HER mother, father, and sister on a dais up the hill from the river. The black-sailed ship slowly wove its way down toward the palace. Did the black sails represent plague or sickness? That would be the ultimate revenge for Athens. Send a plague to Crete, wait for it to take hold, and attack the island. But if that were King Aegeus's plan, why would he announce it with black sails? Perhaps the sails did not represent illness but sorrow.

Fourteen Athenian youths disembarked. The young women each wore a single plain garment that covered their breasts, while the young men wore shorter chitons. No matter how many times Athenians came, it always struck her as odd that men needed to cover their chests as well as women. She could understand that men feared the power of women's breasts, but men's breasts had no power. Still, what flesh she saw of these strangers did not disappoint. Despite being pale, the boys were well muscled. Their hair varied in shade from sand to tree bark, and one girl's hair shone bright as amber.

The Athenians stared in awe at the grandeur of Knossos, the sun shimmering off their oiled hair. Unable to control their surprise, some of the boys craned their necks and gazed open-mouthed at the grand structure.

Athens had no palace or temple to compare to Knossos. Foreigners always commented on the size of the buildings, as if they had been built by giants. Despite the anxiety in the pit of her stomach, Ariadne stood up straight, proud of her land and people.

Two of the young men seemed unable to shut their mouths until another boy patted their backs to prod them to join the group walking toward the raised platform. The Athenians murmured to each other in their language. Ariadne had learned Greek as well as some Egyptian and Phoenician as a girl. She could understand them, though she doubted they understood Minoan.

A youth with short, curly hair and broad shoulders strode toward them with a firm sense of purpose.

"If this is the king's son, his name is Theseus," Alexa whispered from behind. "They say he's son of King Aegeus, but also of Poseidon."

Ariadne put a hand to her lip to hide her smile. What foolishness! Every cuckold was told his wife had taken up with a god. No wonder it was easy for Medea to send him to his death. His claim endangered her own son, and Ariadne's cousin would not have that.

"He was not raised in Athens," Alexa continued. "He grew up in Troezen where his mother was the daughter of a king. They say King Aegeus left sandals and a sword under a boulder. If the boy could move it, he would show himself to be the chosen one."

She could easily imagine the broad-shouldered Athenian moving a giant boulder. He was built like a wrestler, stocky and thick, so different from her own people. The sea salt and wind had undone some of the perfectly coifed hair he had surely been sent off with. His light brown hair fell to his shoulders in wavy locks. He appeared both royal and rugged.

Son of two fathers, a king and a god. He did not radiate divinity, yet there was a sense of ease about him, the kind that came with authority. Some of the Athenians wobbled toward them on unsteady feet. A chestnut-haired girl stumbled and fell. When she rose, Ariadne could tell she was trying not to cry as her throat and cheeks reddened in embarrassment.

How plain these sacrifices appeared standing before her own people. Her father grinned, regal in his robes of purple—more gold on one hand than the entire group of Athenians had together. King Minos even wore gold in his beard and wavy black hair. Pasiphae, Ariadne, and Phaedra wore gold strands entwined in their hair in addition to their jewelry. Even Alexa, a novice priestess, wore more jewels than these noble sacrifices. Aside from a few bronze rings, it appeared the Athenians were unadorned, though she noticed leather cords around their necks. Whatever they wore under their chitons was jewelry of protection rather than of status. Their parents had sent them off with prayers and baubles, knowing they would never see their children again.

Even without jewelry, they made an attractive group. Despite their fear and awe, they held their own appeal. King Minos eyed the beautiful girls, their limbs shining in the light. Queen Pasiphae kept her face impassive, but Ariadne did not doubt that several of these lovelies would warm her bed before their time to die.

Theseus walked toward the royal family on steady legs, leading the procession. "King Minos," he said, bowing. "Queen Pasiphae." He stood up straight and stared a moment too long. "Princess Ariadne. I am Theseus, son of Aegeus, at your service."

This was the little king the goddess would have her go with. She wanted to command Talos to take his dagger and end his life now. But even as this fantasy played through her mind, a surge of attraction overcame her, as if the goddess had attached a thread from her heart to his.

When she gazed past him to the harbor, she was aware of him. Though Theseus did not stare at her breasts, she knew he wanted to. That was no surprise—all the Athenians were both appalled and intrigued by bare breasts. Yet a furtive glance at his face told her Theseus's attraction to her was as strong as hers to him.

"Why are your sails black?" King Minos asked.

"Sire, my father grieved greatly that I chose to come here. He bid me..."

"You chose to come here to die? Why would you do such a thing?"

"Forgive me, Sire. I spoke too quickly. Allow me to relay pleasant tidings from my father. He has sent not only the tributes you demand, but also gifts of a new drink called wine as well as textiles woven by high-born ladies. He also sent sheep and pottery, and we brought acrobats.

"Delightful," Pasiphae said, eyeing his muscular shoulders. The golden strands of his hair glistened in the sun. He was not a typical Athenian beauty, yet there was something about him that made Ariadne almost believe he could be the son of a god and a king.

"Come, we will celebrate your arrival," Pasiphae said, standing. King Minos had not forgotten the Athenian's first blunder of admitting he had come here willingly. No one had.

The Athenian sacrifice bowed his head, but he raised his eyes once King Minos had turned. He stared at Ariadne's breasts and then directly into her eyes. Desire shot through her, and she let out a gasp.

"Are you well, sister?" Phaedra asked.

"Yes," Ariadne said, wondering whether she was about to faint. "Quite."

ALL WAS READY IN THE BULLRING. THE ATHENIANS STARED AT the grand venue, their fear palpable. The girl who had tripped earlier began to cry.

"Hush, Iris," a dark-haired girl said, sounding on the brink of tears herself.

"Come, come!" King Minos said. He relished the fear and uncertainty of the Athenian tributes. Would they be killed now? Each day they lived in uncertainty while King Minos savored their growing fear. Her father knew how to cultivate a spectacle— it could not be rushed. He would keep them for three months and send them into Asterion's lair at the full moon.

Though the bullring was a favorite game for the Minoans, the Athenians had no idea whether they would be forced to play. Ariadne could almost see the fear coming off the Athenians, as if a soft mantle of rust-brown hung around them in a cloud. Pasiphae seemed to inhale their dread. She appeared taller, younger. Her immortality shone brighter than the gold in her eyes. Ariadne had no taste for it.

"Since you are our guests, we offer entertainment. Come sit in our best seats," Ariadne said, pretending not to notice her father's scowl.

"All is well," Theseus said to his people. "Come." With a few words he calmed them. His gaze swept over the group of Athenian youths, and though he did not speak, she saw how their lives and safety weighed on him.

She turned to find her seat, not wanting to see the Athenians or think about their plight. The performers stopped their practice of doing cartwheels and flips when the royal family and the Athenian sacrifices entered. Some of the Athenians gasped. They had never seen the human body like this. The bull-dancers wore nothing but golden armlets and codpieces, a tradition that went back generations for all performers. The girls had small breasts and taut, muscular bodies. The boys were lithe, ready to leap higher and farther than one could imagine.

Ariadne glanced at the full arena as she followed her parents to their seats under a saffron canopy. Those who could afford to had bought seats, and those who hadn't assembled outside. Even if they couldn't see, they could hear the music and savor the excitement.

These were her people. They depended on her like no other. How could she betray them?

The musicians began the bull-leaping song. Tamar strummed the lyre as the sistrum player set the beat. Then the pipe players announced the entrance of the bull. The crowd cheered as White Foot strode in, his long horns painted gold, his hooves flashing in the sun.

An intake of breath made her aware that Theseus sat next to her. His hazel eyes widened in awe, and his thigh brushed her skirt. His chiton left the tops of his thighs exposed. She had an odd desire to grab him above the knee to feel his flesh warmed by the sun.

"What a terrifying creature. Does that bull eat men alive?"

Ariadne stifled her laughter. Theseus thought White Foot was dangerous. The black and white bull they had trained since he was a calf a danger!

"Yes," she replied, glad for a little joke. "He eats the losers, and when no one loses, we feed him criminals and captives."

The blood drained from Theseus's face. "Does your father plan to sacrifice us today?" he asked.

She did touch his thigh then, a brush of her fingers against his warm skin. "No. Not today. Not tomorrow. He will allow your fear to lessen. He will enjoy your company. And you will enjoy your time here before the sacrifice."

Theseus gripped her hand and pressed it to his thigh. He sighed with relief. When he met her gaze, he smiled as if she were a co-conspirator.

"I am heartened to make your acquaintance, Lady Ariadne," he whispered and let go of her hand.

"My sister is to be referred to as Priestess." Phaedra had seated herself on the other side of the Athenian. "Ariadne is the High Priestess of Crete and the most powerful woman in the land. She sacrifices men to the goddess when she demands it."

Theseus's hand went to his waist where he would have normally worn a dagger. Ariadne stifled a laugh, though she did not appreciate Phaedra's words.

"Do not listen to my sister," Ariadne said, ignoring Phaedra's pout.

She glanced at the pretty girls and comely youths who had accompanied Theseus. She wished her father would be content with this tribute and not demand their lives. He could marry them off to nobles, make peace with Athens, and forge a bond of allyship.

But that would not happen. Why had Theseus chosen to come here? He could not simply be a fool who had been played by her cousin Medea, could he? No, his eyes were wise, scheming even, the color of honey. Would his kiss be sweet?

Ariadne tried to focus on the bull dance, to ignore the Athenian. He was nothing more than an attractive youth with wide shoulders and an easy grin—a bit cocky. Still, she pitied him, having come all this way, offering his own life in the hopes of satiating her father's unquenchable vengeance. She sighed and turned her attention to the bullring where Agri, one of the most renowned bull leapers, clasped White Foot's horns. The Athenians gasped as Agri somersaulted onto White Foot's back, stood, and then leapt skillfully to the ground.

The crowd shouted in adoration. The sistrum shook, signaling the next round of dancing.

Theseus's leg rested causally next to Ariadne's. His chiton rose past the midway point of his thigh, revealing the paler skin which highlighted how dark the sun had made him. His tan skin was lighter than parts of hers that had never seen the sun. What would it be like to lift his chiton higher, all the way to his waist?

Where did these thoughts come from? She glanced up into the bright blue sky, wondering whether she would see a smirking god. This was the God of Love's arrow that the Athenians went on about. Had the little bastard truly shot her? Was he in league with the goddess?

She glanced around—hundreds of cheering people in the arena—the bull ready to dance, the acrobats in fine form, the Athenians awed, her father eyeing the Athenian girls, pondering which ones would warm his bed this night. Her mother, eyeing the youths, considering the same. And here she was, her parents' child, barely containing herself from gripping Theseus's strong thigh and pulling his kilt higher and higher.

"Princess," he said, breaking her reverie, "your people are truly talented. Never have I seen such wonders!"

"This is one of many," she said lightly, turning her attention back to the arena.

"I do not want to die," he whispered. "But if the gods will it, I am grateful to come here to do it. Truly I have never seen such grace, such beauty."

She did not turn to look at him, but the tremble in his voice made her pity him. She would be kind to him until the time came. How could she betray her father and mother? All around her, her own people cheered. How could she leave them?

She had sworn herself to the goddess in service to her people. She did not want Asterion to kill the Athenians. She was high priestess, meant to keep the balance between the bull and the goddess. Perhaps there was still a way to do that.

You swore yourself to me, Ariadne. I will have you obey. The goddess's voice was as hard as it had been in the temple. This was not the goddess she had known in her youth. Not the goddess she had honored with honey and flowers. Was this even the same goddess she had sworn herself to?

She had missed the last three leaps. The music was coming to a crescendo. Tanziz, the most famous girl in the troop, was preparing for the big jump. Agri and two boys ran around the sides of the arena with White Foot chasing them, while Tanziz cartwheeled and flipped in the center. The bangles on Tanziz's wrists and ankles flashed in the sun. White Foot's painted horns and hooves flashed. The presence of the bull god was so strong now that even the Athenians must feel it. In the darkness beneath the seating where White Foot and the dancers came out, Ariadne spied a pair of gilded horns. She sensed her brother's presence even before making out that the horns were too high to belong to a bull. Asterion had come out from below.

White Foot was running quickly now, ready to charge. Tanziz ran toward him, sprang off the ground, and executed her famous sideways twist in midair. The crowd roared as Tanziz landed gracefully as ever. Some in the crowd screamed when White Foot turned to charge Tanziz again. This was not part of the ritual dance. Too shocked to play, the musicians stopped.

Agri cried out to get White Foot to come to her, for she was meant to do the final vault, but White Foot had his eyes set on

Tanziz. Tanziz didn't have enough time to grab White Foot's horns, so she flipped as she had before, but White Foot's horn caught her in the side. The crowd screamed out in fear, and Ariadne's blood ran cold. Tanziz's shriek of pain sliced through the air.

Agri ran to distract White Foot and lead him back into his pen. Tanziz landed on her feet and sank down to her knees. Blood gushed down her side, and a broken rib jutted out through her skin. The two boys in their troop ran to carry her away.

This is what will happen if you do not obey me. The goddess's voice came cold and hard. Ariadne could not breathe. Her vision blurred with tears as the arena erupted in shrieks and shouts.

"This can't be."

"She's going to die."

"This has never happened."

"The bull god is falling."

Ariadne could not move. She was frozen in place, aware only of a small strength, a small amount of warmth—her hand held by Theseus.

She glanced into the shadows beneath the arena where she had seen her brother. But he was gone.

13

ARIADNE AND THESEUS

Alexa, Zoe, and Melia were silent as Talos and Manko escorted them back to Ariadne's chambers.

"Poor Tanziz," Melia said.

It was my fault. A message for me. Ariadne could picture the famous bull leaper's broken rib poking out of her side. The girl's screams still echoed in her ears.

"Will she die, High Priestess?" Zoe asked, handing her a cup of mountain tea.

"I do not think she can survive such an injury, but there is a chance." *Great Goddess, if I do what you ask, will you let her live? Will you let my people live?*

The goddess did not reply, but the crescent moon mark on her thigh stung.

"Tanziz knew the risk she took," Alexa said, her voice severe. "The bull god blessed her with greatness, and now she has fallen. Only the gods can decide whether she will rise."

"True," Ariadne said, taking a sip of the tea.

"Here, High Priestess," Alexa said, kneeling before her with a cloth dipped in chamomile. "Let me clean your face. The kohl ran rather badly." She wiped beneath Ariadne's eyes, the cloth and scent soothing. "Tonight will be interesting," she said, unlacing

Ariadne's corselet. "Some of the foreigners are rather pretty, are they not?"

"Indeed," Melia said.

"Did you see one for yourself?" Alexa asked.

Melia's red cheeks answered for her.

"Which one?" Zoe asked. "The broad-shouldered son of the king or..."

"The chestnut-haired girl with the large bosom? I think her name is Echo. I saw you looking at her. I saw her looking at you, too. I think she was wondering what you would taste like," Alexa said, fixing the wayward coils of Ariadne's hair.

Melia put her hands to her face—to hide her embarrassment and to cover her laugh. "Stop, Alexa!" Then pulling her hands away. "Really? Was she really looking at me?"

"Oh, yes—almost the same way the king's son was staring at our priestess."

"He did stare at me with lust, but that is just the look he has. He gazed at my sister and my mother the same way. I think he even set his honey-colored eyes on my father. Theseus did not come here to die."

"But die he will. Will he not, Priestess?" Alexa asked.

"If it is what my father desires, and if it is the will of the goddess. The girl you like, too, Melia. But don't let that stop you from bedding her. These are sacrifices, and we are meant to sacrifice only that which is precious to us. So go to that girl; give her the honor of a short life well lived. Don't let your fear of her death stop you from desire."

She paused as Zoe applied pomegranate juice to her lips and redid her eye makeup. Then she asked, "Alexa, do you fancy any of them?"

"There was a boy with curly dark hair, olive skin. The one who looked the least foreign. His name is Chrysippos. I will bed him if you bid it, Priestess." Alexa grinned.

"I bid you only to follow your heart."

"And you, Priestess," Alexa said, "will you allow the fear of death to keep you from desire? Will you love the sacrifice as the goddess demands?"

What a good priestess Alexa would make.

She pictured Tanziz's bloody rib and heard the screams of her people in the bullring.

"I will always do as the goddess commands. Come. Let us go up to the banquet. It is time to greet our guests."

In the great hall, the partitions had been opened to make enough room for the nobles who had journeyed across the island. Sunlight illuminated the space, shining on the red and saffron meander patterns on the rugs. The freshly painted frescoes of white bulls bowing centered the thrones of King Minos and Queen Pasiphae, which sat empty.

Low chatter filled the room, and scents of roasted meat filled the air. The Minoan guests stared at the Athenian youths as if intrigued by a strange and potentially dangerous animal. Some of the men moved closer and attempted to make polite conversation. The Athenians stood wide-eyed, whispering amongst themselves. Several of the braver boys responded to the Minoans with short words, perhaps giving their names. The girls flocked together like motherless chicks, silent, their eyes downcast.

The redheaded girl, Iris, glanced at the guards and blushed from her chest to the roots of her hair. Ariadne had forgotten that to the Athenians, her soldiers were nearly naked. Yet that did not make them any less fearful.

"How sad it would be to be like that," Alexa whispered to Melia. "The men have stolen their voices along with their power, their breasts, and their vision."

"Indeed," Melia replied, fondling her own half-moon necklace. "I am grateful I was born here."

Ariadne shuddered. To leave Crete, to leave her home.

"Priestess." A male servant carried a large rhyton full of mead. He wore nothing but a short kilt and a golden arm cuff. Melia carried Ariadne's golden cup and held it out for the servant to pour. Ariadne took it gratefully. Mead was most welcome.

She had not sought out Theseus, but he radiated among the others. The Athenian youths gravitated toward him as if for protection. A bronze pin shaped like olive leaves kept his dark blue chiton clasped. The same motif circled his chestnut hair, which had been oiled and shone in the sunlight. His eyes lit up when he saw her, and he paused in conversation with Chrysippos, the curly-haired, olive-skinned boy Alexa favored.

"Sister," Phaedra said, joining her. Phaedra's new handmaiden had arranged her hair artfully, with gems and gold. "Which one will you bed?"

"They've only just arrived." Ariadne twisted the hair ring on her finger, wishing her parents would make their appearance. She glanced at Theseus. Yes, it was as if the goddess had attached a thread between them. She did not want to look at him, yet she could not look away.

"I like the little princeling," Phaedra said. "Oh, and he's wearing a small crown. Are those olive leaves? How sweet, and made of bronze."

"I wonder whether they're shy in the bedchamber," Alexa said, making Phaedra giggle. "Forgive me, Priestess, I must go greet my parents." Alexa walked across the great hall to a stately couple. Her father wore a stunning green cape and leather boots. Long, wavy charcoal hair fell to his waist. Her mother was a glimpse of Alexa in twenty years—just as beautiful, only more confident. They were the image of a fine Minoan family.

Ariadne glanced at her parents' empty thrones—the alabaster one against the wall of painted bulls and the cedarwood one next to it. Both were cushioned with indigo pillows. Her mother's cedarwood throne bore decorations of gold and emeralds. Those two empty seats made her think of her two missing brothers. She turned to Phaedra, to share her thoughts, and found Phaedra staring at Theseus.

Ariadne clutched the cup in her hands and resisted the urge to throw the mead in Phaedra's face. *Must you covet everything that's mine?* Her sudden fury shocked her. She did not want to quarrel with Phaedra. She did not want to desire Theseus.

The lyre and sistrum players started up, announcing the arrival of the king and queen. King Minos wore a cape of murex purple made from Egyptian linen. Pieces of gold, rock crystal, and amethyst were woven into his beard and long black hair. Queen Pasiphae was robed in saffron flecked with gold, the leather belt cinched tight around her waist all the more impressive for bearing nine children. Her breasts still radiated power, and her nipples were painted gold.

The Athenian girls had raised their eyes from the ground and now stared openly, as if unable to look away. Though Ariadne knew it to be untrue, they appeared to be willing sacrifices. If her father had commanded them to walk straight to a guard and bend their heads for the blade, she did not doubt they would obey.

But the Athenians were meant for Asterion, for his bloodlust, and his rites as priest-king.

"Welcome all," King Minos said when the musicians quieted. "Loyal subjects who have traveled from your homes to see the best of Athens, and to our Athenian sacrifices who have sailed the seas to give us their blood."

When this was translated for the Athenians, two of the girls appeared faint, and three silently wept. The boys stood up straighter, but several were clearly fighting back tears. Chrysippos clenched his jaw, anger in his dark eyes.

"Come, little tributes," Queen Pasiphae said. "Let everyone see your youth and beauty. We will feast you and enjoy your life before snuffing it out." At her words, Iris did faint; two girls caught her.

"Bring her," Pasiphae said, her voice hard and bright.

Ariadne pitied Iris as Theseus lifted her into his arms and carried her to the front of the room.

"Have we ever seen a more pale creature?" Pasiphae asked, beholding the unconscious girl. "Enchanting." She stroked Iris's face with her hennaed fingers and patted her cheek to rouse her. The girl opened her eyes, blue as the sky at midday.

"What is your name, child?"

"Iris, Queen." Her voice shook.

"Put her down over there." Pasiphae motioned to the gypsum bench closest to her throne. Ariadne did not know whether her mother wanted the girl or simply did not want Minos to have her. She had clearly marked Iris for herself.

After Theseus carefully placed Iris on the bench, King Minos summoned him and addressed the audience.

"This little lord is Theseus, son of the King of Athens. Turn, boy, and let my people see you."

Theseus faced the crowd. There were some noises of surprise and a tsking sound of shame. What terrible father would send his child to his enemy?

"He's the king's bastard son, but the king's eldest son," an oil producer whispered.

"I heard Medea tricked him into coming here to die so her own son could have the throne," a wealthy farmer replied. Other whispers filled the hall.

Theseus could not possibly understand the words. He rested his hand casually on his waist, his face impassive, scanning the crowd. A slight smile lifted his lips when he saw Ariadne.

"Have the other sacrifices show themselves to my people," King Minos said.

Theseus called to the other youths and introduced them. Some appeared incapable of even saying their names.

The Minoan nobles stared eagerly. Disgust pitted Ariadne's stomach. How could her own people be so cruel?

She had been young the first time the Athenians came, and she had wanted them to pay for her brother's death. But now twelve years had passed. These young people had done nothing to warrant their own deaths. King Minos and Queen Pasiphae were the children of gods. They were unfeeling and petty when it came to the suffering of others. But their heartlessness had impacted the whole of Crete. She could not let this continue.

The music began again, and the banquet started. Male servants carried ceremonial rhytons and poured mead and beer into the guests' cups, while female attendants circulated with flat bread to be used as plates and skewers of squid, anise-goat, rosemary-lamb, and beef stewed with dates and almonds.

The Minoan guests wasted no time in approaching the Athenians. Amid a sea of color, the Athenians stood out as plain but desired. Melia walked over to Echo, saving her from Alexa's father who hovered nearby. Alexa daintily shared a cup with Chrysippos, who appeared ready to follow wherever she would lead.

Ariadne bit at the skewer of squid cooked with rosemary. She saw no way for Theseus to escape the mob of noble women who had surrounded him. Men stood around the fringes, trying to get a word in, but the women blocked them. To bed the Athenian king's son would be a tale to brag about for generations, and if any got pregnant, the child would be a unique blessing.

Pasiphae and Minos sat on their thrones, chatting with nobles. Alexa's father spoke with Pasiphae, who laughed at a jest he made. How long had it been since Ariadne had heard her mother's laugh? King Minos did not notice. He was speaking to one of his advisors, both obviously talking about the blonde-haired Athenian girl. Alexa's father touched Pasiphae's wrist, and Ariadne imagined her mother throwing Minos over to take this Minoan as her husband instead.

"May I join you, Priestess?" Theseus asked, breaking her reverie.

"How did you manage to escape? I thought one of the noble ladies would drag you off."

"I have my ways." His honey-colored eyes seemed to glow.

"Have you had a single bite to eat?" she asked, calling a servant over. Theseus selected some bread and a skewer of lamb.

"Thank you, Lady, I mean, Priestess," Theseus said.

"You may call me Ariadne."

"Ariadne." Her name sounded foreign when he said it—exotic. Who could she be with him? His enemy or his savior?

"Your drink is strong," he said, "and sweet." *Like you*, his eyes said. He appeared his age suddenly, a youth whose story was just beginning.

She did not want to have a hand in snuffing out his life. "Come with me." She smoothed down her skirts, picked up her cup, and wove her way through the crowded chamber, sure he was following. The guards allowed her to pass, and she waited to tell them to grant him permission to leave.

"Thank you, Lady Ariadne," Theseus said, following her down the stairs. With everyone at the banquet, this part of the palace was deserted, save a few guards who lurked in the shadows and those stationed at the doors. She led him into a small chamber with a lit brazier.

"We will not be disturbed here," she said.

He sighed, exposing all the worry and fear he had kept hidden. "I'm grateful to escape. I try to stay strong for my people, but..." He fell silent and laughed softly. "Forgive me, I'm not very good at keeping secrets."

The pity she had felt earlier now blossomed into a desire to protect him and his people. She passed him her cup of mead.

"Lady, do you want me to spill all my secrets?"

"Go on then. Why did you choose to come here?"

He held the cup with both hands but did not drink. "Your people are so different from mine. You do not fear being alone with me?"

"Why, Theseus, son of Aegeus, do you plan to harm me?"

"No, Lady Ariadne, but you do not worry for your virtue?"

She slid her hand to her dagger. "Perhaps this word does not translate well. Or perhaps you are trying to avoid my question. Tell me, why did you come here?"

He grinned as if bested. "I have come to kill the Minotaur."

She nearly laughed before realizing he was serious.

He straightened the circlet of olive leaves on his head. "We have repaid the blood-debt many times over. I have come to ask your father to release my father's debt if I can kill the Minotaur."

Faint noises from the party above came when the wind shifted, but the silence of the corridor, the darkness of the room lay between them.

"If I am ever to be King of Athens, I cannot allow your father to steal our children. At least, that was what I thought before coming here. Now, I am terrified. Even if I could kill the monster, how would I ever find my way out? My friends and I cannot even find our way to our guestrooms. I never imagined a place this big. The truth is, I want to weep at the task ahead of me." He raked his hand through his wavy locks, knocking the circlet to the ground.

Earlier in the banquet hall, she had seen a golden glow about him—his future as a hero and king. But now, she saw another path —one that ended here. Just another Athenian sacrifice.

His father would die of grief, and the young city of Athens would fall into the backwater it was before. All its potential great-ness would be lost. Unnamed artists and artisans would never be born. New styles of art, pottery, and song would fail to exist, and a new way of thinking—a love of wisdom would never rise to great heights. Humankind would not be the same without this youth.

Ariadne pushed the tip of the bull's-horn necklace into her breastbone. Now the goddess gave her visions freely. She bent down and picked up his circlet, her arm throbbing from where she had cut herself in the temple. She saw Tanziz's broken body on the bull-dancing floor.

Ever since Thalia had left, a deep sorrow had permeated her heart. She could not fight the goddess or bear to see another one of her people injured because she did not obey. The attraction to Theseus pulled at her. What a luxury it seemed to just give in to it. The weight of her mantle as High Priestess of Crete slid away. She would do as the goddess commanded.

"Fear not, Theseus. I will help you. Even if it means my own destruction."

His shocked expression changed to one of gratitude. He clasped her hand. "When I first saw you, I felt a spark, as if our destinies were entwined. Help me escape. Come with me. We can marry. I will be King of Athens, and you can be my wife."

She pictured that shining city that could be Athens, colorful marble, statues instead of frescoes, olive branches to crown victors in games, great debates, and above it all, a great goddess, but a strange one. This goddess came from a god and bore the helmet of a warrior. This was not her goddess, yet this was the goddess she would have to obey.

What would it be like to forsake her role as priestess? No more grandeur or power. She would just be a simple girl—another daughter of a king across the sea. Perhaps it would be a relief to not make every choice for the temple.

A golden light shone around Theseus. Ariadne lifted her face toward his, waiting for him to kiss her. His lips met hers, though she felt no spark, no deepening desire. Perhaps this was what it was to be dutiful.

He cupped her breasts, as she knew he had wanted to since first seeing her. She closed her eyes and wished his hands were Thalia's. But the way he touched her was too rough for her to imagine him as Thalia. She had never let a boy paw at her this way. No matter what the goddess said, she need not let it go like this.

She grasped his hands. "Undress," she whispered. She would see every bit of the young man she was giving everything up for.

His eyes widened in surprise, but he did not hesitate to unpin his chiton and drop it to the ground. How pale his body was, and how different from her own people. She could learn to appreciate his bulging thigh muscles, his thick, strong waist, and wide shoulders. His pale cock seemed to strain toward her, and she gripped it in her hand, making him moan.

She glanced at the open doorway, wondering whether she should have him put his clothes back on and take him to her rooms. A guard could see them; someone could walk in.

"Take off your skirt," he said, a slight plead in his voice.

"It's too complicated. I cannot undress as easily as you can."

"Then pull it up, let me…"

She lifted her skirt, and he pushed himself against her. Had he had sex with a woman before? This was what a very young man would try.

"Do you know how this is done, Theseus? I am not yet ready. Get on your knees and worship me as you should."

Disbelief crossed his face. He stared at her as if he had been slapped. "What do you mean?"

"You should pleasure me first. Don't you know what to do?" His confusion confused her. She watched his eyes move down and then up, realization slowly dawning on him.

"You want me to… to…"

"Yes, with your mouth. Do you not do these things in Athens?"

"Only on men." He flushed fully. "I mean, it is only done to men. I haven't done it to men, though many male slaves do."

"We don't make slaves do such things here. It does not feel right if it is done against one's will." She walked across the room. "Perhaps this was a mistake." She fiddled with the hair ring on her finger. A deep sorrow began to build, and she wanted to drink mead and fall into oblivion. Why was she trifling with this Athenian? Perhaps to some he was a hero, perhaps he would one day be king, but right now he was nothing but a disappointing lover.

"No, Lady. This is not a mistake. I can feel a bond between us. The moment I saw you, I wanted you."

"Yes, but your wanting me does not mean what I thought it did. You want to fuck me like you would any girl in any port. While I contemplate betraying all I've known to help you."

She glanced at him—still attractive, still a prince with two fathers.

"Don't worry, little king. I will still help you. But there is no need to go as far as I was going to."

"Ariadne, allow me to try and please you." He stared into her face and slowly sank to his knees. "Tell me what to do."

She walked back to where he was and slowly lifted her skirt. If she was going to give up everything for Theseus, she might as well enjoy it.

14

ARIADNE'S DREAM

In the dream, warm air stuck to her skin. Trees grew everywhere, vines intertwined, the humidity so thick she expected it to burst. The heady scent of jasmine filled the air. Even in the dark night, the trees were vivid shades of green.

She was trying to decipher whether snakes hung in the branches or if what she saw were merely vines when she heard the drums.

Boom. Boom. Boom. A heartbeat from the very center of the earth. A pounding in her blood. She could not move, though it was clear suddenly that she stood in the middle of a road, and a great procession was coming. She should run to the trees to hide.

Boom. Boom. Boom. The sound of bare feet marching in unison. One dance—bringing people together. One goal. Ariadne did not know what it was, only that it was pure and true and something she could not deny no matter how terrifying. The ground shook. She should move, yet she could only stand there, waiting. Whatever it was, it was undeniable. There was no point in running.

Boom. Boom. Boom. Voices now, singing disjointedly. She could not tell whether it was a foreign language or one she understood. She could not even tell whether it was truly music. All she knew was that she, too, wanted to sing along to the words she did not know.

Boom. Boom. Boom. The moon shone brighter. She saw herself from above. A woman with long black tresses falling over her shoulders. She was wearing white, and the moon seemed to focus her light on Ariadne's garment, so even if she wanted to hide, she could not.

The procession approached, moving straight toward her. Fear beat in her heart, but she stood up straighter, wishing she had a dagger.

What a motley group. In the moonlight she made out people of different heights; some of the revelers had animal ears, others tails. Naked, masked women and men draped in vines danced toward her. Some strode forcefully and stood tall like soldiers while others swayed and pranced in celebration.

The man at the forefront promenaded toward her. Taller than the rest, he glowed in the same way she did, as if the moon wanted to illuminate his presence for her. He had his arms wrapped around the waists of two long-haired, dark-skinned girls. Perhaps the man was Greek, possibly even Minoan, but all who followed him who were not deer or wild creatures were people with the same dark skin and black hair. Their eyes were luminous in the light, as if filled with a secret knowledge. The women could not keep their hands off the man, and though a rage began to boil in Ariadne, she understood why they wanted him.

As he and his procession drew closer, familiarity and jealous rage overcame her. That man was hers. Those women by his side had no right to him. Her heart pounded in fury; her fingers clenched into claws ready to draw blood.

When he saw her, his eyes widened. His pace increased, but the women held on.

"What are you doing here?" he asked.

"What are you doing?" she asked, ready to rip the throats from the whores who hung on his arms. Though she stood directly in front of them, the women gazed at her vacantly as if she were not there at all.

"I am making a name for myself, so I can return to you as the god I was meant to be."

She glared at him. His words meant nothing. She didn't know why this stranger infuriated her so.

"Beloved, I've missed you. I have longed for this moment."

"Liar," she spat. Those bitches needed to get off him. He belonged to her and her alone. It did not matter that she didn't know his name. It meant little that she had never seen him before. She was ready to kill them, and possibly him, though she had no idea why.

He untangled himself from the women, and the procession halted behind him. The drums and music suddenly ceased.

"Ariadne." He stepped closer.

Oh, he was striking. Not a typical masculine beauty. No, his cheeks were too high, his eyes too big. He did not wear a beard or have bulging muscles, though his power emanated stronger than any she had known. His lips were too red, and she wanted to lunge at him, to kiss him hard until he bled. But something he said was bothering her. *Ariadne.* Her name.

"You have no right to say my name, stranger!" She wished again for a dagger. She would cut out his heart. She would kill his disciples.

"I do," he said, taking her hand. "Beloved, I do. I have yearned for you every night."

She glanced at one of the women. She could smell them on him, sex and jasmine and other foreign smells she had no name for. The one on his left seemed bored, as if she were stifling a yawn. Neither of the women or the men behind the stranger seemed to see her. They were suspended as if in a dream.

"Yearned for me every night?" she asked, full of fury. "So you fucked these women and thought of me. Oh, it must have been difficult."

The bitch on his left actually did yawn. Her lips opened wide, and her breasts rose as she took in a great gulp of air. That was enough. Before even realizing what she was doing, Ariadne slapped her hard.

The girl shrieked, terror and surprise in her voice. She said something to the stranger in a foreign tongue. He replied in the same language, his tones calming. Ariadne could feel how he controlled the procession behind him. There was a rising urge to draw blood. They had stopped their singing, but the unreleased music was building, ready to burst forth. There was silence where there wanted to be noise. Now, a sudden urge toward violence. The revelers wanted to erupt, if not into dance, then into a fury of bloodlust. Ariadne was ready to lead the fray.

She slapped the girl again.

The girl yelped and stared hard at Ariadne, rage in her eyes. The girl let loose a string of complaints and raised her own hand. The stranger gripped the girl's wrist, bringing it back to her side, and whispered a few words. The girl fell silent but glared at Ariadne, her fist clenched. Her anger flowed back to the band behind her. A dark boil of animosity began to stir.

With a whoosh, a large cat appeared. The leopard bounded toward Ariadne. This creature would surely rip out her throat. But even as she had this thought, she marveled at the leopard's beauty. How poised it was in every movement! It would be an honor to be killed by such a being.

She braced herself to be pushed down and mauled, but the leopard stopped before her, kneeling at her feet. It made a strange sound from deep in its throat that conveyed a happy welcome and turned to face the angry mob. The leopard growled in warning at the stranger's troop, stilling their movement.

"Stop," the stranger said, turning back to her. "Ariadne, do not beat my followers."

"I will. I don't know who you are, but I will not stop until I have blood. I want this bitch punished for having you. I want to beat you for having her while claiming to yearn for me. I don't understand, but this is a betrayal—you here among all these foreigners having an ongoing party when you should have been with me."

The pulse that beat from the stranger was strong, stronger than the pull of the moon, and the anger he roused in her was both unexpected and undeniable. Before she knew what she was doing, she threw herself at him, her nails seeking to rip his skin.

He grabbed her wrists, but even as he held her back, her mouth jerked forward, catching his neck where it met his shoulder. She bit him hard, seeking nothing less than to taste his blood.

He leapt back, pushing her away. The sudden shift of movement made her lose her footing, and she began to fall.

His followers stared at her with wild eyes. She had been affected by his essence, but they had fed on it for days. They wanted nothing more than to kill her, to set upon her like hounds on a deer. All that kept them from swarming upon her body was permission from their master and the leopard guarding her.

But she had upset the balance. As soon as her body hit the ground, she was done for. They would rip her apart with their bare hands. The leopard would attack some, kill others, but there were too many of them. They would get to her and set their teeth on her as she had bitten their master. It was only fair.

As she threw her hands up to try and save herself, something yanked her wrists, pulling her upright. She did not understand how, since the stranger had not grabbed her. Up above, vines streamed from the trees. Her wrists were held aloft, keeping her from falling. She struggled against her bonds, and vines snaked forth from the earth, wrapping around her ankles.

"Bastard," she spat, even as she knew he had saved her life.

He placed his hands, palms down, toward the ground, sending calm to the angry crowd. The woman she had slapped and the others stared at her with malice, clearly wanting to spill her blood. But the stranger had more power than she expected. Surprising, one so slim could hold so much. It was in his hair, she thought, staring at a long, snake-like tress, and in his blood. The magic of his divinity beat lightning quick.

He turned to his revelers and spoke in the foreign tongue. But with the strangeness of dreams, Ariadne suddenly understood his words.

"You will not hurt this woman. She is my wife, most sacred to me. You all know how it is sometimes with the wife."

The murderous crowd suddenly laughed. They did know, even the ones who had once been wives.

"Go now," the stranger said to his followers, "worship me in the trees. Share yourselves with one another, your bodies, your minds, your feelings. Worship me as you will. Go on now."

The crowd moved off, in pairs and threes, some singing, some talking, all animated with excitement. Their god wanted them to be happy. Their god was real, and they would worship him as only they could. She stared at the bite mark on the base of his neck as he came toward her.

"Let me go!" she said, struggling against the vines.

"No." He stepped closer and stroked her throat. "I've dreamed of seeing you again, Ariadne. And if your dream is the only place for it, so be it. A part of you remembers me. A part of you wants me." He cupped her breast. Her nipples were hard, and she wanted to bite him again.

"Let me taste your blood," she said.

"It tastes like wine and lightning. That is what you told me before." He inclined his head away from her, offering the spot she had already bitten.

His skin was pale there, like the moon. Part of her rage dissipated, but her desire for him intensified. She sank her teeth into him again, making him gasp and grip her hips.

"I've missed you," he whispered as she clamped down. His hands clenched upon her buttocks as she sucked on his shoulder, tasting wine and a hint of lightning.

When she released him, she was drunk, not just with rage but with passion. She thought to tell him to cut the vines that held her wrists and ankles, but found herself glad to be restrained in this way. Now at least she would not attack anyone else and could focus solely on the stranger who had grasped either side of her skirt.

"Undress me," she said, the words reminding her of how she had spoken to a handmaiden. How delightful to command a man, a supposed husband, this way.

He unknotted her belt, and her skirt vanished. She sighed to be completely exposed, naked in the moonlight. Her hardened nipples radiated divine energy. These last three years, she had been a ghost of herself. Now, caressed by the breeze, under the stranger's gaze, she rediscovered herself and her power.

"Suck my nipples," she said to the stranger. "Suck me and touch me below."

A soft moan from behind the nearby trees reminded her of his dispersed disciples. Music flitted through the forest as women gasped with pleasure, men sang, and people spoke in their strange tongues. Some of them undoubtedly watched from the shadows, seeing her breasts in the moonlight, the pull of her wrists against the vines. The leopard had remained at her feet and stared at her now with interest.

His mouth was hot on her nipples, his hand caressing her thighs, squeezing her buttocks. She spread her legs as wide as the vines would allow, opening herself to him. His fingers delved into her. She was already wet for him, more than she could ever remember being. He could take her right now, and she would immediately succumb to pleasure.

But no. This stranger who seemed to know her so well continued to stroke her, making her moan for him. Her voice joined a chorus of other women, pleasure coming from the darkness of the surrounding trees. The heavy air seemed to carry the need of his unseen followers hiding in the dappled moonlight.

Opening her eyes, she stared at the jungle around her. There to the right, she could make out a pair of legs amidst the trees. Strong calves, feet planted firmly, knees against the back of another man's knees. A man grunted, the pleasure of his release carried through the heavy air and echoed by the man he shared his pleasure with.

This stranger who called her his wife undoubtedly also dallied with men. As he caressed her below and slid his tongue down her throat, she did not care. All that mattered was that he was taking her here. It seemed a moment worthy of an audience.

"Fuck me," she said to the stranger. "I have come here to find you in my dream to have you fuck me."

He knelt before her and caught her with his mouth, thrusting his tongue into her. She gasped, holding herself open for him. The vines held her up, denying her the chance to plunge her hands into his hair.

Pleasure rose within as his tongue stroked her harder and faster. She moaned from deep in her throat.

He kneaded her buttocks, pushing her deeper into his mouth, taking more of her than she could have imagined. She was aware of herself and the animal noises she was making, aware that some of the lovers in the trees had paused to listen.

The leopard remained nearby, watching with wide, luminous eyes.

"Yes," she whispered, "yes." She wanted to say his name, but she did not know it. Remembering the claim he had made upon her, she gasped, "Husband, yes!"

His tongue stroked her hard, and she forced herself to stay open for him as her pleasure came, flooding her.

Giving her a brief respite, he stood. His black tresses shimmered in the moonlight, covered with a fine gold dust. He was a god. There was no doubt. She did not know which one. Of the foreign gods she knew, he was far too giving of a lover to be Zeus, too confident to be Apollo, too handsome to be Pan, though he seemed to share some of the goat god's power to control crowds. He could not be Poseidon, Ares, or Hermes. No, he was a new god, an unknown god. But she sensed he was like Aphrodite and her horrible son Eros, and like Ares. He embodied something that mortals needed to be released, and like the others, it was a madness. A madness of truth.

"They would have killed me," she whispered, coming to her senses for a moment. "I was so angry. If I had fallen to the ground, they would have ripped me apart."

"I would never permit them to kill you, Ariadne. My pack only kills those deserving of punishment. It is true that most men would punish their wives for being unfaithful. But you are compelled beyond reason to bed that Athenian bastard."

The night went quiet. The air cooled. The revelers were silent now, as if they had all grasped the gravity of their master's tone. Was he saving her so he could kill her himself? Where there had been lust in his eyes, sudden rage lit, and the vines gripped her tighter. Earlier they had appeared as a kind of protection and an enhancement of pleasure. Now they were manacles, the tools of bondage for a cheating wife. No matter that he, this strange god calling himself husband, had slept with half his retinue. That was to be expected.

Through her dream, she vaguely recalled an Athenian, a broad-chested son of a king, a brash boy who would be king himself. *Mortal*, she thought, *that's all he is*. She had slept with the Athenian. She could not recall his name or whether he was any good, only that she had bedded him. She shuddered. This god called himself her husband. He had every right to be angry, but so did she.

"If you had been with me, husband, I never would have looked at another man. You left me, to come to this strange place, and you took all my memories of you. Why did you leave me?"

Her words washed his anger away, and the vines loosened, though they still held her upright.

"I cannot tell you that, Ariadne. Not now. I am only glad to have you here." He kissed her then, his tongue like wine. Overcome by his essence, she swooned in the vines, waiting for him to take her, to kill her, to have her however he wanted.

His long fingers stroked her below, finding her more than

ready. He lifted his purple and gold robe from his body and stood naked before her and all who watched.

His body was stunning. Not a warrior or a wrestler. He had the body of the ideal youth: small, hard muscles, firm thighs and buttocks. Dark, curly hairs stood out on his chest, his nipples the color of wine. The glitter of the curly hair around his groin left no doubt he was divine.

His hand came to her hip, and he traced the line of her body up her breast to her arm.

"Should I release you?" he asked.

"No," she whispered. "I will try to hurt you if you do."

"Every woman is a wolf when the moon is full." His power engulfed her: bloodlust, rage, need, raw emotion. It was all there. Never had she been so unable to control these feelings. She strained against the vines, wanting only to feel his flesh against her own.

He stepped closer. Grasping her buttocks with his hands, he lifted her. The vines around her ankles went slack and then released her completely as he lifted her to his waist.

"You and I are the only ones here now," he said. His words made her more aware of his disciples watching from the trees. *Ghosts, barbarians. None of them matter.*

Once he thrust himself into her, she believed it. He was the only one, her nameless husband. The mysterious god filling her with pleasure. She wrapped her legs around his waist.

As he took her nipple in his mouth, she smelled sandalwood and pine in his hair. She moaned again, the pleasure almost too much to bear.

Rough animal noises rose from the back of her throat. She would not beg him. She would not, but if he didn't finish with her soon, she was sure to lose consciousness. He gave her so much pleasure all at once. It was too much. She wanted to grip him hard and tear his flesh with her nails, but she could only endure as wave after wave of ecstasy washed over her. Darkness began to descend, and she realized she was dying. He was actually killing her, but all she could do was wrap her legs around him tighter and moan, wishing she knew his name.

Ariadne awoke naked in her bed. Instinctively, she reached for Thalia. Gone. She had disappeared almost three years ago, yet some days, she expected to find her there still. It was almost as if she had just seen her friend, but no. She had been having a very vivid dream about a stranger. She wondered whether she had cried out, but Alexa, Melia, and Zoe still slept in their room.

Coming into consciousness, she realized two things: her head pounded as if she had drunk too much, and she was very wet. She lifted the sheet and put her hand to her pubis. Perhaps her moon blood was early. The red beaded necklace she used to count her cycle was at the mid-mark, and she had always been regular. After what she had done with the Athenian, bleeding early would be a relief.

There was no blood. She touched herself, surprised by the slickness under her fingers. She had heard of this happening to boys, but not to women. She lifted her hand in the early morning light. The moisture on her fingers glittered. Curious, she sniffed. It smelled like a man, like wine and lightning.

Wine. She did not remember drinking at all the night before. She had stayed late at the temple, contemplating the Athenian escape. She had not yet figured out how to help them find their way out of the labyrinth or how to prevent Asterion from killing them.

She rolled over. These thoughts could wait. She closed her eyes, picturing the face of the man from her dream. *God*, she thought. He was a god. Despite the pressure in her head, she was still drowsy. *Husband*, she thought and fell back asleep.

15

ARIADNE AND THE MINOTAUR

"King Minos, I have a request," Theseus said one night after dinner. They had eaten their fill of roasted lamb, fennel bulbs, and wild beans roasted with rosemary and oregano and had drunk cups and cups of mead. Ariadne had noticed Theseus watching her father the last few nights, weighing whether it was the right time.

In the last month, the Minoan nobles had returned to their estates across the island. The Athenians often dined with the royal family, drinking the wine they had brought as a gift. Her father's horticulturalist, Silenus, said they would soon have some wine of their own, though it was not ready yet.

Ariadne loved the taste of the new drink. It inspired a different sensation from mead. She enjoyed it too much despite the deep longing it sometimes evoked. She had impetuously summoned Theseus to her bed to ease her pain, though it offered little more than a distraction.

He had not told her what he planned to say to her father. The Athenians were all silent; only Phaedra continued chatting with Chrysippos.

King Minos's dark eyebrows rose, and his black eyes focused on Theseus.

"Speak." Minos gestured with the hand holding his cup. The seal ring on his little finger glittered in the light.

"Great King," Theseus's voice trembled, "my proposal... the reason I chose to come here is if..." Theseus paused and took a drink. "If I can. If it were possible that I could slay the Minotaur, would you agree to end your demand for tributes?"

Everyone had stopped talking now. King Minos grinned, showing his wine-darkened teeth.

"How bold you are, little prince!" Pasiphae said, her voice like a blade. "You come here to our land as a sacrifice and request permission to kill my son."

Theseus kept his face passive and open, though Ariadne could almost feel his heart pounding in fear.

"He is a brash young princeling, wife, eager to prove himself. I'm glad to have learned your secret, Theseus. I've wondered your reason for coming here since you first said more than you meant to upon arrival. How much longer would I have kept you and your friends alive had you not told me?"

Theseus paled, though Iris kept silent. A single tear trailed down her cheek. King Minos let the silence become heavy. Pasiphae radiated fury. Her golden eyes burned as she glared at Theseus.

"This is a matter for us to discuss amongst ourselves," Pasiphae said to her husband and daughters. She glanced at the tributes, eyeing their empty plates. "I hope you were satisfied with your supper, for it has now come to an end. Guards, take our guests back to their rooms."

After a moment of shocked silence, the Athenians rose. Iris bowed her head, so her hair covered her face.

"Quite rude, wife," King Minos said after the tributes had left.

"They needed remain here no longer." Pasiphae nodded as a servant refilled her cup. "I do not want that boy to try and kill Asterion."

"He is quite tortured, I hear." Minos said.

"As are you," Pasiphae said. "As are we all. Yet is it just to kill

160

the Athenian youth? The first and second time, it was necessary, and the third time, too, perhaps. But is this not a bit much, Minos? Why not allow them to return home with a new treaty? Aegeus will be beholden to you and offer more in tax. Asterion can focus his energy on something else. Maybe we can get him to come back to the light."

"Asterion enjoys taking the sacrifices in the name of his brother and in the name of the bull. That little Athenian could not possibly harm him. Asterion has guards down there and weapons. The Athenians have nothing."

"Perhaps you should ask Asterion what he prefers," Phaedra said.

"Your voice does not count here, daughter," Minos said.

Phaedra flinched at his words but did not respond.

"I cannot simply allow them to return," Minos said to Pasiphae. "The boy challenged me. He should die for that, and his companions with him."

"Perhaps it is unfair, Father," Ariadne said. "So many Athenian youths have already paid for their countrymen's crimes."

"But that is how it is, daughter. To belong to a country is to pay for its crimes." He took another sip of wine. "You go, Ariadne. Ask your brother what he wishes."

Ariadne dug her nails into her palms but kept her face calm. She should have gone to visit Asterion sooner.

"Yes, Father." Fear pitted her stomach. "It has been too long since I last saw him. I will go tomorrow."

"Let me go with you, Priestess," Alexa said as she coiled Ariadne's hair. "I have missed the land below where I spent my previous apprenticeship."

"You did?" Ariadne had sensed something of the darkness around Alexa when she first arrived, but it had dissipated quickly. Alexa did not respond as she held out the earrings she had selected for Ariadne's approval: gold hoops with hanging balls of rock crystal.

"You served my brother?"

Alexa glanced away, then slipped the earrings into Ariadne's earlobes.

"Yes."

Did you bed him? Did you plot with him? Ariadne tugged on her earlobe, righting the earring. Who was she to accuse another woman of treachery? If she did as the goddess demanded, she would help to murder her brother. She would betray her whole country. She wanted to rip the earring from her lobe, but even if she were to spill all of her blood, it would not be enough for the goddess.

She followed Alexa down the stairs into the deepest level of the palace. This had been the dungeon when she was a child. Terror and misery emanated from the walls. Criminals were still sent here to die by her brother's hand.

"This way, High Priestess," Alexa said once they reached the ground floor. The place was indeed a maze. It did not follow the same plan as the floors above. The dark red walls made the space appear smaller. She would have been lost without Alexa.

A glimmering light in the distance gave her a sense of direction. In the flickering light, she made out a portrait—luminous eyes, an easy grin—Androgeus. She stopped before his image, understanding immediately that Asterion had rendered this portrait with the blood of sacrifices.

What would Androgeus think of all this vengeance in his name? She had been thirteen when he died and just finishing her apprenticeship as priestess. Androgeus had been twenty, but despite their age difference, she had known him well. He had treated all of Minos's bastard children like full siblings and had been best friends with Asterion. He would have been a kind ruler of Crete, suggesting diplomacy before force.

He would not want Theseus and the Athenian youths to give their lives in his memory, nor for Asterion to become as he had.

He would hate the monster Asterion had become. Androgeus had only ever wanted Asterion to be a strong priest-king. He had longed for a brotherhood with other nations. That was why he had gone to Athens—not just to win but to form bonds with other athletes. It was not the fault of all Athenians that a few of its youths had murdered him. How different the world would be if he hadn't died. Androgeus would have succeeded in making alliances with Athens, with Thebes, in addition to their trade partners in Phoenicia, Troy, Egypt and Numidia. Crete would not need to dominate the Hellenes but could instead trade freely.

"High Priestess?" Alexa asked half-way to the next torch.

Ariadne wiped her cheek and turned away from the painting. The next torch revealed a similar image. As she walked toward it, she kicked something that skittered across the ground. Bones. Human bones littered the area beneath Androgeus's painting.

Stop this, Ariadne. Was that her brother's voice? It had been so long, yet she heard his spirit clearly.

She followed Alexa down a dark corridor but felt a tug on her hem. She gasped, imagining the soul of a victim pulling at her, the bones returning to a spirit ravenous for vengeance, grasping her skirt, and dragging her off into the darkness. Hand on her dagger, she glanced down and let out a soft, half-broken laugh. A loose strand had come unraveled from her skirt. Caught on the corner of an unlit brazier, a red thread led all the way back to the first portrait, showing the way she had come.

She lifted her skirt and ripped the thread, leaving it on the ground. If she lost Alexa, she could find her way out.

An idea began to form.

Alexa waited for her patiently. Her eyes appeared luminous in the semi-darkness.

"This way," Alexa said, though Ariadne did not see where they could possibly go. Alexa grabbed her hand and pulled Ariadne behind her. They emerged into a well-lit room. The brazier made the saffron walls glow. Two guards stood by the entrance and held up their arms in welcome. A young woman whom Ariadne had never seen glanced up in surprise.

"Alexa," she said in recognition. "He is sleeping now. We did not expect you."

"Tell him the high priestess, his sister Ariadne, is here to see him. We will wait," Alexa said, her voice severe.

"Yes, Alexa." The girl scurried away through a portal Ariadne could barely make out.

"Do you come here often?" Ariadne asked, suddenly recalling times she had not been able to locate Alexa in the mornings.

"Sometimes the bull god summons me. Sometimes the Great Goddess speaks to me. I do not question the will of the gods, High Priestess."

"What do you mean?" Ariadne felt the slightest hint of her mother's fury stir within her. She had never been one to be roused to anger, but the tone in Alexa's voice, the secrets her apprentice had been keeping, and her relationship with Asterion incited a wrath she rarely felt.

"I mean only what I say, High Priestess. When the gods speak to me, I do as they bid and do not question their will. Is that not correct?" Alexa appeared guileless. Her wide brown eyes seemed to only want an answer from her mentor, nothing more.

"It is correct. We are merely vessels to do as the great goddess commands." Ariadne wanted to cry as she spoke the words. Instead, she stood up straighter and glanced around the room. At least Asterion still lived like the prince he was. Couches lined the walls. Some of the wooden arms and feet needed to be repainted, and the beautiful carpet was a bit worn, but he lived nothing like a wild monster who subsisted only on human flesh, like the Athenians thought he did. Perhaps she could reason with him.

The clopping of his hooves echoed from the secret passageway. She was not expecting him to wear this bull regalia for their meeting.

Seeing his bull's-head mask in juxtaposition with his bare chest sent chills down her spine.

"Sister," he growled.

"Brother Asterion, I should have come to visit you sooner."

"This is no place for the High Priestess of Crete. She of the Light, Lady of the Wild Things, Lady of the Girls' Blessing, priestess-queen of above."

"Nor should this be a place for you, brother. You are the great priest-king of the bull god. Our people need to see you to remember who to worship."

"After I die, perhaps the next priest-king can live above."

How closely entwined he had become with the bull. This was no longer a role to him. The mask, the sandals had become a part of him. He had become the bull, but she had not become the goddess. The balance between the goddess and the bull had fallen into deep disharmony. She should not have let this happen. Left alone below, he had allowed his sorrow to fester. Bloodlust had become his only comfort. Once the priest-king donned his bull's mask only for sacred ceremonies, but to Asterion it had become everything. He had become the Minotaur foreigners thought he was.

"What do you mean, brother?"

"You know I have always had the gift of prophecy, Ariadne."

"What do you see?" she whispered. He had not offered her a seat, but she could not remain standing.

"We are on the brink of a new age." He paused, his eyes gazing at something beyond her. "Destruction comes to Crete. Why should I not go now? I will join our brother in the afterlife. I will pave the way for the rise of heroes. Our time may have come to a close, but we will not be forgotten."

"Asterion, can we not change what is to come? Would you be willing to let the Athenian sacrifices keep their lives? Let them return with a new treaty. Or even let them stay here. They could marry Minoan nobles. We can be allies with Athens." Her idea appeared so suddenly and seemed so perfect, she knew it could never come to fruition.

Asterion laughed, a deep, rough bark. "Even if I could

summon forgiveness and allow them to keep their lives, the goddess has other plans. The bull of Crete must fall. The great hero must rise. But while I live, I demand their lives. Send them to me soon. I grow tired. I've fulfilled my fate as you are doomed to fulfill yours."

All the hair on Ariadne's neck and arms stood up. She could hardly breathe after hearing his words. Despite the burning brazier, her blood ran cold.

"I am sorry, sister." He clasped her hand. The gold rings on his fingers showed he was still her brother. "Your path is long and complicated, but in the end, you will find happiness. This I know to be true."

"Asterion." She spoke his name like a prayer, wishing she could save him.

"Ariadne, send the little hero to me at the next full moon. We both have our destinies to fulfill. I am ready to face mine."

16

ARIADNE IN THE LABYRINTH

The time had come. This night would mark the third full moon after the Athenians' arrival. Just before sunset, everyone gathered in the arena to watch the sacrifices descend into the labyrinth. With the sacred golden labrys in her hand, Ariadne prepared to lead the tributes. Dressed in white and barefoot, their hair unbound, the Athenians made two lines behind her. Though they stood on the dance floor, there was no bull dancing today, no dancing of any kind as the lyre and sistrum marked a mournful beat.

"Children of Athens, prepare to die for the crimes of your countrymen. The life of my son Androgeus will be repaid with your sacrifice," King Minos said.

Her father's words sickened her as they would have sickened Androgeus. Her parents' heartlessness hit her anew. Minos and Pasiphae were royal, the children of gods. Did that excuse their cruelty? Ariadne had been taught this was the way it must be. But that was a lie. These youths of Athens need not die. She would see to it.

"Do not show your fear," Theseus said to the Athenians. He stood tall, the first in the line of boys, looking every bit a prince. Iris stood taller. Ignoring the tears streaming down her face, she glared at Queen Pasiphae. If she survived, Ariadne did not doubt this girl would spend her life telling stories of the cruel witch-queen of Crete.

"Make your parents proud," Theseus said. "Do not let them say we went into the labyrinth full of fear."

"For Athens," Chrysippos said. The other boys repeated it.

"Come," Ariadne said, leading the way. They followed her into the darkness.

The torches had been lit within the labyrinth—the game had been set. But Ariadne had planned a game of her own. In the guise of checking safety, she had sent Manko to leave a bag near the second torch. She strode toward it and groped in the dark. Nothing.

The Athenian tributes remained in their two lines. Iris stood pale as a statue, but she was not crying. Echo watched Ariadne, ready to do her bidding, clearly waiting for her to speak.

"Go look at the base of the lamps," Ariadne said. Perhaps Manko's idea of the second torch was different from hers. She could not fail them.

"Here," Theseus said, lifting a bag.

"Open it," Ariadne said. "It is yours."

Theseus pulled out two sheathed swords and a skein of red thread. He handed the second sword to Chrysippos and the thread to Echo.

He unsheathed the sword to examine it. In that moment, he transformed from a barefoot sacrifice to a warrior. A golden light of power emanated from him. This is how he would be remembered: a hero who killed the monster, a prince who made Athens great.

"Tie the thread to the first torch and use it to find your way back," Ariadne told Echo. "All of you," she said to the girls, "pay attention to how you go. Remember so you can return to the world above."

"Yes, High Priestess," the girls said. Ariadne's words had lit a spark within them, and they appeared more alive than she had ever seen them.

"Theseus, Asterion will not be easy to kill. But he will not expect you to be armed. He can't see well through the bull's mask. Do not let him separate you. You must all stay together if you want to live. If you do get parted, follow the red thread back to the entrance.

"No one will be watching the dancing ground tonight because no one has ever come out. The gates will be open. You remember the way to the river?"

"Yes," Echo and Chrysippos said.

Theseus, Echo, and Chrysippos had accompanied Ariadne and her handmaidens on a picnic a few days before. Ariadne had purposefully pointed out the white flowers along the way that led from the palace to the river.

"I will alert your crew and have a boat ready to take you to port."

"Ariadne," Theseus's voice broke as he took her hand, "thank you."

"Thank you, High Priestess," the others said, their fear turning into the will to fight and survive.

She clasped Theseus's hand and wished she could be the girl reflected in his eyes. If she were only the infatuated daughter of the King of Crete. If all she were giving up was her family and her home for this hero. There was so much more to her story that would remain forgotten. None of that mattered now. Now was the time for action.

"May the goddess bless you." Would this be the last benediction she gave as high priestess? She turned and left the tributes in the labyrinth.

The blue of the twilight sky shone bright after the darkness of the labyrinth. The arena erupted in cheers when she returned to the dancing ground. The sistrum and lyre played a somber yet firm tune reserved for times of dark acceptance.

When the music stopped, King Minos and Queen Pasiphae rose.

"It is done," Minos said. "Athens will not forget who owns the seas. The riches of Egypt come to us alone. Now, go to your homes and make libations to the sacred bull, for through his power, we stay strong."

Ariadne followed her parents out of the arena. Back in her rooms, she moved as if in a daze, trying to keep herself from thinking that this would be the last moment in her bathing chamber, her last moment with Zoe, her last time choosing her jewels. Whatever she wore now was all she would take with her.

She and Alexa joined her parents for a somber dinner in the small dining chamber.

"I see the Athenian princeling left something behind," Pasiphae said when Ariadne entered.

Her mother had been watching and paying more attention than Ariadne realized. She froze. What did her mother know? Gold sparks lit up her eyes as Pasiphae rose from her throne.

Ariadne stood rooted in place. Pasiphae walked toward her, grinning, her teeth white as bull's horns.

Ariadne glanced at the sacred dagger on Pasiphae's belt, wondering whether the witch-queen of Crete would spill her own daughter's blood. It was no less than she deserved. She wanted to fall to her knees and beg her parents' forgiveness. *It was the goddess. The goddess made me do it, and I had to obey, or she would have made it worse.* Even as she had this thought, she wondered whether it was true.

Pasiphae cupped Ariadne's belly, her warm palm thawing Ariadne's fear.

"How long have you known, daughter?"

"I was not sure until now, Mother." She swallowed, relieved. Her mother only knew one part of what she had done.

"Is she with child, wife?" King Minos asked.

"Indeed," Pasiphae said. "One of a divine line."

"Wonderful!" Minos said, lifting his golden cup. "Good thing you chose that little princeling to bed, daughter. All of Crete will rejoice that the high priestess is with child."

"Did the little prince know before he went to his death?" Pasiphae asked.

"No." Ariadne would have to tell him tonight. She had suspected pregnancy but had told herself stress was the reason she hadn't bled.

"Too bad. It might have eased his death to know," Pasiphae said and then turned her attention away from her daughter.

"And you, Alexa. You also have a radiant glow." She touched Alexa's small belly. Her hand stayed there. Her smile widened. "It is Asterion's." Pasiphae beamed, happier than Ariadne had seen her in a long while. "How wonderful. Does he know?"

"Yes," Alexa said. To Pasiphae Alexa sounded shy, deferential, but Ariadne heard the sorrow in Alexa's voice. Nausea hit her then. She told herself it was her condition, but it was what she had done. What she still must do.

"High Priestess." A servant brought her a bread bowl of lentil lamb stew. She did not feel hungry, but she must eat to keep her strength for the long night ahead. Another servant poured wine.

"This is almost the last of the Athenian wine," King Minos said. "But Silenus says we'll have our own vineyard soon enough."

Ariadne held a sip of wine in her mouth, savoring the flavor and the deep sorrow that overcame her. This was her last dinner with her parents. The last time they would see her as their daughter. The meal was almost over. She swallowed the wine, fighting back tears.

"Where's Phaedra?" she asked. If only they could be reconciled. Phaedra had always resented her for becoming the high priestess when she could not. But it was not Phaedra's fault she had no powers of her own. Alexa would take care of Phaedra once Ariadne was gone. At least Phaedra had her friend.

"She's probably sulking," Pasiphae said. "She did love that Athenian prince. You know how she's always wanted what you have, Ariadne. She begged us to spare his life, but we simply couldn't do it."

"Only if he bests Asterion," King Minos said.

"What?" Pasiphae's fury came on like the blazing sun hiding behind a cloud. "What do you mean?"

King Minos gripped his golden cup, steeling himself for battle, then spoke gently. "The Athenian could never beat Asterion, but I agreed that if he did, he could leave with his life."

Ariadne and Alexa rose in unison. They did not exactly run out the door, but they moved quickly. Pasiphae's rage was like a summer storm: it did not come often, but when it did, it could rain devastation that would not be forgotten.

Ariadne glanced back as her mother threw her golden cup full of wine directly at her father's head.

Minos bellowed back, a secret fury of his own ripping through the room.

"Manko and Talos, stay here and make sure the king and queen do not injure each other," Ariadne said. Both her body-guards paled. No guard wanted to get between the royal couple, especially when they were enraged. "I will be fine, but I worry for my mother... for my father. Gather more guards if you need. Go now." She had not known how she would rid herself of Manko and Talos in a way that would hold them blameless for her crimes. This disruption was the perfect excuse.

Pasiphae let out an acrimonious shriek, and something heavy thudded to the floor.

"Go!" Ariadne shouted, turning away from the small dining chamber.

Alexa raced down the corridor next to her. When they came to the hall of shields, Ariadne stopped. "Alexa, I must go out of the palace grounds. The goddess summons me on some business I cannot speak of."

She expected Alexa to argue or demand to attend her, but Alexa clasped her hand.

"I know, Ariadne. The goddess told me. Worry not for Crete. I will keep your vigil."

Ariadne meant to reply, to express gratitude or even shock, but her feet moved away from her perfect handmaiden. She nearly ran down the corridor, trying not to think how this was the last time she would descend the grand staircase, and this was the last time her father's guards would bow to her as she exited the palace gates.

A small boat waited at the river to take them to the great port. The Athenian ship had docked there to await the news the tributes had been sacrificed. The crew was ready to sail back to Athens at first light; their black sails would alert Athens it had been done.

But no one waited for her on the small dock. Theseus and his friends had not come. This was the moment she had feared. Had Asterion killed them after all? If Theseus didn't come, should she take the boat anyway, go off to the unknown? Perhaps she could find Thalia. Perhaps... that idea was beyond foolish. How could she ever find Thalia? How could she ever forgive her? No. No, if Theseus didn't come, she must return to her rooms. Pretend all was normal.

"Were you going to leave without saying goodbye?" Phaedra stepped out of the darkness near the boat. The glint of her bodyguard Tios's dagger reflected in the light.

"Sister, I was looking for you." Did her voice betray her fear? "You were not at dinner."

"No, I was packing. Too bad you couldn't bring anything."

"What are you talking about?" Ariadne did not sound convincing, even to herself.

But before Phaedra could reply, Tios spoke. "There," he pointed toward the gates. "They come."

The full moon shone down on the river and the horns of consecration crowning Knossos. Ariadne clutched her bull's-horn necklace. Figures in white raced toward her. For a moment, it seemed they were ghosts, and she was in the Underworld. A breeze caressed her face, and the mark on her thigh stung.

"Get ready," Phaedra said to both the oarsman and Tios.

"Halt!" a guard shouted from the top of Knossos.

Ariadne's blood ran cold. Of course the tributes had been seen. Of course the guards would spot them.

The Athenian youths neared the boat just as three guards flew out of the gates. Theseus's white tunic was bloodied. She could not tell whether it was his own blood or Asterion's. He limped badly as he ran behind the rest. Chrysippos seemed to have fared worse; a fresh gash marred his beautiful face, and his right arm hung limply.

"Get in the boat quickly," Phaedra said. The moon reflected the light from Tios's dagger and armbands. Could any of the Athenians stand and fight with him? No. A cursory glance told her they were spent with fear and exhaustion. Ariadne went to stand next to Tios.

"This is sanctioned by the high priestess!" Phaedra shouted. "King Minos has agreed to let the tributes go."

The first guard to reach them stopped short, shocked to see Ariadne next to Tios.

"High Priestess," he saluted her. "We heard the alarm sounded."

"A mistake. Did you not hear from my father that the youths would be allowed to leave if they escaped the labyrinth?" Her heart pounded as she spoke. Behind her, Phaedra helped Chrysippos and Theseus into the boat.

"Go now. Return to your post. The announcement will come in the morning." Her confidence confused the guard, who took a step back but did not retreat.

"My sister speaks the truth," Phaedra said. "Why else would King Minos send a guard to assist them?" She gestured to Tios. "Do you doubt the words of the high priestess?"

"No, Princess. It is only..."

"Return to your post," Tios said, his voice firm.

The guard conferred with the other two and slowly, glancing back several times, they retreated into the darkness.

Ariadne wanted to sink into the earth. She and Phaedra had likely just sentenced those three guards to death.

"Ariadne, get in the boat. Unless you'd rather stay and face mother's wrath?" Phaedra hissed.

Ariadne forced herself to step up onto the dock. There was little room, and Phaedra had already taken a seat next to Theseus, who appeared ashen and fragile.

"Are you injured?" Phaedra cooed.

"I am fine." He patted Phaedra's hand and took stock his fellow Athenians were all on board. Would he have noticed if Ariadne weren't there? Had Phaedra already replaced her? After all she had sacrificed, she could clearly see how interchangeable one Minoan girl was for another. Perhaps how interchangeable any woman was for another in his eyes. *I carry your child,* she wanted to scream at him. But this was not the time. Tios helped push off and jumped in, landing lightly. The oarsman moved them steadily down the river to their black-sailed boat.

The Athenian crew was ready to depart the next morning with the sad news that the youth of Athens had been slain. The captain had remained awake, burning a lamp and drinking mead.

"Great Athena, Prince Theseus, you're alive!" the captain shouted upon seeing them.

"We must go quickly. We are pursued," Theseus called back, creating a flurry of motion. The captain kicked at the sleeping crew members, commanding them to their stations. Ariadne, Phaedra, and Tios clamored on board, followed by the Athenian tributes. They all tried to get out of the way as the sailors worked to unfurl the sail, which sounded especially loud in the darkness. The rest of the crew went below, slipped in their oars, and rowed away,

"I will pour libations to the goddess for your safe return!" the captain said when they began to move. "She blesses us with the light of the full moon so we can move away from this cursed island. Careful there!" he shouted to one of the sailors wrestling with the black sail. "We have no time for mistakes!"

Ariadne and Phaedra stood at the bow, the Athenian girls clustered behind them; all of them attempted to give the sailors space to work. The Athenian boys who were well enough offered to help, but the captain barked at them to move to the sides.

Amid the noise and chaos, all Ariadne could see was her home. The giant horns of consecration that crowned Knossos shone in the moonlight. She would never see them again.

I do this for you, Great Goddess. Ariadne pushed the tip of her necklace into her chest, wishing to draw blood. This was the biggest sacrifice she had ever made for the goddess, and yet Phaedra had come willingly.

"Why did you want to come, sister?" Ariadne asked.

"Do you not want me here, Ariadne?

"No, I'm glad you are here with me, but I didn't expect you to come. How did you know?"

"Theseus told me. He asked for my help."

The hair on the back of Ariadne's neck rose. How many times had Phaedra met with Theseus?

"Alexa said she had a vision that my fate lay in Athens. Once you were gone, there was no chance of me being the next high priestess, so I chose a life of adventure."

"Theseus said he would marry me."

"I know." Phaedra took her hand. Ariadne noticed her sister had a ring on every finger. She probably had a bag full of jewels. "I hope you will help me get settled in Athens once you are queen. Perhaps you will find me a suitable Athenian husband?"

Ariadne's fingers began to tingle. When she squeezed her sister's hand, warmth spread from her hand to her wrist, all the way up to her shoulder. Then, as clearly as she saw the dark sea before her, she saw Phaedra sobbing alone in a foreign chamber. No frescoes adorned the walls; only one simple carpet lay on the floor. The bed appeared small, and the furnishings had no gold paint, no paint of any kind. This must be a chamber in the

Athenian palace. Alexa had lied or omitted the whole truth. Phaedra's fate might lie in Athens, but it was a miserable fate. She would be far more unhappy there than she had been on Crete. Ariadne opened her mouth to warn Phaedra to tell her to turn back, but the look of delight on her sister's face stopped her. Theseus limped toward them.

"Ariadne, Phaedra, are you well?" Theseus asked. He appeared diminished, exhausted from escaping the labyrinth, but still determined. "I am so grateful for all you have done. Both of you."

"Of course. It is an honor to help the Prince of Athens. Here are your things, just as we discussed." Phaedra pulled his clothing and his crown of bronze olive branches from her satchel.

"Ah, you brought my sandals, too," he said, carefully placing his crown on his head. "It is a relief to not return dressed as a Minoan sacrifice."

When had Phaedra made these plans? Before she could formulate a question, Theseus continued.

"Now that you're on the ship, you must cover your breasts. Women do not hold as much sway in Athens as they do in your land."

"Oh, yes, Theseus, of course." Phaedra pulled a plum-colored linen shawl out of her satchel and handed it to Ariadne, taking a turquoise one for herself.

Ariadne wrapped the shawl, which smelled of sandalwood and myrrh, around her chest and tried to quash her anger. Clearly the goddess had forced her into leaving with Theseus as punishment. But what had Ariadne done to deserve this?

She twisted the hair ring on her finger, noticing that Phaedra had replaced hers with a gold one. All Ariadne had now were the jewels in her hair, her bull's-horn necklace, her red carnelian beaded necklace, golden earrings, bracelets, and her rings—one a snake biting its own tail—and the odd hair ring she had found when Thalia disappeared. She had been the second most powerful woman on Crete, and now she was completely at the mercy of this Athenian prince.

Once Theseus ensured their breasts were covered, he limped over to the Athenian youths who huddled together on the deck. Echo drowsed on Iris's shoulder. Chrysippos sprawled in semi-consciousness. Tios tended to his wounds while the other boys looked on helplessly.

"How is he, Tios?" Theseus asked.

Ariadne went over and crouched next to Chrysippos, touching his fevered brow.

"He will live," Tios said, binding his broken arm with a clean strip from the boy's tunic. Chrysippos moaned, and heat shot up Ariadne's arm.

"He was very brave," Theseus said, louder than necessary.

The fire from Chrysippos's brow seemed to lick Ariadne's fingers, and she sensed a vision coming. She closed her eyes, not wanting to see his future. Was the boy going to die here? Was he going to return home to discover heartbreak? But the vision that came to her was not of his future, but of his past. In the flickering torch light of the labyrinth, Asterion loomed above him. Chrysippos's heart pounded so wildly he could barely hear the Minotaur speak, "Perhaps you will be my last kill."

Chrysippos waved his sword at Asterion, who delicately plucked it from his hand. When Chrysippos tried to hit Asterion's bare chest, Asterion grabbed his arm, breaking the elbow. Chrysippos's scream echoed down the corridors. He fell to his knees, sure he would die of fear if not murdered by the Minotaur.

That was when Chrysippos saw Theseus. Thank the gods his friend was here. He would save him from the monster. But Theseus did not step between Chrysippos and the monster.

"Up, up, Athenian. I will not have you die on your knees. Rise and die like a man, like a boy worthy of sacrifice."

The monster grabbed Chrysippos's wrists to pull him to standing. That was when Theseus stabbed Asterion in the back. Asterion bellowed in pain and anger, slashing Chrysippos's cheek as he turned to face Theseus.

"Ah, the great hero," Asterion rasped. "No one will know of

your cowardice and how you did not keep your blood debt. No, they will only remember that you slew a great monster. Only you and I know how badly it was done. Did you send your little friend here as bait?"

"The time has come to end your reign of terror on my people!" Theseus shouted.

"Oh, yes. It is your time to shine, little hero. Too bad you will never know contentment."

"Lies!" Theseus yelled.

Chrysippos staggered, doing his best not to fall. He had the oddest desire to step between Theseus and the monster, to save the monster from the sword Theseus raised. But he dared not. Chrysippos was no hero. He could barely even watch.

The vision faded as Ariadne dropped Chrysippos's hand and sank onto the deck next to him.

"High Priestess, are you well?" Tios asked.

"I am high priestess no longer, Tios. I no longer know what I am." Her hands trembled, full of magic she did not know how to wield.

"Theseus," she said, her voice breaking, "did you kill Asterion honorably?"

He stared at her as if not quite recognizing who she was or what her question meant. "Yes, of course."

She was a coward and a hypocrite. Had she helped him kill her brother honorably by giving the Athenians swords and a way out?

"You are so pale, Ariadne. Are you unwell?"

"I am not used to being on the sea." She did not mention that the visions and her pregnancy made it much harder.

"Perhaps when we stop to change the sails, you and I can get off and sleep on solid ground." He offered his hand and helped her up. His old kindness had returned. She told herself all would be well.

When the boat anchored, the Athenians did not awaken. Theseus had changed into the clothes Phaedra brought. He appeared every bit a returning hero.

"We'll change our sails and wait until dawn to be on our way. The captain doesn't want to continue in the dark. We are far enough from Crete now that we can wait here. Come ashore with me, Ariadne."

Sailors usually swam ashore, but since this was a royal ship, they took a small raft and a blanket. The shore was unremarkable, but it was the first island other than Crete that Ariadne had set foot on. She felt so different here, more alive and alert. Theseus found a spot near some seagrass that offered shelter from the wind and arranged their blanket.

"Ariadne, you have helped make me a hero." He took her hand, and a warmth filled her. In her mind, she saw him wearing a crown of gold, Athens growing from a small town to a great city. Pottery and discourse, games and education would all become possible because of Theseus. She saw him on a throne, crowds cheering him, his name spoken for generations. But she did not see herself in this vision. A wave of nausea rolled through her, and she let go of his hand.

"What happened?" he asked, a hint of terror in his voice. "Your eyes... they turned golden." He moved back. She wanted to laugh at his fear.

"I had a vision. It is so strange. On Crete, I tried to speak to the goddess, to have a vision or any hint of what was to come, but as soon as we left, this ability has grown in me."

"What did you see?" he whispered.

She wondered whether her eyes still glowed golden, or whether that only happened while was seeing the future. "You are to be king of Athens. A hero for your people." Should she lie? Tell him that she had seen herself by his side as a great queen of Athens? She could make herself a part of this future, tell him that under their rule, women of Athens would become as equal as women in Crete. But instead, she grasped his hand and put it over her belly. "I am pregnant, Theseus. I've slept with no one but you."

He pulled his hand away. "This is how you tell me?"

"Yes. This is how you know it's yours. I thought you would be pleased."

Theseus frowned. "I am pleased. I am just not used to thinking of women as sleeping with anyone else but me. You understand in Athens, if you bed another, the punishment is death."

Ariadne caught her breath. Some married men on Crete felt this way, but this was not the law for royalty.

"Oh." Ariadne pulled her shawl tighter around her shoulders. "So men do not force themselves on their slaves in Athens?"

Theseus's brow furrowed as if he were talking to a very stupid child. "Men can do what they will, but women must remain faithful. As you will remain faithful to me. Will you not, Ariadne?"

"Of course," she said, imagining throwing sand in his eyes, tackling him to the ground, and slitting his throat. How dare he speak to her this way? She was the High Priestess of Crete. No. She had been the High Priestess of Crete. Now she was just a woman pregnant with this man's child, at the mercy of him keeping his word. How she wished to end his story right now. She could change the path of fate and end his life, avenging Asterion and changing history. But no. What would the goddess do if she killed this precious Athenian hero? What would happen to Ariadne and the child?

"It has been a very long day. Let us sleep, for we must leave before the sun rises to continue on to Athens," Theseus said.

Ariadne lay down, letting her fury smolder. Having visions had drained her more than she realized, and she fell into a dreamless sleep.

PART THREE
ON THE SEAS

17

DIONYSUS LEARNS BETRAYAL

HALICARNASSUS

Dionysus stood on the busy quay trying to remember how to behave among mortals who were not his followers. The wind whipped at his long hair and purple cloak as he waited with his amphora of wine and chests of bounty from India, holding Thalia's leash. The stares of sailors and fishermen told him he was not succeeding in appearing as a regular mortal seeking passage to another land. The boys who cleaned the nets, the girls who helped with the catch gawked at him. Word spread, and soon more people came from the town to stare, until Dionysus felt he was naked in the marketplace—a slave for sale. He had forgotten what it was to be a stranger.

He stroked Thalia behind the ears and wished he could ask her advice. She had decided to travel as a leopard, saying it was much safer than traveling as a woman. She had selected her red leather collar.

A crew returned from town and began to board their vessel near Dionysus. Perhaps this ship would give him passage.

"Sir," he asked a rugged Ionian. "Can you take us to Crete?"

The sailor paused, staring at Dionysus's purple chiton. "You haven't heard?" the sailor asked, rubbing his unkempt beard. A wind blew from the sea, sending a shiver down Dionysus's spine.

"What's happened?" Dionysus asked.

"Oh," the sailor sighed, ready to impart some juicy gossip. "A great sorrow has befallen the land of the labrys. An Athenian prince has killed the savage Minotaur."

Asterion. Dionysus grasped the bull's-horn necklace that had once been Asterion's. The news did not surprise him, but the pain of loss stung.

"Crete's sway over Athens is done," the Ionian continued. "They will send tributes no more. It is said that Crete has lost all her power and King Minos weeps. Few ships sail to Crete today, but see there? Third boat down, red mast?"

Dionysus followed the man's gaze to a to a medium sized cargo vessel with a prow shaped like a fish and faded blue paint on the hull.

"I hear the crew from Tyrrhenia does what others won't—for a price. You seem like a man who can pay."

Dionysus had the porters carry his trunks down the dock. Two sailors loading an amphora of oil on board paused to stare at Thalia. A seaman with wild, dark hair jumped off the boat to stand near Dionysus. He held his hand to his eyes, shielding them from the sun, and appraised Dionysus and his possessions.

"Hello, young sir, are you looking for something?" The man's wild black beard almost completely eclipsed his face.

"Can you take me to Crete? I can pay well for you to take me and my pet cat."

"Ahoy, Captain Medon!" the first man shouted up to the boat. "We have a young lord here who wants to sail to Crete. What say you?"

"We don't sail for Crete, Dictys. You know that."

"Come take a look, Captain," Dictys said.

The captain also had a long, black beard, brushed into a point.

He stroked it, smiling, as his eyes danced over Dionysus, Thalia, and his three trunks of treasure. He flashed his remaining teeth in a grin. "Please, come aboard, young lord. We will take you wherever you want."

Even after all this time among mortals, Dionysus did not understand them. He had first sensed lust from the sailors, but once they heard the promise of gold, everything changed. He watched as they loaded his wine and crates onto the ship. Thalia pulled at the leash, away from the boat, her green eyes flashing at him. Sometimes the feline got the best of her. It must be her fear of water that made her growl as he pulled her onboard.

"It is an honor to have you," Captain Medon said, ordering two others to stow his goods. "And your, what did you say? Your pet cat. Charming."

"She is priceless. Ensure none of your men tease her. I would hate for any of them to die."

"Worry not. No harm will come to your valuable pet. We have a space for her below, if you'd like to escort her?"

"She will not go below. I'll tie her above. Show me where a good place might be."

Thalia hissed at the captain as Dionysus tied her to a rope securing crates of pottery. All who passed gave her wide berth. She paced as far as the leash allowed. He did not recall her being this agitated on other voyages.

"Worry not, Little Leopard. Soon we'll be on our way back to your mistress. Our exile is done." He sat on the deck next to her and scratched her under the chin and jaw until she settled.

The memories of all he had accomplished in the last three years warmed him. He had devotees far and wide. Everyone had heard of wine now. He had turned a river to wine in India and made those who were once his enemies drunk. He had been a commander of a large army—of wild women and loose-limbed men. Wild creatures had come to him from the jungles to join his troop: snakes, panthers, and great horned cows. Widows and orphans joined his procession, for all were welcomed. The battle to be accepted had been hard fought, but he had won, and now, with the recognition he had longed for, he was finally able to return.

THE TYRRHENIAN SAILORS FINISHED LOADING THE SHIP AFTER much yelling in their language. The crew worked to unfurl the heavy canvas sail. Thalia flinched at the noise as the men lowered the red cloth. After they angled the sail in the right direction, they rowed away from the dock. The boat lurched toward the open sea. The current carried them on their way. Their eagerness to embark matched Dionysus's.

Dictys and several other seamen walked by, staring at him with eager grins. Perhaps they anticipated their payment when they arrived on Crete. He would not worry about the strangeness of these sailors. Mortals were so peculiar in their various ways. Even being on the Phoenician vessel he took from Crete had been odd at first. It had been odd in Tyre and Sidon.

He would not dwell on how he missed Ahumm or his other followers. Soon he would be reunited with Ariadne and Silenus. That was all that mattered. He had wonderful gifts in his trunks —silks, spices, and jewelry for Ariadne. He had found the perfect ring to replace the odd hair one he had left her.

Would she remember him? The hair ring might make her forget him, yet she had come for him in her dream—and her passion had been fierce. How jealous she had been! Seeing her fury had given him strength and made him miss her even more. She was his true wife. She had come to find him in her darkest state of unconsciousness. Their destinies were unquestionably linked. He would be with her soon.

He had enjoyed sampling what the world had to offer in India, but his heart yearned for the High Priestess of Crete. Despite the beauties he found abroad, none matched her power. Being with her was like drinking the moon, like listening to poetry recited from the wine-dark sea. He had enjoyed himself with many, but there was only one moon in the sky, and Ariadne was the one who shone for him. Would she forgive him?

"She will rejoice to see you, Lord. I do not know what she will think of me. I would rather die her slave than be without her as a free-woman," Thalia had said before transforming herself into a leopard and bringing him the red leather collar in her teeth.

The wind had died down. The boat rolled lazily, and the heat from the sun made him drowsy. The Tyrrhenian sailors had appeared so eager to leave port, but now the boat hardly moved. He jumped up and peeked over the side—not a single oar. They were just floating.

He should have kept his retinue, hired his own crew. Yet his own people were not the best at completing their tasks. They tended to cause chaos, revelry, and bloodshed. The vision of a party ship—worshipers embracing, drinking, and dancing instead of rowing hard—made him smile. Paid sailors untouched by his divinity had seemed like the best plan when he had left his followers on Tyre.

"Are you comfortable, my Lord?" the navigator Acoetes asked. A man of middle age, he had a kindly face, a weathered brow, and a piercing gaze.

"Why are we not moving?"

"Perhaps, my Lord, you'd like to change your destination. It is not the best time to visit Crete. Where is home for you, my Lord?" Acoetes asked. "Perhaps we can take you there instead. Perhaps you have family who eagerly await your return and would be pleased to see you alive and well?"

The navigator was clever in a way Dionysus knew little about. He had a clear sense of direction, an internal compass, an understanding of direction the same way Dionysus understood grapes and the fury of women.

"My home is with the High Priestess of Crete, Ariadne. Take me to her, and I will pay the amount we agreed on."

"From what I hear, Ariadne, daughter of Minos is no longer on Crete. They say she helped kill the Minotaur and betrayed her own family to journey with Theseus of Athens."

"What?" Artemis had promised him Ariadne. Betrayed. Ariadne had betrayed her own family as his half-sister had betrayed him.

Nothing but seagirt, loss, and abandonment ahead. He did not often have premonitions, but this one came clearly. A lonely isle of seagirt.

"Where did you hear this?" Dionysus asked.

"Down at the docks. A Phoenician coming from Crete. All are eager to say that Crete has fallen. They won't be demanding Athenian tributes again."

Dionysus had thought his journey over, his quest fulfilled. A great victory had been his and now, and now... uncertainty. He must find her. If she preferred the Athenian, he would leave, but not until she told him herself. Should he go to Athens, of all places?

Acoetes's hairy eyebrows rose in surprise at something behind Dionysus. A hand clamped down on his shoulder. A second pair of hands grabbed his arms, wrenching them behind his back.

Across the deck, Thalia growled.

"Don't," Acoetes said to the sailors behind the young god.

"But he's so pretty," the captain said, coming around to face Dionysus as his men bound Dionysus's wrists. "And here we are in the middle of the sea. A band of sailors and a handsome, rich youth. Surely you are from a wealthy family. Tell me, boy, will someone pay a good ransom for you? Someone in Crete? Perhaps King Minos himself?"

Flecks of salt coated the captain's thick forearms as he gripped Dionysus's shoulder. Dionysus was too stunned to say anything but the truth.

"No." Was Silenus still in Crete? His foster father had wandered off many times, and his old mentor was never good at keeping coin. "No one there remembers me."

"Well in that case, you'll earn a good price as a slave. But before we sell you, we can have all the fun we want." He caressed Dionysus's throat. "We'll get a fine price for the leopard when we dock in Rhodes. Such a creature is rarely seen in these parts. We will start a bidding war."

"Captain Medon." Acoetes's voice wavered, but he continued. "I do not wish to speak against you, but there are laws we must abide by. We took him on as a passenger and made an agreement. If we do not heed it, what are we? I beg you, honor your word."

"Acoetes, hold your tongue, or I'll have Dictys cut it out. After I'm done with the boy, I'll give you a few lashes to remind you of your place."

Acoetes clenched his fists and said nothing as the captain went behind Dionysus and cupped his buttocks.

"Ah, Dictys, what a tasty piece you suggested bringing on board." The captain squeezed a cheek roughly. He moved Dionysus's hair aside and whispered, "I will be the first to have you, then Dictys, then the others will draw straws. I thank the gods who blessed me with such a pretty boy." He laughed, his breath reeking of sardines and rotten teeth. "And to think you're the one paying me!"

A shudder ran from Dionysus's buttocks up his spine to his jaw. He had played many roles in his life: an orphan, a youth, a man, a god, a husband, the leader of an army, and now a helpless captive.

Though he still did not understand humans, he had learned from them. Ariadne had taught him love; Thalia, grief and loyalty. This man taught him betrayal. He had trusted a mortal at his word, and now the man promised to rape and sell him. Perhaps gods needed to visit mortals like this more often.

The captain slid his callused hand up the back of Dionysus's thigh, raising his chiton. Dionysus did not struggle. He let the fear flow through him, let the terror beat hard in his heart, rousing a desire for vengeance that fed his divinity.

Music floated on the breeze. Lyres, pan pipes, and drums sounded, though no musicians played. This had happened before when Dionysus's very blood buzzed with power. On land, his godhood drew players, dancers, wild women and men of the forest, but here, on the boat, no one came, for there was no one there with him except Thalia.

"Thalia." He did not have his thyrsus within reach, but perhaps he did not need it.

Tendrils of vines shot out along the deck; grape leaves festooned the mast, twining around the oars. Wine rained from the sail. The grinning faces of the sailors transformed into expressions of confusion, then horror.

Dionysus tipped his head back, closed his eyes, and whispered, "Release." At his words, his bonds and Thalia's leash evaporated. She growled from deep in her throat. The sailor nearest to her took one look, screamed, and jumped overboard.

She lunged at Dictys, biting his thigh and severing his artery. She lapped up the blood, licked her maw with her rough, thick tongue, and surveyed the rest of the sailors.

As Dictys screamed and tried in vain to staunch the blood, Captain Medon dropped Dionysus's chiton and backed away.

"A jest only, little lord," the captain said, holding out his hands in placation. "We will take you wherever you wish to go."

The captain's rough touch still burned Dionysus's buttocks, and rage overtook him as he let himself transform. Thick, brown fur sprouted over his skin. The shoulder Captain Medon had grabbed grew large, as did the rest of his body. Sharp claws sprang from his paws. He had not taken on the form of a bear in a long time, but this was perfect for the moment. He lifted his snout and roared.

The sailors shrieked. Captain Medon fell to his knees. Dionysus and Thalia moved on him as one. The captain cried out in horror.

"Forgive me. I did not know you were a god!"

This set a new fury in his heart, and he grasped both sides of the captain's head and gave a quick tug.

The remaining sailors screamed and climbed onto the bow. The music continued as vines writhed on the mast, blood and wine flowing on the deck.

"Gods forgive us," Dictys said, dragging himself to the bow. "The cold sea will offer more kindness." He leaned his bleeding body over the edge and fell with a plop. Others followed him, standing on the bow and jumping into the sea.

"Forgive me, Lord," Acoetes said, turning to embrace his death. "I did not want this, but I will pay for their crimes as well." He stepped onto the prow.

Dionysus growled and sent a vine to wrap around Acoetes's foot so the helmsman could not jump. Dionysus began to speak, but only growls came out. His body changed, getting smaller; his skin smoothed, and his sharp claws became nails. Once transformed to his mortal form, he was dismayed to see he had torn his clothing. He did not care about the chiton, but his beautiful purple cloak from Tyre had been split down the back.

A whimper from the helmsman brought his attention back to the one Tyrrhenian left of the crew.

"I will forgive you, Acoetes. You alone spoke wisely."

Acoetes stared, his mouth wide open, as Dionysus strode to the bow to survey the floundering seamen. Though they could all swim, they would not survive in the middle of the ocean. "I will not forgive these men, but they will have a chance at redemption."

One sailor gasped for breath and went under. He thrashed about, churning up foam. The man did not come back up for air, but a gray tail splashed the deep blue water. The other sailors cried out as their skin turned gray, their faces grew long and pointed, their legs merged into tails. Their shrieks turned into squeaks. Acoetes watched, his mouth agape, as his former crew members transformed into dolphins and chattered around the boat.

"Come." Dionysus helped Acoetes down. The navigator fell on his knees and clutched the god's thigh in supplication.

"Forgiveness, my Lord. I did not...."

"You are forgiven. Now rise and take me to my destination. I have changed my mind. We will not go to Crete, but to Naxos. I don't know why, but my destiny is there."

❦ 18 ❦

ARIADNE ON NAXOS

Ariadne sat on the beach, her knees drawn up to her chest. Her tears had dried, and a calm sorrow set in. She had been a high priestess, a princess, and now she was nothing more than a traitor. Even if she had a boat, she could not go back to Crete, and she could not go on to Athens.

A day had passed with no food or water. She should rise from this spot, walk along the beach, and try to see whether the island was inhabited. Yet she could do nothing but sit and wish to die.

Visions filled her mind of her corpse, swinging from a tree on the beach. That surely would make the goddess happy. One final sacrifice. Perhaps she would be remembered as the Goddess Who Hangs—She Who Swings.

She twisted the odd hair ring on her finger and stared out at the horizon. The last three months with Theseus now felt like a horrible dream. How could she have betrayed her family and given up everything that mattered to her? But she had done it for Crete. The goddess would have hurt more than the bull leaper Tanziz if Ariadne had not obeyed.

She stroked her belly. Why had she slept with Theseus? She had been willing to obey the goddess to save Crete, even if she was remembered as a traitor, but she had not needed to bed the

Athenian. He was not even that good of a lover, not like...who? She had never allowed her passion to betray her duty. She had never... had she? Had there been another man? Another lover, a husband she had sacrificed to the goddess? Had there once been one who was worthy?

Hunger and thirst obscured her thoughts. She must find a source of clean water or decide to end her life. Yet she could not move. Thalia's face, her green eyes full of love and devotion, floated into her mind. Phaedra had said the girl ran off. But now, Phaedra... Phaedra had allowed Theseus to leave without her. That little bitch. Her sister had been her enemy all along. Betrayal ran thick in their veins.

She stared out at the sea, and a vision formed: Of Theseus sneaking away from her and waking the oarsman. Of them rowing away in the dark. And of them forgetting to change their sails from black to white.

"You will be the death of your father, Theseus." Her voice came out jagged, but the words made her smile. Theseus had promised to change his sails to white if he lived. In her mind's eye, she pictured the Athenian ship returning with blackened sails. The image formed of King Aegeus, overcome with grief, throwing himself in the sea.

Ariadne stood, letting the sand from her fist slowly fall with her words. "My curse will come to fruition. Theseus, you will be King of Athens, but grief will be your crown. And you, sister, Phaedra, traitor. You will be his wife, but happiness will not be yours."

Ariadne took a full, deep breath of the sea air, releasing her curse and anger on the wind. She was done with Theseus and Phaedra.

She closed her eyes and breathed, taking stock of her body. Hunger, sorrow, but also a new power. She hadn't had a vision this strong in years. She had not gone to a sacred cave or drunk a special draught. Perhaps it was this place, or perhaps it was not being on Crete. The idea made her smile, and she stared out at the sea. The turquoise water rose and fell, darkening further out. On the edge of the horizon, she noticed a ship. For a moment she imagined Theseus returning—claiming it was a mistake, some kind of mix up. And she imagined plunging her dagger into his breast. But the ship was not Theseus's. This ship had a blue hull and red sails which billowed with wind as the ship came closer to shore.

Her own people were pirates. She knew what someone like her father would do with a woman alone on an island. If this was her fate, let it come. Perhaps she would use her dagger after all.

The odd hair-ring on her third finger suddenly irritated her skin. She had worn it for years, and it had never bothered her, but now she needed to remove it. The boat drew closer; vines crawled up the mast, surrounding the oars, moving them at a fast pace. She had gone too long without food or water. Boats did not row themselves. Ships like this needed a hearty crew, yet there appeared to be only two men aboard. Two men and... and some sort of animal, a big dog or perhaps a large cat.

Fears of pirates no longer worried her. This ship was god-touched. It was going to come ashore farther down the beach, and suddenly she found herself running. The sand against her feet made her move terribly slowly. She wanted desperately to be faster. It did not matter how dry her mouth was or that she was running toward a strange vessel. She must be there when they came ashore.

When the ship neared the beach, one of the men dropped anchor. Ariadne stopped directly in front of them, aware of her shawl billowing around her head, her hair floating, and the breeze on her skin.

She pictured herself again, hanging from the tree, and this mysterious long-haired man climbing the tree and cutting her down, taking her body into his arms and cradling it, giving her back her life, giving her back her former self, giving her love.

Tears streamed her cheeks. The ring itched on her finger. She could not bear to wear it for another moment. She wrenched it up, twisting and pulling. It tightened and would not go past her knuckle. The two men and the cat, for it was a giant cat—a spotted lion or a wing-less griffin—were in the water, wading toward her.

She hardly saw the sailor or the cat, for the sight of the man between them made her draw her breath. A tall, dark-haired man; the curls in his hair seemed to match the swirls of the grapevines. She wanted only to stare at him, but she had to get the ring off. The final tug bruised her knuckle, but she didn't care as she pulled it off and dropped it to the sand by her feet.

The cat let out a loud purr, which should have frightened her, but it did not. Tears flooded her eyes as the cat began to run toward her, transforming into a spotted creature with a woman's face. A face Ariadne knew and loved. The paws became hands and feet, the powerful thighs and forearms, a woman's, until the woman/cat rose from all fours and stood before Ariadne naked, surrounded by her long, golden hair.

"Thalia," Ariadne breathed, embracing her friend.

The warmth of Thalia's naked chest pressed against Ariadne's cold bosom. Their arms wrapped around each other as if they could become one. Thalia's tears dripped onto Ariadne's shoulders.

"Mistress," she whispered, "my priestess, my goddess." Thalia smelled wild, like the sea and spices Ariadne did not know, and like blood. There was a different look in her eyes, a fierceness she had not had before. A chill shot up Ariadne's spine. It was not the wild cat, but the woman who was the leopard who gave her pause.

"Ariadne, how I have longed to see you again. I never wanted to leave you. Your sister tricked me, but my master took care of me. He kept me for you."

Ariadne gripped her friend's waist. And Thalia slid her hand around Ariadne's. Thalia's hair tickled Ariadne's wrist as she stared at the man Thalia had called her master.

"Dionysus," she said, stunned to remember all, "my husband."

"Wife, Ariadne, how I have missed you."

He was the most beautiful man she had ever seen. Every black curl hung perfectly, cascading down his shoulders. His dark brown eyes shone slightly green in the sun. The smile on his lips was of one who had done the impossible.

She was married to a god! She had been married to a god and forgotten. She had been married to a god and betrayed him with a foreigner. She had... She swayed, and Thalia gripped her tighter. Her once favorite slave had grown stronger than Ariadne ever imagined.

His power of earth and wine was familiar—the seductive unfurling of vines filled her mind as she imagined leaves shooting up from the soil with clear purpose—to please the god, to create a special fruit for him, to assist the fruit into becoming a gift.

He grasped her hand, to slide her from Thalia's side to his own. But she could not relinquish the woman who was a leopard.

"Dionysus, husband. There is much I do not remember and more I do not understand."

"Your goddess made me leave you. She threatened to kill you in childbed if I did not relinquish my rights on you. She said I must leave you for three years, to allow you to love another."

The goddess had done all this? If Thalia's arms had not been so strong around her waist, she would have fallen.

She could die giving birth. The goddess still controlled that.

"Mistress, you look faint," Thalia said. "Acoetes, go get her some water and whatever food you have."

Dionysus grasped her hand. She wanted to hold him tight, to throw herself into the love she had for him before. But the child in her belly was not his. What husband would forgive that?

"I'm sorry, my Lord. I am only now remembering."

He bent over, picked something out of the sand, and held the hair ring she had just discarded up to the light.

"Did you wear this the whole time?" He appeared delighted to find it.

"Yes, I only took it off when your boat approached."

"Did it work? Did you truly forget me?"

Was he happy or sad that she had forgotten him? She could not tell. Perhaps he didn't know either.

"I did. It is strange to remember now. I felt your absence, yours and Thalia's. I did not know what it was, an emptiness in my heart, a deep sorrow."

A splash of burgundy rolled down Dionysus's cheek as he squeezed her hand. Tears. She was married to a god who cried tears of wine.

Acoetes returned with water and passed a cup to Dionysus.

"Beloved." His voice both familiar and strangely accented roused her. "Have some water." He offered her a golden cup. The water was sweeter than any she had tasted. She glanced up into his eyes and felt seen for the first time in ages. She was not the High Priestess of Crete or the daughter of Pasiphae and Minos. To this god, she was Ariadne, the mortal he had chosen as a wife. The mortal he had chosen to return to.

"Lord," Acoetes said, pointing toward the hillock behind them. "Look!"

A throng of people wended their way down to the beach. Sounds of flutes and festive singing resounded as the villagers descended. In coloring and manner, they looked like Minoans, with light brown skin and black, curly hair, but their clothing showed them to be shepherds and fishermen.

Dionysus pulled her to him and held her close. His scent brought back delightful memories. She wanted to burrow her face into the crook of his neck and stay there, but they must greet the people who came toward them.

A man in a red kilt with long hair led the procession. "The god has arrived!" he cried. "He has come by boat as prophesized." Two youths played pan pipes, and three women sang.

"Didn't I tell you they would come, Palitia?" the man in the red chiton said to the gray-haired woman behind him. Greeting Dionysus, he said, "Lord, we welcome you. The gods have blessed us with their presence." He bowed before Dionysus, raising his hands in supplication. "I am Chalkio, priest of Naxos. I dreamed of the God Who Comes last night."

As the people surrounded them, Acoetes fell to his knees before Dionysus. "I swear to the sea and to the sky, he is a god like no other! He punishes the wicked and shows mercy to those willing to serve. I will sing your praises always, Lord!"

"Up, Acoetes," Dionysus said, pulling the helmsman from the sand.

"We are honored you have chosen Naxos," Chalkio said.

"I am Dionysus, the Twice-Born God. Ariadne, the Mistress of the Labyrinth, is my wife."

He was about to give her divine lineage: daughter of Pasiphae and Minos, High Priestess of Crete. But if word got out she was here, her father would send guards for her. They were not far from Crete, and certainly this place, what did they call it, Naxos? This place had no way to protect her.

"We have come to celebrate our marriage," Ariadne said loudly, interrupting him.

The crowd cheered. Ariadne stood up straight. Would these people believe they had come to this tiny island purposefully? Had she and Thalia been alone, perhaps no one would believe them. As it was, the people did not look at her or Thalia directly, but they could not take their eyes off Dionysus.

"You are most welcome here," Chalkio said. Then an awkward silence fell. Only the sound of the wind and waves was heard as Ariadne realized the problem.

A little girl wearing a necklace of seaweed stared at Thalia. A young boy gazed at her open-mouthed while the adults pretended she was not there at all.

"Husband, perhaps you could give Thalia your cloak." Ariadne would have offered Thalia her own shawl, but these women covered their breasts.

Dionysus gave her a quizzical glance, and his eyes darted back and forth between Thalia and the villagers until he realized the problem. When he did, he laughed and whispered, "Oh, mortals and their silly ways."

"Thalia," he said to get her attention, then to Chalkio and the others, "is a priestess of the Mistress of Wild Things. Sometimes we forget the ways of men." He slid off his purple cloak and handed it to her. "I hope her nudity has not caused anyone difficulties."

Thalia wrapped his torn purple cloak around herself loosely. Ariadne resisted a mad urge to laugh as men and women struggled not to stare.

Dionysus grinned. "We do not mean to impose, but we were drawn to this island. Tonight we will have a party that will be spoken of for generations!"

"We are honored to have you," Chalkio said. The youths began playing their pipes and the women sang, "All hail Dionysus, the God Who Comes!"

The women surrounded Ariadne and Thalia, singing wedding songs and offering their own cloaks against the wind. Ariadne was safe now. The long night she had spent alone on the beach seemed a strange dream. She had thought herself so close to death and yet, here she was, reunited with Thalia, reunited with a husband she had completely forgotten. No, his memory had been erased by magic; the fault was not her own.

They followed the procession up to the village. Sheltered in trees, Naxos Town appeared hidden, though they could see the coastline clearly. She had never seen a village like this. Some houses nestled in hills; most were small wooden huts, a few structures of stone, and in the distance, a bright marble building, probably a temple.

"This way, High Priestess," the gray-haired woman called Palitia said. "I am honored to have you as a guest in my house. I will stay with my sister to allow you privacy."

"Thank you for your kindness." She tried to sound grateful and hide her shock. This small stone house was what they were offering her? She had never seen people live this way. Even the farmers out in Crete had proper two-story houses. The inside was dark and smelled of mud and unwashed clothing.

"Here is the hearth. The basin has fresh water," Palitia said.

"The Goddess Who Comes," a middle-aged woman cried outside the door. A full procession of women and girls amassed outside. They wore plain dresses of undyed wool and covered their breasts. Their thick, black hair was bound, with no adornment. Was this how the rest of the world lived? Eking out an existence on a small island, far removed from the gods?

A chorus of women's voices came from the doorway.

"Blessed be the goddesses who came to our shores," women cried.

"Come," Palitia said, brightening.

Women and girls huddled around the doorway since the house was too small to admit them. Their eyes lit up on seeing Ariadne and Thalia. Each woman and girl carried gifts: bouquets of wildflowers, a blanket, a lamp, a bundle of sticks for the hearth, a small jar of honey.

"For the Mistress of the Labyrinth, honey," an old woman said, offering it in her wrinkled hands.

Ariadne accepted with a sad smile. She was no goddess. If she ever had even been close, she was one no longer. She had not come to this place with purpose. She had merely been deposited. Abandoned. What kind of goddess is abandoned?

"For the Goddesses Who Came," a little girl said, handing Thalia a basket of cheese. "Thank you for gracing our shores, wise ones."

Radiant, with her tangled golden hair and Dionysus's purple cloak, Thalia appeared every bit a goddess. A golden light surrounded her, and her green eyes, always a wonder, now shone with a luminosity of another world. Thalia had gone beyond the realm of mortals. She was a magical creature now.

"Thank you for your kindness," Thalia said. "We are glad to celebrate with you."

Once the women of the island were satisfied the strangers had enough sustenance, they went to join the rest of the village. Dionysus and Acoetes had unloaded an amphora of wine, and the herdsmen prodded their finest sheep to the center to be sacrificed. Revelry, bloodshed, and song were the last things Ariadne wanted. She had thought she would die a silent death, and now silence was all she craved.

"This will help, Mistress." Thalia held out a plate full of cheese and bread drizzled with oil. "Eat slowly so you are not sick."

"I never thought I'd see you again, Little Leopard." She clenched her friend's hand harder than she should have.

"I worried you would think I had betrayed you."

Ariadne was the one who had betrayed everyone: her country and family, her god husband, and even Thalia by believing she had run away with a man. She tasted bile in the back of her throat and hated herself anew.

"Phaedra will be punished," Ariadne hissed. "I've cursed her, and..." She was about to say that since she was pregnant, her curse would be even more powerful, but she could not share this with Thalia.

Without the hair ring to beguile her mind, she remembered everything about Dionysus. He might be a new god with new ideas, but he was a god still. It shamed her that she had slept with Theseus—not because she had shared her bed with another, but because the Athenian had been unworthy.

When he discovered she was pregnant, would Dionysus abandon her all over again? Leave her here for the goddess to pick off with her arrows? Would he keep her as wife, tucked away on some far-off island while he went back to forging an army of worshippers, or would he kill her himself for sleeping with another man—a mere hero who was not even divine?

"You look so tired, Mistress. Come lie down."

Thalia put the blankets on the bed and lay down. Ariadne nestled her head on Thalia's small bosom. There was much to discuss, but she did not want to talk. Held by her oldest friend, she succumbed to sleep. It was the deepest, most relaxing sleep she had had in three years. Here was safety and comfort. Here was a friend and lover. More than a warm, naked body, more than a protector. Though Ariadne slept long, Thalia did not leave her side. Thalia's hair brushed her shoulder, and for a while, she was vaguely aware of a strong paw resting on her breast. She dreamed of Thalia changing from woman to beast, from lover to friend, from friend to familiar.

When she awoke, it was night. She turned in Thalia's arms and rested her cheek on Thalia's chest. "How I've missed you," she whispered. "I did not know I missed him, though I felt an emptiness, but you..."

"I curse your sister for making you think I betrayed you. Did... did you believe I ran off?"

"Not at first, but Phaedra convinced me. She brought men who had seen you. I sent Manko to inquire by the docks, and people had seen you on the ship."

Thalia scratched at the bedding with her nails. "Phaedra sent me to that boat with her man Tios. She said the captain had something to give to you. After I got on board, Tios whispered to him. The captain said the gift for the high priestess was below deck. When I got there, he bound and gagged me. He said the Princess of Crete gave me to him as a gift. I screamed and fought, but there was nothing I could do."

Rage beat in Ariadne's veins. Tios must have made sure Thalia stayed on deck for long enough for others to see. Then, he went back to the palace to lure Dionysus onto the same boat. If Phaedra was before her now...

"I never abandoned you, Ariadne."

Ariadne was shaking with rage and horror. What must Thalia have been through?

"Did he hurt you? Did he..."

Thalia stroked her wrist. "He was about to rape me when Dionysus rescued me. He transformed me into a leopard." She grinned wide. Her teeth shone brightly. Ariadne had noticed a change in her eyes in the light of day. Now, in the flickering lamp light, they were still more gold than green. More like a leopard's eyes than a woman's.

"Don't let anger upset you now. You must rest for the sake of the child."

"How did you know?"

Thalia ran her hand from Ariadne's throat, down her breast to her belly. "I have known your body most of my life. I see the swell of your breasts, Mistress." She cupped one gently, teasing the nipple. "I see the small, hardly noticeable roundness of your belly, yet your arms are thinner; your buttocks have gotten smaller. You've lost weight, and your belly should be smaller, too, but it is not." She cupped Ariadne's belly and stroked her mound through her skirt. Ariadne reached up and fingered Thalia's pink nipple, then grasped both her breasts in her hands.

"How I've missed your pert little breasts, Thalia, and your tongue upon me."

Thalia bowed her head so her long golden hair engulfed them. She pressed her lips against Ariadne's. Ariadne had shared a bed with Thalia, but never had the girl been so forceful. She parted her lips and allowed her slave to have her way.

Thalia's hungry mouth moved to Ariadne's neck, and Ariadne thrust her hands into Thalia's hair. She still smelled of foreign spices, of sea air, and of wild cat. As Thalia's tongue worked its way down Ariadne's chest to her belly, she wondered whether her tongue were rough, whether, like her eyes, she had retained a bit of the cat.

But now Thalia was at her mound; her hair tickled Ariadne's sides, and she parted her thighs to let Thalia lick her long and hard.

The bull's horns of Crete flashed through her mind, the double ax, a butterfly, a symbol of her home.

"No," Ariadne said. The release she desperately wanted was not one she deserved. "Thalia, stop. We cannot. I cannot." She reached out and took Thalia's face in her hands, pulling her up.

Ariadne's desire swelled, and she was barely able to restrain herself from writhing against Thalia, begging for what she could not have.

She could not stay here with the woman who was a leopard, her first and most faithful lover. She stroked Thalia's cheek with her thumb. Her pinky strayed over the girl's lips, and Thalia parted her mouth, sucking on the tip. Ariadne shuddered, wanting her all the more.

"Did you bed him?" Ariadne asked, trying to enflame some of her old anger, to make herself feel something other than arousal quashed by shame. Even as she asked, she knew it was not a fair question. Thalia was a woman and a slave; Dionysus a man and a god. The choice was not Thalia's to make. "Did he bed you?"

Thalia sat up. Her hair cascaded in waves, and for a moment, Ariadne could have sworn she saw spots in the blonde curls. "Since I have become a follower of the Twice-Born God, it is difficult not to speak the truth. Do you wish me to speak?"

Ariadne shuddered. What Thalia said next could shatter what was left of her heart. She was not sure who she would be more jealous of, but the thought of her bedmate and her husband together did not entice the rage she had hoped for. Instead, it deadened her, as if she were fading. They had been together for three years while she had been alone.

Thalia dropped her blanket to the floor and went to pour some wine.

"It is not just the drink," she said, kneeling to offer Ariadne a clay cup. "It is the way the Master compels us to speak the truth, to discover a part of ourselves we did not know about. For some it is violence; for some it is sex or poetry. For me it was something different."

Ariadne took her cup in both hands. She wanted to be strong enough to face this without a drink in her hands, but it was all too easy to picture Thalia embraced in Dionysus's arms. The god could transform himself into a leopard and mount her, his powerful forearm around her spotted chest... Ariadne took a long drink.

"I do not want to know. But tell me."

"Though the Master desired me, he refused to allow himself to take me to his bed. I was often naked in his tent, but despite the desire in his eyes, we never touched. Our love for you stood between us. I was the only thing he would not allow himself." Thalia blushed slightly.

Ariadne surprised herself by laughing. "Oh, I never expected chastity from my husband. I have met men and gods before. I spent my whole life with my father and all the bastards he got on slaves, nobles, and priestesses. As for Dionysus, I remember now who I married. Women, men, I know his tastes. He was faithful for the brief time we were together, but you cannot change a god's nature. Dancing and orgies are part of his godhead—as are blood, wine, and transformation. And he certainly has transformed both of us." She sighed. "I am not as I was, Thalia, and you, my darling, are far more than you were when I last saw you. He gave you freedom. I can see that now. A freedom I could never have given you."

"No, Ariadne." Thalia's eyes blazed, and she grasped Ariadne's wrist tightly. "You gave me more than any other woman could have. You saved my life. You gave me friendship." Her voice became rough until Ariadne could hear the leopard in it. "You shared your bed and your heart with me, a slave. A foreigner. Your countrymen saw nothing but a whore, a novelty, easily bought, easily tired of. But you alone looked at me and saw a girl, a friend who could warm your bed, but not just for a night. I was not a quick sale for you.

"I will forever value the love you gave me, just as I will forever beg your forgiveness for leaving, though it was the last thing I wanted to do. I want to supplicate myself to you. I want to beg your forgiveness with my tongue. I want you to punish me however you see fit, and I would savor any bit of pain you give me. But I will deny myself all these pleasures, for I know you must be reunited with your husband, the Twice-Born God. The

God Who Comes. He has come and come and come to many lands, and now he has come to this place, to this land, for you. Go to him now."

"But..." How much easier it would be to lie back and let Thalia have her way. How much less intimidating to spread her legs for her former slave, to see what that leonine tongue would feel like. "But how? How do I reconcile with a stranger?" *Especially with another man's child in my belly.*

"My lord is the Twice-Born God, the Undying God, the God Who Is Torn Apart and Reborn. He has always been a stranger. But he is no stranger to you, Ariadne. I saw that the first day. You knew each other instantly. Go find him now. Reconcile. He yearns for you. We have come all this way for this. Go."

19

DIONYSUS, THE GOD WHO COMES

The drums beat steadily. After all his travels, wars, and misunderstandings, gaining and losing followers and fighting and being accepted by foreign gods, the easy acceptance of the people of Naxos warmed his heart. He had come here for Ariadne. He had wanted nothing more than their reunion, yet she was closeted with Thalia while he was being worshipped.

How he wanted to slip on the garb of a woman, make his beard vanish, and follow his wife and Thalia. But she did not want him now. Though it pained him, he forced himself to remember he was a new god. A god who could wait. Even if it drove him mad.

In the center of this charming little village, the best of the sheep had been sacrificed and butchered. The scent of roasting meat and rosemary filled the air. Youths played panpipes and sang poems. As the sun set, Chalkio instructed novice priests to light torches. The fire seemed to dance in time with the music. Acoetes had unloaded the magical amphora of wine from the ship. Dionysus contemplated carrying his trunks up to the village, of offering Ariadne the gifts he had brought from India. He couldn't wait to see her in the dresses and jewelry he had chosen for her. Perhaps tomorrow or the day after. He had left his vines onboard the ship. They would protect his possessions.

"Shall I serve the wine, my Lord?" Acoetes asked.

"Yes, let the revelry commence."

The villagers brought cups from their houses. They chatted excitedly and helped Acoetes pour the wine. When the amphora emptied, all Dionysus needed to do was picture it full, and it was. He hadn't even needed his thyrsus to make vines on the ship. Even now he could sense them, there waiting for his command. He had never known he had such powers. Yet he did not delight in them without Ariadne.

"It is all that I hoped," Chalkio the High Priest said, disrupting his reverie. "Lord Dionysus, grape wine is truly a gift, as heavenly as nectar. Surely this is what the gods drink on high."

"Not yet," Dionysus said. "It is a gift—one I give gladly. But be warned, Chalkio, like all gifts, there is a darkness to it. Some transform happily, and some turn to violence. Mix it with water, and don't drink too much. I will teach you how to transform the grape."

"So you will stay?" Chalkio's eyes lit with excitement, and he dribbled wine on his ash-colored beard.

"For a little while, if my lady-wife agrees." After some time here, they would journey on. Ariadne had never been off Crete before, and there were many wonderous places he couldn't wait to show her.

"We are honored to have you, Lord Dionysus, for as long or short a time as you wish to stay."

Dionysus took a sip of wine himself. This batch was particularly delicious, fitting for a celebration. If only Ariadne were here to enjoy it with him. The people of Naxos did not seem to notice her absence.

Chalkio watched his people drink and dance to the music. His cheeks reddened, and his eyes focused on the women of his village, who with each beat seemed to shed more of their clothing.

"Go on, Chalkio. Join your people. This is the proper way to worship me."

"Yes, Lord. If you command it," the priest said with a hint of laughter in his voice.

Dionysus watched from the periphery, slowly sipping from his cup. Women and boys danced nearer to him. *Take me, Lord,* their eyes and bodies said. One older woman ventured close and took his hand, trying to draw him into the center. He smiled at her and dropped her hand. He did not feel like dancing with anyone but Ariadne.

"Lord Dionysus," Acoetes said, bringing his thyrsus. Dionysus was about to thank him. He had carried his thyrsus on all his journeys, but he had purposefully left it on the ship, aware that he did not need it as he did before. But before he could speak, Acoetes stripped off his tunic.

"I committed crimes against the gods by allowing the other sailors to take you on board, Lord Dionysus. Let me pay in blood for my sins."

The music quieted and then stopped. The boys playing the pan flutes appeared in need of a break, and revelers passed them cups. The dancers circled around Dionysus and Acoetes, eager to see what would happen.

Dionysus felt no need to punish Acoetes but recognized how much the man, and indeed all his new followers, wanted it.

"Acoetes, you are the only Tyrrhenian sailor who was worth saving. You are worthy of my lash." He raised his staff. Tendrils sprang from the thyrsus, and vines came down, whipping Acoetes's shoulders. A man in the crowd moaned at the sight, and Dionysus felt the satisfaction of his new followers upon seeing this act.

Acoetes's back already bore scars from captains he had sailed under. Each strike of the thyrsus, no matter how light, no matter how thick his scar tissue, aroused him. Dionysus brought the whip down harder and harder until Acoetes became completely erect. The navigator stood before him, as hard as a satyr and as eager to find a partner as the other mortals gathered around.

"Acoetes, go fulfill your destiny." Dionysus spoke not just to the navigator but to his new followers. "Find lovers tonight with the stars as witness. Spill your seed amongst mortals or on the earth. Find your own way to worship me, as only you know how. Go!"

Acoetes swayed on his feet, staring at Dionysus with love, with awe, and then with glassy eyes that did not seem to see the god at all. Unseen drums boomed. The boys who played the pan pipes started up again, this time joined by music that echoed from the trees. Those who were still dressed dropped their clothing where they stood, hips swaying, feet moving to the drums as if responding to the pulse of the earth.

Pick me, pick me, their bodies seemed to say, not just to the navigator, to the outsider, but to each other, to themselves. One woman cupped her own breast, as if to show what she had to offer, but then, so intrigued by her own body, she continued to touch herself, to stroke her nipples, and slide her hands down her midline to her mound. It was as if she were all alone then, as if she had chosen herself and had no need for anyone else. A boy on the brink of manhood stared at her, as entranced by what she did to her body as she was.

Suddenly aware of those around him, Acoetes strode toward a woman who danced alone. Touching her shoulder, he murmured something Dionysus could not hear, but he did not need to. It was an invitation—one the woman and the man next to her accepted.

Dionysus need not stay any longer. He wove through the undulating bodies and walked toward the darkness of the juniper trees, seeking solitude. This was the effect he had on mortals, all but Ariadne. Why was she not here with him now? Once her memories returned, he thought the spark he had been forced to extinguish would rekindle. But no, she was changed. Alive still, but damaged. Had the Athenian hurt her? Dionysus clenched his fist, wishing he could smash it into Theseus's face—a face he had never seen, but one he hated.

The young god expected Ariadne's feelings to mirror his own, yet they had not. He had given her all day and most of the night to remain closeted with the woman who was a leopard. He could only imagine what they had done together, the intimacy of women without men. His imagination ran wild as he pictured the women he desired most reunited. He had sworn to wait patiently. But she had not come.

He let out a laugh—a short bark of surprise. He was jealous! Jealous of a beautiful slave with the heart of a leopard. He, a god, twice-born, immortal, and at this moment he wished he were a slave, kneeling before his wife. He was foolish, but he did not wish to be a jealous god.

He pictured their naked bodies, writhing together in the dark —Ariadne pinching her nipples, Thalia moaning for her to do it harder. What would it be like to take the part of his wife's female lover?

Deception. Zeus would have thought nothing of taking Thalia's form and finding pleasure this way. Dionysus might not know much about love, but he knew that would be wrong. He had begun their courtship with—well, if not deception, then omission. He would not continue this way.

Then what? He would go to her, take her some wine, some meat, a honey cake. Perhaps she would be willing to sit with him under the trees. Perhaps she would be willing to talk. It was not the best plan, but it was all he could think of.

He had been staring at the crowd of mortals, some dancing, some making love, others drinking or drumming. On the other side of the clearing, a woman appeared wearing nothing but a blanket, the coils of her dark hair in disarray. Even in her obvious distress, her beauty outshone everyone else's. Dionysus felt drawn to her like no other. He tried to see the aura around her, to sense her energy, but the halo around her blurred as if someone had extinguished her flame. She approached a half-naked woman and asked a question. The half-naked woman took her hand, trying to entice her to dance, but she stood there, repeating her question. She was looking for someone—for him. Understanding came quickly. The woman he was drawn to, the stranger with the dimmed light, was his wife.

Here, Ariadne, I am here.

Across the clearing, she raised her head, pulled her hand away from the woman who wanted to dance, and turned in the opposite direction.

She must not have heard him. This made him sadder than he could have imagined. Out of all the sorrowful events in his life, this did not even count. Yet, if the connection between them was broken.... What had he been doing? Who was he? He had left the mortal he loved at the command of a goddess. He had forsaken love to keep her alive, and now she did not see him.

He put his hands to his face, embarrassed even in the dark to shed tears over such a small thing. He strove to be mature, and yet, here he was, hiding, unsure of everything.

"Are you here?" Ariadne's voice came from his right. She had circumvented the crowd to find him. Warmth rushed through his blood, as if newly infused with wine.

"Yes, here." He reached his arm out and found her wrist.

"Are you watching your people? Do you not want to be in the center as they worship you?"

"No. I've had enough revelries. I wanted to be alone to think."

"Oh." She pulled her wrist away, hurt in her voice.

"I wanted to think of you, Ariadne." He clasped her hand, intertwining his fingers through hers. "I have missed you, Beloved. I have come all this way to retrieve you."

She leaned her head against his chest.

He untied his cloak so it fell open. Then, holding the two parts in each hand, he wrapped them around her. The night air was warm, with the first bite of cold as the seasons shifted toward winter.

"I know what this has cost you," he whispered in her ear. "Had

I never entered your life, perhaps you would still be High Priestess of Crete. Unwittingly, I made you sacrifice all that you were. It was not my intention. I wanted you for myself, but I did not want you to lose it all. Ariadne, can you forgive me?"

"Me, forgive you?" She let out a laugh, a loud howl that filled the night air. It burst free so suddenly, and the pitch was so melodic, that others took it up as if it were a game. Dionysus gazed up at the stars, listening to his followers echo the mad laugh.

"How can you forgive me?" she asked, her voice broken. "Do you know what I did? I betrayed my people, my father, my mother, my station. I allowed a foreigner not only to escape but also to take me and my sister with him. I helped him kill my brother! And now I discover that all that time I was married to you! Your wife, Dionysus, and I bedded another man—one who was completely unworthy."

Her wretchedness broke his heart. He was about to tell her that Theseus didn't matter, that he himself had chosen to let her be with another rather than let her die. But she went on in misery.

"I have lost all I was, abandoned not just by a mortal, but a weaselly Athenian." Tears coursed down her cheeks. Her breasts heaved, and she twined her fingers through her hair as if those winding strands were all she had left of the snake that had once been worshiped with her.

"Ariadne, I have already hurt you enough. To me you are blameless. You did not ask to turn against your goddess. Loving me made you culpable. You are the only priestess who could stand by my side."

"I am a priestess no longer. I am nothing now. I have lost it all. I am grateful for your return, the memory, all that I was once. All we could have been."

"You will always be a priestess. How can you not know your power?" He grasped her wrist, pulling it away from her hair, and placed his finger on her pulse. "I feel it with every beat of your heart. You may not be a priestess of your Great Goddess whom I call Artemis, you may no longer live on Crete, but you wield power stronger than any mortal woman. You are the granddaughter of the Sun.

"Asterion knew what would happen. He wanted release. Once he met me, he knew what was to unfold. That's why he gave me this." He clasped Asterion's necklace. "A part of him, of who he was before, a powerful priest-king is with us still. We will pour libations and continue to honor him by not forgetting he was more than a mythic Minotaur."

Ariadne touched the tip of Asterion's bull's horn, digging it into her finger.

"You were a pawn in the game of the gods," Dionysus continued, "but now you are free. It is not easy to leave your home, to venture abroad, but despite your sorrow, a light radiates from you, a power greater than you had on Crete."

She smiled weakly but did not meet his gaze.

"You are still my wife, Ariadne." He touched her belly. "You carry my child."

She stared up into his face. "Your child? How is that possible?"

"You don't remember?"

Her brow furrowed in confusion. He enjoyed memorizing her expression, for she rarely appeared perplexed. Did she truly not remember? He took her wrists and gently pulled them above her head. The blanket fell, and she allowed him to keep her in that position.

The bracelets on her wrists, the jewels in her hair, her earrings and necklace, made her nakedness even more exquisite. Her honey-colored skin bathed in the moonlight; the swell of her breasts and the small mound of her belly made him sigh aloud.

"I was so surprised that night in India when you came to me. Your fury." He transferred her wrists from two hands to one and stroked her jaw. She lifted her head, offering him her neck. He lowered his head to kiss her, first on the lips, then on the throat. He kept her arms raised; she had so enjoyed it the last time.

"Every one of my followers wanted to rip you to pieces, but I would not permit it. I will not allow any harm to come to you, Ariadne. You are mine."

She embraced him, pushing her breasts against his bare chest. She kissed him fiercely. "I am yours, Dionysus. Your wife, your priestess, and I am honored to be carrying your child." She nipped at his neck. "But I don't forgive you. Not yet. Not until..." She raised her arms, putting her wrists together. "...you give me pleasure like you did that night in India. Only then will I consider forgiveness."

He grinned and sent vines from the earth to bind her. He would have her forgiveness this night.

"MASTER, THERE'S A BOAT COMING! FROM CRETE." THALIA'S voice came out rough. She had run all this way to find him and Chalkio up in the hills. He had been searching for fertile soil to create vineyards.

"We must go," he said to Chalkio, turning to follow Thalia.

"There is a goat path we can take," Chalkio said. "Follow me."

"Ariadne said to tell them she died," Thalia said as they followed Chalkio into the trees. Dionysus heard the terror in her voice. There was no way Ariadne could return to Crete. He did not know what her parents would do. He did not want to imagine their anger.

When they reached the goat path, the boat, bearing an image of the sacred bull of Crete on its sail, was approaching the shore.

"Go, Thalia." At his words, she transformed and raced down the path. Dionysus picked up her clothing and rushed after her.

By the time they got down to the beach, the ship had anchored, and two men waded to shore. Though all of King Minos's guards appeared similar to Dionysus, he recognized these two, Ariadne's bodyguards.

Two fishermen were busy cleaning off their keel on the shore.

Manko reached them before Dionysus could. Thalia stalked on the other side of the boat, crouching down low. The fishermen pointed to the village above, and Talos and Manko gazed up to where Ariadne was. Dionysus was contemplating whether he should transform into a villager or invite them up for some wine. He glanced at Thalia, wishing he could ask her. She nuzzled his leg, and her movement caught Talos's attention.

"Lord Dionysus," Talos said, taking a step away from the god and his leopard. The Cretan guard was not the same proud soldier Dionysus had known. Stripped of all jewelry, Talos appeared almost naked. He had a black eye, scabbed knees, and bruises all over. He must be in great pain after walking through the saltwater.

"Is it true, Lord Dionysus? Is Ariadne here?" Manko asked. He had also been beaten and was missing his golden armlets, earrings, and rings.

"And if she is?" Dionysus asked,

"We have been charged with finding her and bringing her back to Crete."

"And if you don't?" Dionysus stroked Thalia's head gently.

"King Minos will execute us," Manko said as if he were speaking of someone else.

"Well, we don't want that," Dionysus said. "You were so loyal to my wife."

"We are still, Lord," Talos said.

Just then a man splashed from the boat into the sea. Frantic flailing in the water ensued though the seafloor was not deep here. Talos turned around and yelled, "Put your feet down. You can walk." There was a flurry of motion, of wet tunic and wild hair, and then Dionysus began to laugh as Silenus found his footing and waded to shore.

"Old friend, you appear to have swum here instead of coming by boat." He ran to his foster father and embraced him, not minding how wet the old satyr got him.

"Little Liber," Silenus said. "It has been a rough journey. I barely escaped."

His foster father's bald patch had grown, and his stubby nose appeared redder, but his eyes and smile were the same. "Minos has gone quite mad. He has been drinking these last five days and beating the guards who let your wife escape. When he heard King Aegeus of Athens threw himself in the sea, he called for a big celebration. They say Queen Pasiphae has cursed him and is mourning for her son. I jumped onboard without his leave as these boys left Crete. If he realizes and remembers I left, he'll be looking for me."

"But the vineyard is good?" Dionysus asked. "They will have wine?"

"Yes, yes," Silenus said, struggling to remove his wet garments.

"Well, I see you were not starved in Crete." Dionysus patted Silenus's belly. "Are the men on board faithful to you, Talos?"

"They are seamen of Crete, used to doing what they're told. Is she here, Lord?"

"Perhaps," Dionysus said. "Thalia, go run up to the village; tell them we have guests. Tell them there will be wine."

And wine there was. And a joyous reunion. The Cretan crew happily swore allegiance to Ariadne.

"We have two boats now," Dionysus said. "We can stay here no longer. I know exactly where we shall go." He chose not to say aloud that their destination was Lemnos, where his friend Hephaestus had offered him refuge. He spent the night explaining to Chalkio and his followers how to harvest grapes. Dionysus needed to leave, but his gift would stay behind and grow.

20

ARIADNE'S ADVENTURE

LESBOS

"You can be whoever you want now," Thalia said their last night in Lesbos. "This is what I learned as a leopard. I didn't know until I transformed. Before, I was Thalia, servant of Ariadne, High Priestess of Crete. I would have been happy with this my whole life, but once I left Crete, I realized I was so much more. You now have this freedom, Mistress."

Exhausted from her pregnancy and their travels, Ariadne had returned early from the festivities. The lyric poets of Lesbos had composed poems for Dionysus and Ariadne. Tonight Dionysus would award prizes to the best.

Thalia handed Ariadne a cup of mint and chamomile tea, which she took gratefully.

"I am high priestess no longer, but the wife of Dionysus. I will be the mother of his children." She stroked her belly. The midwife she had consulted suspected Ariadne was carrying twins.

Ariadne intertwined her fingers with Thalia's. "I will only transform into a wife and mother, not a leopard."

"Out here, you can be who you want, Ariadne. You've lived

your whole life beholden to your parents, to the goddess. Now you can be the goddess."

"Don't speak that way, Little Leopard," Ariadne whispered. Dionysus assured her they were safe, but she sensed an animosity in the ether, as if the goddess searched for her. Had her father believed the lie reported on Naxos, that she had died there? Did he send his boats to hunt the seas for Talos and Manko? Did he think they had failed to find her and fled to foreign shores, or did he guess they had found her and changed allegiance?

"Do you feel different here, Ariadne?"

"Of course. I'm with child… and I am free of responsibilities."

"I can feel your power growing as we move away from Crete. On Samos and Chios, new worshippers begged to join us."

"That is Dionysus, not me. He grows stronger every day. When we docked in Lesbos, drums beat with no players in sight. Young men ask to accompany us, though Dionysus will not tell them where we are going."

"Ariadne, don't deny the goddess within. Women and girls come to him, but they are drawn to you just as they were drawn to your mother. The midwife and her daughter who will sail with us tomorrow want to follow you. The novice priestess from Chios vowed to become the new priestess of Ariadne, Mistress of the Labyrinth. The leopard in me is telling you to relish this time. You are powerful. Become who you were meant to be when we reach our destination."

Ariadne kissed Thalia's hand. "I am so lucky to have such a wise leopard advisor. I will do my best to follow your counsel."

The next morning, Ariadne dreaded getting back on the boat. The crew slept on the deck as though dead from imbibing too much the night before.

"Up, up!" Dionysus shouted.

Acoetes jumped to attention, then promptly ran to the prow and vomited over the side. Some of the other sailors laughed, though they also appeared unwell.

Manko and Talos assisted Ariadne and Thalia to the boat

while Dionysus made sure all was ready. The two ships they had taken from Naxos with a skeleton crew were almost full. They had skilled sailors now and were able to leave more quickly than Ariadne had hoped.

Ariadne sat in a proper seat on the Minoan ship, protected from the sun. She drowsed for most of the journey and awoke nauseated. The fresh air offered relief, but the movement of the boat intensified her discomfort.

As soon as she awoke, Thalia fetched her mint tea. Dionysus returned with her, ducking under the shaded awning.

"It won't be much further, Beloved," Dionysus said. "Once we are in Lemnos, we'll be safe." Thalia brought a cloth soaked in chamomile and dabbed her brow.

"What is Lemnos, Master?" Thalia asked.

"It is an island on top of a volcano sacred to Hephaestus. After Zeus gave birth to Athena supposedly by himself, Hera made Hephaestus without Zeus to prove that she, too, could make a child on her own. But he was born with a clubfoot. Hera thought him so ugly that she tossed him out of Olympus. Thetis rescued him from the sea and helped him recover, as she later rescued me. After his recovery, he returned to Olympus. The Olympians begrudgingly accepted him, until he intervened in a fight between Hera and Zeus. The King of the Gods threw him from Olympus a second time. He landed on Lemnos, where the people nursed him back to health. In exchange he taught them the skills of the forge."

"Do you know this Hephaestus, Master?" Thalia asked.

"In my youth, I sought shelter with Thetis under the sea. I do not know how long I stayed with her, but one day she took me to Hephaestus's forge beneath the ocean. His talent amazed me. Having been so unappreciated, he embraced my compliments. He and I have much in common—we both only have one parent. And we are gods who are not accepted on Olympus."

Dionysus glanced up to the skies. Ariadne wondered whether Zeus watched—whether the goddess she had angered watched, or whether the gods had ceased caring. Dionysus returned his attention to Ariadne and Thalia. "We both have skills that help mortals transform one thing to another. He told me that if I ever needed a place to seek shelter, I would be welcome on Lemnos."

Ariadne's nausea had lessened, and a swift joy overtook her. They were starting a new life. She was with Thalia and Dionysus, Talos and Manko. This would be a good beginning. For the first time, she began to think about where they were going instead of what she had left behind. Feeling better, she stood and went to the prow. Now she felt the exhilaration of being at sea. Crete and the past were behind them. They would continue on as a family.

"It is lovely, isn't it?" Dionysus said as the volcanic island came into view. "I'm so glad to bring you here, Beloved. I'm sure there are wonders here to rival Knossos, and you'll be safe from any harm."

The sea calmed around the island, and Ariadne sensed the divinity hovering over this place. The clear water reflected the calm skies.

"Are those giants guarding the port?" she asked, squinting ahead.

Dionysus grinned. "It does appear so. Do not be alarmed by anything you see here. Know I will protect you."

He clasped her hand and turned away, calling out to Acoetes. "Tell the men below that their faith in me will be tested. No harm will come to them if they do not panic but obey."

Acoetes sent a deckhand with the message and steered toward the giants. Talos and Manko stood up and flanked Ariadne. Thalia appeared, silent as a cat, and entwined her fingers through Ariadne's.

"This place feels magical, Mistress." She lifted her head and sniffed the air. "I smell metal and eggs. I can almost make out the energy of the volcano and its desire to help transform mundane objects into the sacred."

As they neared the port, the pair of bronze giants standing in the water showed themselves to be statues of the lame god. He had a large face, obscured by a wild beard, a broad chest, and huge hands. Every detail of the statues appeared real. And then the thick arms moved, barring entry. A deckhand screamed, and the row master shouted from below to halt. Terror rose up from below deck.

Thalia wrapped her arm around Ariadne and her other hand around a rope to steady them as Talos and Manko stepped closer. Ariadne felt a thrill but no fear.

"Abandon ship!" a frantic sailor cried, and two Cretan sailors leapt into the sea.

The ship would not be able to stop before crashing into the statues. They would all be destroyed.

"Trust in Lord Dionysus!" Acoetes bellowed above the panic.

Just then Silenus and Dionysus shouted out in unison, the loud braying of a donkey. The arms of the bronze giants immediately pulled back, allowing the ships passage. Ariadne and Thalia turned to each other and started laughing like they hadn't laughed in years.

As the ship pulled into port, they could hardly stand, not because of the movement, but because they kept hearing braying in their minds.

"That's the secret code," Ariadne whispered to Thalia, and they burst into laughter all over again.

The rest of the crew was not nearly as amused. Acoetes appeared as if he might be ill, and the deckhand who had screamed sank onto the deck, unable to move. Talos and Manko gripped Thalia and Ariadne as if to hold them up, but Ariadne realized that they needed someone to hold. She wanted to tease her bodyguards, but clearly they found no humor in fearing their deaths.

Dionysus returned from the prow holding Silenus, who had never been light on his feet.

"Did you like that, wife?" Dionysus asked, wiping a tear of laughter from her cheek.

"Very much. I take it the donkey is sacred to Lord Hephaestus?"

"Yes. It is easier for him to go about on one."

The port city of Lemnos came into view. The sand was a light shade of saffron, beautiful against the blue of the sea. Brick-roofed houses stood in the port, and higher up the hill, marble structures with golden domes glittered in the sun. In the distance she heard drumming—the sound of hammers beating against metal. The whole island was the god's workshop.

A crowd gathered at the harbor. From the ship, Dionysus shouted out to them, "Go tell your master Dionysus has arrived!" Two boys turned and ran up the path toward the volcano that crowned the island. "Ah, it is as magnificent as he said. Even your Daedalus cannot compare to the Smith God."

"No," Ariadne said, eyeing the bronze statues. "It is truly impressive."

After Acoetes docked, Dionysus helped Ariadne disembark, while Talos and Manko followed with Thalia.

The movement of the bronze statues had drawn attention. People came toward the ships of Dionysus. Excitement swirled in the air, for anyone who made it past the statues was a friend.

"Welcome to Lemnos, Lord. We've sent word of your arrival to Lord Hephaestus," a black-haired man said.

At first it appeared to be an island of only men, but then women came out wearing red and brown dresses and carrying jugs of water.

"Welcome to Lemnos, Mistress," an older woman said.

"Thank you." Ariadne took the copper cup in both hands. Before she took a sip of water, she gazed at the craftwork. A man with a twisted foot fell through the sky to the sea below. To the side, an idyllic island where cows grazed peacefully. Though the man falling was only part of the scene, she felt his pain and the serenity of the island. They had cups like this on Knossos—grand scenes on the cups for royalty—but this was what was given to strangers in the harbor. The cup itself was a magical object. It created such deep emotion in Ariadne, she almost began to cry in sympathy for Hephaestus's fall from Olympus.

When the crew disembarked and stood together, Ariadne thought of chastising them for doubting Dionysus, but their shame-filled faces told her that was unnecessary.

One of the sailors who had jumped from the ship swam slowly toward the harbor and then lay upon the shore, gasping for breath.

"I give his life to you, Ariadne, for he is one of yours," Dionysus said.

The Cretan sailor remained on the saffron sand, as if waiting for a death blow. Ariadne could easily have Talos kill him. Her heart filled with pity at the thought of killing one of her countrymen who had given in to fear. Instead, she would offer him to the god.

"Talos, go tell him I will spare his life, but he will become a devotee of Hephaestus."

Talos walked toward the sailor. Dionysus stroked Ariadne's wrist. "So wise, my wife." She grasped his hand, filled with happiness. This would be a new chance for them, a new land where she need not kill her husband, where they could have children and live among friends.

A burly man strode toward them with a polite smile. "Lord, Lady, I am Milos. I will be your guide. Please come this way."

While Acoetes made sure the boats docked, six men escorted Dionysus, Ariadne, and their small retinue toward the glittering golden domes. The path was paved with marble and clearly well-trodden. Though they moved away from the disgraced sailor, Ariadne could not stop thinking of how he had thrown himself from the ship. She understood his fear, but his actions shamed her. She was glad to leave him below, or she might have changed her mind and killed him. It was the pregnancy. Sometimes rage descended. Like the cravings for figs or honeyed goat cheese, she was susceptible to rage, nausea, and moments of worry.

They climbed up out of the port town. A steep trail lay above them, and Ariadne gasped for breath.

"Lord, Lady, the donkeys are just here," Milos said.

The small troop of brown-haired, pale-bellied donkeys stood under the shade of their small stable.

Silenus danced toward one donkey and began stroking her ears while he clicked his tongue. The donkey nuzzled his hand.

"Ah, she likes you," one of the guides said. "And she doesn't like many people. You can ride that one. Lord, Lady, please take your pick. The rest are more docile than the one your friend fancies."

Silenus made a low braying sound, and his donkey responded, until it appeared they were having a conversation.

"I thought you were done with having wives," Dionysus said, lifting Ariadne onto her donkey.

"I made no such promises, Little Liber," Silenus said, awkwardly scrambling up the donkey's side.

Dionysus let out a hearty laugh as Thalia, Manko, Talos and their guides mounted their donkeys and began their journey up to the crest of the volcano.

With each step up the steep ascent, the view became more stunning. The yellowed rock created a brilliant orange mixed with gold, as if amber and honey had been frozen in time from previous eruptions.

The pounding of hammers echoed above them. A deep, horrible stench engulfed them as they made their way up. Ariadne reached into her satchel for her mint leaves.

"This is the scent of eggs I caught in the harbor," Thalia said, coming up alongside her.

Plumes of gray smoke wafted out of crevices, their scent foul and strong.

"Do we approach the Underworld, Lord Dionysus?" Talos called out. His duty to protect Ariadne outweighed his normal deference. He and Manko flanked her and Thalia closely now. She sensed no fear but appreciated their protection, especially since all she could do was savor the scent of the mint and try to push the nausea away.

"I don't believe so, Talos, but if we were, you need not fear it."

"We're going to Lord Hephaestus's workshop," Milos called back. "He doesn't allow just anyone up here. Only friends. He has spoken highly of you, Lord."

"He has tormented all of us with his tales of your new drink, Lord," another guide said.

"Look," Thalia said, pointing ahead to an opening in the side of the mountain where a portion had been dug out. Bronze statues of Hephaestus stood near the mouth of the workshop, and the hammers beat out a song of creation. On a nearby table, bronze swords and shields lay in the bright sun.

Milos let out a low, long, coded whistle, and the bronze giant statues moved away from the cave opening.

The guides halted the donkeys, dismounted, and led them to a nearby tree where they tied them up in the shade.

"Are you well, wife?" Dionysus asked, lifting her down. Touching him brought comfort.

"It is the babes," she said. "They do not like this smell."

He held her in his arms longer than need be. Seeing the flecks of green in his eyes reflecting her own light gave her a moment of peace. The smell was no longer so strong.

A clanking sound pulled their attention away. Dionysus put Ariadne down. Thalia had leapt off her donkey as soon as she could and stood nearby.

The hammers ceased, and a flash of gold rippled inside the cave. Blinking into the light of day, Hephaestus, seated in a chair held by four golden women, came to greet them. The God of the Forge had a blunt face covered with a wild black beard and equally wild, wavy hair. His broad chest swelled with muscles. His strong forearms and hands were black with soot, as was his red tunic and thick leather apron.

"Twice Born!" Hephaestus bellowed when he spotted Dionysus.

"Twice Fallen!" Dionysus shouted, running toward his friend. "You appear much taller than the last time we met."

"Indeed! I have grown four golden women bearers and a golden chair instead of regular feet." Hephaestus's laughter reminded Ariadne of a rock crumbling. "I am honored to host you."

"And we are honored to be here. Allow me to present my lovely wife, Ariadne, Mistress of the Labyrinth, her companion Thalia, and my foster father..." He glanced around, not seeing Silenus. "My foster father is here somewhere."

"An honor to meet the wife of Dionysus," Hephaestus said, though his eyes lingered too long on Thalia.

Ariadne marveled at the golden women who held up Hephaestus's golden chair. She had never imagined such a thing. Statues come to life, their eyes were made of marble with pupil insets as if they could actually see. They strode together in unison when Hephaestus commanded it, though how he controlled them, she could not tell.

"Very impressive. The statues at the harbor were incredible, but this is even more original. And such craftsmanship," Dionysus said.

"The automatons are some of my finest work. I cannot wait to show you more, Twice Born. In fact, I am working on one of my most exciting pieces just now. Come, come see." His golden women turned around with perfect symmetry and began to move toward the opening of the workshop.

"Bring your friends," Hephaestus shouted over a broad shoulder.

Dionysus waited for Ariadne and Thalia before stepping forward. The heat emanating from the workshop was warm and inviting, not the kind of heat Ariadne had expected from a volcano.

"He must be using a spell of protection. He has always had a way with fire. Even under the sea, he could make gasses and flames shoot out. Quite a good trick," Dionysus said.

Inside the workshop, bronze torches gleamed. A small army of blacksmiths stood by the forge, pumping the bellows, smelting, and hammering. The cords on their forearms stood out as they hammered and poured. Ariadne noticed their blackened leather aprons before realizing that they all appeared to have only one eye.

"At long last, a fellow god has come to visit," Hephaestus said, his voice bellowing over the hammers. Those who could, stopped their work and stared. These men exuded such strength and force, as if their one purpose was to transform metals from the earth into bronze, silver, and gold, to make what appeared to be mere rocks into statues, weapons, and furniture. Ariadne absorbed their stares, undaunted by their power. Thalia, too, stared back, standing casually, as she often did, but Ariadne knew she could pounce at the slightest provocation. How small and naked Talos and Manko appeared in this darkened place.

"Polydorus," Hephaestus called. A giant man with red hair came, wiping his hands on his leather apron. In the flashing light of the torch, Ariadne made out a tan colored patch over his left eye.

"Offer our guests some refreshments: water, beer, and some bread and cheese. My apologies, ladies, for not having comfortable couches to lounge on, but we do have some nice chairs." He pulled a gigantic, filthy cloth off several lumpy objects, exposing a small seating area.

The first golden chair had the paws of a lion for feet. The armrests had lions' faces, and the top headrest featured a lion's mouth wide with a roar. Dionysus was about to sit in it when Hephaestus called, "Oh, not that one! That one bites. Lady Ariadne, please sit here." He gestured instead to a wooden chair with shining gold faces on the arms and headpiece. When Ariadne sat, the golden faces began to sing. Ariadne's heart lightened, and her nausea disappeared completely as they all paused to listen to the joyous song.

"How lovely, Lord Hephaestus," Ariadne said as Polydorus

brought her some water in a golden cup. She held the cup in her hands, marveling at scenes of the very workshop she was sitting in. The details of the forge and the one-eyed men working took her into another world. She drank a sip of the clear water, refreshed.

Thalia sat upon a chair that had the paws of a lion, but no snarling face. The chair playfully cavorted around the area, not going too far in any one direction. Thalia let out a series of giggles, the like of which Ariadne hadn't heard in years.

"Ah, and you, Twice Born, would you be so kind as to try my newest chair—a throne I have made for someone special." He lifted a heavy cloth off a covered object. Gold so bright it rivaled fire glowed from underneath. The throne was a magnificent reproduction of a peacock. A lifelike peacock face hovered over the backrest rendered in gold. Brilliant onyx stones made the peacock's eyes appear alive. The seat was pure gold, and behind the back of the chair, a tail of silver, gold, bronze, and copper spread out. Between the delicately crafted web of metal feathers, emeralds, lapis lazuli, and turquoise jewels sparkled with all the grandeur of a real peacock.

"Oh, Twice Fallen, you have outdone yourself. This is exquisite." Dionysus strode around the throne, delighting in the fine filigreed work on the back. The feet appeared to be real replicas of birds' feet, and Ariadne wondered if this chair could walk, too.

"Will you sit?" Hephaestus asked.

"I hesitate to do so, old friend, for I think I know your mind."

Hephaestus hooted. "Ah, you know me well, Twice Born. I promise not to keep you."

"I will see this magic, and I will be pleased with your work, but perhaps my wife's bodyguard Talos would be more suited for the role."

"Talos." He eyed the slim Minoan who stood alert, his hand near his dagger.

"A mortal? No. I'm afraid it might kill him. I need to try it on a god."

"Give me your promise then," Dionysus said, taking Hephaestus's large hand in his own. Hephaestus's blackened hand was so much larger than Dionysus's. Soot was embedded in his palm, and Ariadne could hardly distinguish his blackened nails from his fingers. The Smith God grinned, his uneven teeth shining through the darkness of his wild beard.

"I swear on the River Styx, and more importantly on my forge, that I will let you go when you ask. And further, Twice Born, I welcome you and your people to Lemnos. I invite you to make your homes here and raise your children. Though we may not be related by blood, you are the closest thing I have to a brother." Flames glowed in Hephaestus's eyes as he spoke, and the green fire in Dionysus's eyes kindled in return.

"Wife, Thalia." He glanced about for Silenus, who was not there. "You heard my brother-god's pledge. Make sure he keeps it."

"Twice Born, I will be careful not to anger your wife or her friend, for they both have formidable powers just under their skin." He looked into Ariadne's eyes. The familiar sensation of her new power kindled within, and she knew her own eyes were glowing with gold.

Hephaestus's ability to control the volcano, to wield the hammer, to create these glorious works from gold, bronze, and silver was formidable, yet Ariadne sensed nothing but love for Dionysus from the Smith God.

Dionysus went around to the golden peacock throne and inspected it from the front. He glanced at Hephaestus and sat.

"It does need a cushion," he said, easing into it. "How do I look? Regal? Perhaps like the Queen of Heaven?"

Hephaestus grinned at him, and suddenly golden threads sprang from the throne, tying Dionysus fast. Talos and Manko lurched to his side but couldn't do anything to free him.

"So tight," Dionysus said. "Quite a trap."

"Please, Twice Born, try your best to escape."

Dionysus glanced seductively at Ariadne and then Hephaestus, wiggling in his seat. The gold filigree held fast. He could not rise.

"Can you transform?" Hephaestus asked, not hiding the excitement in his voice.

Dionysus closed his eyes a moment and summoned an inner strength. Ariadne had seen him do this countless times. It was the same for Thalia now. She need only imagine her leopard self to become a leopard. But Dionysus remained in his mortal form. His fist clenched against the armrest, and the peacock's tail began to quiver. A vein pulsated on his forehead, and golden sweat glittered on his brow.

"What magic is this, Hephaestus?"

"Quite good, isn't it? I had to go to a sea-witch for it. It cost me a bit of gold, and several wild nights, but it was well worth it. Is that all you have, Twice Born?"

"Try vines, Master," Thalia said. The ragged edge in her voice suggested she was ready to transform herself and bedevil the Smith God if he did not keep his promise.

Dionysus closed his eyes to summon his vines. As it often did lately, Ariadne's mood changed. She had trusted Hephaestus a moment before, but now she saw him as another vengeful god, ready to ruin her happiness. It took all her restraint not to jump up and pummel him like a mad woman.

Having Dionysus bound infuriated her. He had told her how easy everything had been for him, how quickly he could run, how swiftly he could swim, how easily lovers came to him—until he met her. But seeing him trapped, a god diminished, hurt her in a way she could not name. How cruel this game seemed. She placed a hand over her belly. What kind of monster was she to bring children into this world where gods jested with each other in such a way? Where kings like her father ruled over mortals and decided their fates, and goddesses grew fickle and despised their priestesses.

Just as she was about to rise from her chair, vines sprang from the earth, sliding between the filaments that restrained Dionysus. The web loosened ever so slightly, and Dionysus began to slide up, out of the throne.

Hephaestus hooted with surprise. The vines pulled the filament. Just as Dionysus was about to escape, the golden peacock head let out a plaintive scream of alarm. Dionysus was so startled, he fell back into the chair. Hephaestus and Polydorus dissolved into laughter. Ariadne's fury rose until Dionysus himself began laughing, too, and then, her concern changed. She heard the peacock alarm again in her mind, saw his shocked face, and laughed with him.

"Well done, Hephaestus," Dionysus said, reddish-purple tears leaking from his eyes as he continued laughing. "Ariadne, Thalia, did you see?" He imitated the sound of the peacock. Once, twice. The third time, Hephaestus joined in, and then Silenus staggered into the workshop, making the cry of the peacock himself. He appeared oddly transformed and unstable. When he walked toward them, Ariadne saw that he had ass's ears.

"Oh-ho, is this? Can this be..." Hephaestus said.

"Allow me to introduce my foster father Silenus. Silenus, this is the twice-fallen smith god, Hephaestus."

"An honor, sir," Hephaestus said to the old satyr. "I have heard many good things about you."

"And I you," Silenus said. "Thank you for your kind welcome to your island. May I inquire why the Lord of the Vine is wrapped fast in that peacock contraption?"

"Just a favor," Dionysus responded. "Though my friend is about to cause some serious trouble, I offered to help. Let me try once more." He closed his eyes to summon the vines. More rose up from the earth, joining the ones entwined with the golden filament. The vines pulled the golden binding away from his body, loosening the ties on his legs and arms so he was able to wiggle out, up, and stand on the seat. The peacock face screamed, but, expecting it, he didn't flinch as he leapt off the golden throne and onto the ground.

Hephaestus guffawed and clapped his large hands while Polydorus appeared dismayed. Ariadne and Thalia whooped in joy.

"Well done, Twice Born! I had thought my gift ready to send, but it appears I still have more work to do. But that is for later. For now, you and your people are here, and there is much to celebrate!"

Dionysus grinned but appeared drained from his escape. Ariadne wanted to offer him her chair, but he must appear strong in front of the others.

"Here, Twice Born, sit here." Hephaestus gestured next to him, to a simple wooden chair with a well-worn cushion.

"Does it bite?" Dionysus asked.

"Not that one. It neither bites, not runs, nor sings."

Dionysus sat down slowly, accepting the cup of mead that Polydorus offered. Two of Hephaestus's blacksmiths carefully covered the golden throne with the heavy fabric. The small seating area grew dim without its light.

"Now, let's get you settled. How many of you are there?"

"About sixty. I tried to keep it small."

"I would welcome more if you need it. I know just the place for you to make your new home. Some of the golden domes above are empty, and they are the perfect place for a god and goddess to start a family." Hephaestus's eyes lit on Ariadne, and she felt herself blush, as if he could see her clearly—not this woman who covered herself, but the High Priestess of Crete who she had been. "We have a fine midwife here. She delivered three of my own children, though perhaps you brought your own. We also have caves sacred to the goddess of childbirth. The hospitality of Lemnos is the finest, as you will soon discover."

"Thank you, Twice Fallen," Dionysus said, rising to clasp his hand.

"Not at all, Twice Born. Welcome to your new home."

21

DIONYSUS AND THE PEACOCK THRONE

Two years later

Lemnos was the glorious land Dionysus had hoped it would be. Hephaestus had given them the most splendid palace to live in. The Smith God called it a house, a temple for the new gods. Dionysus felt he was in Olympus—this was as close as he wanted to be to heaven. Here on earth, with Ariadne by his side, he enjoyed every day.

Ariadne had borne him twins. Staphylus and Oenopion happily toddled about, causing mischief. Dionysus loved playing with them, teaching them new words, and watching their dark eyes sparkle with understanding.

Instead of leaving the boys with their nurse, Dionysus took the twins with him to the vineyards. The volcanic soil created magnificent wines. Silenus said his growing divinity made the vines ripen more quickly than they would for mortals. Even though the vines were young, the wines were already better than he had imagined.

Even if they couldn't understand, Dionysus told his sons everything about viniculture. They played in the soil and watched the vine tendrils shoot up, yearning for the sun. They helped water, though they often spilled. They witnessed the dormant vines and the pruning.

"The vines appear dead, but deep beneath the soil, they are getting the food they need to grow strong, so when they come back to life, they will be full of flavor," Dionysus explained. Staphylus was playing with a worm, but Oenopion paid attention to his father's words.

"Grow," Oenopion said to the soil. "Like mama's belly."

Dionysus laughed and picked up Oenopion. "Yes, she's growing a baby. The vines grow into grapes that we turn into wine, just like you'll grow into a man." *And I've grown into a father.* He tickled Oenopion. His son's giggle made his heart soar. What a fool Zeus was to think pleasure was only in having a woman and leaving her alone with child.

Before meeting Ariadne, Dionysus himself had been an uncaring fool. He had never given a thought to the countless bastards he had likely gotten on mortal women. He had not been a father to those children, but he would be a father to Staphylus and Oenopion, and to every child he sired after. His own father was King of the Gods, but he had not taught him how to be a father.

"Phaestus," Oenopion said, pointing.

Hephaestus rarely came out to the vineyards, but he came now, riding a donkey.

"Didn't want to get your throne dirty?" Dionysus said, grinning at his friend.

"The golden throne was not made for trodding through soil, Twice Born. I hope you have plenty of that delicious wine. Tonight we celebrate."

"Hephaestus, you didn't."

"I did. I've sent my mother her gift. I was remiss in thanking her for the life she gave me. What a coup for her! She gave birth to me without the help of Zeus or any god, yet being imperfect, she tossed me from heaven."

"Mothers are not perfect," Dionysus said, putting Oenopion

down. "Why bother with those Olympians, though? You are far more capable than they." Dionysus had meant to discourage Hephaestus from sending Hera her gift, but it had slipped his mind. Now it was too late.

"I am, and it is time they know it. They will beg for me, and I will not come—I the twice-fallen, twice thrown from Olympus. They will not forget me again." Hephaestus grinned. The fire in his eyes lit, but then, he caught Dionysus's furrowed brow. He urged the donkey a step closer, careful of the rows of dormant vines.

"You do not care for this mischief?"

"You are like my brother, so I must tell you my concern. I came to Lemnos for your kind hospitality, but I brought my wife to conceal her and give her shelter in a safe place, away from the Olympians—for there are those who wish to harm her in order to harm me."

Hephaestus glanced at Staphylus, his hands and mouth covered in dirt, and at Oenopion scrutinizing the dry vines.

"I have my own sons here on Lemnos. We are well protected, even from the gods."

"You sent the gift already?"

"Yes, on flying golden horses. It will be delivered before sunset. It clearly says it is a gift to the Queen of Heaven. How envious the other gods will be! They will all want their own. They will be overcome with jealousy, and Hera, my beautiful mother, will lord it over them. Proud as a peacock herself, she will strut about, fuss about where it should be placed. In the great hall, of course, next to Zeus's throne. Should she replace her old throne, the one that served her all these years? But yes, yes of course. This new throne, the perfect replication of a peacock, must take center stage. She will have them move her old throne, push Zeus's throne off to the side a bit.

"Aphrodite and Athena will be jealous. Hermes will grin wryly. He knows Hera has enemies, as all gods do. He alone will wonder who sent such a glorious gift. Only the God of the Ways will silently observe the unforgivable gloating, the envious stares. Zeus will suppress his resentment that such a fine throne was not sent to him. He will guess that perhaps I made it; he will glance at Athena, the god he made without Hera, the inspiration for her to make me. But he will not think to warn her.

"It will be time for either a celebratory meal or a meeting when the other gods assemble. If there is no reason to feast, if the mortals below have not sacrificed enough, then Artemis or Apollo will shoot some of their arrows across the seas so that some poor chump or a once rich village will suffer, and in their suffering, they will offer a sacrifice, and then the gods will feast on smoke and ambrosia.

"And that is when Hera, Queen of Heaven, will sit in the glorious golden throne I spent years perfecting for her."

Dionysus could picture it all as Hephaestus described. He tried to suppress his own resentment. He had never been to Olympus, never even met his father, the King of the Gods. Of all the Olympians, he had only met Hermes and Artemis. One was a friend, and the other his enemy.

He had no wish to become an Olympian himself. Why even have such a thought? None of Zeus's bastards by mortals could even enter the great kingdom in the skies. And why would he want to live among them when they were petty and cruel? Still, the scenes Hephaestus had described stirred a longing in him to be among the other gods—to be there to catch Hermes's eye, to watch Aphrodite's longing and observe Athena's vexation. He pushed these thoughts aside and picked up Staphylus, who was about to eat a worm.

"And what will happen then, Twice Fallen?"

Hephaestus hooted. "You know what will happen then! She will be held fast, shackled in a way she never imagined, chained to her lovely throne, a queen for all time! She who created me on her own and then decided I wasn't complete enough. She who shackled me to this life and tossed me from on high, but being born an undying god, I am bound to live forever while she barely spares me a thought." Darkness descended over Hephaestus's broad face. A line as deep as a crack in the earth furrowed his brow. "And when I returned to the sky and defended her in a fight with Zeus, he flung me down again. Did my loving mother come to find me? Did she send Iris the Rainbow Messenger or Hermes to thank me for intervening on her behalf or check on my injuries? No. She's probably forgotten about me completely. Once, she had a son on her own to show her husband she, too, could conceive without his help. What need does she have for me now?" Hephaestus's voice had grown bitter, and a spark flashed in his eye. Dionysus wondered whether this was what his friend had for tears. He brushed the dirt from Staphylus's mouth and shifted him to his left side to clasp Hephaestus's soot-blackened hand.

"I understand, my brother. I worry for my wife and sons, but I understand why you had to do this. Let her suffer a bit of the pain she has given you. You know Hera is no friend to me. She's attempted to kill me twice. You have accomplished a great deed that you have spent countless days on. Tonight we will celebrate and honor your vengeance." Perhaps with time, Dionysus could persuade him to release Hera from her throne, but it would not be today. Hephaestus grinned, and the darkness left his face. "Thank you, my friend. I know of all the gods, you understand my pain and my fury."

Dionysus felt a spark in his own eye. He had always tried to quash this pain, this longing to be accepted by the other Olympians. It could not be more clear that Hephaestus was right: they were gods who lived among mortals and were happy among mortals. Artemis, too, was like this—away from Olympus most of the time. He had really believed she would understand him.

"Tonight we will raise a glass to each other—two gods on an island who are like brothers. We will laugh below as we delight in the chaos you have caused above. But it will happen a lot quicker if you'll help me with these boys." He handed Staphylus to the God of the Forge. "Will you take him back to his nurse? I'll get Oenopion."

Hephaestus took the dirty toddler on his lap, letting him pretend to hold the reins. "You're a good father, Twice Born, and a good friend."

They raised many glasses that night, to Hephaestus, to Dionysus, and to Asterion.

"I wish I could have met the famous Minotaur of Crete. He would have been welcomed here," Hephaestus said, reclining on his couch outside Dionysus's temple.

"His fate was to die, brother, unlike ours. But you would have liked him, of that I'm sure."

"And he would have liked you," Ariadne said to Hephaestus.

How radiant she appeared in the torch light, wearing one of the many garments Dionysus had gotten her in India, this one a ruby red skirt embroidered with golden birds and a loose saffron chemise.

"With your permission, Lord Hephaestus, I would like to build a monument to Asterion here. A labyrinth, a maze for worshippers to walk to find themselves. We could make it here, near Dionysus's temple," Ariadne said.

"Brilliant! I heartily approve." Hephaestus raised his glass. "To Asterion, the Cretan priest-king who did not forget his hatred." Sparks lit his eyes, and Dionysus could feel Hephaestus's rage at Hera.

"My brother did live entrapped in his hatred, but I do not think it served him well," Ariadne said softly. Though incredibly drunk, Hephaestus listened. "He missed out on much, not just the light above ground, but on love, on a child. He could have lived to rule Crete, but he chose to become consumed. Lord of the Forge, you know how one object can change into another. The hottest fire can melt the strongest sword and turn it into a beautiful statue. I loved my brother, but I did not love his choices."

"You speak wise words, Ariadne, but I cannot hear them now. Tonight I celebrate my vengeance. I stoke my anger."

"Very well, Lord." Ariadne stood, her shape outlined by the firelight. "Then allow me to get you another drink."

They began work on Asterion's labyrinth the next day. Hephaestus and Ariadne drew designs in the dirt until they reached an agreement. Once the workers recovered from the revelry, they began clearing the land and moving the stones.

They had accomplished much in the last three months, especially since it was the cold season. Ariadne spent her days with her women, establishing her own temple and coming to the worksite to talk to the foreman. Dionysus liked to meet her at mid-day and watch the meander path of the labyrinth grow from an idea to a physical presence. And he loved watching Ariadne tell the burly foreman what was to be done, to watch how these mortal men responded to his wife. They knew she was a goddess.

It had rained the day before, and now soft, puffy clouds graced the bright blue sky. Dionysus noticed a speck, a familiar fluttering. Soon the mortal men working on the labyrinth shouted and pointed up.

"Ariadne," Dionysus called, walking toward her. He was propelled by a desire to protect her, but also to show her off. When he reached her, he instinctively placed his hand on her belly. It would only be a few more months.

The speck in the sky descended toward them. A man—a god, wearing a winged helmet and winged sandals that crisscrossed up his strong calves. In his left hand, he held a caduceus, a short staff with two snakes intertwined.

"Hermes," Dionysus said, flooded with joy at seeing his first friend.

The silver-eyed, bronze-skinned god fluttered above, a sardonic grin on his upturned lips.

"Ah, Twice Born, I came to quell trouble. I am not surprised to find you at the center of it," Hermes said as he descended.

"For once, this mischief was not my making. It is so good to see you, my brother." As soon as Hermes's winged sandals touched the ground, Dionysus embraced him. Hermes's scent of clouds with a bit of sandalwood sparked so many memories of centuries before that tears came to Dionysus's eyes.

"How has it been so long?" Dionysus asked, wiping the wine-tears from his cheeks.

"I've watched over you, Twice Born. You might not have seen me, but I did not forget you. I have seen how you have grown into a god and a husband." He bowed to Ariadne.

"Lady, it is an honor. You are the most splendid consort to my beloved little brother. And..." Hermes trailed off, distracted by the sight of Thalia walking up to the worksite.

"Exquisite," he whispered. "Dionysus, you've outdone yourself. A woman who is a leopard."

Thalia came toward them, the leopard in her stride and in her eyes as always.

"I take little credit. Thalia was a leopard all along. I only released her from her human form. Thalia, this is Hermes, the God of the Ways."

"Well met, Lord," Thalia said, unbothered by his silver eyes boring into her.

Hermes blinked, took his gaze from Thalia, and said, "I come as the Messenger of the Gods today. Our father great Zeus has demanded I bring Hephaestus to Olympus to unchain his mother." A hint of laughter marred the last word.

"Of course," Dionysus said. "I tried to prevent him from sending his gift, but he was obdurate. I will take you to his forge, though I doubt he will change his mind."

"If anyone can persuade him, you can," Ariadne said. "It is only a matter of getting him in the right mindset."

"As always, my wife gives good counsel." Dionysus adjusted his myrtle crown, which had slid back when he gazed up. He led Hermes away from the building site and toward Hephaestus's workshop.

"It is so good to see you, little brother," Hermes said.

"It has been too long. Silenus is here... somewhere. He met me in Crete, but often goes off—I half think he has a donkey as a wife and a foal of his own."

Hermes laughed heartily. "I half understand his desire. Sometimes it is easier to live as an animal than a man. Oi, what is that smell? Is there an entrance here to Hades I don't know about?"

"Hephaestus says it's called sulfur. I'm curious to see whether I can use it with wine. It is useful in many ways once you get past the smell."

"Little brother," Hermes said abruptly, "this situation with Hera and Hephaestus, although comical, is quite serious. I would like you to think of yourself in all of this."

Dionysus went cold, silently cursing Hephaestus for endangering Ariadne and their sons.

"You can benefit from this. The Olympians are offering a reward for whomever can free Hera—or get Hephaestus to free Hera. The prize is Aphrodite's hand in marriage." Hermes paused and took in the view of Lemnos and the deep blue sea. "This is a charming isle. I'm sorry to pull you away from it. But I know what you've always longed for, and you could do worse than being married to the goddess of love and beauty."

The idea was tempting, but only for a moment.

"Who would not want Aphrodite for a wife?" Hermes asked.

"Any god with sense. I have a wife. She may not be recognized widely as a goddess, but she is one to me."

"Yes, I can feel your happiness. She has helped change you. Yet you are still not recognized as the god you are."

"Perhaps not by the Olympians, but every mortal who tastes wine knows I am divine. And every mortal who does not recognize me knows my vengeance."

"The Olympians should know it, too. I will tell them you will not help unless they give you and Hephaestus what you both want —a throne on high."

Dionysus gazed down to the harbor and the dark blue sea. He and Hermes had just passed the gold-domed temples he and

Ariadne called home. These mortals did not question his godhood. True, others across the sea might mock him. He would return to battle after Ariadne had their next child. Would being acknowledged by Olympus—the thing he had longed for since birth—really matter now?

He clasped Hermes's hand. "It is kind of you to think of me this way, brother. Let us see what Hephaestus has to say first."

They turned away from the view of the sea and walked toward the cave. The beat of hammers echoed toward them, and a bronze automaton stood at the entrance. Twice as large as a mortal man, he glittered in the sun and came menacingly toward them.

"Calm, Talos. We come in peace," Dionysus said. The automaton stopped, turned, and went back to the entrance of the cave. "Hephaestus built him in the likeness of Ariadne's body-guard—the resemblance is impeccable."

Once recovered, Hermes grinned. "A man made of bronze. Is there nothing Hephaestus can't do? Well..." He glanced up toward the sky. "Let's hope there isn't."

Inside the cave, torches burned bright. The hammering of anvils reminded Dionysus of a dance. How he would prefer dancing and revelry to this fight among the gods. Hermes's very skin shone in the dark. His eyes glittered silver as he took in Hephaestus's workshop. It had changed much in the last three years as Hephaestus's interest moved from thrones to chariots.

"Oh ho! I was wondering when they'd send you!" Hephaestus's bellow rose above the blows of the hammers. Sweat glistened down the Smith God's broad chest as he swung one final blow and limped out from behind his forge. "The answer is no, God of Ways, but go ahead and beg me to come to Olympus. I want to hear it."

"Your skill is beyond compare, Hephaestus. The gods on high would all be honored if you would come join them."

"Will she beg? Will he apologize? That is all I want to know." Hephaestus rubbed the sweat from his eye. He brushed his wild hair off his face, leaving a streak of soot on his forehead.

"Your goddess mother is most eager to see you. She is terribly sorry for past misunderstandings. The King of the Gods, Zeus himself, begs you to return to Olympus and free his wife."

Hephaestus laughed, but there was no humor in it. "Ah, I see your tongue is made of silver and matches your eyes. Well said, but my answer is still no. Let her suffer as I suffered. She wanted a golden throne instead of a deformed son, and now she has it."

"She does. Are you not the slightest bit curious to see how she struggles in your bonds?" Hermes asked.

"I can picture it perfectly in my mind. I need not ever return to on high—I've been thrown off twice."

"You are right, Twice Fallen," Dionysus said. "Leave him be, Hermes. He has made his decision, and we must respect it." Before Hermes could protest, Dionysus addressed Hephaestus. "Would you mind if Hermes stays the night? He was my first friend, and I have not seen him in centuries."

Hephaestus glared at Hermes, scrutinizing his perfect feet, his winged sandals and helmet.

"When I return to Olympus without you, I will tell them all how impressive your island is. I've never seen such buildings as what I saw when I flew down. I've never seen such crafts as the ones you have here. They will lament your absence even more."

"Fine," Hephaestus said. "But only for tonight."

The party would begin at sunset. There had been many nights of celebration of the new god and his goddess, though not for the last two moons. The labyrinth and children had taken up so much of their time, and in the winter chill, people had wanted to stay inside. Dionysus stood outside his temple, watching his supplicants light the torches. They had become experts on delighting him with their worship. Acoetes and some other sailors were hauling giant amphoras of wine while the women roasted the fish and prepared the feast.

Tonight the weather had warmed up. Soon shipping season

would begin, and those who wanted could journey across the sea. Dionysus felt the tug of adventure on the winds. But he had no desire to jump aboard a boat. He had found his home. Yet Hermes's promises taunted him. Did he want a throne on Olympus? From what he understood, the other gods didn't live there all the time. It was more a symbol and an honor. To think he, a bastard son of Zeus and a long dead mortal, could even entertain such a thought.

"Master," Thalia said, surprising him. She had gotten so quiet upon her approach. She was the only one he didn't see coming—at least, that was what he hoped.

She wore a red dress, dyed by the Lemnian clay—a special color between brown and ocher. Her freshly washed hair hung in well-defined curls, though some of her spots darkened the blonde hair.

"You look lovely, Thalia." He had no doubt Hermes's presence had stirred this within her.

"I only want to look my best for one of your parties, Master," Thalia replied. When her eyes met his, they shared an image of her in her leopard form, gnawing the forearm of an enemy solider. They both burst into laughter. How many times had he seen her lips smeared with blood or wine? He hadn't seen her this clean since he had first met her on Crete, when she had not yet become a leopard.

"Husband." Ariadne came toward him wearing an indigo gown patterned with flowers and birds and embroidered with silver thread that he had brought her from India. Though she wore less gold than when they had first met, her radiance shone twice as bright. Talos and Manko stood behind her. They had relaxed their stance, though they remained forever alert. That was one reason Hephaestus was inspired to create his own Talos like Ariadne's protector. Ever vigilant, Hephaestus called him, a faithful guard.

"What is your plan?" she asked softly.

"I'm not sure yet, but I will attempt to get Hephaestus to free Hera."

"You will go to Olympus," she said. Concern clouded her eyes.

"Do you have a premonition about this?"

"No." She placed a hand protectively on her belly. "I know it is important to you. I want you to be acknowledged as the god you are. This appears to be the time. Just return in time for this child to be born, if you can."

"I will." He put his hand on top of hers. Just then the baby kicked. He put both hands on the side of her belly, feeling the movement.

"She's strong," he said.

"He is," Ariadne replied. She was sure the goddess would never allow her to have a daughter.

Knowing how much she wanted one, he hoped she was wrong.

"Little Liber!" Silenus called, staggering toward him. Hermes followed; the bemused grin on his lips broadened when he saw Thalia.

"Did you reminisce with Hermes, then?" Dionysus asked.

"It's been centuries. So grand to see him again!"

Upon hearing his voice, satyrs from the temple came out to welcome Silenus. He capered off with them to help prepare for the celebrations.

The drums started when the sun set, and the dancing began immediately. The priest of Hephaestus had already slit the throat of a bull in honor of all three gods on the island, and the scent of roasted meat mixed with the wine being freely poured and the perfumed bodies dancing.

Hermes paid little mind to the maenads and satyrs dancing in honor of Dionysus. Instead, he attended to Thalia, peppering her with questions about being a leopard. Ariadne reclined on one of the couches Hephaestus had donated. He had quite a few that had not worked out. This one did not walk properly, but only crawled slowly when activated. Dionysus had furnished them with faded purple pillows and checked she was comfortable before going to find Hephaestus. He was still in his workshop, though most of his blacksmiths had gone home.

"Twice Fallen, come join the revelry. I have a special wine I am eager to share."

"Fine, but I will not go free Hera."

"I am not asking you to do that, simply to come with me and have a pleasant evening. Some of my maenads are said to be almost as beautiful as Aphrodite herself. I think a woman's touch is just what you need, Twice Fallen."

Hephaestus put down his hammer, wiped his hands on his leather apron, and grabbed a towel he kept nearby. He wiped the glistening sweat from his broad chest and thick neck.

"It is always hard to refuse an invitation from you, Twice Born."

By the time they returned to the temple, the orgy had already begun. Hermes and Thalia were nowhere to be seen. Ariadne lay on the couch, half-drowsing, as a girl from Lesbos massaged her feet.

Hephaestus grinned from atop his golden throne carried by his golden women as he allowed a topless redhead to fill his golden cup. He had changed out of his work clothes and washed a bit, though soot still blackened his fingernails, palms, and fore-arms. He took a long swallow.

"Ah, this is a fine brew! Worthy of the gods themselves!" he bellowed and drank it all down.

"More, Lord?" the redhead asked. She stared at Hephaestus's muscular chest. *God-struck*, Dionysus thought, pleased that his friend was getting what he needed.

"Yes," Hephaestus said, taking her hand and pulling her up into his throne. "So much more."

The moon was high in the sky when Hermes and Thalia returned to the temple. Thalia's dress was rumpled, and her hair had become wild and full of pine needles. Hermes appeared a bit out of sorts without his winged helmet or caduceus.

"Did you lose your snakes, brother?" Dionysus asked.

Startled, Hermes clenched his fist and glanced back the way they had come.

"I'll find them," Thalia said. She pulled off her dress, handed it to Hermes, and transformed into a leopard.

"How I have missed you, brother," Hermes said, taking another drink of wine. He slid his arm around Dionysus's waist and whispered, "Where is Hephaestus? Can you get him to come?"

Dionysus did not answer, but he staggered with Hermes to a dying fire where Hephaestus, out of his golden throne, lay with two wild women asleep on his chest.

Hephaestus cocked an eye open. "A nice party, Twice Born."

"I see you have enjoyed yourself. But are you satisfied?"

Hephaestus eased the sleeping women off his chest, lowering them to the bed of moss below. "I'm never satisfied," the Smith God said, rising unsteadily.

"Do you think the great Aphrodite herself would satisfy you?" Dionysus asked.

Hephaestus lurched into his golden throne and fell into the seat. "I don't know, but I'd love to find out."

"She is a sight to behold," Hermes said. "The most beautiful of all the Olympian goddesses..."

"You could have her for your own, Twice Fallen."

Hephaestus hooted at this. "The most stunning of the gods with the most hideous! How the gods would laugh at that!"

"You would be the one laughing at them," Dionysus said. "You would be showing how powerful and worthy you are. They will give you Aphrodite's hand in marriage if you free your mother."

A hint of bitterness left Hephaestus's face.

"They will accept you as one of their own," Hermes said. "If you come with us, I will bargain for you. If you release your mother, they will give you and Dionysus a throne. And they will give you Aphrodite as a wife."

Sparks danced in Hephaestus's eyes. Dionysus had no idea if the Smith God would erupt in anger or laughter. Hermes stiffened, preparing for anger, but then Hephaestus slowly moved his head in agreement. "I can't promise to free her, but I would like to see how my mother struggles in her bonds, and perhaps I'd be willing to hear what the gods of Olympus have to offer."

Hermes grinned and began to summon magical glowing mist to help transport them. Naked, Thalia padded over with Hermes's caduceus in her hand, his winged helmet askew on her head. The snakes on the caduceus were not holding onto the stick tightly, but they appeared still functional.

"What a vision," Hermes said, exchanging his helmet and caduceus for Thalia's dress.

"Are you leaving, Lord?" Thalia asked, eyeing the mist slowly cocooning them.

"Yes, I must return to Olympus. Lord Hephaestus has agreed to journey there and see how he feels once we arrive."

"You'll look after my household, Thalia?" Dionysus asked.

"Always, Master. I will tell her that you left." She held her dress in her hands, but did not put it on, letting them watch her as they drifted up off of Lemnos and toward the sky.

Olympus appeared far less exciting than Dionysus had imagined. Hovering above the clouds, floating in Hermes's magical orb had been more thrilling than setting foot on the highest mountain. A distinct lugubriousness hung in the air like a heavy raincloud. He had expected bright blue skies and golden sunshine, but the heights were shrouded in shades of gray and white.

The marble buildings that dotted the land appeared drab and blocky compared to Hephaestus's delightful feats of architecture. The houses he saw—he suspected they were meant to be palaces —didn't even have golden caped roofs.

A disappointment—like so many other realizations. The thing he had always wanted was just a bleak home for unhappy gods. Crete, Thebes, Lemnos, the battles he had fought in India brought more delight than this place.

Still, he could sense more power than he had ever encountered. And his father was here. A familiar dread shot through him. Was he worthy? Why had Zeus never come to meet him before? What would it be like to meet the god who had killed his mother? The father who had taken what was left of baby Dionysus and kept him in his thigh, acting as mother and father both, then abandoning him. He understood Hephaestus's anger and applauded his cleverness. But if Hephaestus did not free Hera, the gods would not stop coming to Lemnos, and Dionysus could not have that.

Hermes led them toward the grandest marble building. Dionysus felt the fear and rage before he saw Ares stride toward them. The God of War wore the short tunic of a solider. His muscular thighs bulged, and his calves were covered in greaves molded to fit his form. His breastplate shone, and he held his helm in the crook of his arm.

"Brother Hephaestus, so good of you to come," Ares barked. "Can I convince you to free Mother?"

Hephaestus did not respond. He stared at Ares's perfect feet in his well-crafted sandals. Confusion and grief washed over his face, and Dionysus sensed his desire to flee Olympus.

"That is solely for Hephaestus to decide," Dionysus said.

Ares glared at him. Dionysus summoned the strength that had sustained him through his campaign in India and met the God of War's eyes. He was not afraid.

"Ah, the new god we've heard so much about. I never thought you'd come to Olympus."

"I go where I please, especially when accompanying my friend Hephaestus and when invited by my brother Hermes."

"Well met, then, New God," Ares said with a hint of respect.

"Come, my brothers," Hermes said, continuing toward the palace. The white marble columns appeared dull. The whole place had a sense of abandonment. Dionysus imagined Hera screaming and struggling. Her impotent fury must have driven the other gods away. Even her attendants appeared to have abandoned her.

A great sorrow descended upon Dionysus when they entered the empty throne room. An intricate rug, woven with gold and glittering like stars, lay before a half circle of thrones—all of them empty except the most exquisite—the peacock throne Dionysus had been trapped in his first day in Lemnos. And there sat the Queen of the Gods, bound with golden filament, unable to change her shape or flee.

Hera's cold beauty shone hard through her wrath as she glared at Dionysus and Hephaestus. Then she composed her face, erasing her vitriol. Her large brown eyes opened wide and filled with glittering tears.

This was the goddess who had killed Dionysus's mother and pursued him as a youth. She had denied him a mother, a childhood, a place of his own. And yet, she had made him who he was. Hera killing his mother had made him become the Twice Born god. He hated her, knew how malicious she was. And yet, she appeared so miserable, so helpless, he could not help but pity her.

The hall filled with attendants who brought lamps. The other gods appeared: Ares and Athena then Hestia, Apollo, Demeter, and Aphrodite. Iris the Rainbow Messenger stepped out of the shadows along with the three Graces.

Fortunately, Artemis was not in attendance. He suspected she rarely came to Olympus. Zeus must be taking full advantage of his wife being bound to her throne. Perhaps he would be kinder to Hephaestus after this. Poseidon and Hades were in their respective kingdoms, unconcerned that their sister suffered.

Aphrodite radiated beauty. Desire pulled at Dionysus. Hephaestus stared at her far too long. Indeed, it was part of her godhead to stir carnality. Her diaphanous blue dress hinted at the pleasures she promised. Her magical girdle caught the light of one of the lamps, and Dionysus found himself unable to look away. When he met her gaze, she stared at him with lust. All other thoughts drained away. This ravishing goddess had her eyes set on him. She wanted him, and unquestionably, he wanted nothing more than to be with her.

Hermes pinched him, hard. Dionysus scowled. He was being a fool.

"Son," Hera said, her voice breaking, "finally you've come to free me."

Hephaestus stared at his mother as if in a trance. Rage, sorrow, and pity swept his face. He ran his large, dirty hand over his beard, attempting in vain to tame the wild hair that stood in every direction.

"Brother Hephaestus, we are quite impressed with your skills," Athena said. "The throne you made your mother is, though terribly cruel, a feat of craftsmanship. And this chariot you've fashioned for yourself, these spectacular golden women—your work is utterly beyond compare. There is no question in my mind that you are a true Olympian. Come home, brother. Let the gods themselves delight in your skill. Let us be the beneficiaries of your unsurpassable work."

"Wise Athena speaks the truth," Apollo said, stepping forward. How beautiful Artemis's twin was. His bronze skin radiated with a light of its own, and his golden eyes shone. Dionysus wished he could leave this place with Apollo, sit on a cloud, and discuss ideas he was only beginning to consider by being so near the God of Light.

"It is time to free your mother," Hestia said. "It is the right and dutiful thing to do."

The other gods echoed their agreement.

Dionysus stepped closer to Hephaestus. "All of Olympus will show their gratitude if you do this." He put his hand on Hephaestus's and pulled him forward a step. Sparks filled Hephaestus's eyes. Dionysus's felt his friend's pain—the rejection, the sorrow, the loss, and now the begrudging acceptance after Hephaestus had shown his skill and demanded attention.

"I made you myself, my son," Hera said. "I created you out of pure desire to have a child of my own. Every parent makes mistakes. Please forgive mine. It is time for us to be reconciled.

Time for you to come home to Olympus and have a throne of your own here in this hall."

"Go, Twice Fallen," Dionysus whispered. "Get yourself a new destiny."

Hephaestus glanced at Aphrodite as his chariot lurched forward. He moved toward Hera, bound fast in her throne. Dionysus suspected Hephaestus's beard hid his grin. How small and pitiful the great goddess appeared. She who had caused such sorrow and suffering to the children of Zeus. Dionysus momentarily wished she could stay there forever. This was a brilliant punishment that he only admired fully as it was about to end.

Hephaestus stroked the peacock's head. He ran his thick fingers along the crown of the feathers and squeezed the middle three feathers together. Hera's bonds were released. She momentarily froze, then jumped up.

"Well done!" Athena cried.

"Clever Hephaestus, you have made the right decision. Welcome to Olympus," Apollo said.

"You are a good son," Hestia said. "You have done your filial duty and will be rewarded."

"Join us here on Olympus, son," Hera said, her strength quickly returning. Already the color had come back into her face. Was she plotting to hurt Hephaestus? No, Dionysus sensed that she genuinely wanted him to live on high.

"And," Hermes added, "there were promises of Lady Aphrodite's hand in marriage."

Hephaestus grinned foolishly at the goddess of love and beauty; Ares scowled.

Aphrodite raised her eyes from below lowered lids and serenely glanced at Dionysus. Lust pulled at him, but he inspired enough lust on his own. He did not need her for a companion. She was enchanting and powerful, but her divinity depended on manipulating others. Ariadne had a power that required help from no man. Dionysus had no desire to stay here. He did not want to make a permanent home for himself here. He belonged on the earth, teaching mortals to make wine, discovering new vintages and ways to preserve his gift.

"I do love a wedding," Hera said. "Marriage is just what our dear Aphrodite needs." She glanced at Dionysus, clearly having no idea who he was. "What is your name?"

"I am Dionysus, the Twice-Born God of Wine. But I have only accompanied my brother Hermes and my friend Lord Hephaestus. Hephaestus is the one who chose to free you. He is the one who will wed Lady Aphrodite."

Hera's face lit up in a smile. Aphrodite frowned, but Hephaestus was watching his mother's reaction.

"Perfect!" Hera cried. "My son, you have returned to free me and marry a beautiful goddess. She is a worthy prize!"

"Wonderful," Demeter said, though Dionysus could clearly detect *Better her than me* in her tone. Hestia also cheered, and the two goddesses rallied around Aphrodite.

"Should I go find Lord Zeus?" Iris the Rainbow Messenger asked.

"No," Hera said. "I'll find him myself after the wedding. I made Hephaestus myself, and Aphrodite was born from the sea. Neither are his children, and I am the Goddess of Marriage. Let them be wed now."

Before Aphrodite can escape, Dionysus suspected Hera was thinking.

The wedding between the two gods was far from elaborate— Hephaestus drunk, still dirty from the forge, and Aphrodite appearing bored and resentful. Still the clouds parted, and Mount Olympus now emitted an atmosphere of celebration. Dionysus considered offering wine from his magical wineskin, but he wasn't sure of his place. Hephaestus went off to Aphrodite's house, and the rest of the gods mingled, gossiping about the terrible juxtaposition between the couple.

"He's so skilled, but so ugly," Athena said.

"I wonder what Zeus will say when he finds out," Iris said.

"He won't say much when Hera finds him with his latest

nymph," Demeter replied. "He's going to be in for it, thinking she's all tied up. He's going mad down there, bedding all manner of women."

Dionysus wandered toward Apollo, wishing he could talk to him, not knowing what to say.

"Come, brother," Hermes said. "Let's go talk to Hera."

The Queen of the Gods appeared completely recovered. As she had spoken the words of the marriage vows, her strength had returned full force.

"Great Hera," Hermes said, "Dionysus did not ask for the hand of Aphrodite, but I would like to request he also be given a throne here in Olympus for his part in freeing you."

She stared at Dionysus now as if seeing him for the first time. Her large brown eyes were incredibly beguiling.

"Oh, Semele's son. I see now. I had forgotten you were still alive. And what are you the god of?"

"I am the god of transformation, of wine and revelries."

"And the mortals honor you?"

"Yes."

"They pray to you?"

"Yes."

"Yet your mother was a mortal, and one easily tricked, if I recall correctly."

Dionysus swallowed his anger. It had been nothing for Hera to play her part in killing Semele, nothing for her to attempt to kill him, and yet he had come here to free her. He was beginning to regret it.

"Yes," he said, doing his best to keep his face passive.

"How are you a god?"

"I do not know. I only know I am. Hephaestus is a dear friend of mine. I have known him for centuries. I see the change in vegetation, in the vine and in women, and I draw it out, just as I was able to draw out the desire in your son to free you."

She narrowed her eyes. Her expression hinted at a smile from the polite challenge of his words.

"It was most kind of you to convince him to do so. Now that I am free, I will no longer persecute you. But alas, you are not one of us, and even if you were, we simply do not have another throne. There are twelve Olympians and twelve Olympians only. That is how it is and how it will always be. Your place is on earth, son of Semele, among the mortals, tending to the vine. Hermes can escort you back." She turned away.

Dionysus pushed down the bile, ignored the old scab she had ripped open. Of course he was not one of them. How had he ever thought he could be? He felt like a young child again, staring up at the heavens, wondering whether his father was there and whether he would ever come for him. He would not. Not even here in Olympus would Zeus meet him.

"Come, brother," Hermes said softly. "Don't let that old bitch disparage you." He led Dionysus away from the drab palace. "The gods are fools," Hermes said as magic mist began to encircle them. The wings on his sandals and helmet began to flutter, and he slid his arm around Dionysus's waist. "This will not be the last time you are on Olympus. I am sure of it. The other gods will recognize you. Now apparently isn't the time, but this is not over."

"Leave it," Dionysus said, having mastered his tears. "I am content below with my vines and those who care for me. I will return to Ariadne and to adventure. Soon I will return to war and make sure all mortals know me for the god I am. I need nothing from Olympus."

✿ 22 ✿

ARIADNE: SHE WHO SWINGS

LEMNOS

A YEAR LATER

"I will return soon," Dionysus said at the port. The sun was just beginning to rise. The soft pink clouds suggested it would be a good day to depart.

Ariadne bit back her bitterness and glanced down at the baby at her breast—Thoas, another boy—a message of displeasure from the goddess. She could not cry now, with Dionysus about to board his boat full of men eager to fight for him. She did not want him to leave. As his high priestess, she could not play the role of the clingy wife, lost without her husband. Yet she sensed doom in his departure, as if she would never see him again.

Seeing her sorrow, he cupped her face. "I wish I did not have to leave you, but Thalia, Talos, and Manko will not permit anything to happen to you or the boys. And Hephaestus, when he is not in Olympus arguing with Aphrodite, watches over you. All of Lemnos loves you and your new labyrinth."

She leaned her check against his palm, savoring his touch. "Curse this Perseus of Argos. What a fool he is to invite you to war. I only wish I could go as well." She detached the baby from her breast and burped him. Little Thoas was the perfect mixture of his parents. Dark-eyed, with curly black hair, he smiled serenely.

"I wish I could take you, Ariadne. If Thoas were older, I would. It is safer for you both here."

She imagined giving Thoas to a wet nurse and leaving with Dionysus, but the sense of dread followed her even in this fantasy. Something terrible was about to happen, but she could prevent it no more than she could prevent the passage of fall to winter.

On the boat, Acoetes shouted orders louder than usual, gently hinting it was time to go.

"I will not be gone long." He took her hand one last time.

"Don't be like Silenus," she said, attempting to make light of the pain clenching her heart.

"I will never forget you." Dionysus opened his eyes wide in shock. "I mean I would never forget you the way he forgot me. I will return as soon as I can."

"Go. Make Perseus believe in the new god. Make all of Argos worship you." She hoped he didn't hear the tears in her voice. She didn't think she could keep them back much longer. She turned away, wiping her eyes, as he boarded the boat.

She could not stay on the dock to watch the boat sail away; besides, she would be able to mark its progress from the hills above.

As they headed away from the harbor, the mark on her thigh began to tingle. Odd, she had felt nothing since the goddess had demanded she help Theseus. She had thought that spot to be dead, like her thread to the goddess. Manko and Talos helped her mount her donkey, then passed her the babe to slip into her sling. Thalia could not bring herself to ride other creatures. As she always did, she pulled off her dress, handed it to Ariadne, and transformed into a leopard.

Ariadne grinned as Thalia raced up the mountain. No one feared her here. Thalia could be herself without worrying about being killed or stolen. Lemnos had truly become their home.

Ariadne had much to do today at the temple. She had decided to see if they could recreate some of the frescoes she had grown up with. In the temple, they could paint a scene for the women, one showing what herbs to pick and depicting the stages of a girl's transition to womanhood. Her novice priestesses had been astounded when she told them of the first blood ceremony and the red beaded necklace they used on Crete to keep track of their cycles. They all wanted to institute the same practices and were eager to have their first ceremony among the girls who had had their first blood.

While Dionysus was gone, Ariadne would have an assembly of women—of all ages—to discuss the cycles in women's lives. Every woman she told thrilled at this idea, and it stirred her own certainty that this was the right path. Ariadne had been surprised to learn this was not usually done on Lemnos or Lesbos or Chios or any of the places the women who had joined them were from.

The more women she talked to, the more shocked she was how fragmentary women's knowledge was of their own bodies. Some understood how to avoid pregnancy; others did not. Maia, the midwife from Lesbos, knew a great deal. When she told Ariadne about the Egyptian practice of preventing pregnancy by inserting a suppository of crocodile dung and sour milk, Ariadne realized she needed to have a women's symposium.

She spent the day in the temple planning the symposium for the next full moon. If she could fill her days, perhaps she would not miss Dionysus so much. Back in their bed, sleep did not come. Worry gnawed at her, and she tried to ignore her sense of dread. She nursed Thoas, gently dislodged him, and tried to go back to sleep.

The mark on her thigh stung suddenly, as it had after Dionysus had boarded his ship. She had felt nothing all these years, and now... and now. Slow understanding seeped into her sleepy mind. The goddess had given her a reprieve—three years and three years only.

Ariadne had three sons. The goddess would never permit her

to have a daughter. The line of her foremothers, from Io to Europa to Pasiphae, would end. The power of the priestess had been lost to her line. And soon the goddess would come to end Ariadne herself.

The goddess had kept her word to Dionysus—mostly. She had not promised to let Ariadne live long. Dionysus was gone; Hephaestus was in Olympus with Aphrodite. Now that the goddess knew Ariadne was on Lemnos, she would have her revenge. She had not killed Ariadne in childbed, but that did not mean the goddess would let her live.

Calm descended as it had before she slit a throat for sacrifice. It would be so. There was no point in trying to fight. She understood Asterion's acceptance of his own fate now. Ariadne had not received a prophecy, but the understanding came as cool and firm as a rock inside a sacred cave.

She slid her arm out from under little Thoas. How she wished she'd be able to watch him and his brothers grow up. But the urgency of the pain threatened everyone she loved if she did not leave the bedroom. She covered him and Thalia and crept out of the house.

In the garden, she cupped Dionysus's favorite vine, a little tendril shooting forth. "Tell your master his wife is in grave danger. Tell your master I love him. Spread my message along the vines; flow to where he is. Tell him..." She did not know if this would work, but it was all she had.

She stared up at the crescent moon, waiting for the goddess. Ariadne had dreamed of the Great Goddess coming to her since childhood—but not like this. She had never imagined it would be like this. The goddess took many forms. To the Hellenes, she appeared one way. Theseus had described her as a gray-eyed maiden armed with a breastplate bearing the face of a Gorgon, a great helmet on her head. He said she was the god of his city and his own protectress. Dionysus had said she was a young girl, always on the hunt, Mistress of Wild Things.

It did not matter what she was called or what guise she went by. To some she was the Mistress of Snakes, of the Underworld, of the Moon, consort to the Sky King or the Lord of the Seas. She was all the same. She brought life and took it. The seasons of the earth and the stages of a woman's life all belonged to her. She was the earth herself—matron of the arts, creator of crafts, killer of deer, women, and men, Little Bear, Mother of All. She was here, and she was angry.

Though Ariadne could not yet see her, she felt the goddess's energy and her fury. Ariadne dropped her shawl to bare her breasts. She raised her arms as she had been taught to do when addressing the Great Goddess. But she wanted to fall to the earth and beg for another day, another moment—to just once more allow her child to suck at her breast. To just once more kiss her husband, to say goodbye, to…. A terrible burning came from the crescent moon on her thigh. She gasped and dropped an arm, pushing on the mark with her thumb.

"You were beloved to me, Ariadne, daughter of Pasiphae. Your mother disappointed me. I hoped you would redeem her. And for a moment, it seemed you would." The goddess appeared incredibly young and strong. She wore a quiver on her back and carried a bow in her hands.

Ariadne pinched the mark on her thigh, attempting to dull the pain. "All I ever wanted was to please you, Great Goddess. That was all I ever strove to do."

"Until Dionysus came."

"I tried to refuse him."

"You did." The goddess floated to the ground. She reached out an arm, pale as the moon, strong as the wind. Her finger caressed Ariadne's cheek, her touch cold as the dead.

"You did try, and you did obey me when I told you to bed Theseus and help him destroy your people."

Ariadne fell to her knees, aware of the tears streaming down her face as the goddess wiped one away with the tip of her finger and licked it.

"Why did you have me turn against my people, Goddess? Didn't we do all you wanted? Didn't we worship you as you liked?"

The goddess took one of Ariadne's breasts in her cold hand. "You did. Until your mother chose to permit your father to live. He was meant to be king for a year—a great year, but still, she should have sacrificed him to me, son of Zeus or no.

"Disappointed, I turned my sights on Attica. The Hellenes' star is on the rise. They are the ones I have chosen to allow to worship me now. Your people have been very useful, but the earth turns; time moves on. I consulted with my brother's oracle. Soon your fine island will be destroyed. Your labyrinth imagined as only a myth. Yet Athens will persevere. I have chosen those men to keep my power strong."

Ariadne gasped, the pain of the goddess's words as great as the burning in her thigh.

"You have chosen men? Men over the women who have kept your worship for generations?"

"Women will always worship me. They will pray to me when they have their monthly blood and when they are pregnant, and I will reward or punish them as I see fit. But it is the men who make war. And the winners of war will be the ones to spin the tales. I will not be forgotten!"

Ariadne stood, fury burning in her fingers. She had been subservient to the goddess all her life, and her life mattered not at all. "You are not the goddess I worshipped in Crete. You have changed."

"Yes, those who want to survive, change. I need not kill you, but I shall, for vengeance. Your husband had the gall to come to Olympus and ask for a throne. He tricked me into thinking you were already dead, but once I heard that he refused to marry Aphrodite, I suspected there could only be one reason. What pain your death will cause him! And the mortals of this isle, who have begun to worship you, will return their prayers to me."

"Why do you hate Dionysus so?"

"He trespassed in my territory, and he fancies himself a god.

He would make you a goddess. I need no more goddesses, but since you have been so obedient to me, I will allow you to choose how you are to die."

Ariadne dug the tip of her necklace into her chest. She could scream or draw attention, but if she summoned Manko and Talos, the goddess would only kill them, too.

Should she walk into the sea? Perhaps a bull made of foam would somehow save her. She could jump from the heights, hoping Hermes or one of Hephaestus's winged chariots would catch her.

The goddess grinned, her teeth shining like blades. "I offer you three choices: snake bite, hanging, or being turned to stone."

Ariadne shuddered. She did not like any of those. She did not like any of this.

"Hanging," Ariadne said. "The most sacred way to go. A reflection of She Who Hangs, one of the goddess's many names. An idea of the goddess I worshipped in my youth, not who you've become." She glared at the Huntress, who smiled as if provoked.

Her form changed to one of a maiden, to a woman made of silver, to a huntress, to a bare-breasted Minoan holding snakes. The goddess bore Ariadne's form and spoke. "To die in the air, with your feet off the ground, your body floating in air. Neither on earth nor at sea.

"Your people once told stories of the sacred epiphany, of swinging up and up, raising consciousness until it could be raised no more. After you rise so high, Ariadne, both in consciousness and body, the only way left to go is down."

The goddess transformed back into the Great Huntress. She gripped the red-beaded necklace Ariadne had worn since her ceremony of first blood and pulled, snapping the thread. The beads scattered on the ground.

"Hanging is a good choice," the goddess said, producing a silver rope. As if made from stars, it shone with an unnatural light. "A good way for a former priestess to die."

23

DIONYSUS WARS WITH PERSEUS

ARGOS

"Halt!" Perseus yelled from above, flying on his winged sandals. His golden breastplate shone in the sun. Dionysus's troops paused, surprised by the hero's flight. Perseus's men stopped their battle.

"Cease!" Dionysus shouted to his men. They were glad for the rest and lowered their spears, though all kept their shields nearby.

Staring up at the hero's firm, tanned thighs, Dionysus noted that Perseus made a fine warrior. His short leather skirt created a pleasant view from below. Dionysus especially appreciated the way the winged sandals complemented Perseus's muscular calves.

"You will not take my kingdom!" Perseus yelled.

"I don't want your kingdom. I only want your people to know the joys of my gifts, of which there are many," Dionysus shouted, gesturing with his thyrsus.

"Why did you send madness on my women?"

"To show you a bit of my power. And I only did that after you refused me."

"It's said you made them rip the babes from their breasts and tear them apart!" Perseus's rage betrayed his fear.

Dionysus shrugged. "If any of your women did that, it is not my doing. I merely permit mortals to feel what they really want. Come down, little hero. Come have a drink with me."

"How would you feel if your woman was to die?" Perseus asked. "What if she were turned to stone?"

How annoying the little hero was. He had killed one Gorgon, turned a king and a sea-monster to stone, and now, he thought himself impenetrable.

Dionysus had let this go on too long. He had hoped to cajole Perseus, but this insult could not stand. Still, the mortal's words had the desired effect. A cold fear began to grow in Dionysus's belly. The thought of losing Ariadne again. No. A shudder ran through him, and he wanted to throw down his sword, turn from the battlefield, and return to Lemnos as quickly as possible.

He could not abandon the soldiers who had followed him. There were bodies to be buried, and he still had not convinced Perseus to accept him.

The mortal above him now bore a smug smile as he reached into his leather pouch. Dionysus shot a vine from his wrist up into the sky. He had a moment's hesitation between wrapping it around Perseus's neck or his waist. At the last minute, he decided not to kill him just yet. They were brothers, after all.

"What!" Perseus exclaimed as the vine twined itself around his waist. Dionysus didn't let him finish. He yanked.

The hero tumbled to the ground, his winged sandals keeping him from crashing completely. His men lurched into action, but Dionysus's troops stood between them. Perseus's general gave the signal for his men to stand down, waiting for a command.

"Do not speak of my wife being turned to stone, little hero. I've been kind to you and your kingdom so far, but if you rouse me to fury, you will be king of wild women. Your only subjects will be the corpses of your men." He spoke loudly and felt the fear his words caused the fighters of Argos. They had reason to be afraid of their women. Dionysus gazed out at Perseus's men, making them remember how they had treated their wives and slaves. The soldiers' faces showed their horror. They could not fight him now even if their general, who had thrown off his helmet to clutch his head, commanded it.

Perseus appeared unaffected by the memories Dionysus had summoned. From what Dionysus had heard, Perseus was a good son and husband, or perhaps his winged helmet protected him.

Perseus reached into his leather sack and pulled out the Gorgon's head. Dionysus instinctively looked away, into the hero's eyes. They were black as onyx. Perseus grinned arrogantly.

"For shame, Perseus. This is what you call a weapon? The head of an innocent you murdered. Could you not let her rest?"

"It is no stranger than your weapon, God of Wine," the hero snarled.

"No, I suppose it is not. I wonder whether it will affect me." The thought of Ariadne turned to stone made him question his divinity. Could he fail to protect her again? If the head of a dead Gorgon was to be his undoing, how powerful was he?

Perseus slowly raised the Gorgon's head to eye-level. "Let's find out."

Dionysus looked. Poor Medusa. Locked in a silent scream for eternity, the snakes in her hair writhed lazily, as if tired of this game. What had she done to deserve such punishment? Ah, yes, she was once a mortal woman who was found desirable by the gods. The same crime his mother had committed, and Perseus's mother, too.

"We are not so different, Perseus. Are you not my half-brother? Though it seems I am divine, and you are not."

Perseus stared in shock, his mouth agape. Dionysus could almost see his thoughts on his face.

"No, no. Don't look at her yourself. You've seen the damage she has wrought. Don't end your own story here."

"How is it you're divine and I am not?" Perseus asked after returning the head to his leather pouch without glancing at it.

Dionysus had mused on this many times over the centuries. In his wandering, he had come across some of his father's many sons.

He understood how the Olympian gods were divine. They were children of gods and Titans or goddesses and gods, but all the other sons of his father with mortal mothers were demi-gods or heroes.

"Gods pull the strings." He moved his fingers as if pulling a dancing wooden doll, and at the same time, called vines to surge from the ground. He was able to call the seeds, to make the vines grow and spring up from the earth now. Perseus stepped backward at the sight of the vines that had yanked him to the earth. "Heroes do the gods' bidding. You are a great Gorgon-slayer because the gods wanted you to be. They set you a task, gave you their gifts." He gestured to the winged sandals, leather pouch, and sword with his thyrsus.

"However." He made the vines dance. "Gods do what they want."

"But..." Perseus began.

"You think it was your idea to kill the Gorgon? I've heard your tale, and it sounds to me like the goddess wanted her dead—you were a convenient way to have it done." Dionysus paused. Goddesses had set his own story in motion as well. Hera's hatred had killed his mother, forced his nursemaids to hide him in a cave. Artemis's hatred had inspired him to find Ariadne, and his love for her had made him challenge himself to become the god he was now. He raised a finger to make the vines grow a little more just to watch Perseus flinch.

"Forge a peace with me, little hero. Taste my wine; try my gifts. Let us bury our dead and call a truce."

"It is no truce if you win," Perseus said, but the fight had gone out of his voice.

"It is a truce if you do not lose and your men live. I do not want to conquer your land or take it as my own. My only desire has been to share the gift I bring. I will leave behind skills your people will enjoy."

Perseus stared at him as if entranced. "I will try your drink. I will stop fighting you. Come, sup with me in my great hall and be my guest. I invite you and your..."

A flash of saffron caught their attention. Perseus drew his sword. Dionysus raised his thyrsus. An arrow suddenly flew at Dionysus, who moved a moment before it would have struck him. And the goddess stood before him.

"Bastard of Zeus, we meet again." Artemis appeared as a young girl. Her yellow chiton shone in the sun. Her bow glittered in her strong hands. She glanced at Perseus. "Ah, another one of my father's bastards—this one obedient. I'll let your woman live."

Dionysus went cold. He knew then, even before Artemis uttered her next words.

"I renege on our agreement—or rather, I've changed my terms. You stayed away for three years, and so I gave her three more years of life. But that was all I owed. I did not promise more than that." Her arrows remained in her quiver, her bow was still in her hand, but it was as if she had struck him clean through the heart.

He wondered whether the Gorgon's head was slowly working, for he now stood as still as a statue, unable to move at all. His face formed into a mask of tragedy, and he had a vague thought of this horrible pain being shared with others. Every soldier on the battlefield should throw down his arms, fall to the ground, and weep for this horrible loss.

His wife, the mother of his children, the shining light of his heart had been taken from him. He had given up much, had changed and become a god for her, and now she was gone. He did not need to hear the goddess's next words, but she spoke them anyway.

"She chose the manner of her own death. She was getting too popular with the mortals, and you, bastard son of Zeus, coming to Olympus, demanding followers, you are getting too cocky."

Artemis grinned, savoring his torment. If she could have drunk his tears, she would have. She would feast on his sorrow. But he would not let her best him. His mask of tragedy turned to one of comedy. This was it. This was his way to the heavens. He would not be bested by this bitch. He would not let her arrow find its mark.

His mouth lifted into an obscene smile. He had gone mad before, wine-mad, furious with rage, thirsty for blood. But not this time. This was not madness but clarity. The future lay before him. His path shone brightly in his mind, and he saw exactly what he must do.

"You have had many women, Artemis, but you have not known love. Your women are devoted to you, but to you, they are the same. I've heard how you tire of them—kill them in your jealousy. You may be a cruel goddess, but I will not be such a god."

"You're not a god at all," she sneered. "You could not save your woman. You could not save your mother."

His mad grin grew wider. "You're right. I failed to save them. I sought you to find a comrade, and all you offered was hatred. I saved Hera from being bound, and she could not properly thank me. Yet I am a new god, one who forgives and grows. So thank you for giving me the chance to prove myself. I will do what no other god has. I will go to Hades and bring them back. I will ascend to Olympus, and it will all be because of you."

PART FOUR
THE UNDERWORLD

24

SHE WHO WAS ARIADNE

Her spirit hovered near her body hanging from the tree, swaying slowly in the wind. How long ago had it been that she had pumped her legs on a swing in Crete, trying to find an epiphany and understand her goddess? How impossible that seemed now. She would never understand her goddess—never understand anything ever again.

At first light, Thalia crept out from their house. "Ariadne?" She scanned the garden and gasped, making out the body in the dim light. She stood below the swaying corpse.

Thalia. The spirit tried to touch her friend's face, but her hand didn't make contact. This was what it was to be dead. She was only a memory. Insubstantial. She remained with her corpse, but she was nothing.

Thalia blinked and wiped her cheeks. She took a shaky breath and shuddered.

"Ariadne." She raised her arms as she would if calling upon the goddess. "I will always honor you. I will ensure you are not forgotten. To me, you were always a goddess."

Ariadne's form glowed with a golden light upon hearing Thalia's words. She imagined herself as a constellation in the sky, as eternal as the gods. That was all she could hope for now. To be dust remembered.

Thalia kissed Ariadne's cold foot, knelt below the corpse, and transformed into a leopard.

The branch she could not reach as a woman was just a leap away for a leopard. The rope she had no knife for was just a few swipes with her claws. She grasped it in her mouth and bit down, severing the rope, but not letting her mistress's body fall to the ground. Slowly, she lowered the body, almost losing her balance several times.

When the body was on the earth, Thalia leapt down and let out a roar. All her grief rose from her throat as she bellowed her sorrow through the trees. She cried out again and again until unseen drums boomed.

All through the village, women stopped cooking, weaving, and working in their gardens. They streamed toward Thalia. Upon hearing her roar, some had undone their hair, and now, seeing the body of Ariadne, High Priestess of Lemnos, on the ground, the silver rope around her neck, they ripped open their gowns or unpinned their chitons. Their cries joined Thalia's growl as they knelt before Ariadne, making a circle around her corpse. Some screamed and rubbed dirt in their hair or smudged their faces; others clawed at themselves.

"Why, High Priestess?" women screamed. This was what the goddess wanted, to punish those who had failed to worship her. The spirit who had been Ariadne realized now what the goddess had planned. The goddess surely grew strong on this misery.

The spirit watched, honored by their grief. She wanted to float back to her house, to see her children one last time, but she could not move away from the corpse. Word spread to the men, and the wailing resounded through Lemnos.

How precious all the mundane parts of her life seemed now. She longed to nurse Thoas or listen to Oenopion ask why again and again while she watched Staphylus dig in the mud. Those simple times with her children were done. She could never hold them again. She would never go to the temple to check on the three novice priestesses she had begun training or share her bed with Thalia. She would never see her husband again.

Her spirit let out a soft, unheard sob just as Hermes floated above the ground, carried by his winged sandals and winged helmet. The caduceus in his left hand pulled at her soul as if he had her life-thread wound around it.

"Lady Ariadne, please come with me." His words were a formality, but a break in his voice betrayed his sorrow.

"Hermes, I do not wish to leave this place." She doubted her words would change anything, but she wanted to know whether she still had a voice.

"And I do not want to take you." He glanced down at Thalia, screaming in grief, and looked away quickly. "I have taken countless souls to the Underworld, but if I could do anything to prevent this, Lady, I would. The longer we stay here, the more painful it will be. Come." He grasped her hand. To the God of the Ways, her form was still tangible.

They floated away from her corpse, away from the house where she had lived with her husband and children, away from Thalia, away from Lemnos.

"Dionysus will not forgive me for this, but what can I do? I lead the dead to the Underworld. The goddess killed you. I cannot leave you above ground with the living. I shirked my duty to take the dead to the Underworld once before. If I ever do it again, Zeus will punish me greatly." Hermes's smooth voice calmed her, and seeming to understand this, he continued. "I will not blame Dionysus for it, but that was when I got in so much trouble. After my father birthed Dionysus from his thigh, he instructed me to take baby Dionysus to safety. I found the most glorious cave on Mount Nysa for my little half-brother. The beds were made of grass, the nymphs dressed in nothing but dew drops. It was in the loveliest valley, and I might add I did such a good job keeping his location secret that people still don't know where I hid him."

The God of Ways had not struck her as an easy talker. When she had met him a year ago, he was quick, decisive, and quiet. Perhaps he was only like this with the dead, for the dead excel at keeping secrets.

"I was meant to drop my little brother off and be on my way, but the nymphs compelled me to stay. A day, a century, who can say?" He paused, and she imagined how pleasant that time had been. Hidden from the gods, the only time to have peace.

"When Silenus arrived to watch over Dionysus, I should have returned to the needs of the gods, but I did not want to. Never had I enjoyed such idyll. Even as a young boy, Dionysus created enchantments. And when he invented wine, and Silenus taught him to cultivate the grapevine, naturally I had to stay. What trouble I got into then, Lady! In the mortal realm, the souls piled up. The clever ones figured out how to cross over; cowards assembled outside the gate, unable to find the courage to go inside. Others rambled across the land as vengeful ghosts.

"Father Zeus was furious, Hades even more so." He laughed, a quick bark that held little humor. "I do not control the seas or cause earthquakes. I do not cause the grain to grow, but by taking souls to the land below, I fulfill an important task. Without me, the lives of the living would be chaos."

This whole time, Hermes had been leading her on the wind. They had flown away from the sun. She did not know where they were now. The clouds seemed to be descending from the sky to cover the land. They flew into the mist, which became a thicker fog, until she could only make out Hermes' luminous silver eyes. She gripped his hand, glad to still feel anything.

"You are so lovely, Ariadne. Did you know Dionysus could have married Aphrodite when he convinced Hephaestus to free Hera? He did not want her, for he had you."

Dionysus had told her about his time on Olympus, but he had not told her that. Love, bitterness, and sorrow mixed. She had always known he loved her, but to want her more than the goddess of love and beauty! Even though she understood that a godly marriage was not for him, that he would be an unsuitable match with Aphrodite, the pain of this knowledge, of how her death would hurt him stung.

When they landed, Hermes set her on the ground. He walked her toward the gaping black mouth of a cavern.

"You will be remembered, Ariadne, by gods and mortals alike. Here now."

This place could not be more different from the cave her husband had grown up in. The fog outside turned everything white and gray. The opening of the cave gaped, sure to swallow anything whole. She wanted to cling to Hermes, to beg for one more moment, for one more chance.

"Please," she gasped. Her fear took control before she could stop herself. She clutched his wrist, fighting the urge to kneel and grasp his calf in supplication. Foolishness. He could do nothing. But her panic did not care. Would he push her in? Thrust her inside and float away? This was his duty. He had brought count-less souls to the next plane. What would her fear matter?

"Don't." Hermes's voice was a sharp command. He clasped her around the waist, and together they entered the darkened cave. "Don't be afraid, Lady. You have the strength of a goddess."

She held her tongue this time. He thought well of her. She could not let this last memory a god had of her be of groveling, no matter how badly she wanted to.

"Ariadne," he whispered her name. She guessed he was not supposed to address her by it now that she was a shade. "Your husband has always been a fighter." His breath was like honey in her ear. "You know how Hera tried to bring an end to the infant Dionysus. You know how determined his father was about his birth. You know how strong the young godling was himself. He refused to be killed. He finished maturing in Zeus's thigh. He will not give up on you. He will not abandon you. So I tell you what I told his mother Semele: eat nothing in the land of the Under-world. Have this cake. I took it today from an altar. There is magic in offerings given by those they were meant for. It will sate your hunger. In the Land of the Dead, you will not yearn for anything but your husband. Wait for him."

SHADES OF GRAY. SHADOWS. CHARCOAL, COBALT, JET. ASH. HER memories disintegrated. She had taken a small boat across a river. And then she floated amidst others like herself, souls lost to the day. A vague memory of being... something. Someone. Daughter, lover, mother, wife, priestess. Priestess, so close she had been to the goddess once. Goddess. The goddess had killed her. That she remembered.

She followed a river that did not make a sound. There were few sounds here, just as there were no colors, no scents. As soon as she had these thoughts, she forgot them. Once there had been colors. The color of the sea and sky—she did not recall the name for it. The color of wine and the nipples of her lover, that name, too, was gone. The color of trees and grass, of her female lover's eyes. Once she had been part of a world so beautiful. Once she had been alive.

Now she was no more. She existed only as a forgotten memory —not even able to remember who she had been—only flashes. The feel of her husband's hands upon her body. The movement of a child within her belly and then the pull of his suck upon her breasts. She had created life, nourished children. And she had killed. The memory of slitting the throats of animals, the hot blood. She had been powerful in life—and she had been a pawn, like all mortals under the will of the gods.

What had she done wrong? Why had the goddess killed her? She had refused to kill a man. No, no that was her mother—that man had been her father. She, this shade who did not remember her mortal name, she had loved a man—a twice-born god, child of the moon and sky. She had loved him when she was vowed to the goddess. That was why. But mortals died all the time, usually without reason. She tried to hold fast to these memories, but like the river she followed, the thoughts flowed away from her. She did not know where they went.

She came to a place where other shades gathered. Vague forms of people, some made of spider silk, others of smoke, of shade. Shadows who moved without the sun.

Who are you? she asked one.

The shade turned. A woman? A man? She could not tell.

I am ash upon ash only. Forgotten, even to myself, consigned to exist here forever. Who are you?

Ariadne. The name came quickly in response to the other's question. She savored the knowledge of who she had been, holding it in her mind as she had once held honey on her tongue. *Daughter of Pasiphae and Minos, High Priestess of Crete.* A moment of pride. There were shades here who had done little in their lives— who had lived a short while and accomplished naught.

She had been royal. She had been holy. She... *Betrayer of Crete,* the wisp of a memory said. *Despised by the goddess,* another voice said. *The goddess killed you with good reason,* a gnarled tree seemed to croak. She glanced above, wondering whether the furies would descend on her. She did not think she had murdered anyone without sanction, but had she not broken her parents' hearts, betrayed the trust of her people, and committed adultery against her husband? In the eyes of many, she deserved punishment. In the eyes of many, she was the villain. Perhaps it was better after all to forget and become obscured by oblivion.

In this land, time was forgotten. No moon waxing or waning, no sun to rise and set; even her own body had ceased keeping time. She had no monthly blood to mark time; she had no blood at all. Her hair would never turn to gray; wrinkles would never line her skin. Had it been days, months, years?

In the world above, her memory was celebrated. She guessed it was the woman who was a leopard who poured the libations over her grave—or perhaps her husband's maenads danced and spilled blood in her name. When they did these things, her shade grew vibrant, surging from a gray wisp to a boldly outlined iron.

At times her dress bloomed cobalt, her hair returned to onyx, her hands flickered as if they could be solid. At these times, she imagined taking a deep breath—the sensation was so real, she could almost feel her lungs fill with air. The air here was stale, the scent dank, but having the sense of smell, the memory of color thrilled her. The moments never lasted long, and the memories of the joy fled as quickly as the sensation of life came.

Sometimes she thought to journey back to the entrance—to the river. She could find a way to go back with the ferryman and wait on the bank until the sensation came again. Perhaps the women above would sacrifice a heifer in her name. All that blood would give her strength to return to the land of the living, if only for a day. But as soon as she came up with a plot to cheat death, the idea flew away, leaving her with a sad sensation of confusion and loss.

Still, she knew who she was—who she had been. She had met many who no longer remembered their names.

I was the wife of Dionysus. I was High Priestess of Crete. The first thought gave her comfort; the second stung like a bee. She did not remember why. *I was the Mistress of the Labyrinth. I was a lover, a wife, and a mother.* She had been other things, too, but these things were the most important. These memories she clung to, even in the long times between the sacrifices taking place above.

She drifted to a gathering of women. They sat silently by the river near a cypress tree.

I was Ariadne. Who were you?

The shades of the women did not respond. They seemed made of smoke, as if they were about to disappear forever.

Were you mothers? Daughters? Wives? Do you remember your names? Ariadne's shade asked. She tried to make out their features. *You were more than this once. Do you remember?* She approached the woman closest to her. A sadness emanated from the soul, but little else. On a whim, Ariadne reached out her hand, not expecting to touch anything, but when she fingered the other woman's wrist, she felt an almost intangible substance. She saw for a moment a child's face, smiling up at his mother. The woman whose wrist she touched gasped and shimmered. Her form grew darker and more defined. Her eyes had been blue, her hair dark brown.

"I was from Thrace, wife of Gelon. I had three babies and died giving birth to the fourth."

The shades of the other women gathered around her. This was the most excitement Ariadne had felt in the Underworld. She touched another woman who had floated too close. This woman, too, glimmered, and Ariadne felt her anger.

"I died on Pylos at the hands of a cruel master." The woman's face transformed from a smoke-gray shadow to one covered in bruises, one eye swollen shut, a necklace of bruises around her throat. "It was long ago. I wonder whether my master is in this place. Perhaps I can find him." She turned and moved away, more quickly than Ariadne had seen any shade move.

Great Lady, the other shades called, *please bless us.* They surrounded Ariadne, reaching out to her.

"I was High Priestess of Crete, daughter of King Minos and Queen Pasiphae, wife of Dionysus, mother of three sons. Remember who you were," she said, touching them. She had spoken aloud for the first time since coming to this place. *I have a voice, and I give a voice to all of you.* A tingling pain came from her eyes, and she wondered if she could cry real tears.

"Great Lady," a crone croaked, her hand feather-soft in Ariadne's, "what magic is this?" She held up Ariadne's hand in her own. Not only had the crone grown darker and more defined, but Ariadne had as well. She could almost see her skin tone. Her indigo dress, a gift from Dionysus from India, shone with color—the brightest colors she had seen in this place. The shades of the women around her had grown vibrant, though they still retained their gray hues; their faces had become distinct, their eyes focused.

"My name was Eos. I was from Thessaly."

"I was called Gaia. I had three daughters. I wonder whether they're here!"

"I was married to a fool, but I loved his brother." This shade, a gray-haired woman, giggled, and the others began to laugh, too. Other shades, who had simply been drifting, began to come over, drawn by the noise.

Ariadne stared at her hands, marveling at how clearly she could see them. What had she done? How had she done it? Silently, she moved away from the women, going in the opposite direction of the shades swarming toward the noise and the color.

*A*RIADNE, *K*ORE CALLS YOU.

She floated across the shadowed grass. Having grown up in Knossos, she always had a firm sense of direction. Even here in this dizzying space of eternity, she sensed the direction from which she had come. Though the sound was nearly imperceptible, she found the river and followed. The water was unlike any she had ever seen, a blue-black surrounded by gray. It flowed almost undetectably.

The river branched in three directions, and she followed the one to the west. When she was a child, Daedalus had shown her two magnets drawn to each other. This was the way her soul was being pulled now. A great palace loomed in the distance—the home of the Queen and King of the Dead. It was the Queen of the Underworld who called to her now. Ariadne did not have a true physical body, only the intangible memory of her form, yet the phantom pain of a magical mark, a crescent moon on her thigh, pulled her toward the palace.

The columns of the palace gleamed bright in the gloom of the Underworld. As she drew closer, she saw the columns were giants' bones: the bones of Titans who had died battling the Olympians. Now Hades held his empire up with the bones of his enemies. A wise strategist. Her father would have done the same. Everything about the palace warned visitors to go away. Yet fear was not an emotion she recognized any more. She was dead. All her regrets and triumphs were behind her.

Strange colored lamps lit the way to the main gate. It reminded her of Asterion's labyrinth. Was that what the afterlife was—a labyrinth, a path? Or had that been her life, and now she was trapped within the center, or had she found a way out?

The palace itself shone against the light of the flames. Aside from the Titans' bones, the palace was made of a pure black polished marble. It was bigger than Knossos—perhaps bigger than Crete itself. The immensity of the palace had no end. She gazed up to decipher how many floors it had, but a heavy gray mist engulfed the higher floors. It could be four stories or twenty.

Shadows white as bone guarded the perimeter. These former soldiers were the closest thing she'd seen to corpses. If she had been mortal still, her skin would have risen in gooseflesh. Some of the soldiers wore their armor, and some continued to bleed from their wounds.

"Please, Lady," a man gasped. Fingers made only of bone reached out to her; dry mouths begged. These were the unburied, the unmourned, the forgotten. She could picture Hades standing by the river and pointing out these lost souls to Charon. "That one, and him, and him." They would be allowed to cross, to guard the palace, but they would have no peace, for no one above remembered.

Guards stood by the gates, solid forms with luminous eyes. They did not speak to her or bar her entry. She was expected.

The Queen of the Dead met Ariadne in the entryway holding a lamp.

"Dark Maiden," Ariadne said, saluting her in the Minoan style. She could not make out the Queen of the Dead's face through the shadows. For a brief moment, she saw her own face as it had been in life, then Persephone's face changed to a girl crowned with flowers, filled with light, and changed again to a dark goddess, though the light in her black eyes remained.

"Welcome, daughter of Pasiphae. I have been eager to meet you."

To ask why would be rude. Out of all the souls who came to this place, Ariadne doubted her own importance. Persephone grasped the shoulder panel of Ariadne's dress and fingered the indigo fabric.

"To see such a color here. Truly you are gifted."

"I don't even know how I did it. I just began talking to some women, and they..."

"The dead do not speak. My husband will not care for this. Come." She took Ariadne's hand in her own and then paused to hold their hands up to the light.

Persephone's hand was delicate and pale. Exquisite rings of diamond, ruby, and emerald set in gold adorned her fingers. Ariadne still wore the memory of her rings, the snake biting its own tail and the seal ring she had worn as high priestess. Her skin was darker, and in the torch light, it appeared to glitter.

"You are the granddaughter of the Sun. There is immortality in your veins." Persephone studied her. "But there is more to it than that. You have great power over mortals. You help them find their way. Come with me. There is someone I want you to meet."

Ariadne followed Persephone down a dimly lit corridor. They passed shades of guards and servants. Torches lined the hallways, their fire making the jewels in the walls glitter in the flame. They ascended a stairway made of giants' bones, up and up and up into the women's quarters.

"I have heard much of your husband, the new god," Persephone said. "His devotion to you is known far and wide."

The memory of a blush stirred, and Ariadne smiled at the thought of blushing and of her husband.

"He is unlike any other. We were parted too soon."

"You are not the only one who lost him too soon." Persephone strode past giant couches of amethyst and rubies. The shades of lovely ladies wove great, glittering tapestries, but all was swathed in dark colors, tones of smoke, charcoal, and jet. Occasionally,

Ariadne made out a shade of blue-gray, or a hint of eggshell or alabaster. Some of the weavers shimmered bright as bone, but only Ariadne carried true color. She was surprised it had lasted so long.

They walked on for what seemed a very long time until they came to what could only be the very back of the women's quarters. In the gloom of this last chamber, Ariadne made out a small shade, crumbled like a spider corpse.

"Semele," Persephone said, clasping the shade's frail hand, "you have not been forgotten. This is Ariadne. She was a high priestess as you were a priestess. She, too, is beloved by the gods."

Ariadne took Semele's hand. "It is an honor to meet you after all this time. Indeed, you have not been forgotten. Your legacy lives on."

The crumpled shade of the woman shimmered with light, with color, with hope. A beautiful face shone from the gloom and sorrow. A young girl's green eyes flashed for a moment before retreating to tones of gray. When Ariadne took Semele's hand, she felt her own power in a way she hadn't in the Fields of the Dead.

"Your son has become a great god."

"Son? The babe who burned with me?" Semele croaked.

"He lived, Semele," Persephone said. "Dionysus, the Twice Born God, lived and thrived. He has become immortal."

Ariadne could not say what exactly she saw, but Persephone seemed to transfer a part of herself into the shade of Dionysus's mother. Semele uncurled and strengthened, growing strong as she pulled energy from both Ariadne and Persephone. Ariadne did not need to see her colorless clothing or her smoke-colored skin to know she had been drained of her power. She had her own well of reserve, her own strength to draw from, and she was glad to share her strength with her husband's mother. Even as a shade, she could help women; even as a shade, she would triumph.

$\not{\mathcal{X}}$ 25 $\not{\mathcal{X}}$

DIONYSUS DESCENDS

Finding the way to the Underworld was no easy task. Dionysus wanted to ask another god for help, but Hephaestus would not know, and Hermes would forbid him from entering Hades. This was his trial and his alone. He set out, as he had many times before, but this time not to fight or bring wine but to bring back his wife and mother.

His mother. Stories of her beauty and shining light had haunted his childhood. He spent countless nights wishing on the moon, eager to believe the rumors that she was a moon goddess. He had imagined his mother as the moon staring down on him, that rain and mist were her tears over their separation.

One day, my son, we will be reunited. One day I will cup your cheek and hold you close. Until then, I can only gaze down and miss you. He had heard her voice the first time he drank wine, and then, the pain being too much, he pushed away those early memories, forgot the old wound. He never imagined he could journey to the Underworld, but now he would seek her out.

His reverie was interrupted by a blur of motion. Something streaked toward him. He grabbed his thyrsus and readied himself for a threat. Was this Hera? A mortal foe? Another king who would not accept his gifts of wine? No. This creature was low, running on four legs. He grinned as he made out the form of a leopard, racing across the rocky slope.

She stopped before him and transformed into a woman.

Her naked form had always been lovely, but now, every bit of flesh on her arms and legs was muscle. She had once been soft and pale, her hair clean of brambles. Her nails were long and coated in dirt, and her hair would have appalled any matron. Yet Thalia had come into her true self, and that made her even more breathtaking.

"Thalia, how many times have I told you the dangers of running about like that?"

"Master, I am not sure which form is more dangerous for me if I am going about on my own."

"Well, having roamed the earth as a man, I have to agree." He clasped her bare shoulder. "Please, be careful. I can't bear to lose you as well."

A blush came into her cheeks. Her green eyes brightened at his words. She touched his hand on her shoulder a moment before stepping back.

"Master, I met a devotee of the Mysteries. He said he would be willing to show you the way."

"Little Leopardess, that is the best news I've heard in... how long has it been?"

"It's been a year since my mistress was killed," she said, her voice rough.

He added this to the other years they had been apart. Far too many.

"Come, Master. Ride me, and I will take you to this man. I'm sure you can persuade him to show you the way."

Dionysus grinned as his most faithful servant transformed herself back into a leopard. Her naked limbs became haunches and forelegs, her fingers and toes curled into large spotted paws, and long, golden hair covered her body. She was ready to run faster than the wind. He stared at her, enamored by the beautiful creature he had helped her become, and thought of the words he had said to Perseus. He had not created her but unleashed what she truly was. That was part of his power—not to create but to unleash. He stroked her bowed head, scratching her between the ears until she purred, the sound rich and strong. She lowered herself so he could sit astride her more easily. He made himself light and gripped her shoulders tightly as she began to run.

THE INITIATE OF THE ELYSIAN MYSTERIES HAD ONLY ASKED FOR a promise in exchange for telling Dionysus the way. Dionysus found the entrance just as the initiate had said and began his descent. As the air cooled and the colors faded, he plotted how he would retrieve his wife and mother. There were no stories of gods or mortals going willingly to Hades, let alone returning with someone.

The slope became steeper and steeper. His feet slipped in his sandals, and the tops of his thighs burned. How long had he been walking? He imagined Hermes bringing souls this way, easily floating above the slope. This was one of the many barriers to keep the living out. A mortal could never endure this descent, but it was one of many challenges Dionysus was willing to face for his wife and mother.

His thoughts turned to his unknown uncle. The King of the Underworld was not known for honoring requests or being magnanimous. Once Dionysus found Hades, how could he possibly get permission to return with Ariadne and Semele? Would the offerings he had brought be enough? Could anything be enough for Hades?

Silenus had told him how Zeus, Poseidon, and Hades had drawn lots to decide who would rule each realm. Though Hades was the eldest brother, he had drawn the worst lot. Relegated far from Olympus, the King of the Underworld remained a mystery.

And what of Hades' wife Persephone? Of her he had heard many things: that she had been abducted by Hades, that she drew her own power from the Land of the Dead, and that vegetation died with her disappearance and returned with her reemergence.

Dionysus reached a place where the ground leveled off. He could not tell whether he strode on hard packed earth or black stone. A dark river flowed silently, showing him the way. An eerie quiet enveloped him. How could a river be silent? Cocking his head, he listened harder. There was a sound to it, like a hand slowly running over fabric. The faintest hint of splashing as an old man ferried a boat away from the shore. Dionysus watched the boat drift down the River Styx—Styx, once a Titan who had become a river, just as Crete had once been a princess. He thought of all the seeds he had planted in the earth above, of the infinitely complex gift he had given humanity. Had he come here to die? Was his time above through?

This place, this terrible calm, the loss of color that surrounded him, brought forth the deepest sorrow. This was the other side of wine, not the joy, not the exuberance, not the desire to dance or even the thrill of violence. He did not lust for blood or yearn for sex; he wanted only to sit by the river and weep.

Pity filled him. Poor mortals. They struggled so—for so long and so hard, and for what? Just this? Death and quiet oblivion. If they were lucky, they would be remembered as a place, a river, a star, but most were forgotten. His own sweet Ariadne would be remembered as a high priestess, as a daughter of a king, but what of someone like Thalia? There was no record of her life. No fresco commemorating what she had done, her acts of bravery or kindness or the horror she had endured at the hands of men. No one would know she had ever lived. And Ahumm, his faithful Phoenician sailor, who would remember him? Did it even matter? Did anything matter?

He found himself sitting on the damp earth, trailing his fingers in the water to see if it was real. Drinking from the river Lethe would erase all memory—what a fine idea. He would follow the River Styx until he found Lethe and drink; then he, too, could be lost in oblivion. All his heartache forgotten. The sorrow of his long, tragic life just a poem for the bards to sing. Mortals would honor him forever in drink, but he himself would not have to bear the pain—the hatred of the goddesses, the loss of his mother, the neglect of his father, his inability to protect his wife. After all he had done, this seemed the perfect ending. He rose, barely remembering to pick up his basket.

No sun shone in this place, but had it grown darker? The cavern had shifted from smoke to slate. Soon it would all be obscured in fog. Soon he would forget everything.

"Little Wanderer?" The voice of a god hit him like the slap of cold water. He blinked and turned to find Hermes leading two shades to the ferry landing.

"What are you doing here, Dionysus?" His first friend sounded cross. His silver eyes shone brighter than anything in the cavern.

"I..." Dionysus raked a hand through his hair, upsetting his myrtle wreath. What was he doing here? "...I came to retrieve my mother and my wife. I came to ask my uncle a boon."

"Did you now?" Hermes strode over to him, the souls forgotten. "How did you even find your way to this place?"

"It wasn't easy."

"Why did you not ask me?"

"Would you have brought me here?"

Hermes stroked Dionysus's cheek and ran his hand down his beard. "I do not know. But I'm glad I found you when I did. You do not appear to be well. In fact..." He wiped under Dionysus's eye and brought away a glistening ruby tear. "It appears you were weeping." He brought his finger to his lips and tasted the tear. "But look how powerful you've become. Crying wine, descending to the Underworld without a guide. You mustn't question your divinity any longer."

Had Dionysus not been enshrouded in grief, Hermes's words would have cheered him. But the shadows still closed in, and he yearned for help.

"Will you guide me?"

"Twice Born, I cannot. I should retrieve you from this place and return you to the upper world, but you know I am your true friend."

"My first friend. My brother." Dionysus clutched his forearm.

"Stop your sorrow. Focus on your task. Do not be distracted by the regrets of these souls. You were overcome by it." Hermes's lip curled in what was almost a smile. "You've always been too sensitive."

Dionysus closed his eyes, savoring the silken warmth of his friend's skin under his fingers. Hermes was right. He was unprepared. He had struggled to find his way to this place but had not planned what would happen once he got here.

"Thank you, brother. You saved me, even if you won't show me the way."

"I need not show you the way. You have made it here. All you need do is find Hades and persuade him to relinquish two souls." Hermes tried to hide his grin, but his lips turned up at the ridiculousness of the task that lay ahead.

Dionysus fought back more tears. What a fool he was! How would he ever get Hades to give him back Ariadne and his mother?

"Dionysus, I didn't want to bring Ariadne here, as I did not want to bring your lady mother. I told each of them not to eat or drink anything from the land of the dead. I had hoped that Zeus would try to retrieve Semele, but he did not have your courage.

"Here, take these honey-cakes. They're fresh. I just stole them from the temple between picking up souls. I see that you have brought gifts as well." He eyed Dionysus's basket, then turned his attention to the river. "Ah, the ferryman returns."

A hooded shade poled a flat-bottomed boat slowly toward them.

"Take this coin, and three more for the way back," Hermes said. His silver eyes shone with undying light, his teeth flashing bright in the gloom. Dionysus yearned to go back with him, to return to the land of the living, but he could not give up now.

Hermes held out his muscular arms and embraced him. "Great Hades is lonely in his realm. He has suckled nothing but the bones of regret and loss. Give him something to be jovial about. Give him a reason to repay your favor. Go now and do what no god has done before." He kissed Dionysus full on the lips. Though the kiss was brief, Dionysus came away feeling he had taken some of Hermes' light.

Hermes's eyes shone less brightly as he adjusted Dionysus's myrtle wreath. "Go, Little Wanderer. The God of Ways blesses your journey."

Hermes's kiss filled him with strength. He was no longer alone or a stranger. He was known. He had friends. Renewed, he stepped onto the dock amidst the shades. Freshly dead, they maintained their mortal form—transparent versions of who they had been before. An old man, a young girl, several soldiers all crowded onto the boat when the ferry docked.

The ferryman, Charon, reached out a bone-white arm from his tattered, once-black cloak and plucked coins from the mouths of the dead. Dionysus handed him a coin and got on. The ferryman's immortal eyes shone with a haunted light—not a flame, but a hint of the moon and stars.

As the ferryman poled his boat down the river toward the realm of the dead, Dionysus observed the light in the shades begin to dim. The shadows that had masked his eyes earlier descended again, only this time, he had Hermes's kiss on his lips; his half-brother's silver eyes shone in his mind. He pictured Ariadne's deep black eyes and the way they glowed golden when she had a vision or felt her power. He would find her. He would retrieve her and his mother. He would do what had never been done. Not even Hades would stop him.

When the boat docked, the shades drifted off. The girl and the old man went in one direction, the soldiers another.

Transparent shades floated near the dock, reminding Dionysus of leaves stuck in a whirlpool. They had nowhere to go, no destination and no impetus to move on.

"Lord Charon, where can I find the King of the Dead?"

The ferryman startled at his voice. Dionysus instantly regretted speaking in this place of silence. The shades turned toward him. Some began to drift over.

Charon's glowing eyes bore into him. Dionysus tried not to pay attention to the skeletal face, the hooked nose, or the wave of terror the ferryman caused in him. Silenus had told him that Hades's ferryman was the son of Night and Darkness. Dionysus had forgotten until this moment. There was no doubt of Charon's parentage. Had the ferryman ever eaten? Had he ever spoken a word to a mortal? Was he used to the moans and complaints of the dead and unable to hear or respond?

I am a god. I do what no god has done. Dionysus gripped his thyrsus and stood straighter, allowing the ferryman to look him over. Charon's gaze on his body was like a touch, and he struggled not to shudder.

"You are not dead," Charon said, his voice rough with disuse.

Was Charon going to force him back on the boat and to the other side? Should he run?

"And yet, you have died. Curious."

"I'm here to visit my uncle and my mother."

Charon lifted his thin lips and bared his teeth in a lurid grin. "Ah, your mother. Yes. Well, Undying One, the king and queen's palace is that way." He lifted his pole, dripping with dark water. "Follow the road made of giant bones. Careful of the dog." He turned back to his boat, plunged his pole into the water, and pushed away from the dock.

With confidence he did not feel, Dionysus strode in the direction Charon had indicated. Gray mist engulfed him. Shades swarmed toward him. If they had still been living souls, he could have given them his gift of transformation. He could have changed their sorrow to joy, but his gift did not work on the dead.

There was nothing for these spirits to transform into anymore. They floated to him as a moth does to flame, aware of his light, of his vitality and its difference.

I should have listened to my mother, the shade of a child thought.

Aristos, is that you? the shade of a young man asked. *I have been waiting here for you, my love.*

Son? a woman with a swollen belly said. *Is that you? Have you found me all grown up? Can I hold you at last?*

Other voices came, drowning him with their sorrow and regret. He thought of Hermes again, focused on Ariadne, and held his thyrsus upright. He took one step, then another, pushing the thoughts of the shades away. *You've always been too sensitive,* Hermes had said. Dionysus blocked out the thoughts of the shades. He pushed away the pleas and questions and continued up the road made of giants' bones.

In the mist, it was difficult to make out what lay ahead. Charon had warned him about a dog, but he had not expected three. When he saw that it was one dog with three heads, he nearly laughed aloud, which would have woken two of the sleeping heads. He slipped his hand into his basket and pulled out one of the barley cakes, placed it on the ground in front of the dog, and backed into the mist.

The dog who was awake snapped up the barley cake. The sound of it eating made Dionysus glad the other two slept.

In the fog, the palace of Hades loomed as a shadow in a world of shadows. Giant bones stood upright, columns glittering white in the darkness. Their light drew him. He pushed away the fear creeping up his neck. From the gloom, four shades of soldiers stepped forward. Unlike the others he had encountered, these were not transparent or formless, but seemed to be made of shale and bone.

"Halt, stranger. Who dares to come uninvited to the palace of Lord Hades?" The guard's voice was like the clanging of metal in this quiet place, and Dionysus jerked and then stopped before him.

"I am Dionysus, nephew of Lord Hades. I come bearing gifts."

An eerie light illuminated the guard's eyes, like fire reflecting off a cat's eye. He seemed able to peer into Dionysus's very soul.

"You are not one of the dead. You are not supposed to be here."

"No. I have come to speak to my uncle. Will you let me pass?"

The guard turned to another soldier. "Go, tell this news to our master and see what he says."

When the shade went inside, Dionysus stood in awkward silence. Of all the men he had encountered, this was a first. They could not speak or drink or fight or fuck.

"Do you remember who you were? Do you have any messages for those above?"

The light in a guard's eyes blazed and then returned to its eerie light. "I have not thought of that for a long while. No one can send messages to those above, and even if you could—there is no one above left for me. For any of us."

A great sadness crept off him at these words. There was no questioning the certainty. This was life for mortals: a brief period, easily forgotten.

"Yet you serve a purpose still. You four were chosen to guard this place. King Hades trusts you in this. That is also an honor."

The main guard's eyes flared again for a second. *But what is this compared to one moment of being alive?* the shade thought. Dionysus wanted to tell him just retaining his own thoughts was more than the other shades had. But he had not come here to argue with the dead and comment on their various gradations of despair. Truly, he did not know whether it were better to exist silently floating in the shadows or remember all that had been lost. Soundlessly, the guard who had gone inside with the message returned.

"King Hades bids you come."

Two of the guards led him through the antechamber and into the grand throne room. Devoid of frescoes or colorful paints, the walls glittered with jewels. Flecks of gold, chunks of diamonds and rubies encrusted the walls. Shades of royalty, their diadems still perched on their heads, stood in attendance, outlining a path to the raised pavilion where the King and Queen of the Underworld sat.

The royal pavilion was held up by columns made from the forearm bones of giants, wrapped in silver and diamonds. The stairs and platform were carved from rock crystal. An enormous amethyst served as a couch, cradling Hades as he reclined on a cushion of black wool. Persephone sat upright next to him, her eyes fixed on Dionysus.

Dionysus noticed similarities between his own physical features and those of his uncle—the curl of their hair, the keen gaze of the eyes. Hades's black beard glittered like obsidian in moonlight. Dionysus wondered what his father looked like.

"I hear you are one of my brother's bastards," Hades said by way of greeting.

"Yes, King of the Underworld, that is one thing I am."

"I have heard you are called Twice Born, yet here you are in the Land of the Dead."

"Yes, my Lord, that is one thing I am not. May I call you uncle?"

Hades glanced at his wife. Persephone's pale face remained calm, but she stared at Dionysus longer than was proper. Her gaze seemed hungry for him, and despite her husband's noticing, she did not look away.

"I suppose you may, for you are indeed my brother's bastard, semi-divine and still-living."

"Thank you, Uncle. I have come bearing gifts."

"And I suppose you come to ask a favor as well?"

"Yes, but first, may I offer you a drink? I have taken the grape and made it wine..."

"Tell me what you want."

"Other than to meet you and the Queen of the Dead." He stared at Persephone, who held his gaze. No, he must focus on his mission. "I've come for two women, Uncle. Two mortal souls, both with the qualities of the semi-divine. I have come to offer a gift in exchange for returning them to the world above."

Hades paused as if he had misheard and then burst into laughter. "You come to my very throne to take what is mine?"

"No, Uncle. I come bearing gifts and hoping to make an exchange. I offer you revenge on two goddesses. Restoring the lives of these women will irk Hera and Artemis. I know you have no love for those who frolic above, free to lounge in the sun and travel wherever they desire."

Hades glanced at Persephone, and Dionysus wondered whether he had said the wrong thing. Persephone's lips turned up in the hint of a smile, and Hades appeared slightly amused.

"Ah, revenge on my sister Hera would be a fine thing. But I have no grudge against Artemis. In fact, she sends me many souls. She kills women in childbirth, and she kills freely. Often I receive two shades at once. And I would not want to anger her twin brother Apollo."

Dionysus bowed his head. His myrtle wreath shifted, and he pushed it back. "I see. Well, Uncle, I have also come to give you what no one has."

"And what could that possibly be? You glimpsed some of the jewels on your way to this chamber? All the gold, iron, diamonds, any gem from the earth belongs to me. I possess the soul of every mortal who ever lived." He raised his large hand; a huge piece of labradorite glittered on his first finger as he gestured to Persephone. "I have a beautiful immortal wife and many slaves. What can you give me that no one else has?"

"What do you receive from these shades you rule over?" Dionysus wondered if the flame in his uncle's eyes was mirrored in his own. Heat grew between them, warm then hot. Would his uncle cast him out, or did he feel this connection, too?

"Their lives, their spirits, their memories are all mine," Hades replied.

"And do you use those well? Do you savor each new life, relive each memory?"

"No," Hades sighed. "They are little more than detritus to me. What do you come here offering me, godling?"

Dionysus gently lifted the amphora out of his traveling pouch. "This is of one of my gifts, Uncle. I have many more. For now, please allow me to offer you the drink I have created. It is unlike anything you have tasted before.

"I offer you what no other can—the gift of change in an unchanging world. I have transformed the grape into a drink that will change your own feelings. I call it wine, and it will change your perception."

One of Hades' soot-black eyebrows raised as if he had not even remembered he had feelings for centuries.

"And, after you drink, you will rest like you have not rested in a long while," Dionysus added.

Hades' eyes smoldered with surprise. He let out a laugh, like rock breaking.

"Come, then, godling, sit with us and let us try your drink."

Dionysus did not know how much time had passed. His magical amphora refilled itself numerous times. Hades had offered him food, but Dionysus knew better than to take it. With nothing to eat, even he found himself rather drunk. Queen Persephone had partaken, and now a rosy glow illuminated her pale cheeks.

"Son of Zeus, how are you divine when so many of my brother's bastards are merely heroes?"

Dionysus swirled his wine in his cup. "Wise Uncle, my divinity was not given to me but earned. I have never met my lord father. I made my way on my own. Hunted by Queen Hera's wrath, I have always been an outsider—a stranger to mortals and gods alike. The Queen of the Gods sent madness to my first stepfather. Fleeing his rage, I jumped into the sea, and the Titaness Thetis took me in.

"I am not only a god of wine. I am the God of Transformation
—twice born, re-formed, born of my father's thigh, born with
horns, born unknown." He glanced at Persephone. "I have made
my own way and my own rules. I alone among the gods can break
free from the chains of the past. I have transformed not just the
humble grape into wine but a bastard boy into a god."

Hades chuckled. His black eyebrows rose in amusement, and
he raised his chalice. "Ah, youth. Your father, Poseidon, and I
once spoke so. We would be different from our father, different
from the generation of Titans that went before us. We would
become our own gods, set the stars to align our own fate. And I
suppose we have. I don't believe any of us have eaten our own
children as our father did." He took a sip of wine and shuddered.
"Being kept in your father's thigh is a better way to be born than
being eaten by him."

"There are many ways to come into this world," Persephone
said. "It is what we do once we're here that matters."

"Truly, our birth is not the important part. It is the survival,"
Hades said. "I was like you once, nephew. All young gods are. But
as we grow older over the centuries, we realize the nature of one
is the nature of all. We are not so different from the generation
before us."

Hades stared into his chalice, swirling the dark wine. "Your
skill is admirable. I'll give you that." He raised his chalice to his
lips. "This is better even than ambrosia—and you made this? Very
impressive."

"I transformed it, Uncle. As death transforms a mortal to a
memory and time transforms the memory to a myth or a
forgotten life, I transformed the grape into a potion to help with
sorrow, to fuel the blood, and feed desire."

"Tell me again why you came here, Dionysus," Hades said.

"I came for my mother." He glanced at Persephone, a beautiful prisoner in the Underworld. The maiden forced to live in the
darkness half the year, a girl who had become queen to the King
of the Dead.

Hades glanced at his wife, love in his eyes. "Who does he mean?"

"Semele," Persephone said. "Daughter of Cadmus and Harmony, a priestess of the moon from Thebes. A great beauty, a wise woman. Zeus loved her more than Hera, and for that, she died." Her voice was soft and sad, as if the story broke her heart. "She is here in the palace, one of my ladies, though after all this time, refusing to eat, she has grown so weak, I can barely find her. There is only the faintest trace of her shade. We should let him have her, husband. It will infuriate Hera and bring chaos to Olympus."

Hades laughed more freely, as if it were a skill he was remembering. His deep voice rang out, echoing through his onyx halls. Then he laughed again at the sound of his merriment, clearly so foreign, and appreciated.

"You may have her, nephew."

"Thank you, Uncle. And, I beg you, allow me to have my wife as well. I will give you anything you desire in exchange." Dionysus stood and knelt before his uncle's throne, allowing his shoulder strap to slip down and expose his chest. How long had it been since a living being had offered himself to the King of the Dead?

"Oh, youth. What are you, a mere 500 years old? Certainly, less than a thousand." He stroked Dionysus's neck. "Supple and alive, and so different from your father. He would never offer himself like this." He twined a lock of Dionysus's hair around his finger.

"You offer yourself so easily, as if you lose nothing through submitting. My brothers and I were not like this. The slightest hint of deference, and we thought we had lost our manhood. You seem oddly stronger than that. You make me question too much. It is a tempting offer, yet what would I lose in taking you?"

"Let the boy have what he wants, husband," Persephone said. "Give him his mother and wife both. His wife has helped shades speak. She has made colors bloom. It is better if she is no longer here."

Hades's eyes went from Dionysus's chest to Persephone's lips. Dionysus sensed the King of the Underworld wanted them both —he wanted all—every soul, every jewel. Dionysus had experienced this insatiable feeling when drunk, this longing for everything that would never be enough. He understood his uncle more than he would have liked.

"Husband," Persephone said, bringing Hades's attention back, "if you give him his wife, I will come to you early next year and stay late. I will do it every few years, enough to confuse the mortals, and I will bring you gifts from above. In fact, I will bring you wine. Come, now, godling," she said, rising. "I will take you to your mother."

Dionysus did not rise from his knees, for Hades had not let go of his hair.

"Not so quickly, dear wife. I will accept your offer and allow him to take his mother. But..." He released Dionysus's hair. "For your wife, I will have a trade. Give me something alive that you love in exchange for her."

Thalia. She was the first living thing to appear in his mind. He loved her dearly. She would gladly give her life in exchange for Ariadne's. Losing her would hurt too much. Hades wanted this exchange to hurt, though the King of the Underworld would suffer nothing to return Ariadne to the world above.

"Whose life would you give to retrieve your wife? One of your followers perhaps? A priest? A lover? I've heard about your wild women, ripping apart babes and husbands alike. Perhaps one of your wild women or one of your satyr friends? Surely they would not mind dying for their undying god."

Dionysus bowed his head; his myrtle wreath shifted. Ariadne had told him how her first husband had been honored to die for the goddess. One of his own devotees would be more than willing. A devout follower like Acoetes or Ahumm would do for Hades. But what kind of god would Dionysus be to sacrifice one of his own?

He adjusted his myrtle wreath. He was the god of vegetation, of transformation. Humans were not the only living thing he loved.

Remaining on his knees, he clasped Hades's hand. "As you wish, Uncle. I will give you a living thing dear to me, a long-time companion. I will be sorry to lose this, but it is yours now." He lifted the myrtle wreath off his head and ceremoniously handed it to Hades.

"This myrtle is a living thing. It will no longer be sacred to me but to you. It will continue to live here in the Underworld with you."

Hades accepted the crown with shock and then amusement.

"So quick-witted, son of Zeus. I will take your offer, though it is not what I meant. Go, quickly, before I change my mind."

"You were brave to come here," Persephone whispered after they left the great hall.

"I regret that I did not think to find my mother sooner. It did not occur to me until Artemis killed my wife."

"Perhaps you were only waiting to become strong and wise enough for such a journey. Your mother would be proud." Persephone met his gaze in the flickering light. "I've heard much of your life, Dionysus. I have listened to all that is said of you. I'm sure Zeus has done the same. Now, let us find Semele."

Dionysus followed her deep into the cavernous palace. Hades's abode appeared to go on forever. Persephone led him to a set of stairs made of polished rose quartz which glowed dimly.

"I do not think it inappropriate to bring you to the women's quarters, for you have masqueraded as a girl before," Persephone said as they began to ascend. "Or perhaps that is incorrect; perhaps it is inappropriate for you to be in the Underworld at all, so it is not wrong to take you upstairs."

"It is true. I have been in the women's quarters many times. It is always an honor to see women free of the domination of men.

Among my own followers, this is how my worshippers are, free and able to do what they wish."

Persephone almost laughed. "Sadly, the shades above have far less freedom and joy than your initiates. Your devotees are free to be who they truly are. They are the pinnacle of life, whereas my ladies are done with life completely."

They reached Persephone's chambers. Despite the grand nature of these halls, sorrow hung heavy. This was the best a mortal woman could hope for—to be taken in by the Queen of the Underworld and allowed to serve her. A wave of hopelessness rose over him. But there was beauty in this place still. Even in the unchanging Underworld, he could bring change, and from what Persephone said, it sounded like Ariadne had, too. He would find her soon.

Two of Persephone's women sat weaving on a splendid loom using golden thread that shimmered in the light. He stepped closer to examine the image and immediately recognized the palace at Thebes looming in the background of the tapestry. The central image was of a maiden encircled in smoke; a glowing rod of lightning flashed brighter than anything else in the tapestry. Above the lightning, the face of a god hovered, silver tears leaking from his eyes and into his curly black beard.

"She wove this scene over and over again until she faded. When Ariadne revived her, she began again," Persephone said.

The shade before him continued to weave as if he were not there. He glanced around the room for Ariadne, desperate for her, but understanding his duty now was to his mother. Though mostly transparent, she bore many of his features.

He knelt before her. "Mother? Were you called Semele in life? Were you the daughter of Cadmus and Harmony?"

Her eyes, which had once been green, focused on him, trying to comprehend his question.

"She is weak, Dionysus. She has eaten nothing all these years," Persephone said. "You would not be able to see her at all if your wife had not given her strength. Semele, this is your son." Persephone touched Semele's hand, infusing her with light.

The green in Semele's eyes grew bright, and her chestnut hair shone in the gloom. "Son? My baby who survived?" She saw him now.

Tears welled in his eyes. He forced away thoughts of what it would have been like to have a mother, to have taken milk from her breast instead of drinking goats' milk fed to him by rain nymphs, to have grown up as her cherished son, the grandson of a king. No... there would have never been a happy story for them—not with Zeus as his father—not once Hera found out.

Semele squeezed his hand. "I thought you had burned up with me, too young to even become a shade. I never imagined meeting you. And here you stand, a lovely man. Did you die early, or is this the form you chose to take for eternity? What is that coming from your eyes? Son, are you bleeding?"

Dionysus wiped at his cheek.

"No. I am well, Mother. I am..." Happiness and sorrow mixed, and he could not utter the next words.

"He is a god, Semele. The newest god in Hellas. He has traveled far and wide and been worshiped by many. But this is his farthest journey, to the Land of the Dead, to find you and his wife Ariadne, the one who gave you so much light," Persephone said.

His tears flowed freely now. Rivulets of wine ran down his cheeks. He did not trust himself to speak and was grateful that Persephone spoke for him. His happiness would be complete if Ariadne were here to share it with him.

Watching him, Persephone seemed to read his mind.

"Ariadne, come," Persephone commanded. And now he saw his wife rise from behind an amethyst couch. Though she was transparent and gray, the tiniest hint of gold shone in her eyes.

"Wife." He rushed to her the way a man was never supposed to do in the world above. He did not care. He made his own rules, followed his own code now.

"Dionysus," Ariadne said, her voice little more than a whisper.

He reached to embrace her, but she was intangible.

"Help me." He was not sure whether he was speaking to Persephone or Semele. Semele took his and Ariadne's hands, so they formed a circle.

"You have enough immortality to share. Give some to your mother and wife," Persephone said.

Dionysus thought of the vine growing from seedling to ripe, plump grapes. He imagined the tendrils of his immortality coiling around the souls of his mother and wife, giving them the strength they needed to return to the world above. Like the grapevine, they would return after appearing dead. They would survive, undying.

Semele and Ariadne glowed with color now.

"Semele of Thebes is dead," Persephone said. "I rename you Thyone. And you, Ariadne, will be Dionysus's immortal wife as I am Hades' immortal wife—may you have eternal happiness."

Golden tears glittered on Ariadne's cheeks. His mother Thyone's beauty shone strongly now. He could feel their happiness flow through him. Persephone smiled serenely, as if finally completing a task she had hoped to achieve for centuries.

"My husband gave you permission to return to the land above. I advise haste. Come now." Persephone led them down the stairs. It had seemed to take a long time to climb up, but now, all four of them immortal, they almost seemed to fly. At the great doors of the palace, Persephone grasped Dionysus's and Ariadne's wrists.

"I will see you again. In the spring I shall bring you flowers."

DIONYSUS AND ARIADNE RISE

They emerged from the darkness of the cavern leading from the Underworld. Ariadne blinked into the haze, grateful to draw breath. Two shadows awaited them in the blue-gray light.

"Mistress!" Thalia ran over and hugged her tightly.

"Little Leopard." Ariadne held her friend, inhaling her scent. "I thought I'd never see you again."

Hermes approached them. grinning. A golden object shimmered behind him.

"I did not doubt you, Dionysus. Shall we call you thrice-born now?"

Laughing, Dionysus embraced his brother. Ariadne studied Thalia. New lines and freckles marked her skin.

"How long have I been gone?" Grief and fear rose suddenly.

"Three years."

"My sons…"

"They are well cared for on Lemnos."

Though she had left through no fault of her own, she was overcome with guilt and regret.

"I've missed so much." She had not been a mother to her children, a priestess to her followers, or a wife to her husband.

Thalia wiped Ariadne's cheeks, her fingers glittering with Ariadne's tears. "You returned from the Underworld. No one has done that!"

Ariadne glanced back at the cave. Thyone stood in the pale light, gazing at her own hands in wonder.

"Someone else has done it as well." Ariadne tucked away her remorse. How foolish. She had been gone for three years. How long had Thyone been dead? She had missed all of Dionysus's youth. She had never even had a chance to nurse him. Now she returned to a world long lost to her, and instead of grief, she greeted it with amazement. Ariadne would do the same.

As Hermes came toward her, his silver eyes glowed.

"Lady Ariadne, did I not say I hoped to see you again? And Semele, it has been centuries."

"She is called Thyone now," Dionysus said, pride lighting his eyes. He had a mother. For the first time in his life. He appeared brighter, stronger, and unconquerable. The ache Ariadne felt for her sons was replaced with happiness for her husband.

"An honor, Lady. Welcome back to the land of the living," Hermes said.

Thalia did not speak but bowed politely to Thyone.

"Thank you, God of Ways. It is a pleasure to return." Thyone shone with her new immortality. Ariadne never imagined the crumpled shadow she had first seen could radiate this kind of beauty. She understood why Zeus had loved Semele and why Hera had been so jealous.

Dionysus clasped Ariadne's hand and brought it to his lips. He stared at her as if they were alone in their bedchamber.

Desire coursed through her as she remembered what it was to be alive. To feel his tongue on her skin, his hands on her thighs— she wanted him as desperately as the first time they had met. No, more fiercely than that because then, he had been a stranger. Now she knew the pleasures he could give her. Images of lying with him under the sun, of him kneeling before her while her wrists were bound and his followers watched, of the two of them alone, lying among the grapevines. She was ready to strip off her clothes for him.

Hermes coughed softly. Dionysus let go of Ariadne's hand. The smile on his lips hinted at later pleasures.

"I made an agreement with our father, Twice Born. Zeus said that if you succeeded in returning from the Underworld, he would welcome you to Olympus. When Hera argued that there could only be twelve Olympians, Hestia offered up her seat. She says her place is in the hearth of every mortal who worships her. She need not have a seat above. You are to be an Olympian, my brother, finally acknowledged as the god you are." He clasped Dionysus's forearm.

"Now that I've done all the work, they acknowledge me," Dionysus said. "How like the Olympians. Still, thank you, my brother."

"Where is your crown of myrtle?" Hermes asked.

"Hades offered me Ariadne's life in exchange for a living thing I loved. It was not a difficult choice."

"So clever. I'm sure the King of the Underworld did not appreciate that little trick. Perhaps it is best not to dwell here. Let us fly to Olympus. Thalia, if you will?"

Thalia transformed into a leopard and padded over to the front of the chariot so Hermes could harness her with golden chains. Ariadne noticed the chariot then, a golden boat, clearly made by Hephaestus.

The sleek leopard and the golden chariot made a beautiful image, but Ariadne worried for her friend.

"Pulling us will be too much for Thalia," Ariadne said.

"Worry not, Lady. She will not actually carry our weight. You will see." Hermes helped Thyone up and offered his hand to Ariadne. Dionysus climbed next to her, sliding his arm around her waist. A cloud of mist engulfed them. The wings on Hermes's helmet began to flutter. He took the reins, and Thalia began to run.

"Within this magic orb of mist, the laws of weight and gravity do not apply. Hephaestus made this chariot so you could ascend to Olympus in style."

The chariot lifted off the ground, the magical orb floating up like a bird taking wing. They rose above the dreary mist that surrounded the cavern to the Underworld, flying into the golden sunlight.

The sky had never been more blue. It was almost the exact shade as the frescoes of Knossos, and now Ariadne flew surrounded by that blue and those she loved. She took a deep breath of clean, fresh air, savoring being above ground.

As the chariot rose higher, Ariadne glanced down to see Argos, a fortified palace, the walled city. They continued their ascent, and she appreciated the beauty of the sea, the coastlines turquoise and the water gradually darkening away from the land.

"Lovely," Thyone said. Ariadne noticed a musical aspect to her words. Perhaps it was her accent, or perhaps this was how people had spoken generations ago.

As Thyone turned back to smile at Ariadne and Dionysus, the connection between the three of them pulsed in Ariadne's veins. Through death and divinity, they were irrevocably linked.

Thyone's joy at being alive again invigorated Ariadne, entwining with her own elation. The wind lifted her hair off the back of her neck as they continued to ascend. She caressed Dionysus's inner wrist.

"We were in the Underworld, consigned to a murky existence, dead for eternity, and now we are immortal in a flying boat, pulled by a woman who is a leopard," Thyone said. "We are going to Olympus to meet the gods, all because of you, my son, and you, daughter."

"The absurdity of life, death, and fate could not be clearer. The random lot of mortals, the fickle ways of the gods, the luck of some and the tragedy of others," Dionysus said.

"I think of this often, Twice Born," Hermes said. "Some sink so low while others rise so high. And now you who have been to the depths of the Underworld ascend to the greatest heights."

Thyone began to laugh at this, a musical sound Dionysus, Ariadne, and even Hermes could not resist. They joined in, echoing her mirth. Thalia turned her leopard head back and let out a roar that was a laugh all her own.

"The irony of it all. The pain and the joy," Dionysus said, grinning madly. "Perhaps I will create a new form of art—a performance where mortals can be entertained by the comedy and tragedy of life." He wiped a wine tear away with his finger. "The two seem connected in a way I had not fathomed before. Perhaps I will call it theater."

"Delightful," Thyone said.

Images from Dionysus's mind flashed through Ariadne's: a stage with people wearing masks—not just telling stories, but pretending to be the characters. This wonderful new idea thrilled her—to sit and be entertained in such a way!

"You give mortals so many gifts," Ariadne said. Once spoken, her words shocked her, for she no longer counted herself among mortals. She studied her free hand in the sunlight. Golden beads of divinity glittered on her skin.

You have always been a goddess to me. How many times had Thalia said that to her? And now the words of the woman who was a leopard had come true. She turned to Dionysus and kissed him full on the mouth.

He embraced her; their bodies pressed together, not caring how improper such behavior was. Time lost all meaning. All that mattered was Dionysus's mouth upon hers, his hands caressing her.

"We are approaching the peak of Mount Olympus. You might want to compose yourselves," Hermes said. "I'm going to fly over so you can see your new home and all the gods will see us coming. Dionysus, you will find it much changed."

Ariadne adjusted her dress and smoothed down her hair. She had no idea how she appeared, but the way Dionysus gazed at her made her think Aphrodite herself would be jealous.

Below their chariot, glorious gold domes capping marble

palaces shone in the sun. Clearly this was Hephaestus's work, for it mimicked the home Dionysus and Ariadne shared on Lemnos. Each building appeared unique to its owner.

"That pink marble monstrosity is what Hephaestus made for Aphrodite as a wedding gift," Hermes said.

Ariadne did not think it so horrible, though the golden statues of giant clam shells with huge pearls in the garden did appear a bit much.

"That slate building capped with a helmet belongs to Athena, and the one with the golden sun is Apollo's. That great palace obviously belongs to Zeus and Hera." Hermes gestured to the largest building, which had a painted statue of Zeus sitting in his throne next to a smaller statue of Hera in her peacock chair. Upon seeing the image of the King of the Gods, Ariadne felt both Thyone's excitement and Dionysus's apprehension.

He was about to meet his father for the first time, the father who had carried him in his thigh and then abandoned him. She clasped her husband's hand, proud he was returning to Olympus to take his seat at long last.

"That simple barracks-like building is home to Ares." Past the squat house, Hermes gestured to an immense forest thick with fir, cypress, oak, and almond trees. "The modest palaces among the trees belong to Demeter and Artemis, when they choose to stay on high—which is not often. I don't know where Hestia stays when she comes; she is always by some hearth."

"Kind Hestia has given up her throne for me?" Dionysus asked.

"Yes, she does so happily. She prefers the company of mortals to Olympians. The mortals honor her always, for what is a home without a hearth? She is the first to be sacrificed to and the most benevolent of all the gods. She does not especially enjoy her time here."

As Hermes circled the chariot above, preparing to land, the Olympians and their attendants came out to greet them. Demeter and a troop of tree nymphs emerged from the forest. Ariadne glimpsed Zeus also slinking out of the forest before Hermes turned the chariot and set it to land before the great meeting hall.

Hephaestus limped out of the hall, beaming. He shone with a divine light he had not possessed on Lemnos. Ariadne rejoiced to see him walking instead of using a donkey or magical device. Perhaps at last he had been accepted for who he was.

"Twice Born, welcome to Olympus!" His booming voice drew the other gods, who surrounded the golden chariot.

"Lady Ariadne, it is so good to see you again. Twice Born, this must be your lady mother, Seme..."

"Hephaestus," Dionysus interrupted, "allow me to present my mother, renamed Thyone. She and my lady wife now share my immortality."

Hephaestus's jaw dropped. "I did not know such a thing was possible. Ah, Twice Born, to think you doubted your divinity when we first met? It is a pleasure, Lady Thyone. Welcome. I know Zeus will be pleased to see you."

Ariadne wondered how Hera would respond. At least she could not kill Thyone again. She glanced at the gods surrounding them, relieved Artemis was not there. The goddess probably had no desire to see her enemy accepted by the Olympians.

Demeter came toward them with her troop of tree nymphs. Her resemblance to Persephone and the crown of wheat adorning her dark hair told Ariadne exactly who she was. "Welcome to Olympus. I can feel that you've seen my daughter—all three of you. Is she well?"

"She is," Thyone said.

"Goddess, she thrives. She rules wisely and has more strength than those above realize," Ariadne said.

"Thank you. I'm glad to hear this from a woman's mouth."

The other gods and their attendants drew closer. Ares and Aphrodite, Athena and Apollo watched from a distance, taking in the scene. Hera stood alone staring at Thyone, glaring at her youth and beauty, which seemed to shine even here among the gods.

And then great Zeus strode forward. His shimmering white chiton covered one shoulder, clasped with a silver eagle pin, exposing half of his broad chest. Beneath his glittering crown, black hair cascaded to his shoulders. The waves in his hair were matched by his perfectly coifed beard.

"My son," he said, holding out his arms, "and your lovely mother and wife! Welcome, welcome! We are honored to have you. Disembark from this glorious sky-boat Hephaestus made for you." He offered a hand to Thyone. "My dear, it has been too long. You appear as enchanting as the last time I saw you centuries ago." He lifted her by her tiny waist and helped her to the ground. Dionysus jumped down from the chariot to assist Ariadne.

"Lady Ariadne, I have heard much of your beauty," Zeus said.

"Thank you, Lord. It is an honor to be here," Ariadne said, though she did not care for the insatiable lust in his eyes.

Zeus turned to Dionysus. "And you, my son, how proud I am of your accomplishments. When I scooped your essence from the ash that was your mother, slashed open my thigh in my grief, and let you mature inside me, I never imagined you would grow to be the newest god of Olympus, the only one born of a mortal mother."

These were the words Dionysus had wanted to hear all his life. His father acknowledged him, welcomed him, and recognized his godhood. Yet what right did Zeus have to this pride? All Dionysus had done, he had done on his own. Ariadne kept a smile on her lips and let her husband speak.

"My mother is mortal no longer, great Zeus. She is reborn as Thyone. I have shared my immortality with her and Ariadne."

Zeus considered this, impressed. "Well done, my son. Thyone, my own goddess wife Hera and I welcome you to Olympus."

Hera pinched her lips and scowled but said nothing. Thyone did not even seem to see her. She stared at Zeus with devotion.

"Come, my son, see your new throne, and later, the new home Hephaestus built for you."

Dionysus, Ariadne, and the gods followed Zeus into the great hall, where the thrones of the Olympians sat in a semicircle. A glittering golden throne decorated with vine leaves and clusters of grapes made of amethyst sat on the end.

"It's stunning, Twice Fallen," Dionysus said.

"I began working on it when you first came to Lemnos. I promise it will not bite or bind you," Hephaestus said.

Dionysus chuckled. Ariadne noticed that Hera and Ares did not think this a funny joke. She did not care what the other gods thought. She and Thyone beamed as Dionysus sat on the plush purple cushion.

"Perfect," Zeus said.

"Marvelous," Aphrodite said, seeming to admire the throne, but gazing at Dionysus's thighs. Ariadne did not mind. Being married to a god the Goddess of Love and Beauty lusted after did not bother her, though she worried about the heartbreak Aphrodite would cause Hephaestus.

"And I did not forget you, Ariadne," Hephaestus said. He reached into an unseen pocket in his leather apron and produced a sparkling silver crown. The silver shone with the luminous quality of stars and lit the great hall with a quiet light. He held the crown out for the Olympians to admire. Seven perfectly shaped diamonds twinkled in sparkling silver.

"Hephaestus, your skill is matched by your kindness. I am honored to have your friendship," Ariadne said.

Aphrodite shifted her gaze from Dionysus to her husband. The disregard she had for him changed suddenly to pride, as if her husband's accomplishments were her own.

Hephaestus handed the crown to Dionysus, and he rose to place it on Ariadne's head.

"When I met you, you were a priestess and a princess, but you are the queen of my heart." He placed the crown on Ariadne's head, nestling the end pieces in her hair.

"I am proud to call you husband, and to be married to the newest Olympian," Ariadne said.

He grinned, ecstatic. He had gotten everything he had ever wanted. She noticed Apollo gazing at Dionysus and had a vision of the two of them having endless discussions about the nature of man and morality—perhaps even this new idea of theater.

Dionysus grasped Ariadne's hand and strode out of the great hall.

"Come, Twice Fallen, show me where you were thrown."

Hera glowered at him as Hephaestus limped forward, with the other Olympians following. It might take a mortal half a day, but the gods only walked a little way to the edge of Olympus. The sun had set. The clouds glowed with golden light, shades of white and yellow, light and deep pink, so warm—the complete opposite of the colors of the underworld. Down below, a tapestry of landscape unfurled under the darkening sky: green lands, rocky landscapes, houses clumped together, a scattering of temples, the wine-dark sea encompassing islands.

"Is this where the gods stand to look down upon mortals?" Dionysus asked.

Zeus stood nearby, watching Dionysus quizzically.

"Yes, this place has the best view," Zeus said. Ariadne could picture Ares greedily watching battles and Demeter noticing nothing but the crops, Hera staring down trying to find Zeus hiding from her, Aphrodite looking for handsome men or vain women.

Dionysus did not look down. He gazed at Ariadne and then glanced at the darkening sky. "I want to remember this night forever."

Once he spoke, Ariadne knew exactly what her husband would do. Without him asking, she lifted the crown off her head and handed it to him. He held it carefully, positioning it just right. He closed his eyes, summoning a newfound power, and gently flicked his wrist.

The crown remained in his hand, but the diamonds were gone. When they gazed out to the sky, there they were, set as stars.

"This night will be remembered forever in the heavens. Let

every mortal and every god who looks upon the crown of Ariadne know of the love of Dionysus and Ariadne, and the happiness of the newest Olympian."

Aphrodite sighed at this romantic gesture, despite herself. Hephaestus hooted.

"Truly you are an Olympian to set the stars," Demeter said.

The gods gazed at the night sky, but Ariadne found her eyes drawn back to the earth, to the isle of Lemnos. Dionysus took her hand, knowing her thoughts. How she longed to see their sons, to hold them in her arms, to see how their faces and limbs had grown long, to memorize every detail of their new little bodies.

Yet at the same time, these emotions did not tear her apart as they would have before. She thought of a clay pot, soft and malleable, put into a kiln and made hard—this was what her divinity had done to her. She still had feelings, but they were hard and distant. Was this how Demeter felt, being separated from Persephone? The Goddess of the Grain watched her, a sad smile on her face.

"Let us return to the great hall," Zeus said. "I'm eager to sample this new drink." The King of the Gods strode back toward the center of Olympus, and the others followed. Demeter walked toward Ariadne.

"Strength, little goddess," Demeter whispered. She stroked Ariadne's forearm and walked back to the great hall.

Dionysus and Ariadne stood alone on the edge of Olympus beneath the starry sky. Before she could ask when they could return to Lemnos, he spoke.

"I miss them, too, Beloved. I will not be like my own father, uncaring and absent. We will spend a few days here, give them a party they won't soon forget. Then we'll return to Lemnos, to our sons and followers."

Ariadne kissed him full on the lips. She smiled up at her crown in the stars—their love remembered for eternity.

"A good plan, husband. Now, let us drink."

AUTHOR'S NOTE

The myths of Dionysus and Ariadne are complicated and contradictory. This book came about partially in response to the well-
known Athenian tale that Pasiphae, maddened with lust, made
Daedalus create a wooden cow so she could climb inside and have
sex with the bull from the sea. This made me start thinking more
deeply about how the Greek myths we know are the stories of the
conquerors and the ones who lived to record their version of
events.

The Minoans lived during the Bronze Age, between 3000
BCE to 1100 BCE. Their stories and surviving art and architecture have fascinated generations for millennia. I was curious to
try and discover what could have "really happened." Of course,
like many of the peoples lost to history, there is no way to know
for certain.

I was inspired to tell the story of Ariadne from a Minoan
perspective instead of the common Athenian version where she is
a daughter of Minos who betrays her father and her people for a
hero who then abandons her.

I wanted to break away from the traditional story and explore
some of the contradictory myths—that Dionysus was Ariadne's
husband before Theseus and that's why Dionysus had Artemis kill

her, that Perseus killed Ariadne with Medusa's head, that Dionysus saw Ariadne for the first time on Naxos and told Theseus to abandon her because he wanted her for himself—or that Athena told Theseus the same. Two of these versions offer Theseus an excuse for his inexcusable actions. He needed to go on to be the cultural hero of Athens, and impregnating a girl who gave up her whole life to save him and then abandoning her on some random island doesn't bode well for a hero.

But in all of the stories, Ariadne is a pawn, a side note. In many versions of the myth, Daedalus does all the thinking—he tells her about the thread to help Theseus out of the labyrinth. Ariadne is used and deposited by Theseus and swooped up or murdered by Dionysus. I wanted to give Ariadne agency, as she surely had in Minoan times, and I wanted to put Dionysus back in her story.

I was also inspired by the idea of the Minotaur. Along with the Pasiphae "bull-fucker" story, this seemed like very good propaganda for the Athenians to tell about an enemy. The Minotaur—the monster in his maze—is such a powerful image, and the idea of the hero Theseus killing him in the Minotaur's own labyrinth to protect Athens and his people is compelling. I had an image of a Minoan priest-king wearing a bull mask during a ritual and then thought, what if there was no real half-man, half-bull creature, but a man mad with grief who just kept wearing the mask? There are also many references to Dionysus being born with horns, so the connection between Asterion and Dionysus came up naturally.

There is no mention of anyone like Thalia in any of the myths. Dionysus has often been shown with a leopard in ancient art. The idea of Thalia just came to me, and as the novel progressed, she transformed into what she truly was. I hope you enjoyed reading her character as much as I enjoyed writing her.

ACKNOWLEDGMENTS

I'm so grateful to the following people who came on this very long journey with me. First, Planaria Price and Joann Lo, who literally came with me to Crete—one of the most amazing places I've been. John Leopold, my ninth-grade history teacher who first taught me about the Minoans and Myceneans, and who was a fantastic online friend. I'm so grateful that he got to read this book in its infancy and give me feedback before his untimely passing. Laura Perry, whose incredible knowledge of the Minoans has inspired me countless times. Her Facebook group Ariadne's Tribe: Modern Minoan Paganism has been a great connection to the Minoans as well as the Modern Minoan Pagan movement, which serves as a testament for how enduring this ancient culture is. I was thrilled to have her edit this book. Amalia Carosella, a fantastic historical fiction author who read an early draft and gave great feedback. Erin Davies, Historical Fiction Reader, who was not only an early reader but also started a Historical Fiction Zoom Happy Hour that really helped get me through the pandemic.

Huge thanks to my long-time writing group: Eric Wat, Lisa Hernandez, Dana Collins, and Brett Tam, who read this whole novel over the course of what must have been years. My dear friends, Saharra Sandhu, Sheri Lupoli, Mia Hopkins, and Ariel Senseman, who held my hand through many drafts. Luis Romero and Jessica Cale, who gave me so much feedback on cover design, and my amazing new cover designer Diana Kohne. I'm incredibly grateful to my husband Kevin, who gave me time and space to write and took care of our children when I went to Greece and all the times I needed some space. He also is fine with naked statues of Dionysus around the house and has recently come to enjoy wine.

Reference Books and Inspiration:

Bacchus: A Biography by Andrew Dalby

Dionysus: Archetypal Image of Indestructible Life by Carl Kerenyi

Gods and Robots by Adrienne Mayor

The Search for the Origins of the Viniculture of Ancient Wine by Patrick E. McGovern

The Minoan World by Arthur Cotterell

The Civilization of Ancient Crete by R.E. Willetts

MORE BY ZENOBIA NEIL

Turn the page for an excerpt from
The Queen of Warriors:
Alexandra of Sparta Book One

PROLOGUE

EPHESUS, WINTER, 244 BCE

Alexandra knelt before the priestess in the darkened cavern amid the flickering lamps. She had been to every temple from Isfahan to Ephesus and sacrificed to no avail, but she had never expected to find herself here.

"What do you want from the goddess?" the priestess asked, eyeing her with distrust.

Alexandra was fairly sure the priestess knew who she was—who she had been—but she did not think the old woman would turn her in for the price on her head.

"I wish to break the curse that haunts me." She spoke from low in her throat, an intimacy between the two of them. This was the secret she had longed to say aloud for the last three years, and here it was. She stopped herself from saying what else she longed for—to find any of her men who still lived, especially Aristos and Nicandor, and ask for forgiveness before she died.

The priestess's one blind eye and one seeing eye passed over Alexandra's muscles and scars. The old bitch had made her strip for this ritual, and now she stared, her eyes lingering over Alexandra's golden necklaces, bracelets, and rings.

"The goddess cannot break the curse," the priestess said. "But if you wish, I will ask Hecate to open the gate. Then you may speak to the one who cursed you. Then you can beg for forgiveness."

Alexandra was not one to beg. She did not fear living men. But Hecate, the triple-headed goddess, the keeper of the crossroads, the goddess of witches—Hecate—the name was like an ice-cold blade on her naked flesh.

Yet Alexandra had traversed all the way from deep within the heart of Asia Minor to come here to Ephesus. She had expected the great temple of Artemis to be her destination, but she had been summoned to this cave shrine of Hecate.

She would see it through. "I seek only one of the dead. Will others cross the gate?"

The priestess grinned, exposing her broken teeth. "That depends on your crimes, warrior woman. If those you killed lay unburied and haunt the land of the living, longing for vengeance, they may come through as well."

"Can they harm me?"

"They are merely shades. It is for you to account for the lives you've taken."

Alexandra lifted her chin. "I regret not a single one of the men I killed, only the deaths I failed to prevent. For those I repent, and for those I am willing to pay, with my life if need be."

"It will not be that easy." The priestess withdrew a dagger from a sheath on her waist. The sacrificial blade was short and dark, bronze instead of steel, and had been forged long ago. "Your people know the goddess yearns for mortal blood, as do the shades of the dead. Take this and give them what you will." She handed Alexandra the dagger, hilt first. "Though I can see you are shrouded in sorrow, it is not your time to die yet. Don't cut too deep."

Alexandra approached the black goddess stone on her knees. She raised her left arm, whispered a name, and cut her wrist so the blood began to flow.

The priestess drew a circle around Alexandra and the stone. She pulled a pouch from her robes, uttered an incantation, and sprinkled an herb over the lamps. Soon the scent of myrrh and honey mixed with the iron smell of Alexandra's blood filled the cavern.

Once the gate to the Underworld opened, the priestess left. Shades of fallen warriors filled the sanctuary, shouting oaths no louder than the wind. Alexandra stared at them, trying to find a familiar face. Though she had lost enough blood to swoon, she swayed on her knees, her back straight, and spoke loudly to the shades.

"If I killed you in battle, you died honorably. If it shames you to have been killed by a woman, know I am not any woman. I am of Sparta—any of my countrymen would have dispatched you just as quickly. Go from this place now, drink from the River Lethe, and find peace."

The shades did not leave, but they quieted. Her skin prickled with gooseflesh. It was not only fear. Despite the smoke and flames, the temple had grown cold.

One shadow who had been silent all along now grew strong on her blood. Though still transparent and dark, it gained form.

Suddenly able to see the shade, tears came to her eyes.

"Beloved," she said, her voice breaking, "forgive me. I did not mean it to happen. Tell me what to do. I will give you my life if you wish it."

The shade gazed at her with a mixture of love, bitterness, and vengeance.

Vishanti, the shade said, the sound no more than a whisper. *I cursed you in love, and only by love or justice can you break the curse. You must right the wrongs you have done and face your deepest fear. Return to Rhagae and pay for your crimes.*

Alexandra swayed on her knees and brought her hands to her face, allowing herself to sob only once. She had planned to return to Sparta. After all this time, she had been about to journey across the sea, to finally go home. But it seemed the gods had other plans for her.

1. ARTAXERXES'S PRIZE

RHAGAE, SPRING, 243 BCE

"You must go," Alexandra said to the noseless man. She had released her slaves and those who followed her in Ephesus, but the noseless man and her Persian handmaiden, Dari, had insisted on accompanying her to Rhagae.

"No, little queen. I have lived with you and fought with you. If the gods will it, I will die with you."

"Horses," Dari said. "They found us."

Ten Persian chargers galloped toward them. The sun glinted off their breastplates and shields painted with golden lynxes.

Alexandra and the noseless man drew their swords as the riders surrounded them.

"Are you the Queen of Warriors?" a Persian archer asked in common Greek.

This made her laugh. As if any other Greek woman would wear a leather dress and breastplate under her cloak. As if any other Greek woman would stand in Rhagae and hold a sword.

"What do you think?" she asked, staring up at him. Standing back-to-back with the noseless man, they turned in a circle, pointing their swords. "Who among you will be my last kill?"

The archer could have shot her then. But he didn't. There must still be a price on her head if she was taken alive. Four riders dismounted.

Let me die to the sound of sword song, she thought as she ran at one of the Persians. He dropped his shield, and she beat him back, waiting to be struck from behind. Instead her opponent succeeded in slicing her left bicep.

"Don't kill her!" a Persian shouted in Aramaic. A rider came from behind and threw a net over her. She struggled to free herself but was knocked to the ground. Still grasping her sword, she scrambled to rise, but a man gripped her shoulders hard, squeezing her cut bicep.

"Drop the sword."

"No." She would die with it in her hand. But when they stepped on her wrist, she relented. She scanned the ground for the noseless man and Dari but saw nothing but horse hoofs.

After she was disarmed, her wrists were bound. They blindfolded her and forced her up onto one of the horses, in front of a rider who gripped her tightly.

"Artaxerxes will take care of you," the Persian said in common Greek. "Soon enough, we'll see your head on our gates."

Artaxerxes had taken Rhagae two years earlier, killing the Greek satrap she had helped put in power, but what worried her more was that Artaxerxes had once fought for Red Wind, the man who had been her undoing and put the price on her head.

"What have I done?" Alexandra asked lightly.

"Do you deny being the Queen of Warriors?" the Persian asked.

"Once, long ago. But no more."

"No," the Persian growled in her ear. "No more." The horse slowed, and he dismounted, pulling her down roughly. She stumbled but did not fall. On the wind, she heard word being relayed that she had been caught alive. They were keeping her here so the people could assemble.

The jubilation of the crowd could be heard from a distance.

Shouts and laughter, as if it were a festival day and she the main entertainment. A long rope was wrapped around her bound wrists and given to another horse rider. She feared being dragged for a moment, but then she remembered the price on her head. This was a processional; everyone wanted to see her alive before her execution.

Focusing on her steps, she listened to the movement of those around her. There were perhaps ten men whose job it was to guard her, to keep her from escaping, and to prevent the crowd from killing her.

"Hail Artaxerxes, the Golden Lynx of Rhagae!"

It must be this Artaxerxes who held the other end of the rope, leading her into the city as his prize.

As she walked, she shook out her hair, loosening the blindfold. Through a sliver of vision, she followed the rope to Artaxerxes, who sat astride a bay stallion. The sun shone off his silver Greek helmet. Long black hair cascaded down his back, loosely bound in a braid. In typical Persian style, he wore leather trousers and had a bow slung across his back—if only she could get it, this would all be over quickly.

"Murderer!" a man in the crowd shouted.

Another laughed. "The Terror of the East no more!"

"Ahura Mazda has heard my prayers. The Queen of Warriors will die in Rhagae," a third cried.

It was true she had once been known as the Terror of the East, a Greek woman fighting for a Greek king to keep his Persian subjects loyal. Her advisor, Nicandor the Little Red Fox, had sent out rumors she was merciless and fierce, holding no weakness in her heart, for she loved no man. Though many had tried to win her love, none had succeeded, losing their lives and armies to her instead.

"Death to the Queen of Warriors!"

The crowd was rabid. She could almost smell their bloodlust.

She reconstructed the road she trod upon from memory, paved and wide enough here for four horses. Ignoring the jeering mob, her mind filled in what she could not see. The province of Rhagae was not incredibly large, but it was well situated on the trade route and very rich. With sturdy gates and the snowy Elburz Mountains to the north, it seemed impossible to breach. But she and her army had found a way.

"This is the Queen of Warriors?" a woman asked in Aramaic. "I thought she'd be taller and her hair golden."

"Where are her horns?" a girl asked.

"I heard she's an Amazon," another said. "They say she fights as well as a man."

"Well, she has muscles enough like a man," the first said. "And look at that gash on her arm!"

"I hope King Artaxerxes pours salt on it before he impales her," the girl said.

The Queen of Warriors . . . She had not thought of herself that way since losing her cavalry and all her men at Aegis three years before. But now she slipped the persona on as she would a well-worn pair of sandals she had long ago discarded. *I will die as the Queen of Warriors, as I was meant to.*

She sensed the danger a moment before it came. A stone flew through the air and pelted her leather breastplate. Another hit her boot, and a third struck her forearm—that one stung. The guards moved to protect her, their scent of sweat, myrrh, and leather enveloping her as they raised their shields. A few stones pinged against metal, but then a deep voice announced that anyone who hurt the Queen of Warriors would lose a hand. The crowd quieted. The danger had passed. She raised her head high, remembering who she had once been.

"It will take more than a few pebbles to kill the Queen of Warriors!" she shouted in her battle voice, then laughed as the guards scrambled to protect her.

Soon the heat of the sun was replaced by the cool of the fortress. The rope went slack for a moment, then was taken up by another. Artaxerxes must have dismounted. Was he leading her into his fortress to exhibit her to his men?

"Stairs," a guard growled, grabbing her elbow and leading her up.

She pictured the oxblood columns holding up the great archway which led into a vast courtyard and attempted to recall the layout—the audience chamber, the dining halls, and the stone stairs leading to the maze of rooms on the upper floors. She had not thought of this fortress in years, but she tried to envision where she was now—and to guess in what room her torture would take place.

Sensing a moment of laxity on the part of the guards, she elbowed the one nearest her and almost pulled off the blindfold before another caught her from behind.

"Watch her carefully," a Judean said. The sound of a Judean in charge surprised her, and she was unprepared when a potion was brought to her lips.

"Drink," the Judean commanded. She clamped her mouth shut and struggled until a blow to her stomach made her gasp in pain, and a bitter liquid was forced down her throat. She choked and sputtered, then fell into a deep sleep.

The Queen of Warriors awoke in the dark, bound and blindfolded. The sword cut on her bicep throbbed and her body ached, but she lay still, taking stock. A sentry smelling of onions stood near.

She had been bathed and stripped of her jewelry. Her ruby-encrusted gold bracelets and her jeweled necklaces were gone. They had left only her mother's ring, a silver snake biting its tail, and her golden earrings. Perhaps they would rip them out when they cut off her finger to take the ring.

The leather dress she had worn under her chiton had been removed and replaced with a sleeveless silken gown. The gash in her arm had been disinfected with myrrh and sewn together. If Artaxerxes had ordered her wound tended to, he had plans for her. She would have to speed her death and deprive him of his fun. Though her wrists were tied, she could easily remove the blindfold. She was barefoot, but her feet were unbound. All she need do was wait.

"Are you sleeping?" a man whispered in common Greek. She did not answer. He hovered above her, his onion fumes telling her exactly where he was. Quickly, she interlaced her fingers and brought her forearms together. Using her fists like a hammer, she hit him in the throat, threw off the blindfold, and hit him again when he tried to strike her. As he struggled for air, she tripped him, knocking him to the ground.

Two small lamps flickered in the darkness. As she knelt to search the guard, the rug shifted beneath her feet. The sleeping potion still flowed in her veins. She groped for his sword only to find the sheath empty.

Whispered laughter came from the shadows. The other men in the room had been perfectly still until now.

"Very nice. We were hoping for a show of your skill."

She could not see the man the voice belonged to—an educated Persian used to speaking common Greek.

Still crouching, she spun around.

His curved sword was at her throat.

She lifted her wrists to the blade, but her unseen captor antici-pated her move and pulled his sword away, so she fell with her wrists still tied. Others in the room laughed. She struggled to rise, but a boot on her buttocks stopped her.

"Put the blindfold on." He lifted the blindfold off the floor with his sword and dropped it into her hands. She extended her arms to pull the blindfold over her head, and the pressure of the boot relaxed. She rolled away, then quickly jumped up to attack the man behind the sword. When she reached where he had been in the shadows, there was nothing but air.

"Take her," the voice said.

Rough hands grabbed her by the shoulders and held her firmly. She kicked one man in the belly as another blindfolded her and a third hoisted her back to the bed. She expected to be struck, but instead, they forced her bound wrists up over her head, bending her elbows and pulling her wrists down. There was a tug as they attached her wrists to a rope around her waist, pinning her arms behind her head. Her ankles were bound together. She kicked, but her feet met only air.

"A nice attempt. Some of my men doubted you were the famous Queen of Warriors. No one believed you would return here." Her captor spoke from low in his throat. His accent reminded her of another voice. A voice that haunted her dreams. "Do you know where you are?"

"Rhagae." She said the name tenderly.

"Yes. Rhagae has only recently thrown off the yoke you put on her back. The people have not forgotten how you took the city by trickery eight years ago, murdering the satrap Darius and his family and impaling men of noble families."

She pulled at her ropes, wishing she could see his face to gauge what kind of man he was. This must be Artaxerxes, the Persian rebel who had taken over the territory she had held for the Great King.

"What you say is not true. The satrap Darius summoned his death when he rebelled against the Great King. I was kind to Rhagae. I didn't put all the men to the sword or enslave the women and children as anyone else would have. I allowed those who pledged themselves to the Great King to live. And as for the nobles you speak of—they swore themselves to me while plotting my death. I gave them no more than they planned for me."

"Those you slaughtered would not have called you merciful." His voice was raw with anger. He took a breath and seemed to calm himself before coming closer. "But where have you been, my queen? We have all been looking for you. These last three years, no one has seen you in the flesh until now." His hand, cool and dry, caressed her throat.

She tried to appear calm. *Never let them see your fear,* Nicandor the Little Red Fox's voice said in her mind. Even as a ghost, he advised her still.

"How much is the price on my head?" she asked.

"Three gold talents if you are captured alive, relatively unharmed."

A single talent was more than a common man could expect to see in his life, enough to buy a battleship or feed an army for a year.

"A fine amount. I'm flattered." He would keep her alive then, deliver her to the highest bidder. "Who will pay you these many talents?"

"No one. I am the one who set the price."

"But it was Red Wind who put the price on my head, and Red Wind is dead."

"Yes." He trailed his fingers to her chest, where he could surely feel the pounding of her heart. "I heard you were dead too, my queen, yet here you are."

She tried to ignore his hands, to push away thoughts of what he would do to her. This was what Nicandor the Little Red Fox had tried to prepare her for, what Lysander and Caiaphas had warned her about.

"Are you Red Wind?" she asked, unable to keep the terror from her voice.

"No, I am Artaxerxes." He spoke his own name as if caressing a lover.

"But you knew Red Wind? You were in his army?"

He made a noise low in his throat. "Why?" he asked, speaking almost in a whisper. "Are you looking for someone? Someone you left behind when you gave your army to Red Wind at Aegis?"

She clenched her fists and gritted her teeth, her blood pumping with rage. "I did not give my army to Red Wind!"

"We all know how you abandoned your army, leaving the men loyal to you to die. It is said they crucified your generals Caiaphas and Lysander."

She had heard the rumors, like a knife searing her flesh every

336

time. There was no reason to doubt it was true, but she could not help but ask, "Were you there? Did you see it yourself?"

He paused and lifted his hand. "Yes. It took Caiaphas the Cruel almost three days to die, and there was much rejoicing."

She winced as if struck, glad her eyes were hidden. This Artaxerxes must have been an officer in Red Wind's army. Surely if Red Wind lived, he would be here now—unless he was on his way and Artaxerxes was keeping her for him.

"Why did you come back now? Is there someone you seek?"

She had searched for Nicandor the Little Red Fox and Aristos since she had lost them. If she could only see them once before dying . . . but what if they were his slaves? She did not think she could say their names without tears. Images of Caiaphas and Lysander on the cross flitted through her mind. She should have died at Aegis with them.

"Tell me," he said, laying his hand on her throat, "why did you return to Rhagae after all these years?"

She laughed bitterly, hoping to mask the grief that had overcome her. "Well, Artaxerxes, it appears I have returned to Rhagae to die. How is it to be done?"

He did not answer. Instead, he trailed his fingers over her collarbone and down the length of her arm as if touching a coveted gift.

"Though some of my men and all of Rhagae would like me to kill you immediately, I need not. I have the luxury of doing with you what I wish."

"You will have to kill me. I will belong to no man."

"No, Alexandra of Sparta? We will see about that. It is said you killed your first and second husbands and took their armies for your own. Is that true?"

"It's a good way to acquire an army, Artaxerxes. Perhaps you desire to be my third husband?"

A man in the room laughed though Artaxerxes did not.

"My army would not yield to you so easily."

"No. I suppose they wouldn't." She tried to laugh, to appear strong. *Keep him talking,* Nicandor's ghost counselled. *Discover his plans and try to thwart them.* "So what will you do with me?"

"My men would like me to march you through the streets naked and in chains, others suggest I let the populace whip you to death in the bazaar, and those who remember what you did eight years ago suggest I impale you so your death takes three days. What you have done with your own captives? Did you let them go to an easy death or torment them for years?"

I showed mercy to many. I was not the monster Nicandor had me pretend to be.

"They say when you took Rhagae, you killed the royal family, the satrap Darius and his wife, his niece and nephew. Is this true?" His voice moved away, and she heard the sound of steel leaving a leather scabbard. A quiet sound only a trained warrior could hear, the way a mother recognizes her child's cry from a distance.

What he described was not exactly what had happened, but there was little point in correcting him.

"Yes," she hissed. Better to let him think the worst of her.

"This is a lie." The cold steel of his sword slipped beneath her gown, resting gently on her leg. She held still, waiting for the bite of the blade against her flesh as the sword slid beneath the fabric and up her thigh until it rested above her hip.

The silk yielded easily as he slit open one side of her gown.

"It is also said on the night of the red moon, you humiliated a Persian boy in front of your men."

"There are many stories about me," she said. "Only some are true."

"But I will have the truth from you, for you belong to me now."

Though she tried to maintain a calm demeanor, her heart pounded wildly. Yet the risk of coming here was worth it if there was a chance of breaking the curse.